Whatever happened to Rosemarie?

A novel based on a true story.

Vera Christa Doederlein (Döderlein) Hastie

With an Afterword by
Christa Hastie

Book reviews play a crucial role for authors.

Thank you in advance for taking a few minutes
to write and post your review of this novel:

www.MissingGermanGirl.com

For Rosemarie

Prologue

Vera and her family had lived in Canada for seven weeks when her little sister, Rosemarie, disappeared. Until they'd arrived in Montreal, Vera couldn't imagine living anywhere but in the tiny village of Birkenfeld in the Enz district of Baden-Württemberg.

The majority of Vera's childhood was marred by World War II. But that wasn't what she'd remember about her homeland. They say pain has no memory and she would have believed that right up until the last time she saw Rosemarie. Vera learned at a very early age that heartaches have no timetable, no calendar. Pain has no date and no regard for time or distance. You don't forget to feel.

There had been plenty of pain in Germany during the war. But there had been more joy than any child could have asked for. Vera spent summer days in the local river with Rosemarie while Günter and Hilde, their older brother and sister, watched them from the banks. Even when food was scarce during the height of the war, she helped her mother bake bread and would turn a few pieces of meat and potatoes the size of big grapes into a meal that almost satisfied the whole family.

Vera's parents told her and Rosemarie that they were heading across the Atlantic. She imagined a life without the childhood friends she'd known her whole life. She pictured how difficult it would be to make friends when she didn't speak the language. She thought of everything she would miss about Germany. It never occurred to her that she could have to live her life without her sister.

1

Four Weeks Before The Disappearance

Vera had never been so sick. Not even when her whole family had the stomach flu. She had also never been on a ship before. So when a storm hit a thousand miles off the eastern coast of Canada, Vera cried for her mother. But Hilda was just as ill as her daughter and couldn't lift her head off the pillow. So Vera called for Rosemarie, who was two years older, but couldn't really do anything to help her other than hold her little sister's hand when she cried and vomited.

"Why are we even on this ship?" Vera asked, although Rosemarie, at the age of almost fourteen, had no idea. "Where are we going?"

"I heard Mama and Pappa talking last night. He told her we're going to a place called Montreal in Canada."

This made Vera cry harder. "But why? Why did we leave Germany? What if they don't have rivers to swim in and bakeries to visit?" Back home in Birkenfeld, Vera and her siblings spent every summer playing in the Enz—a bubbly, clean river that ran through the south side of the village. Kids loved to climb and jump off the boulders. The river was deep enough for them to hold onto a rock and pretend to swim. Every June Vera told herself that one day she was going to learn to swim for real, and then she wouldn't need the rock any longer. "What if Pappa has to go away again? He just got home."

"I know!" Rosemarie exclaimed. "He was gone for a hundred years."

It certainly felt like it'd been that long to Vera and the rest of the kids. "It was six years. But it might as well have been forever." Vera held her stomach as she felt another roll of nausea hit. "I hope the bad guys don't take Pappa away from us again. I don't even know why he was gone so long."

"It wasn't his fault." Rosemarie touched her sister's hand, trying to comfort her. "That wallpaper hanger made Pappa fight in the war for Germany. And then when he was trying to get home, France made him stay there for a really long time. I think I heard Mama say they captured him."

"What's a wallpaper hanger?" Vera asked.

"You know that's what Mama calls Hitler. We're not allowed to say his name in front of her."

"Oh. That's right. But why was Pappa trapped in France for so long?"

"I don't know. And every time I ask, Mama tells me that it's over so we don't talk about it. She told me to be grateful that Pappa made it home alive."

"Then I guess you can't ask her why we're on an awful ship sailing across the Atlantic Ocean on our way to a place where we don't know anyone but Günter and Ruth."

Vera and Rosemarie's big brother and his wife had left Germany the year before. Vera only hoped that they were going to Canada to visit them and would eventually go back to their motherland. Vera tried to push herself up in bed to talk to her sister, but even that slight movement made her vomit. Fortunately, Rosemarie knew what was about to happen and shoved an old, aluminum bucket under her chin. When she stopped retching, she said to her little sister, "Mama says there's nothing left for us in Germany. That Canada is going to be the start of something wonderful."

"Mama never lies to us. So if she says it's going to be wonderful, then I guess we have to believe her." Vera made another sick noise, and Rosemarie crawled into bed with her and stroked her little sister's hair.

As Vera tried to sleep, she thought about the watercress that grew wild and plentiful on the banks of the Enz River back home in Germany. There was always enough for the whole town and Vera loved how she'd play with all the neighborhood kids while their mothers picked the herb for salads and other dishes. Rosemarie and Vera frolicked in the knee-high water, kicking, laughing, and splashing each other while mothers made their way to the banks to tear off the crispy, firm watercress from the river's edge. If Hilda couldn't be there to watch her two youngest daughters, their sister Hilde would sit quietly on the river's edge and keep an eye on them. Being seven years older than Rosemarie and ten years older than Vera, she was almost like a second mother to them. She was introspective and kind, and often played with dolls while she waited for her sassy sisters to get out of the water.

When Vera awoke next, she felt somewhat better. She rolled over, expecting to see Rosemarie curled up next to her, but she was alone. Cautiously, she swung her legs to the side of the bed and tried to stand. Not only did her stomach feel more settled, but the ship was a lot steadier. She thought that perhaps they had passed through a terrible storm and the worst of it was over.

She knocked on the adjoining door to her parents'

room, expecting to hear her mother's weak voice telling her she was too sick to get up. Hilda, too, had been terribly seasick since they'd left Germany. Instead, Hilda pulled open the door and hugged Vera. "My darling girl. Would you look at us? We're both feeling better." Hilda's skin had gone from a sallow green to a healthy peach.

Vera peered around her mother. "Where are Pappa and Rosemarie? I wanted to tell Rosemarie that I am feeling better."

"They went to the dining hall for breakfast. Would you like to join them?"

Vera had barely eaten anything since they'd boarded the ship days before. "Oh yes, please. I am starving. It's such a good feeling to be hungry again!"

Hilda took Vera's hand and together they walked down the long, narrow corridor. Vera took the quiet moment to ask her mother questions she'd been wondering about since the cold, September morning a few days before when Hilda told Vera and Rosemarie to get dressed in the clothes she had laid out for them.

They'd gotten in their new car and their parents had driven them to a tavern at an inn. It was the first time they'd ever been out to eat. They'd even slept there and then the family drove to Cologne. They stopped at a historical church and admired the artwork before getting back in the car and driving to the harbor of Bremen with the vast ocean in front of them.

"Mama," Vera said as they walked. "Why are we really on this ship? I don't even know what Arosa Kulm means. What kind of name is that for a boat? Where are we going and why did we bring so much stuff with us? Are we ever going back to Germany? And what about Pappa's car? He loved that car so much. And now it is gone. How will we get around town when we get back to Birkenfeld?"

Hilda glanced down at her daughter, remembering

how upset Oskar had been when he'd come back to the inn in Bremen without the car and without the money he was counting on when he sold it. The man Oskar had arranged to sell the car to didn't have all the money he'd promised, so Oskar had pushed the car into the ocean. Then he'd told Hilda that he was too proud to give up the car for less than what it was worth. And if he couldn't take the car with him to Canada, then no one could have it. Hilda felt like that was excessive and foolish, but she knew better than to question Oskar's actions.

"Oh Vera," Hilda said as they walked down the empty hallway. "We should really talk about this with your father and your sister. You've always been the inquisitive one. Asking all the hard questions." She stepped faster and told her daughter to pick up the pace so they could join Oskar and Rosemarie for breakfast. "For now let's just be thankful that we're feeling better and can actually eat something."

"Okay Mama," Vera said. "But I have one more question. Will this dining hall have grapes hanging from the ceiling like the restaurant where we stayed right before we got on the ship?"

"You mean the Rathskeller Tavern and Inn?" Hilda longed for German food and the familiarity of the language at that moment. "I don't know. But remember how good the food was and how comfortable the beds were? And it was only a few minutes from the ship. Pappa sure did do a good job finding us the best place to stay." Hilda was trying to distract her daughter. She didn't have any idea how she and Oskar would explain to their kids the real reasons they'd left Germany.

Hilda mussed Vera's hair and urged her forward. They'd just gotten in the dining area when Vera saw her father and her sister. "Rosemarie!" she yelled. "Look at me! I feel so much better." Rosemarie turned toward the sound of her sister's voice and Vera knew in that moment that she'd never need another friend again, as long as she had her sister.

Rosemarie ran toward Vera and hugged her hard. "Look at you! You must be feeling well. You haven't gotten out of bed at all before now."

Vera took in the room around her. Chandeliers the size of her kitchen table in Birkenfeld hung from the ceiling and crisp linens were folded in the shapes of birds and flowers. Vera had never seen anything like this before, and for a moment she thought that perhaps everything would be okay. "Come on," she called to her sister. "I am starving. Let's see what they have." She turned toward tables of food. "Oh my, Rosemarie. Look at this. All the food is laid out in front of us." She approached the first table covered with bread, muffins and pastries. The next had chafing dishes with little candles burning beneath each one, but she didn't dare open them.

Oskar approached Vera and stood beside her. "This is called a buffet. Once we are seated, a waitress will tell us it's our turn and we can come up here and take whatever we'd like." Rosemarie's eyes got big and her stomach growled. "And the best part is you can come up as many times as you'd like."

"But not too many," Hilda answered. "It's not ladylike, after all." Hilda touched her stomach, thinking about all the nights she'd gone to bed hungry during World War II. She never wanted her children to experience what she went through. She always made sure Günter, Hilde, Vera and Rosemarie had enough to eat, even if it meant she went without food for a day or two. "On second thought, go crazy. Eat until you feel like your tummy will explode."

Rosemarie and Vera took off toward the buffet and stared at each dish as though they'd never seen food before. Oskar took Hilda's hand and said, "Look at those beautiful little girls. There were years when I was a prisoner in France that I thought I might never see them again. And now that we're here and we're safe, about to start our new lives in Montreal, it's like everything bad that ever happened was just a dream. Or it was something we had to live through so we could appreciate all that we have now."

"I agree," Hilda said. "But at some point we need to tell the girls why we left Germany and that we're not going on vacation. That we're actually moving to Canada."

"Give it time. I think once they get settled and realize how much better Canada is, they'll forget all about Germany."

"I should hope not." Hilda motioned for her children to join them by the front of the restaurant. "Don't forget that Hilde is still there."

"Did I hear you mention Hilde's name?" Vera asked, as she came to them from exploring the food. "Why didn't she come with us? You keep saying what a fun trip this is going to be."

Oskar and Hilda exchanged looks, then Oskar spoke. "You know your sister is married now. She has her own life. She chose to stay in Germany with her husband and precious little Gabriel. I'm sure they'll come visit as soon as we get settled."

"Settled?" Rosemarie glanced at Vera. "Are we staying in Canada?"

Before Oskar could think of what to tell Rosemarie, the hostess showed up and led them to a table. Once they all sat, she told them to feel free to visit the buffet as many times as they'd like. The girls were so excited to eat all they could that they quickly forgot to ask any more questions.

A line had already formed for the food and as they waited their turn, Vera remembered the process they had to go through to get on the ship. "Doesn't this guy behind us look like the man who inspected our little books? He's got the same pointy nose." She pointed so Rosemarie would know who she was talking about.

"He does. And he's skinny too. But he wasn't looking at little books. Those were our passports."

"What's a passport?"

Rosemarie remembered learning about them in school. "It's something you take with you when you go to a new country. I hope we don't lose them or we won't be allowed to go back to Germany."

Vera frowned. "I don't think we're going home ever again."

Rosemarie eyed her sister. "I know what you mean. Something strange is happening. I just don't know what it is yet."

After they ate, Hilda asked her daughters if they wanted to see the rest of the ship. "Yes please!" Vera was excited to explore the long, roaming corridors.

"Great." Hilda eyed Oskar. "Your father will take you. I'm still quite tired."

The girls finished their meals and waited while their father spoke to a couple at a nearby table. Before the war, Oskar had been a translator and spoke seven languages including German, English, French and Italian. Vera recognized that her father was speaking English to a skinny guy who looked about the same age as Vera's parents.

After a few minutes, Oskar returned to his family. He kissed Hilda on the cheek and then made an elbow for each girl to hold and all three went exploring the ship. "Does this ship really stay on top of the water Pappa?" Vera was confused.

"Ships are built to stay on top of the water." He was touched by his daughter's naivete.

"So none ever sink?" asked Rosemarie.

"Not exactly." He remembered hearing stories

about the unsinkable Titanic that had gone down forty years before. "But let's not focus on that. We have a lot of ship to explore." Many people were coming and going. They made it onto the deck and the wind was biting.

Oskar led them to a bunch of chairs. "Out here, see? There are lounge chairs. You can sit and watch the ocean or just take a breath and read. Now that you're feeling better," he looked at Vera, "you'll be able to relax up here if it's not too cold."

"Look!" Rosemarie pointed straight ahead. "You can't even see where we came from. No land in sight at all. Wow. Just think!"

"Think what?" Vera asked. The sky was overcast and a chilly wind caused them to hug themselves trying to keep warm. The promenade was also full of people looking through the windows. All the lounge chairs were occupied. They all just walked around taking in what was on the ship. The girls were excited. Rosemarie, especially, because she had her sister back. Finally, they went back to their room.

The ship gently rolled back and forth. "Vera, doesn't that feel like we're on a cloud?" asked Rosemarie.

"It feels nice and it's putting me to sleep." She rolled over in her bed and fell asleep.

When they woke they took special care of their hair and made sure their stockings were pulled up properly without any ridges. Their mother looked so pretty in a grey, long-sleeved dress with a white lace collar and a small white hat and white gloves.

"Girls, take a look at my nylon seams. Are they straight?" Hilda turned so the backs of her legs were facing her daughters.

"Yes," said Rosemarie right away while Vera spent a longer time staring at the seams.

"I can't wait to be older so I can wear your shoes." Vera admired her mother's black Mary Janes.

"Well, hmm, mmm, my dear sister. I'm the oldest, so therefore I get them first." Rosemarie pointed at her own chest.

"Don't worry you two . . . soon you'll have shoes like that." Hilda patted each of her daughters on the head and turned them toward the door.

A siren screeched and someone said something with a bullhorn.

"Something is wrong." Hilda opened the door. People were wearing orange jackets and running down the corridor and up the stairs to the deck. "Girls, there're orange jackets at the foot of your bed, hurry up and put them on." She put on her own vest. "We're going now. Hold each other and don't let go. No matter what. Understood?"

"Yes. Yes. Let's go and find Pappa. He's probably just as scared as we are," Rosemarie said. As they got to the upper deck, someone on the P.A. system was announcing that it was a drill and everyone would be allowed to return to their cabins in just a few moments.

Hilda gathered her girls. "Nothing to be afraid of. We just had to practice what to do in case something goes wrong. No need to worry." Just then the ship hit a big wave and it rolled from side to side. "Oh. I am not feeling so well." She put a hand to her stomach. "Come on, let's go back to our rooms. We should all rest."

When they got back to their rooms, Hilda lay down for a few hours, but was feeling well enough to go to dinner with Oskar and the girls.

Later that night they ate spaghetti for the first time. After dinner Rosemarie and Vera took a walk around the promenade and Vera got queasy and grabbed her stomach. "Oh no. Not again! I thought I was done being sick."

Rosemarie pointed to an open window. "Here, Vera, come on, this window is open, you can puke out into the ocean!"

Vera stood on green pipes running along the bottom of the wall. It just made her tall enough to get her chin above the bottom rim of the window and she started to vomit. Unfortunately the wind was not kind to her and blew it right back in her face. "Help me to our room." Vera was disgusted with herself and was happy to get back to their cabin. "Mama," she said. "It's happening again. Why am I so sick all of a sudden? I was feeling so much better."

"It's the ocean and the waves," Hilda said. "Be prepared for it to get worse. I believe in a few days the weather will turn even more sour."

"Don't say that, Mama," Vera said. "I'm not sure I can feel like this much longer."

Rosemarie rubbed her sister's back. "It's okay. I'll help you."

Vera grabbed Rosemarie's hand. "Thank you so much. I don't know what I would do without you."

"It's okay. You'll never have to find out."

On the fourth day of the trip, weather came across the Atlantic. It was so terrible that Vera and Rosemarie could hear the loud speaker saying that no one was allowed on deck. Vera was finally feeling better again, so she and Rosemarie asked permission to walk around.

"Absolutely not," Hilda said. "Haven't you heard the announcements? We're supposed to stay in our cabins."

"No Mama. It's okay. We promise to stay down here. We just want to wander around the halls. We've been cooped up for so long. We need to stretch our legs," Vera said. "Please let us go. We won't be long."

Hilda eyed her daughters, assessing the situation. "Fine," she finally said. "Promise me you'll be careful."

"Thank you, Mama!" Rosemarie clapped her hands and they ran off. The ship went back and forth, from left to right and every which way. It was hard for them to keep their balance and each time they started to topple, they squealed with delight. When the sisters were far down the corridor, she turned to Vera and said, "Come on. Let's go up on the deck. No one will be there and we'll have the whole outside to ourselves."

"Didn't you hear Mama? We're not allowed on the deck."

"Oh live a little," Rosemarie shot back. "Come on. It'll be fun."

Vera considered this for a moment. "Okay. Let's go!"

They climbed the stairs and the cold air bit at their cheeks. They sat on the lounge chairs as the loudspeaker repeated the same warning. After a few minutes, Vera was shivering and bored. There was nothing to see other than gigantic waves that threatened to come over the bow. She was about to tell Rosemarie she wanted to go back when she noticed a ship worker going through a door. Wondering where it led, she jumped up and ran after him. She grabbed the door handle, but a gust of wind ripped it from her grip and she was swept toward the bow of the ship.

"Help!" she screamed, but no one could hear her above the ferocious wind. She grasped for a bar and held on as tightly as she could. But the bow dipped into the water and she was submerged into the icy ocean. She was lifted up into the air toward the sky and quickly back into the coal black water. Terrified, she wet her pants. She continued screaming and Rosemarie rushed to her. But it was too slippery and she was too scared to help her little sister. She knew she needed to get help, but she didn't want to leave Vera. So she screamed as loud as she could. It seemed like an eternity, but it was really within minutes that a crew member rescued Vera.

Rosemarie barreled toward her sister and almost tackled her, she hugged her so hard. "I'm telling on you! You're so stupid! You could have died! What were you thinking? Thank god you're okay. I was so scared." Vera was in such shock that she couldn't answer her sister. She was thoroughly soaked, shivered and stared straight ahead. "Are you okay? Are you with us? Come on! You need dry clothes." Rosemarie took her by the hand. They kept their eyes down to avoid the curious gazes of other passengers.

The girls entered their parents' room and Hilda pushed herself up in bed. She hadn't eaten very much for days and was still weak. "Vera what on earth happened to you?"

Rosemarie laughed. "The question should be what on ocean happened to her?"

Vera didn't ever want to lie to her mama, but what could she say? "I was stupid. I went outdoors when I shouldn't have." Then she told her mother everything that had happened.

"This is all my fault. You poor child. You must have been terribly frightened. Get undressed, Vera. Rosemarie, would you please get her purple sweater and black skirt? Everybody is fine and that's what's most important now. From now on I'll make more of an effort to be with you girls. Has anyone seen your pappa?"

As if on cue, the door opened and Oskar stood there. When he saw Vera, wet and shivering, he rushed to hug her tight. "Someone told me Vera had an accident. What happened?"

"Darling." Hilda eased out of bed while she spoke. "Vera fell and got all wet. No one got hurt. But you, Rosemarie, need to take care of your younger sister a little better."

"She doesn't listen!" Rosemarie protested.

Hilda gave her a stern look. "I bet she will from now on, won't you?"

Vera hung her head. "Yes Mama. I am sorry. I will be a better listener from now on."

After a total of eleven days, Vera and her family finally made it off the ship. It was very cold as they stepped down the staircase while crates full of their belongings were brought to shore and stored in a warehouse. Just like when they boarded the ship, they stood in a long line, waiting to have their passports checked.

2

Early 1939

The Baden-Württemberg region cradled Birkenfeld and its farmland that produced some of the best cherries, grapes and apples in Germany. Children were taught early to show gratitude and appreciation to Mother Nature with a festival with dancing, singing, eating sauerbraten and spaetzle, knackwurst and broetle, sprudel and beer. The townspeople played games and men danced and clapped their hands on their knees and on the sides of their lederhosen. Dark green hats with feathers stuck on the side completed their festive look. Girls and ladies of every age wore the Black Forest costume—black full skirt with a fitted bodice and a white blouse with short puffy sleeves, a cherry red half apron, white stockings and black shiny shoes. They donned natural colored wide brimmed straw hats with red pom-poms sewn on top. They danced around the pole holding streamers while someone played an accordion.

Günter and Hilde loved to watch the men try to climb the greased pole, hoping they'd win a prize if they reached the top and ripped off the warning sign that read "Halt! Do not climb further!" There was nothing the siblings loved more than going to that festival and being so involved in their small, friendly town. Years later, when Rosemarie and Vera were born, Günter and Hilde couldn't wait for them to get big enough to go with them to the riverbanks and the festivals.

On the way home from the festival, Günter and Hilde walked through a suburb called Kleine Höhe, which meant little height, as in the one little hill among the flat farm land. It was about a forty-five minute walk to the center of town and they wandered in and out of the birch trees on their way. The trees swayed and waved their leaves in the breeze like a pianist playing staccato. The kids loved the ruffling sound of the leaves, and they would lie on their backs pretending to play music. A comb wrapped in tissue paper was all they needed to make music.

Their tiny village was magical for many reasons other than just the festival. Streets were unpaved and past the birch trees were wheat fields with an abundance of blue cornflowers, red poppies, yellow buttercups and a sea of white daisies. All homes were two stories with a red tile roof and dark green shutters. Flower boxes filled with red geraniums complemented the windows.

The front door of the Döderlein house led to a hallway with coat hangers and an umbrella stand. On the right was the kitchen, and straight ahead was the formal dining-living room that housed Oskar's piano. At the end of the hallway, a shiny blond oak staircase led upstairs to the bedrooms and attic.

Walls were papered from floor to ceiling, corner to corner with a soft creamy background and cheery little blooming roses in varying shades of burgundy. The floors had narrow black walnut slats; in the corner stood a black belly stove with its black venting pipe going up through the ceiling.

Günter and Hilde helped around the house as much

as they were asked, especially after Oskar was chosen to fight in the second great war for his homeland. Günter never had to be asked twice to keep the wood and coal box filled. During the winter he carried dry wood and two or three shovels of coal from the basement every few days. It kept the fire going for a few days, spreading its warmth throughout the whole second floor. While Günter helped his father with the wood and coal, Hilde would be in the kitchen helping her mother with food preparation.

Upstairs in the corner stood an armoire painted a shiny, crisp white with a soft grey-blue trim. Another bed was pushed against the wall with a white rocking chair in the corner facing the window. A ladder on the second story landing led to the attic used for storage. Hilda used the attic to dry laundry in the winter and keep wood dry. All year bundles of chamomile hung upside down on a line from one end of the attic to the other. As the leaves, stalks and tiny delicate white flowers dried, the scent of sweet hay permeated throughout the second floor. Hilda believed that chamomile was a great healer of everything. If her children had even the slightest sniffle or stomachache, she would make them tea. There was no argument; they kept quiet and drank their tea or soaked a hurt toe in the yellow water. The kids believed their mother's claims about the chamomile because they were never really sick. To them, it was the best kind of magic.

Some of Günter's favorite moments were spent gathered around the fire with his sister while Hilda told them about their father. Hilda always said he was the most handsome man she'd ever seen. Hilde and Günter used to giggle because they couldn't understand! After all, this was their dad she was talking about. He was just the goofy, hardworking loving father that they'd always known.

Oskar had light brown hair and blue eyes that made

people comfortable before he ever said a word. But he could be stern too—his kids knew which of his looks meant they had misbehaved. He left the house every day in polished shoes, a suit, shirt and tie and in the winter, also a hat.

Once a week Hilda would fill a heavy iron with water, set it on the stove feeding it plenty of coal so she could iron her husband's shirts. Everyone in town knew he was a linguist who spoke, read and wrote seven languages fluently: French, Spanish, Italian, Polish, Russian, English and German. He worked for the French Gendarmerie. His job was in the city of Pforzheim, about an hour away by train.

He often said he respected and liked the people he worked with, received very good pay and wouldn't change a thing in his life. At work and at home, he loved his life. Everyone in town knew of his talents and business knowledge. On warm Sunday mornings some townsfolk would make it a point to walk past the Döderlein house and listen to Oskar play the piano.

When Oskar got home from work, the family would eat dinner together and then after the kids went to bed, Hilda and Oskar would listen to the radio with a glass of wine while Hitler made one of his grandiose speeches of promises and greatness, while denouncing the Russians' threat to invade Germany. Throngs of people cheered him on. The crowd quieted as he spewed about the possibility of the Red Army overtaking Germany.

"How can that wallpaper hanger want to lead us into another war now?" Hilda felt nothing but disgust for Germany's leader. "Why get into another war when we've barely recovered from the last?"

"I don't know. All I can say is that we'd better start working on proving we're Aryan. I don't know what purpose that will serve, but I got papers in the mail that we must have this certification on our persons at all times." Oskar looked worried as he said this.

"You were at work when two men came to our door. I suppose they went to everyone in town. They asked who I wanted to protect Germany from the communists and asked if I knew what a threat the Russians really were to us. I told them that in Birkenfeld we hardly hear or read anything about Russia, we mostly hear Hitler's speeches on the radio. They went on and on and I can hardly remember all the confusing talk of who is doing what, where, how and why. They also tried to convince me about how much Hitler cares and needs our vote. Somehow I felt very intimidated. I just wanted them to get out again, so I signed on the dotted line. I don't even know what I was signing."

"I hope God will help us all. Did you know that by August the nineteenth Hitler had a ninety percent majority?"

"Doesn't that mean he is president now as well as chancellor? Yes, we better make it a point to go to church on Sunday."

"I'm not sure *anyone* can help us now." Oskar let out a sigh and slapped his knee.

"What does that mean for us? Our family, I mean."

"It means he's the dictator of everything, including all the military. Personally, when I hear him I smell a big rat carrying a lot of diseased cheese. It will be just like a mafia Germany—the do or die fatherland." Oskar scratched his scalp and rubbed his neck. Something he did when he was nervous.

"About the Aryan thing? Do you suppose we'll have trouble getting that information together?"

"I hope not. I'm working on it. I don't think my one root from the Netherlands, or yours from your father's French side should create any problems." He turned off the radio.

On the first day of September 1939 Hitler invaded Poland and occupied it within a couple of days. Within a week the mail confirmed that Oskar's number came up to be in the army. It was a dreaded day. He knew escaping the orders would be impossible, but he didn't want to leave his family or his secure job. There were plenty of men who willingly went to war with great gusto, the true fighters, the warriors of the world. Oskar wasn't one of them. He hated the thought of leaving his family and perhaps giving his life for something he didn't even believe in.

But there were only three choices: join when ordered, rot in jail or end up in front of a firing squad. The French Gendarmerie closed its doors within the month and moved out of Germany. Oskar packed his few belongings from his desk and walked to the railroad station to take him home from his office for the last time. Sitting, waiting, staring at the railroad track, the birds settling on wires flying in and out of the meadows and trees that bordered the track, the realization hit him hard. As per orders, he'd soon be on a train to Baden-Baden. His shoulders sagged and sadness permeated his body.

Hilda and Oskar took a short slow walk hand in hand through the narrow farmer's field paths. The scent of grass and old rotting apples smelled sweet. The quiet looks for each other said it all. They had the same look of love for one another as when they first met.

As they rounded the corner on their way home, Hilda turned to Oskar and said, "We need to tell Günter and Hilde that you'll be leaving soon. They're old enough to understand and they need time to process your impending absence."

So the next day, they sat them down and explained about the war and that Oskar would be leaving soon to fight for his country.

"How long will you be gone?" Günter was curious. He and his friends had been talking at school about the war. But he didn't really understand what it meant.

"I don't really know." Oskar pulled at a handkerchief he was holding. "That's up—"

"Pappa will be home before you know it." Hilda interrupted her husband. There was no need to scare the children.

"Will you come home to visit?" Hilde had stopped playing with her doll; her eyes rimmed with tears.

Before Oskar could answer his daughter, Hilda squeezed his hand hard. "I'll be home as soon as I can." That wasn't what Oskar was going to say, but he understood his wife's meaning.

"Well I promise nothing will stop me from being a good person and a good student. I'll make you proud. So you will have a reason to come home." Günter stood up for a hug and Oskar swept him up in his arms.

"I hate to leave you, your mom and your sister." Oskar wiped away a tear. "But I have to do what's best for the country. That wallpaper hanger is a big talker. He impressed the people at the right time after the first great war with this whirlwind economy."

Hilda rolled her eyes. "They say Napoleon was also an impressive talker and look at the damage his army made straight across Europe. I'll bet everybody was happy when his army met Waterloo! Napoleon's timing is just like Hitler's. He took over France and impressed the oppressed; look at the world around you now, oppression is everywhere . . . all over. The depression hurt so many people, even in America. Men, women and children stood in line at soup kitchens and begged for dimes and pennies. Napoleon was put on a pedestal by the peasants and what did he gain for France by killing so many of his own soldiers and enemies, and plundering all over Europe? He was exiled to an island. That's what! Hitler is using the same tactics, scaring the population about communists taking over. In the end, no one really wins."

Oskar flashed his wife a look. "Why don't we continue this conversation a bit later. Perhaps after the children have gone to bed."

Hilda's cheeks flushed. Oskar was right. They shouldn't discuss politics in front of the Günter and Hilde. But it was so hard for her to keep her feelings to herself. She was so passionate about when the leaders of countries behaved so badly.

3

October 1954

Vera tugged on Rosemarie's sleeve. "Where are we going now?" They'd gotten off the ship and finally through customs. Now they were on a train. Vera was so tired. She felt like they'd left home a year before.

"Good God, Vera!" Rosemarie turned her head toward Vera and whispered, "Leave me alone! I'm so stinkin' tired. Ask Mama. Go on. Ask her why we're on this train. Don't ask me."

"Mama and Pappa are sleeping. I don't want to wake them up."

"We should be too. So hush and close your eyes. Leave me alone."

Rosemarie closed her eyes again and huddled her face into the crook of her left arm, not caring why they were on a train. She just wanted to sleep. As she dozed, she remembered a big sign hanging from an ugly dark ceiling in what she thought was called the customs building. In bold black words, it said, *Le Havre, Quebec.*

Just like in Bremerhaven, everyone stood in a line that might as well have been a mile long with their suitcases and bags dangling next to them.

Official-looking men sitting at tables stamped people's papers. Then, thankfully, the line moved forward. Being on the train now felt so good, she didn't care what anything meant or why. She was happy to be relaxing now.

As soon as Oskar had been seated on the train, he started snoring in the same rhythm as an elderly gentleman across the aisle. To Vera, it seemed as though her pappa and that man were in competition as to who could be the worst and the loudest of snorers.

When everyone else was settled, Hilda sat next to Oskar. She soon found a way to keep her head almost comfortable by leaning on one of the bags made from burgundy velvet, and she promptly fell into a bottomless catnap. Knowing their huge wooden crate was off the ship and ready to be safely transported to Montreal, and the children so well behaved in the seat ahead, gave her the feeling that there would never be another woe for her in this world. They made it. They were here . . . in Canada . . . in Quebec riding onward to Montreal.

Now Hilda and Oskar's beloved only son, Günter, and wife, Ruth, would be greeting them with food and shelter. Hilda was so thankful to them for leaving their homeland in search of a better life for them all.

She reached for Oskar's hand. It felt so solid and it reassured her belief that the Hitlers of the world would never again make their lives miserable. Never again would a war control their lives. The idea of being completely free was an alien concept. Hilda almost thought it was too good to be true. That she and her family would never have another bad thing happen to them again.

The train clickety-clacked through the cold night. A lot of people from the same ship rode this train and all were hoping to start a new life, having left almost everything they owned behind. Here and there you could hear a sniffle or two, someone blowing their nose, and a child dribbling words to a patient and overtired mother.

"Montréal. . . prochain arrêt . . . Montréal. . . arrive à Montréal!" boomed a voice over the loudspeaker.

As Vera and her family stepped onto the platform, Oskar motioned for a yellow taxi and it promptly came to their side. A man who looked to be in his early thirties got out, picked up all the suitcases, and stored them in the trunk. Hilda sat in the back with the girls while Oskar rode in front with the driver, chatting in French all the while. The driver was curious about their experiences on the Atlantic and Oskar expressed concern about his girls getting used to their new surroundings and their lack of knowing the language in school. The driver quickly assured him that he knew other immigrant kids in his neighborhood and they took to the city as easily as learning the alphabet.

"My god, mama, where are we going now?" Rosemarie glanced out the window, marveling at how different everything looked.

"Rest now. Soon enough you'll know. It's a surprise, I suppose." Hilda patted Rosemarie's hand and she thought that Hilde would have loved this adventure. But Hilda reminded herself that Hilde was very happy with her new living arrangements and loved being a wife and mother.

"Who are we going to see? I don't understand anything. Why did we take this ungodly horribly long trip? Eleven miserable days and nights. Vera almost got lost in that black water and the way you moaned all the time, I thought you were dying."

Hilda whispered, "It's too important, and besides, it's too much to explain right now. So, both of you, watch the outdoors and see what's happening, or close your eyes again until we get to where we're going—Randall Avenue."

Hilda and Rosemarie sat by the windows with Vera

in the middle of the backseat, all aware of the day's early light breaking out of the night. Unlike Vera, Rosemarie and Hilda didn't pay much attention to the cars rolling by, the many bright lights, and the people holding their coats or jacket collars close to their necks.

Vera whispered, "In Birkenfeld, everything would still be quiet at this time of the morning. I wish I knew where we are. Where are we going?" She yawned, then she reconsidered. "No, I guess that's not true. I've seen Mr. Schloss walk with his oxen down our street to his fields even earlier than this. When it was still nighttime." She saw nothing but tall, brick buildings. "I don't think Mr. Schloss's oxen would like this city very much."

"Vera, who cares right this minute? Huh? Seriously, who cares?" Rosemarie put her finger against her mouth. "Shh."

Oskar and the cab driver chatted amicably as they made their way to Günter and Ruth's apartment. Oskar was getting tired and closed out his story by saying that it was a rough week on the Arosa Kulm. "Ships as old and as unstable as the Arosa Kulm shouldn't be allowed to cross the Atlantic at the end of September. The weather is so terribly unpredictable. As a matter of fact, when my son, Günter and his wife came to Canada last year, he took pictures of an iceberg. An iceberg! Can you imagine? He must have been scared stiff."

The driver laughed. "My grandfather emigrated to Canada from Holland decades ago and growing up he told me stories very similar to your son's. I am very thankful I was born in this great land and will never have to get on a ship like the Arosa Kulm."

"Well, I am glad to be here. But I will not soon forget the waves that were five to ten stories high and how the ship tumbled over and under the waves. I guess this is why the last voyage of the year is in September. Can you imagine having that experience in December or January?"

The taxi slowed and made a smooth stop by the sidewalk. "Here we are, sir." The driver opened his door. "Fifty three seventy Randall Avenue. I'll help you with the luggage in a second."

Vera was taken by surprise by how quickly he got out of his own seat and opened all the car doors saying something that the girls didn't understand. He opened the trunk and carried the luggage up the three steps to the front of an enormous glass door. There were nice houses across the street surrounded by small grassy areas. The few trees within view had already lost most of their leaves. "If my nose is sniffing correctly I would say I detect the scent of a bakery. What do you think?" She looked at Rosemarie who nodded in agreement.

Rosemarie looked around for the source of what smelled like freshly baked bread. She pointed across the street. "What are those white bottles in those baskets?" She waited for Vera to follow her gaze. "Near the front doors. See? Almost everyone has a basket and at least one bottle."

"Looks like milk." Vera rubbed her eyes. "But I'm too tired to think."

Oskar paid the driver and they shook hands.

The driver smiled at Hilda and the girls. He gave a quick wave. "Bienvenue au Canada!"

Oskar opened the large glass door and everyone stepped inside the warm hallway. Oskar pressed a button on the wall and a few minutes Günter arrived, coming from a second set of glass doors. Vera thought it was magic that a mere press of a button would summon her beloved brother.

Günter rushed into his parents' waiting arms. "Oh Mama! Oh Pappa. How I've missed you both!" His voice broke as he hugged his parents tightly. Rosemarie and Vera leaned against one of the other walls and looked at one another, their faces practically glowing. They bounced on their heels, hardly able to contain themselves. They were so excited to see their older brother that they could hardly wait their turn to greet him. Finally he came over and the girls leapt into his arms.

"My sweet sisters. I'm so glad you're finally here." Günter mussed their hair and gave them another hug. Finally, he left to help their father bring in the rest of their luggage. The girls took their rucksacks up the stairs and saw Ruth waiting for them.

"My goodness." Ruth put her hands on her chest when she saw her little sisters-in-law. "I think you've both grown a foot since I saw you last. How was your trip? We were expecting you yesterday. Was there a problem?"

Hilda gave her daughter-in-law a curt pat on the back. "Hello dear. Yes, yes. The trip was quite dreadful. I spent most of the time in bed being seasick."

The girls and Hilda put down their bags and removed their coats. Ruth was ready with hangers and neatly put away the coats in a hallway closet. "Oh, I'm sorry to hear that. Yes, I recall it was a long and difficult journey. Would anyone like breakfast?"

"Thank you, but I think we're all too tired to eat. Would you mind showing us to our rooms? Some sleep would do us all some good."

"May I use the bathroom first?" Vera asked.

Rosemarie poked her sister in the ribs. "She always has to go."

Ruth winked at Vera. "Follow me." She led her down the hall and opened the door for her. "Here you go. And just so you know, the white roll of soft paper right there." She pointed to a small table in the corner of the bathroom. "That is toilet paper. You use it to clean your private parts after you've done your business."

"Wow. That's got to be better than the newspaper

on the ship."

"And even better, if you pull on the chain behind the toilet, it will automatically flush."

"But . . . " Vera couldn't believe her eyes. "Why is there a tub in the same room where you do your smelly stuff?"

Ruth chuckled. "Because we don't have outhouses in apartments. Every single person I know has indoor plumbing."

Vera mustered up all her courage and stepped foot inside the bathroom. Then she lifted the toilet lid. "Oh my!" She looked at Ruth, as if for confirmation of what she was seeing. "There's no scary, dark hole. I don't have to be afraid that I might fall in anymore." There was nothing Vera hated more than going to the bathroom in the dark in Germany.

Vera thanked Ruth and closed the door. She never knew going to the bathroom could feel so luxurious. When she returned to the small living room, she looked at Ruth as she talked to Hilda about where everyone would sleep. To Vera, Ruth looked exactly the same. She still had dirty-blond hair that was cut to the end of her earlobes. And it was still thick and curly. Her dark brown eyes were bright, and their brilliant shine was further enhanced by her flawless skin. Not that she'd tell this to anyone, but Vera secretly admired Ruth's way of talking. She always talked like a sophisticated city lady . . . in High German; not like them in Swabian.

Ruth had a small neat bed ready for Vera in the hallway, and Rosemarie's bed was all prepared on a red couch in the living room. Neither one had any trouble falling asleep. The adults continued to talk for a few more minutes and then went to rest themselves. Günter stayed up and left for work earlier than usual.

It was close to three when Oskar and Hilda woke

the girls.

"We won't be able to sleep tonight if we don't get up now . . . up, up, princesses, can't sleep all day!" Pappa patted their heads and dutifully they obeyed.

"Where's Günter?" Rosemarie asked.

"At work. He'll be home soon."

"Where's Ruth?"

"She's also at work."

"I'll cut some bread for you and look . . . come here. What do you think this is?" As the girls entered the kitchen, Hilda stepped backwards and stretched out her arm and hand as though she was introducing someone on a stage and pointed at a big white and sort of shiny box against the wall.

Rosemarie pressed an index finger to her dimpled cheek. She raised her eyebrows as though she were giving great serious thought to the question. After a couple seconds, she tried to sound extravagantly adult and sophisticated by speaking first in High German, "Mama, I must tell you that I gave your question a great deal of thought. However, I would not want to spoil your fun by not telling us what this white thing here is."

The cute part that Hilda liked was that every time, toward the end, Rosemarie automatically fell back into Swabian, and she never knew it.

"I've never seen anything like it and I'm sure everyone here is desperate to know." She stepped closer to the door. "Whoa! Look at that! It looks like there's a door. Have you tried it, Mama?" She smiled at Hilda.

"Yes, I have." Hilda walked to the door and opened it. "And here's the butter as cold as ice! Come and look. Feel the air! Feel the inside of this box, It's cold. Come. It won't bite."

Hilda held the door open and Rosemarie tested the cold air inside.

"How does it get that cold in there?"

"Günter told me, before he left for work, but I forget now. By the way, this is called a fridge or something like that. Just imagine, food stays cold inside and stays good to eat for days afterwards. Not only that, but guess what? Günter told me that everybody in the city has one in their kitchen."

"That's great, Mama! I mean that's really something. Vera, get rid of that blank look! Come on over here! You need to see this!" Vera felt as though she didn't know where she was and wished she could have stayed in bed. "Come and see what's called a fridge! Hey, it's our first English word!"

"I'll fix you some bread with butter, and I saw that Ruth has cinnamon," Hilda said. "How about that? And chamomile tea. Sit . . . sit, girls."

Oskar was at the table when Vera returned to the kitchen.

"Pappa, Mama, seriously, tell us where we are, how long we're staying, who's feeding our rabbits while we're gone? Vera, don't *you* want to know?" asked Rosemarie, looking back at her parents. "Is it a secret? Can no one know? What about Hilde? Does she know where we are? Is she worried about us?"

Oskar sat upright, shoulders back. "Yes, Hilde knows we left Germany. She took your rabbits and promised to take very good care of them. I suppose now is a good time to explain. Sit back and listen." Oskar took a deep breath. "The reason you didn't know about this trip was because, if you knew, then all of the people in Birkenfeld would have known. You would have told a friend, and that friend would have told another, and so on. For many, many reasons this is the kind of move most people want to keep to themselves. I know you don't understand the many hurdles that are there for people who want to migrate out of Germany, but we do know the problems and pitfalls . . . so we had to keep our intentions a secret from you, our neighbors, even from some friends."

"I—" Rosemarie started to ask a question.

"No," replied Oskar, "don't say anything. Someday you'll understand why we did this. It's for us…you, your children and so on down the line. Someday you'll thank us."

Hilda smiled coming from the kitchen. "I don't mean to interrupt, but this is so exciting. Look how much easier the cooking area is. I can't believe we don't have to chop wood and stoke up a fire just to heat water or cook something. Look girls." Hilda gave a demonstration of the gas stove's ability to light up and close down at a finger's touch by merely turning a little handle. She walked to the sink. "Not only that, hot water comes out of this faucet here, and cold comes out of this one here." Both girls got up to test the water.

"Who would have ever thought of inventing instant dishwater," Rosemarie replied.

"How does the water get hot, Mama?" asked Vera.

"Hmm, that I don't know . . . Oskar, how *does* the water get hot?"

"I'll have to ask Günter." Oskar shook his head. "No idea how a big building like this manages that. I didn't experience that in Italy or in France, even during the good times. I'll have to get back to you girls."

"Ah ha, Pappa! Hold on! Hold on! You told us once a long, long time ago that you knew everything!" Vera piped up, excited and smiling.

"Well, girls, that goes to show you that your pappa can sometimes exaggerate. You'll go to the neighborhood school. We'll enroll you on Monday. You'll learn to speak English and French. And listen, you're luckier than most because after all, you know I can help you. They're easy languages. You'll like your new modern life . . . remember, no matter what, we love you, and everything we did, we did it for you. We sold our house and everything in it. And let's not ever forget that we owe a lot of gratitude to Günter and Ruth for taking the first step into this new country."

"Where are we anyway?" Vera asked, looking uncertain.

"We're in Montréal. It's a city in Canada."

"Hmmm," Rosemarie remarked. "And why did you sell everything? Are we staying here forever?"

Oskar became uncomfortable sitting. Ever since he came home as a POW from France in 1948, he had experienced severe back pain, which Hilda recognized immediately by the slump of his shoulders. "We're going to make new lives for ourselves here."

"Are we going to live with Günter and Ruth forever?" Vera asked.

"We're just here for a while then we'll get our own place. But I promise we can visit whenever you want. It will be so nice to have all of us back together again."

They heard the opening of the front door, and Ruth entered the kitchen carrying a bag of groceries, greeting everyone and offering to make dinner. "Günter should be home in about an hour, about five, so dinner should be ready by then."

Vera ran to her and hugged her. "Oh Ruth! Mama says we can come visit even when we get our own house. Would that be okay?"

Ruth stroked Vera's hair. "Of course, sweetheart. Why don't you and your sister go to your bed and play while I make dinner?"

Rosemarie took Vera by her forearm and pulled her into the living room and toward the balcony door. The city was already dark and house lights illuminated the inky sky. Every so often a dog barked and a cold wind penetrated through their clothing.

"Look at this, Vera. What a wide street. Nice houses and so many cars. And look at that beautiful harvest moon. Big and bright. Did you know that at home, if I kept my head in a certain direction I could look at the moon until I fell asleep? Just about every night. It's like a giant jewel in the sky. One giant pearl. If I died, I would rather go up to the moon instead of heaven. Wouldn't you? I would look down and laugh."

Vera wrapped her arms around her chest. "I'm cold, Rosemarie. Yes, yes, and yes! The moon is beautiful and bright! Like a jewel! But I'm going in before I freeze to death."

Rosemarie stepped inside. "Glad you talked me into coming back in. It was pretty cold out there."

After dinner Ruth stayed in the apartment to clean up while everyone else was ushered downstairs and outside to admire Günter's truck. It wasn't new, but it was clean. Oskar stepped inside the truck and fiddled with the steering wheel. Hilda and the girls giggled when he said, "Vrum, vrum, vrum." Rosemarie and Vera stayed close by their mother's side. It was cold and they wanted to go back inside.

Rosemarie pointed to the left. "See, Mama? Just two doors away is a bakery. Can you see the sign? It's a loaf of bread. Can we go tomorrow just to see what they have? Please? It smelled so good when we passed by."

"According to our papers, a transportation company will deliver our crate tomorrow. Your pappa and I will be busy unpacking. But I see no reason why the two of you can't go." Hilda continued in a softer voice. "Isn't this exciting? Günter has his own vehicle, and this is our second night in Montreal. It's so hard to believe we made it to this special day." But when her girls weren't looking, Hilda looked at the ground to wipe away a tear. She was homesick already. She missed her eldest daughter and grandson and wondered when she would see them next.

To the girls it seemed forever until they all went back inside the apartment. They were cold and tired and wanted to go to sleep. They were grateful when Hilda urged them to get ready for bed. Six days and nights on a rather uncharitable Atlantic, to several hours on train throughout the night, a long taxi ride, and catching up with family turned into a very long week.

38

4

The delivery truck arrived late morning. Two men in navy blue uniforms huffed up the four flights of stairs. Vera heard the commotion and got Oskar. He rushed to the door and held it open for the men to deposit the crate inside the hallway. Oskar shook their hands and gave them each a dollar.

"Okay girls, stand back a little. After being in a warehouse overnight by the waterfront, who knows what might jump out!" Oskar laughed and the girls stepped back. He reached for the crowbar Günter had left him.

"Better yet," Hilda smiled at the girls and turned to Oskar, "do you have any money on you? This is a good time for them to go to the bakery and see what's there."

He stopped tugging and pulling on the crate long enough to check his pockets and pulled out a bill and gave it to Rosemarie.

"Thank you, Pappa," Rosemarie said politely, and they quickly slipped by the crate and out the door.

"Hold it girls!" Hilda waved at her daughters. "Over here . . . over here. I want to talk to you for just a second. Come into the kitchen. Sit . . . sit." Hilda pushed the chairs away from the table and patted the seat with her hand.

"What?" asked Rosemarie.

"I really want you two to stick together, even if you argue and get mad at each other. Above all, do not talk to anyone, except the help in the bakery. You hear me?"

"Yes. Sure." They were anxious to go.

"I repeat. Don't talk to anyone except the people who work at the bakery. And definitely not any of the men sitting in the yellow cars parked alongside the street. This isn't like our village where we knew everyone. Like Pappa explained, Montreal is a big city. We know no one here. But go and see what they have. Get something good for yourselves."

"It's only two doors away. What can happen?" asked Rosemarie.

"Okay if we go now?" Vera asked impatiently.

"Sure girls. Go." Hilda looked each girl in the eye, sure she'd made her point clear.

It was overcast. A cold gust of wind swept hair into their faces. Vera reached for her sister's hand.

"I'm not going to hold your hand. Maybe you want to look like a baby, but I don't. I'm going to be fourteen next month, so I'm not holding anyone's hand." Rosemarie was thoroughly annoyed. She pushed her shoulders farther back and held up her chin.

"Come on. Mama said we should stick together," admonished Vera.

"Stop it. We're here already, so keep quiet and let's check out this bakery."

As Rosemarie opened the door a bell jingled just loud enough for an elderly woman to come out of a back area. She had a yellow kerchief around her head, and her blue eyes were smiling. The sisters saw wooden slanted shelves showing off different kinds of bread. Inside a glass counter were several trays with different rolls and cakes with cream.

"I think they have the same kind of stuff just like back home," Vera said.

"Vera, remember? There is no back home. We're here now, this is our home. So look at all this good stuff. Isn't this great?"

The lady had her hands in her apron pockets and listened attentively. She let them carry on a bit longer. "Young ladies, I'm Mrs. Blatt. What are your names?"

"I'm Vera. Pleased to meet you." Vera spoke in German. She stretched out her hand and stepped forward to shake the woman's hand.

"And you?" She looked at Rosemarie.

"I'm Rosemarie. I'm almost fourteen. How come you speak a weird kind of German?"

"It's Yiddish. Have you ever heard of it?" Dumbfounded, they shook their heads.

"You girls are pretty. Do you live here or are you visiting?"

"We live just two buildings away. Our pappa gave us money so we could buy something to eat."

"My husband bakes everything I have and, believe me, he's the best baker I know!"

"You're lucky. That means you get to eat anything you like any time."

She touched her belly. "It shows, doesn't it! Is there anything that looks good, so I can fatten up the two of you a little bit?"

Rosemarie touched her dimple. "Everything looks good. Hmm. Let's see."

"I'd like to buy one of those Kaiser rolls over here." Vera pointed to the tray.

"Me too, I guess," Rosemarie said.

"That will be thirty cents, girls."

Rosemarie pulled out the one dollar bill and stretched it flat on the counter.

"Hey look, Vera, there's a lady's picture on the money."

"You don't know who that is?" the lady asked.

Both girls shook their heads.

"That's Queen Elizabeth. Isn't she beautiful? If you go to school here, you'll learn all about her, I'm sure. The coronation was just last June."

The girls looked at each other. Each knew instantly that the other had no clue what a coronation was and, as so often before, their eyes had a questioning look—were they really dummkopfs after all? Now they were terribly embarrassed. Rosemarie quickly picked up the change and the small bag off the counter, and without another word, they headed for the door.

"Listen girls, tell your mother that my husband's bread has a delicious crust and I have a machine that will slice it."

"We'll tell her."

The little bell jingled again.

Rosemarie carried the bag and neither could resist opening it to smell the fresh rolls. They walked side by side when Vera tapped Rosemarie on her back.

"What?"

"That man sitting in the third yellow taxi, is that a towel on his head?" Vera asked.

"I once read a book and it had a picture of someone with one of those things around his head. I think people wear them when it's hot. And maybe they don't want to get their hair dirty. I bet he's wearing it today because it's windy. It's not much different than us wearing our berets. But it's not a towel. It looks like a bandage. It gets tied together in the middle of the forehead. Can you see it?"

"No. I'm afraid he'll catch me looking. Remember what Mama said. We're not supposed to make any trouble. What if he doesn't want us to look at him?"

"Then he shouldn't have worn that. It makes him look funny."

"Rosemarie! That's not very nice. I won't tell Mama you said that."

"Good. Then I won't tell Mama that you're looking at strange men."

As Rosemarie finished talking, they reached their apartment building. Rosemarie opened the enormous glass door and they entered their new home.

"Thank you, my queen." Vera curtsied holding on to the hemline of her navy blue skirt. Rosemarie laughed out loud but didn't say anything.

"What's so funny?"

"I had to come all the way to Canada to a bakery with you to graduate from a princess to a queen. In all the time playing in the meadows I don't think you ever called me queen!" Their little squabble was soon forgotten as they were moments from enjoying their rolls.

As soon as Vera pushed the white button next to the mailboxes, the other door opened and they raced up the stairs. Out of breath Vera said, "I won! I won the race." She turned into the kitchen and almost ran into her mother. "Look what we bought!"

Hilda opened the bag and inspected the baked goods. "Good choice." Hilda took a dish of butter from the fridge and handed it to Vera. "Why don't you sit and eat. And tell me all about the bakery." Both girls started to talk at the same time, but Vera gave up, letting her older sister take the lead.

"You'll never believe this in a million years. Seriously, Mama, not in a million!" Rosemarie said.

"Tell me." Hilda urged her on.

Rosemarie told Hilda about the bakery, including that Mrs. Blatt spoke Yiddish.

"I know all about Yiddish. Mrs. Bloomberg, who

used to watch Günter before the war, spoke Yiddish. I believe she taught Günter and Hilde a few words when they were young."

"Yes, and did you know Canada has a queen?" Rosemarie was proud of herself for remembering that fact. "The lady at the bakery told us that. It was interesting and I kind of got what she was saying."

"And how did you speak to her? In Swabian or High German?" their mother wanted to know.

"Kind of mixed. She also told us to let you know that her husband is the best baker she knows."

"She has a lot of good stuff. Can't wait to go back." Vera finished her last bite of her Kaiser Roll. "There's something I'm really curious about."

"We'll never know until you ask!" Rosemarie replied.

"Why do they call this a Kaiser Roll?"

"You'll have to ask your father when he comes back from his walk," Hilda said.

"Oh yeah . . . there was this man in a yellow car who had his head wrapped up in something white. Rosemarie thinks it's a huge bandage. To me it looks like a towel."

"It's called a turban. Men of certain cultures wear them all the time. But don't fret, you'll learn about people and other cultures in school. You didn't stare, did you? You know it's not polite to stare. Right?" Hilda said.

"No, Mama, we wouldn't do that."

"I love you girls." Both kids got a hug. She shooed them away from the table. "You know we opened the crate, and we have a little mess in our bedroom, but I have your clothes in the hall closet and dresser. Now go and take a look to see what's on your beds."

The girls took off and Vera shrieked, "Ah, Snowbell! You beautiful, beautiful Snowbell!" Vera remembered the many Christmases that Saint Gabriel visited their house in Birkenfeld. Mama left the windows open and he'd come to the house on Christmas eve. Oskar called his kids and they rushed into the living room. A green pine tree stood in the corner decorated with silver ornaments, icicles and little bells. Candles were clipped onto the edge of the branches twitching with the slight breeze within the room leaving a glow on their faces.

"See how lucky we are? Saint Gabriel didn't miss our house and he was kind to bring gifts to all our children. I need to close the windows!" Oskar closed the window and pulled the curtains as he spoke. Rosemarie and Vera were mesmerized. Near the Christmas tree stood a doll carriage, white wicker with real wheels. A doll in a soft baby blue dress and cap sat on the chair right next to the carriage. It was the exact doll that Vera had admired each time she walked by the toy store. She had brown braids, dark blue eyes, dark eyelashes and ruby lips. Vera was certain that she was smiling at her and only her.

From the first time Vera saw the doll, she knew that if she ever got her, she'd name her Snowbell. Rosemarie always scoffed at that name and tried to tell her that Snowbell was a cat's name, not a girl's. Really, it was neither. It was the name of a flower that grew while snow was still on the ground. Vera loved those little bells and loved it when the snow around them melted. When they busted through the ground, spring would soon arrive.

Vera was so busy hugging Snowbell, she hardly heard Rosemarie saying, "Thank God I've got my soldiers. Never thought I'd see them again, and my purse, my jewelry, my New Testament." Those too had been gifts from Saint Gabriel. Rosemarie carried her three soldiers to Vera and sat on her bed. Vera kept rocking and hugging her doll. "It looks like Snowbell handled the ship better than us! I'm so glad for you." And just like Hilda, Rosemarie patted

Vera on her hand. For all the times that they bickered, there was no one Rosemarie loved more than her little sister. And Vera felt the same way.

"Your soldiers—hey, it looks like nothing bothers them either." Vera danced around with Snowbell. "I wondered what happened to her. I should have known, Mama wouldn't have left her or your soldiers behind. Can we play and try on your jewelry?"

"No. You broke my necklace, remember? It's probably the only jewelry I'll ever have . . . sorry, but no. You're too careless." Rosemarie adjusted her soldiers in her arms and went back to her bed.

5

Monday morning, Rosemarie and Vera wore their favorite lilac skirts, white turtlenecks, and white stockings knitted by Hilda the previous winter. Small white bows fastened with bobby pins kept their perfectly combed hair out of their eyes. They wore polished dark brown lace up ankle boots. Dark purple jackets with white velvet collars finished the picture for the first day of school in Montréal. The girls felt good and ready for their first day of school in their new country.

While Oskar put on his coat, he said to himself, "I am more than lucky."

They walked two blocks down Randall Avenue past the yellow cabs. Then they crossed the street, turned right, and walked another block, crossed that street and finally, there stood the school. The white building with light green trim had a sign with big green letters across the wide doors that read, *Merton Elementary School.*

Butterflies crept into Vera's belly as they walked past the large gate and the school's big entry came closer and closer. Oskar held the big door open, and soon they found themselves sitting in the principal's office. Neither girl said a word and no one said a word to them. Only Oskar knew what the man behind the desk said. He wrote on some papers, smiled in the girls' direction and handed a pen and paper to Oskar.

Rosemarie and Vera gave each other a confident smile, as they continued to hold their rucksacks. Pencils, rulers, notebooks, and their most important tool, the English-German dictionary and lunches were all they had for now. Hilda suggested that they watch what the other kids did and didn't do. Both agreed to keep a sharp eye on everything and exchange notes later at home.

Vera was in fifth grade and Rosemarie in seventh. A lady came into the office. Oskar stood to shake hands. He turned to the girls and motioned for them to get up. "Listen, princesses, I know you'll be in good hands. I'll be outside the gate at three o'clock when school is finished. So look for me. This lady here—her name is Mrs. Bell—will take Vera to her classroom first, and then she'll take you to yours," he said looking at Rosemarie.

"Thank you, Pappa," Vera said quietly. She missed Hilde so much then. If she had moved to Canada with them, she could have walked Vera and Rosemarie to school. She wondered when she would visit her family.

"Are you all right, child?" Oskar asked.

"Yes, Pappa, and I'm ready to go." Vera turned to Rosemarie. "Don't forget. I'll see you in the schoolyard."

"You'll be okay, Vera. I'll think about you," Rosemarie added quickly. Mrs. Bell smiled at the girls as they walked down the hall. They noticed that the floors were shiny and there were little closets against the walls painted a light green. The lady stopped at a classroom door and indicated to Rosemarie to wait. She smiled and nodded, letting Mrs. Bell know she understood.

When she returned, she ushered Vera through the door and there they were, all staring at her. Mrs. Bell took

Vera by one of her shoulders to guide her toward the teacher's desk. He rose and had a few words with Mrs. Bell, then smiled at Vera, welcomed her, and shook hands. As Mrs. Bell left the room, the teacher spoke to the class. Vera understood only one thing—her name. They kept staring. Oskar had warned his girls that it was kids' natural reactions to stare at new students. It made Vera feel less uncomfortable.

"I'm Mr. Fisher." He pointed to his chest and smiled down at her as he guided her to the back of the classroom to a desk. He opened the top of the desk to show the books and selected one for her to look at. Vera took the book and smiled, and he knew she had understood. A picture of a cute dog was on the cover. He was running with his little red tongue hanging out. Underneath the story began, *Run Spot run! See Spot run? Spot can run!*

Rosemarie experienced much of the same. Kids were staring while the teacher, Mr. Kirkpatrick, introduced her to the class, and she was ushered to the rear of the classroom with some books. Mr. Kirkpatrick talked to Rosemarie for a second or two until she understood to look at the books and try to read. She chose a book about Davy Crockett.

She studied the words carefully. When the bell rang, everyone got up and lunged for the door. Rosemarie was not sure if that meant she, too, should go and was glad Mr. Kirkpatrick indicated that she, too, should leave, and then showed her which outside door to use.

There were a lot more kids in the schoolyard than Rosemarie had ever imagined. Standing on the top stairs outside, she spotted Vera leaning on the fence. "How did it go?" she asked.

"Okay, I guess. Just like Pappa said they would, everybody stared. Everybody."

"Oh sure. What else can they do? It's nothing bad," said Rosemarie.

"Do you think we'll be getting one of those navy blue tunics and white blouses? I noticed they all wear the same shoes. Did you see the penny stuck in the middle of the front of the shoes?"

"I noticed that too. It looks like we'll have to wear a uniform. I guess we should ask Pappa about that. I'm surprised the lady in the office didn't say anything."

"I don't think anyone in all of Canada is dressed as we are! No one knits like Mama!" Vera laughed and stroked her turtleneck sweater and jacket.

"Listen, there's nothing wrong with our clothes. It's just that they have different clothes just for school. Mama and Pappa always make sure that we're taken care of. Right?" Rosemarie asked, raising her eyebrows. "What's your teacher's name?"

"Mr. Fisher," Vera said. "Mister means he's a man. He was really nice. I didn't understand a word he said. But he's nice. I like him."

"Good. Mine is a man also, Mr. Kirkpatrick. He's nice too and he gave me books to look at."

"But you know what I thought the most interesting part of the day so far was?" Vera said with excitement. "Some girls in my classroom wear colored stuff on their fingernails. I've never seen that before!"

Appearing interested, Rosemarie replied curiously "Hmm. I didn't notice. Tomorrow you'll have to show me what you're talking about."

6

Late 1940s

Vera loved everything about living in the Black Forest in Germany. Even during the war, she felt safe in her tiny village. She and her family were insulated from the outside world, protected. When someone wondered why it was named Black Forest, she was the first to explain that the conifer trees grew so close together that rays of sunlight could barely penetrate the thick, green needles, casting the forest floor in near darkness at all times.

Vera remembered reading an article that described the Black Forest as a truly mystical place where sorcerers, witches, devils, composers and the well-known, hand-carved cuckoo clocks were born. Many storytellers wove tales of the famed forest into their books and poems. The Brothers Grimm with Hansel and Gretel, Snow White, and Little Red Riding Hood. Philosophers and poets such as Friedrich Schiller, Johann von Goethe and Wilhelm von Humboldt. They all had set their stories near Vera's hometown.

Cuckoo birds flew freely and happily in the Black Forest. Vera was certain there wasn't a child who didn't know at least one song about the birds. She'd spent most of her childhood happily singing songs about cuckoos. They seemed to be everywhere—both in folklore and in her everyday life. She was amazed at how everyone she knew had a story about the cuckoo bird.

Vera was reminded about the cuckoo birds from Birkenfeld at dinner after her first day of school when Ruth called one of their neighbors a cuckoo.

"What are you talking about?" Vera put down her fork and stared intently at her sister-in-law. "I thought only birds were cuckoos."

Günter looked surprised. "You don't know?" he asked.

"Know what?"

Günter continued talking. "Our neighbor's daughter just had a baby and left the infant with her parents to raise it."

"I don't understand. What does that have to do with cuckoo birds?"

"Female cuckoo birds lay their eggs into another bird's safe and well-built nest. The owner of the nest always raises the babies."

"Really?" Vera was fascinated. "How? Doesn't the other mother bird mind?"

"Well, I'm no bird expert. But I heard that the male cuckoo makes lots of noise to discourage any surprise visits from the owner of the nest so the female is free to lay her eggs without being disturbed. Then when the owner of the nest comes back, she is met with a home full of eggs. And the other female is free to do what she wants."

"Just like your neighbor!" Vera was so pleased with herself that she made the connection. "That's so neat. I love it when things that don't seem like they should go together actually fit."

"Like puzzle pieces." Rosemarie reached across her

sister and put a roll on her plate.

Hilda pulled at her napkin. "There is a lot of old and new colliding in Germany. So much history. And so much of what you kids learned there is relevant here." Oskar cleared his throat and Hilda realized her mistake. She and Oskar had made a point to not talk too much about their homeland. They didn't want their daughters to be homesick. "Oh, but I'm sure there is a lot of interesting history right here in Montreal."

Vera loved history so much. She thought that when she grew up she might be a history teacher. "Maybe!" She wiped her mouth with the napkin she'd put in her lap. "But Mama. Please tell me a story about Germany. I want to know more fun stuff like what Günter told us about the cuckoo bird.'

Hilda looked at the dusty light fixture above the table while she tried to come up with the best story to tell her anxious family. She glanced at Oskar and he nodded, giving her the okay to talk about their old world. She closed her eyes, thought of a story, and then proceeded to captivate her family with her tale.

"Back in Birkenfeld, there was a road named Roman Road in case you didn't know it. There were hundreds of thousands of roads like this all across Europe that helped Rome rule the ancient world. They were often made using soil and hand-made bricks that were trampled down by sheep and goats until everything became flat and even. High praise for their straightness and solid foundations was always given. Perhaps you might have also heard the saying 'All roads lead to Rome?'" Hilda explained.

"What's a Roman road?" Vera asked, fascinated by her mother's story already. "Does it lead to Rome?"

"Once upon a time, yes. It did lead to Rome. As a matter of fact, you've all walked on those roads many times."

"How so?"

"It's right off the asphalted street that you all walked on to go to school which, mind you, that street was built many, many years later. You can imagine they didn't have tar in those days. All those narrow streets we used to walk from our house to the village and back were original stone roadways." Hilda smiled wistfully, remembering the details of her own beloved hometown. "All the weathered tiled roofs and red geraniums blooming in window boxes played up the charm of the old village along the road."

Vera was starting to forget Birkenfeld. She shut her eyes for a moment to try to remember the old, two-story Bavarian style houses with turrets. The first floors of these homes held the farmers' barns, sheds, farming equipment, farm animals, large milk cans, wooden carts, and worn-down wooden bins that held all the fruits and vegetables brought in from each day's trek to and from their farmland located outside the village. Farmers lived on the second floor above and sold their goods to the one store in the village.

Early in the morning farmers led their oxen hitched to wood carts and went to work the wheat fields and acres of fruit trees. Before each day ended, tired and sweaty farmers trekked back home with their produce and equipment in the cart. An old man walked slowly through the streets hauling his weathered wooden cart with a shovel secured on the outside. He'd stop to scoop up the manure left behind from the oxen or horses. He'd shovel it up and dump it into his cart and yell, "Cow manure! Cow manure!" Some of the kids often mimicked him, and they'd call him silly names. He'd stop and pretend to lower his cart, threatening them while waving his shovel at them. The kids laughed and squealed and then ran off. They believed that if he caught you he'd throw you into his cart face down! Adults were interested in the manure for their gardening.

They paid the old man or traded vegetables or fruits from their gardens. Most ladies were always eager to do business with him . . . after all, back in the day, manure from any farm animal gave anyone a green thumb.

During Christmas the old fashioned street lamps circa 1850 were lit up. The center of the village became the look of a holiday greeting card. Hilda once said that nothing much had changed in the village since she was a child, except that when she was little, an old man would walk the streets and yell the time. *Eleven o'clock and all's well. Twelve o'clock and all's well.* He'd do this until the night was over and dawn showed its face. The only time he would yell something different was when the gypsies rolled into town every summer in the middle of the night.

Before they set up their wagons and secured animals under the roof of the threshing machine located on the outskirts of town, folks heard the town crier yell, "Nail everything down! Nail everything down! They're here!" Everyone knew who *they* were. Some people jumped up and secured loose property. Gypsies were best at stealing what they could sell or trade in nearby towns.

"You know," Hilda said, bringing Vera back to the present. "There were also rumors that they stole children, especially the blue-eyed ones." Vera glanced at her sister. Hilda had told them this story before and Vera always worried about Rosemarie because she had blue eyes.

"Didn't a child get stolen a few years ago?" Günter asked. "I remember hearing something about it before Ruth and I left Germany."

"Yes." Hilda surveyed the table, grateful to have three of her four children with her. "It was three years ago. And people are still talking about it. The town folk still wondered whether it was the doing of the gypsies."

One morning, after the gypsies had arrived a few days earlier, Hilda had been working in the garden since sun rise. She stopped to stretch her legs and heard her neighbor Anna coughing. Hilda dropped her hoe and walked to the fence.

"Time for a break?" asked Hilda. Anna stood and brushed dirt off her skirt and hands. Hilda swiped a fly from her forehead. "Did you hear them last night?" she asked, referring to the gypsies. "I was sitting on our doorstep knitting Vera a sweater. I could hear them playing their tambourines and, no doubt, they danced around the firepit being happy."

"Yes, I heard." Anna nodded.

"In a way I'm impressed that people who have so little, can be so happy."

Anna looked into Hilda's eyes. "Ja, ja, a happy bunch; but someone told me that last year they stole a little girl who lived just on the outskirts of the village. I never knew which family. They moved away a short time later. Devastated and overwhelmed with grief, I'm sure."

"Yes, sure … why would anyone want to stay there?" Hilda replied softly as she watched Anna wipe a tear. "I can easily see why they would want to get away! How incredibly painful that must be." Hilda's children meant everything to her, and she could not imagine her life without each and every one of them. "My heart is doing double time right now. Honestly, I couldn't take it . . . never knowing what happened to your child. Look at these goosebumps . . . see the hair stand up?" Hilda raised her forearm.

"It truly must be the worst. It would be kinder to know a child is dead and buried. At least you'd know where he is and you could visit." Anna's voice became almost inaudible.

"Were the police sure . . . I mean . . . I mean if it was the gypsies that took her? Maybe someone else could have been responsible?" Hilda questioned.

"Oh no! I don't believe anyone in Birkenfeld is capable of doing anything as bad as that. No! I simply can't believe that. Oh, well, Hilda, maybe one of these days we'll know more. They say history repeats itself."

"Don't say that!" Hilda was horrified that anyone else might lose a child. "Let's just hope the police find out who did this before another child disappears."

Vera couldn't stand thinking about any child being taken, and suddenly she was afraid of her new city. If she got lost, never mind taken, she was sure she'd never find her way home. "So, does anyone want to hear about school? It was quite a day." She made eye contact with Rosemarie who started talking. Vera was grateful that her sister understood that she had had enough talk about children getting stolen.

Later that night in bed, Vera realized that the mother cuckoo explanation was the first time in a long time that she and Günter had had one of their conversations. Even though her big brother was twelve years older than her, Vera had always felt like she could talk to him about anything. He was the perfect combination of father, brother and friend. She hadn't realized until that moment how much she had missed him over the last year since he'd been gone. And she knew then, that coming to Canada was the right decision. She only hoped that one day Hilde, little Gabriel and her husband would join them in North America. Only then would she feel like her family was whole again.

7

1940

Oskar and Hilda sat outside next to the big leafed rhubarb facing each other. He covered her hands with his and looked intently into her eyes. "You know that tomorrow I'll be on the train headed for Baden-Baden. Hilda." Oskar sucked in his breath. "You'll have Günter and you're strong and smart. Hilde will help you take care of meals and cooking. I know you'll be okay. Just know I'll love you even more every minute, wherever I am and," he smiled pointing to his left, "before those white lilacs over there bloom again, I'll return to you. Remember I'll see the same stars as you."

"Please . . . please be sure to write to me, please." She got up and sat on his lap and put her arms around him begging once more.

"You know I will. Don't worry sweetheart, you'll hear from me." He kissed her with such fervor it took her breath away. "I'll be gone before you wake."

"You'll always be my darling," Hilda whispered in his ear. The night proved that both bodies and minds knew that every caress could be their last one as they made love in slow motion savoring every breath of every moment. After Oskar fell asleep Hilda cried softly into her pillow half the night before she finally fell asleep causing her to wake up too late to give him her final kiss and love. She looked at the spot where he had placed his brown rucksack and jacket the night before.

She stared at the coat hanger and stroked the metal gently as though it were a newborn. She swallowed hard. The thought that Günter and Hilde would be coming downstairs soon made her control her emotions. She forced herself to think of happier times.

As days ran into weeks and months she amused herself, Günter and Hilde by playing a few songs on the piano. The kids even sang with her. Faced with night after night of loneliness, Hilda slept with what she dubbed 'the crying shirt'—the one Oskar wore his last day home. The light blue shirt was rolled into a soft messy ball. Pressed to her face she whispered, "Return to me . . . darling. Be sure to return. We need you. I need you." She wondered where he was, what would he be doing? Would he see the same stars as she? The scent of the shirt quieted her mind enough to finally fall asleep. The aching, churning feeling mixed with the lucky feeling of at least having Günter and Hilde home with her. They were constant reminders of all the good Oskar brought to the world.

Birkenfeld remained isolated from the war. Most people hardly experienced any difference in their lives except for those with husbands and sons who'd been drafted. The pro-Nazi residents showed they were believers in everything Hitler decided by showing off their boys' new haircuts. It was cut short on both sides and up the nape while the hair on the top of the head was left long, sometimes dangling down to the eyebrows.

The only radio in the house was in the kitchen. It sat on a triangle shelf just above a corner wooden bench where Günter ate and did his homework at the kitchen table. The radio was black art deco style. Oskar enjoyed watching Günter's youthful body climb up on the bench and sit partially on the shelf and for some time he was amazed at the tiny little lights inside. He thought tiny people played music or talked in the radio. The radio announcers showered the public with news of great victories and Hitler continued to scream on. When the crowds cheered just as they did before the war, Hilda felt frustrated and turned it off.

A few months after Oskar left for Baden-Baden, Hilda found out she was pregnant. Her neighbors had been complaining that food was scarce. But, so far she had no trouble finding enough for her children and herself. She hadn't been sick at all and was ravenously hungry. So she was grateful her grocer still had plenty of meat and vegetables available. Every day it seemed like her belly grew bigger and before long she could feel the baby kick. Oskar always wanted to feel the kicks when she was pregnant with Günter and Hilde. Oh how she missed her husband in those moments. And she didn't even have an address for Oskar. So she had no way of telling him that he would soon have a beloved third child.

Günter was barely ten when Hilda called him from the kitchen on a cold November day. "Günter I need you to run! Hurry! Run to Dr. Wilhelm. Let him know that the stork is about to arrive. I need him soon. Go darling! Go!" She waved her hand. Günter ran as fast as he could to the center of the village where the doctor and his wife lived. On his way to see Hilda, Dr. Wilhelm stopped at the midwife's house who, thankfully, was at home.

Dr. Wilhelm and the midwife helped Hilda give birth to Rosemarie while Günter and Hilde had a delicious thick slice of wheat bread spread with fresh churned butter and blueberry jam with their friends next door. After a short and easy labor, Hilda beamed with pride holding Rosemarie.

***

At a year old, Rosemarie had fine blond hair, delicate features and deep blue eyes. A year later, her smile could chase the devil away. Hilda could hardly wait to write Oskar that his second daughter had his eyes. Hilda often said, "If you look into the eye of a cornflower, you'll see Rosemarie's blue eyes." Hilda didn't know that this remark would become, more often than not, the only important thought in her daily life that evolved into an unending whirlpool of mystery and unforgiving grief.

Hilda received only two notes from Oskar. The first one was to let her know he was stationed in France and he wasn't allowed to divulge any real information. Finally she had an address to communicate with letters. The second one told of his anxiousness to see Rosemarie and that he'd be shipped somewhere soon, but didn't know where. He'd let her know as soon as he knew and for her not to forget that the white lilacs would bloom again next year. She could tell that both were hurriedly written. She sighed deeply each time she sat by the bedroom window to read the notes over and over, finishing the night by pressing the notes to her lips as often as she'd read them.

One day in November a small, brown envelope arrived with Christmas presents for Hilda's children. Hilde received a little ivory flower delicately placed on a hairpin. It reminded Hilda of the Edelweiss that grew in the Alps. Günter got a black comb and Rosemarie received a doll. Hilda read a note that said, *I don't have anything for you except my constant love with every beat of my heart. As I'm writing this I just received news that I'll be taking the railway to Milan, Italy tomorrow. Much love, Oskar.*

The first real letter came from Italy during the latter part of spring. Oskar wrote that the Italians were great people, despite there being a few shootings that ended with death. He enjoyed Italy much more than France and hoped to stay there until he could return to his beloved family.

The work space he shared with Mario, another translator, was bright, airy and clean. There was a lot of work and he only had to walk a couple blocks to get to his sleeping quarters. Most of the Italian people he met loved to see the Germans. Living quarters and food were good. Nothing much could beat Italian food. Not even the French. Mussolini gave long speeches that Oskar and Mario translated. He was busy all the time. He mostly had to translate Italian into German or Russian into Italian, and vice versa. Oskar was sworn to secrecy and if he divulged even the slightest bit of information that he translated, he could be put to death.

In June Oskar sent a note saying he wouldn't be able to come home in the spring. Hilda was disappointed because, after all, like a ritual last spring Hilda made one bouquet after another with lilacs and placed them on the nightstand that also held her favorite picture of them. The scent of lilacs was magic.

"Why do you make bundles of these same flowers so often? Why don't you put some on the kitchen table?" Oskar had asked once, curious.

"Because darling, lilacs are one of my favorite flowers, and the scent reminds me of everything that is good and clean, such as you." She bent down and gave Oskar a quick hug.

8

October 1954

On the second day of school, Vera and Rosemarie walked to school with Oskar. When they arrived at the front entrance, Oskar stopped and turned to his daughters. "Would you like me to go in with you? I have some time before I have to get to work."

The girls exchanged looks, each checking in with the other. "I think we're good, Pappa." Rosemarie glanced at her sister. "We know where we're going today."

"Okay. Have a good day. I can't wait to hear all about your day at dinner tonight." He kissed each of his daughters on the cheek, gave a small wave and left them in front of the massive brick building.

Vera grabbed Rosemarie's hand and pulled her toward the courtyard where dozens of other kids were waiting for the bell to ring. They stood by the fence and Vera studied the girls who were talking, seemingly all at once. She wondered if she'd ever learn English. "See!" she pointed to her right. "Look at those two girls, right there. The one with the two long blond braids. Do you see her?"

Rosemarie leaned against the fence. "Yes. What

about her?"

"Look at her hands, her fingers. There's bright red paint on each nail. Isn't that wild? I've never seen that before. Have you?"

Rosemarie stared for a second and the girl caught her looking. "Do you see the way she's looking at us? Funny how some of the kids are speechless when they see us coming. But yes, I see her fingernails. I think it's very pretty. What do they eat?"

Just then the bell rang. "Oops! We have to hurry."

"Can you find your way to your classroom?" Rosemarie asked.

"Yes. Sure. See that redheaded girl over there?" Vera pointed. "She sits right next to me, so I'll just follow her. See you!" She waved and dashed up the stairs. She and several other kids were still getting situated in the classroom when the teacher began to talk and handed papers to every student except her. *Hmm*, she thought, *I'll be handed papers soon and know exactly what's wanted.* She reached for her book, *Run Spot, Run.* She loved little Spot.

Rosemarie, in her classroom sitting in the last row against the wall, noticed a boy staring at her. Every so often he turned his head to take a quick peek. She checked her mouth and then her nose just to make sure she didn't have food or something on her face.

"Robert? Are you paying attention?" Mr. Kirkpatrick asked.

Meanwhile, Rosemarie was reading a book about Davy Crockett. She was engrossed with the pictures of Crockett's hat and tried to understand the story, with the help of her English-German dictionary. Time went fast.

The lunch bell rang and the sisters met in the hallway and walked to the lunchroom together. Oskar had given them each two quarters to buy their meals. The hallway was warm and neither Vera nor Rosemarie could believe it. "The kids in our old school should see this. Can you imagine, even though it's already cold outside, it's so warm inside." Vera spun in a circle, noticing all the other kids—none of them were wearing coats.

"I know. No more jumping jacks every half hour just so we can write!" Rosemarie flapped her arms, pretending to do the exercise.

The lunchroom had two cold closets with glass doors, so the girls could see all the drinks inside. Vera opened the door and picked up a small carton with red print, and Rosemarie picked one with brown print. Then they paid an elderly lady sitting at a register.

Rosemarie and Vera struggled to open the cartons. The boy who Rosemarie had caught looking at her showed up at the table. He looked at her and said "Rosemary, look" as he pointed at the arrow and the words, 'Open here' on the box before he tore it open. He handed it to Rosemarie and then he opened Vera's. He said something to a girl who sat at the same table. He left and the girl came back with two straws. She demonstrated what to do with them.

Rosemarie put the straw to her lips, then set it on the table, and closed her eyes. "Oh-la-laaaaa!" She held up the carton.

"What's in it? Goat's milk?" Vera stopped drinking.

"Good God, no. It's the best drink I ever tasted. Here, take a sip. Don't get greedy now! Just a sip. I warn you!" Rosemarie handed the carton to Vera.

Vera took a sip, looked at the carton's print for the first time. "Chocolate!"

They sipped their chocolate milk and chit-chatted. Vera stopped to ask why the boy called her 'Rosemary' instead of Rosemarie.

"One girl in class told everyone that the Canadian version of my name was Rosemary, not Rosemarie. I thought it was unusual too!" Rosemarie explained quickly to Vera as she took another sip of her milk. "Ahh, so refreshing!"

The bell rang and they headed back to their classrooms. *"I seh de widder draussa,"* Vera called to Rosemarie in Swabian. "I'll see you again outside!"

When school ended, they were glad to see their pappa's friendly smile.

On the way home they walked on each side of Oskar and bombarded him about their day. He told them their school uniforms were in their rooms waiting for them. They could try them on when they got home and practice their English.

"Pappa, I'm not sure if it's safe to learn English from you because you sound so different from other people here. No offense, but I can't help but notice it. Why is that? Why are you different?" asked Rosemarie.

"That's because I learned English at the University in Heidelberg. We learned what's considered to be true English, or the King's English. If you were to go to England, that's all you would hear."

"So should Vera and I learn to speak the king's English or is there even a Canadian English, or what?" Rosemarie said. "I mean how should we talk? It's pretty confusing."

"I would speak the way you learn it at school, the way you hear other kids and your teacher talk." Oskar was pleased his girls had a great first few days of school.

They continued walking and chatting, and Oskar was so happy to have his two youngest children holding his hands, so happy and eager to tell him about their new school. The girls seemed content to chatter about things they saw along their walk. Suddenly, Vera nudged Rosemarie and said, "Do you remember the song we used to sing at our old school about May bugs?"

"Yes, of course." And then Rosemarie started to sing in German, "Maikäfer flieg. Dein Vater ist im Krieg. Deine Mutter ist im Pommerland. Pommerland ist abgebrannt. Maikäfer flieg!"

As Rosemarie sang, Oskar sang along with her, but in English. "May bug fly, your father's in the war. Your mother is in Pomerania. Pomerania is burned down. May bug fly."

"What made you think of that?" Oskar asked when they were done singing.

"Hmm. I'm not sure. It just felt good to sing something from back home, I guess," Vera said. "And I kind of miss being able to roam around with my sister like we used to."

Oskar stopped walking and squatted down so he was eye to eye with his daughters. "Try to remember not to say the words *back home* in front of your mother. It will upset her. But I think it's normal to miss things now and then. The important thing is that we're all here and together. We care about each other and have nothing to fear, so to speak. Your mama and I will always take care of you. And most importantly, just give it time. We just got here. Before you know it, Montreal will feel like home and you will have forgotten all about . . . what was that place called?"

"Birkenfeld," the girls shouted at the same time and laughed.

Once inside the apartment, Oskar took the tunics and white blouses out of the hallway closet. "Here you go. I think these are your sizes." Oskar handed one to Rosemarie and the other to Vera.

"I want to try it on. Let's go to the bathroom." Vera bolted with her tunic in hand, and Rosemarie was right behind her. It didn't take them long to change.

"Pappa, are you ready to see us?" Rosemarie called from the bathroom.

"Yes. I am. I'm sitting on the sofa and waiting." He thought in all his life he'd never seen more excited school children than these two. He was grateful. They easily could be fussy or difficult, missing their friends and their old school. He knew that he and Hilda were blessed with delightful children.

When he was a POW in France, after he'd returned from war, only to be sent back out again and captured, he was forced to sleep in the cold mud, among dead bodies. He heard the moaning of men who lay beside him, wishing for death to free them from their living hell. Every night he begged God to let him make it home alive so he could meet Vera. He considered himself so blessed that when he'd been home on leave the last time that God had granted Hilda another pregnancy.

The girls came outside, and with light quick steps, they pranced back and forth in their new uniforms. "What do you think, Pappa?" asked Rosemarie.

"I think I hear your mama at the door. I'll be right back."

Oskar opened the door and took the two bags from Hilda and carried them to the kitchen table. The girls followed their dad into the other room.

"What do you think, Mama?" asked Rosemarie, turning in a circle.

"I think the two of you look like real students, and the uniforms are neat."

"I was just thinking how lucky we are to have these two apple-cheeked kids!" Oskar said.

"A lot of girls wear knee socks. Can we get knee socks?" asked Vera.

"I brought some with us. I'll get those for you. Tell me, was your second day as much fun as your first? I'm so curious. What are your teachers' names again? I know you told me last night. But I still feel a little tired from our trip." Hilda walked back to her room to get the socks.

"Mine is Mr. Fisher and he's really nice." Vera was still twirling in her uniform.

"I have Mr. Kirkpatrick. He gave me some books to look at. But in the afternoon class, we had a woman. I don't know her name yet. I'm not even sure what she teaches. She had red hair just like Doris. When we left the room, I thought she kind of stared at me." Rosemarie mimicked someone staring at her.

"What did you do?" Hilda asked.

"Nothing. I went out with the rest of the kids to go home. Oh Mama, do you want to hear the craziest thing? There aren't any ink wells in the desks. How are we supposed to write? Always with a pencil?"

Vera got excited too. "Oh yes. I noticed that too. But did you notice that all the other kids were using some kind of pencil-pen thing? It's shaped like a pencil, but some kind of ink comes out. The girl sitting in the next aisle to me used it. I wanted to ask her about it. But I need to learn more English first."

"It's called a ballpoint pen. You'll get one soon enough, I'm sure," Oskar said.

It was only in the middle of the afternoon when they put on their pajamas and carefully hung up their uniforms so they'd be ready for the next day. Then Oskar read an article and they copied the sentences. It was important to Oskar that the girls learn English as quickly as possible. He didn't need any reminders that knowledge of languages had saved his life more than once.

Oskar remembered the days as a young man when he didn't appreciate his strict professor in Heidelberg. Maturity forged a fondness for the old gray-haired, tall and slim Professor Schulz with his quick rod. Students who mispronounced words learned quickly that he was not too shy to whack the offender's back or desk.

Oskar was busy helping Hilda in the kitchen, talking and making her laugh. Vera sat on the couch looking at a book and Rosemarie sat next to her wiping off her soldiers and laying them next to each other. They could hear Günter's voice and a giggle from Ruth as they came into the apartment together. Ruth stopped off in the kitchen doorway momentarily, admiring what her in-laws were cooking.

Günter casually walked toward Vera and stopped to look down at her.

"What are you reading?" he asked in German.

"Pappa says it's *Moby Dick*," said Vera.

"That's a great book. We got a letter from Hilde yesterday. Maybe you can write back to her and tell her that you're reading the great classics in school. She will be so impressed!" He took the book from her, looked at the cover, then gave it back to her. "Let me know if you need help with it. English is a bit tricky. But you'll pick it up quickly. You're such a smart girl!"

He walked away from Vera while taking off his leather coat and hanging it on his forearm as he sauntered toward Rosemarie. "I see you still have your soldiers. I'm so glad they didn't get lost in the move."

"I liked it when you used to play with them with me." She offered him one and he took it. "Want to play now?"

"I would love to, little sister. But I need to take a shower first. Then I'll play, I promise." Günter left and went to his bedroom.

When Ruth came into the living room, she had one of her loose-fitting cotton house dresses buttoned up to the neck. This one had big yellow daisies on a dark blue background. She sat on one of the extra chairs and straightened out her house dress, pulling it over her knees. She leaned forward and smiled.

In German she asked, "So how did school go today? Was it as good as yesterday?"

"It sure was different. Do you want to see our tunics?" asked Vera.

"Yes. Go get them."

Vera jumped up and ran to the hallway and produced the tunics.

"Did you try them on?"

"Yes. They fit nicely," Rosemarie replied.

"I bet you both look terrific! You have such nice figures. Are you going to wear the stockings your mother knitted?"

"Yes, the knee socks with the cable pattern. We like them a lot. She knitted them last winter . . . white, dark blue and black. Oh!" Vera clapped her hands. "Do you want to hear the English words we learned?"

"Sure." Ruth sat, looking intently at the girls.

"My dog. My dog is on the green grass. My ball is red. My red ball and my dog are on the green grass." Vera laughed. "I memorized it."

"Before you know it, your English will be better than the teacher's." Ruth laughed.

The family ate dinner together. Then Rosemarie and Vera finished the dishes and tidied the kitchen. They went into the living room while the adults sat at the kitchen table to talk more about the job possibilities for Oskar and maybe even Hilda.

"Come to the window with me." Rosemarie motioned with her hand for Vera to come to her side. "Tell me the truth, isn't this the most beautiful moon? There's something different about a Canadian moon, although I can't be sure what or why. Now here's a challenge for you.

If you had to describe the moon in one other word, what would you call it? I mean, besides the word 'moon'!"

"Hmm . . . uh-ha . . . I need to think. This is tough. I'm not crazy about that round bubble up there like you are." She kept staring up at the moon.

"Come on. What word would you give it?" Rosemarie persisted.

"What about bubble?" offered Vera.

"Why?" Rosemarie asked.

"Because it's round and kind of see-through. I would also pick promise."

"Promise? Hmm. Why promise?" Rosemarie asked.

"I figure that as long as there's a moon, there seems to be a promise for tomorrow. Does it make sense?"

Rosemarie was duly impressed with her little sister. "Clever. Real clever. You're the smart one here, like Ruth. Do you like her?"

"Yes. I like her." Vera nodded.

"Me too."

9

The next morning, neither Rosemarie nor Vera had any trouble finding their classrooms. Mr. Fisher smiled at everyone. After he closed the door, the kids stood and faced the rear of the room. Two flags hung on the wall, alongside a picture of a lady with a crown holding something in one hand. Vera was amazed that they did this without the teacher saying a word. Vera didn't know what was happening, but she did what everyone else did. She placed her hand over her heart and faced the British flag. When her classmates began singing something in English, Mr. Fisher hurried to her desk and handed her pages with something written on them. Vera tried to follow along.

> *God save our gracious Queen.*
> *Long live our noble Queen.*
> *God save the Queen.*
> *Send her victorious,*
> *Happy and Glorious,*
> *Long to reign over us.*
> *God save our Queen.*

Vera started to sit down when everyone began singing again and saluted the Canadian flag.

> *O Canada!*

Our home and native land!
True patriot love in all of us command.
With glowing hearts we see thee rise,
The True North strong and free!

Everyone waited for a few seconds and then sang, "Ô Canada, terre de nos aïeux," saluting the Canadian flag once again. There were six verses printed in French.

Vera mouthed some words and decided French was not her favorite language. The singing stopped after the first verse, and the kids dropped their arms to their sides.

For the third time Vera had started to sit when she realized everyone else was still standing. She shuffled the papers her teacher had given her and found one that looked like they hadn't read yet. The words were written in English and the only one she could read was *Lord's*. Vera watched the other kids as they dropped their eyes and folded their hands and recited something she assumed was a prayer. When they were done speaking, the students sat at their desks and began writing.

Vera lifted her desktop and found a blank notebook, but she didn't know what to write. So she picked up her math book and let out a small groan. Math was not her favorite subject, but she started doing some simple addition. Then she read about Spot again and copied sentences and looked up the meaning of words. Every now and again, Mr. Fisher made his way around the room, checking students' work and assisting anyone who needed help. Vera must have been working hard because before she knew it, the bell rang and it was time for a short break.

Vera found Rosemarie at the fence. "Did your class sing three different songs in French and English, all while standing with their hands on their chests?"

"Yes. I think they might have been the national anthem. But I don't know what the last thing they recited was. Did you notice the picture of the queen on the wall is not the same as the one on the dollar bill?"

"Yes. The crown is different."

The girls stood at the fence watching kids break into smaller groups. Rosemarie felt a longing for home and the friends she left behind in Germany. "Remember I told you that I have another teacher with red hair just like Doris? This morning I found out her name is Mrs. Brent. She hasn't said anything to me so far. She just stares. Like the kids."

"So how did you find out her name?"

"She has a thing on her desk. It has her name on it. I don't know what it's called."

"What does she teach? It's funny because most of the time I don't know what Mr. Fisher is teaching. I just read or practice arithmetic. It's not too bad." Vera thought for a moment. "But where is Mr. Kirkpatrick?"

"I think he just teaches math. I don't understand anything he says. But he tries to help me. How is math going for you?"

"I've just been doing addition. So far it's pretty easy. I'm sure it'll get harder." Just then the bell rang and Vera said, "I'll see you at lunch!"

Lunch came and went, but Vera didn't see Rosemarie. After checking the bathroom she quickly stopped by room five where she saw the red-haired teacher, Mrs. Brent. "Rosemarie?" Vera put her hands out and raised her eyebrows to show that she was questioning.

"Not here. She's not here. Go to Mr. Kirkpatrick's room." Vera didn't understand anything Mrs. Brent said except *Mr. Kirkpatrick*, so she assumed she was supposed to go to his room.

Vera checked her sister's classroom, but didn't find her. She went to lunch and ate by herself. Every time she heard the door open, she looked for her sister. But she never came. Finally she decided that Rosemarie must not be feeling well and was sent home.

For the rest of the school day Vera kept busy writing out words and sentences, saying the alphabet letters with pictures of various things quietly over and over to herself until she memorized them. She didn't have the time to worry about Rosemarie. Mr. Fisher also took a little time with her, pronouncing various new words, and looking at her math papers.

"Very nice, Vera. Nice work," Mr. Fisher said. Vera was pleased that after only a few days of school, she was starting to understand more and more English.

At the end of the day, the bell rang. Vera grabbed her rucksack and put in two books and the lyrics to the songs her class sang that morning. She was anxious to share them with her family. She spotted Oskar and Rosemarie and dashed to the fence.

Vera turned to her sister. "What on earth happened to you?"

Oskar said, "Let's start walking before we get trampled."

They crossed the street and Rosemarie said, "I'll let Pappa tell it to you. It's too crazy."

"Rosemarie came home with a note from the principal saying her teacher, Mrs. Brent noticed she's wearing rouge. He explained they don't allow children to wear things of that nature to school in Canada, so she was sent home. I translated the note, your mama and I had a little chuckle, and I walked back to school with Rosemarie. I simply explained to Mr. Black that due to our particular healthy climate, most kids generally have pink cheeks. Rosemarie therefore does not wear rouge of any kind."

"What's rouge, Pappa?" asked Vera.

"It's a cream that people, especially women, put on

their cheeks to give them more color."

"Do I look like I have rouge on my cheeks?" Vera asked.

"No," said Oskar. "Not all youngsters fall into that category."

"You'll never believe what Mrs. Brent did," Rosemarie blurted.

"What did she do?" Vera asked.

"She stood in front of the class and called my name."

"How did you know what to do?" asked Vera.

"I looked at her and then I pointed at my chest. She made a hand signal that told me to go to her. So I went to the front. She held me by my shirt sleeve. Up here, see? Like this." Rosemarie grasped Vera's jacket at the top of her shoulder seam and pulled it slightly up. "Like that. Then she talked to the class. But she talked so fast I couldn't catch even one word. Once she pointed to my face, and a couple of kids snorted."

"Snorted? Like they were laughing?"

"No. I don't think so. But then she took me to the principal's office. She talked and talked. Of course, I didn't understand anything she said."

"What did the principal do?" Vera was fascinated by her sister's story.

"He just looked at me with these little squinting eyes. Then he wrote a note and made me understand that I had to go home. The girl who sits in front of me brought my rucksack to the office. That's when I knew for sure they meant for me to go home."

"No wonder I didn't see you at lunch, but I sort of thought you were sick and went home. I went looking for you and ran into Mrs. Brent. Oh boy, I see what you mean about the red hair. I said your name and she kept repeating Mr. Kirkpatrick's name. I went looking for him to ask him where you were. But the bell rang before I found him."

"It was all so strange. Don't you think, Pappa? Why would I wear rouge to school? I'm still a kid," Rosemarie said.

"Yes, but misunderstandings happen when you're new in a country. Trying to learn a new language."

They continued walking and Oskar suggested they stop by the bakery and get some of that famous bread the owner talked about. As they walked by a cab, Rosemarie noticed the driver was wearing a turban. "Pappa." She pointed at the driver even though she knew it was rude. "I think he's staring at us. Why does he do that?"

Oskar glanced at the cab and motioned for Rosemarie to put down her hand. "He's waiting for a customer to come along. I'm sure he's just passing the time. I know Montreal probably feels like a big, scary city to you. Especially compared to Birkenfeld. But I promise you the people of Canada are friendly. We're safe here. We don't have to worry about war or crime anymore."

They reached the bakery and spotted Hilda inside. The girls ran ahead of Oskar and the bell jingled at the door. The pleasure of surprise was obvious in Hilda's smiling eyes. She took Oskar by his hand and introduced him to the woman behind the counter.

"My husband, Oskar." Hilda smiled with pride as she introduced him. "And I know you've already met our girls. Oskar, this is Mrs. Blatt, her husband is the fabulous baker."

"Pleasure." Oskar extended his hand.

Mrs. Blatt gave him her hand. "Nice to meet you. Your girls are charming. Before you know it, you'll have to fight to keep the boys away from those two." She spoke Yiddish and giggled like a young girl.

"Oh goodness, we're not ready for that!" Hilda laughed.

"Now girls." Mrs. Blatt turned to Rosemarie and Vera. "How is school going?"

Both replied at the same time, "Good."

"That is excellent. Are you happy so far?"

Vera spoke up. "I like my teacher, Mr. Fisher. He talks slowly to me so I can understand some of what he's saying."

Hilda put her purchases in her burgundy velvet bag and gave it to Rosemarie.

"That's interesting. I, too, have trouble understanding people when they talk fast." She looked at Vera. "Let's see, if I remember, you're Vera. Right?"

"Right."

"Come back soon." Mrs. Blatt walked out from behind the counter to the door and held it open. "It was really nice talking with you," then she looked at Oskar, "and to meet you. Come back any time Hilda, just to talk." She looked at Oskar. "I know you'll like the bread."

On their way to the apartment, Oskar commented, "Nice lady. I'm glad you have her to talk with. The only thing is—"

"What?" asked Hilda.

"There are people who don't know the difference between Yiddish and German. They don't know that it's a language by itself. Germanic yes, German, no."

"Ah, so what. Who cares? Everybody doesn't have to have language expertise. I understand her and she understands me and best of all, I tasted some of the bread. It's delicious. Believe me, you'll like it a lot." Hilda picked up her pace and continued home.

Ruth prepared dough for spaetzle and Hilda made a salad for dinner. When Günter got home from work, he stopped in the kitchen and gave Ruth and Hilda quick pecks on the cheek and moved on to the living room to see his sisters.

"How was your day, girls? Good, I hope?" he asked.

"The morning was good. But then I got sent home because a teacher thought I was wearing rouge. But dad brought me back to school and told the principal that I just have rosy cheeks. It was embarrassing. But everyone seems pretty nice." Rosemarie looked at her brother, happy to be reunited with him again. But it made her miss Hilde even more.

"How about you, Vera?" Günter turned his attention to his youngest sister.

"It was pretty good. But because Rosemarie got sent home, I had to eat lunch by myself. I didn't like that. I felt like everyone was looking at me."

"You'll make friends before you know it." He removed his leather coat and hung it up. "I think you're going to love it here. I'm going back in the kitchen to see if Mama and Ruth need help."

After he left, Rosemarie asked Vera if she missed Germany and their old friends.

"Truth is this," Vera said, "if I think about it before I sleep, I miss things more. Especially Hilde. I really hope she comes to visit soon. I can't wait to tell her about your rouge episode."

"Hmm. Have you noticed that if a student becomes annoying, they don't actually get punished? Can you imagine what would have happened at our old school if our teachers thought we wore rouge?" Rosemarie asked.

"I don't even want to know. But I do know it would have been terrible."

After dinner Hilda asked the girls to tell her about their day. Vera went to her rucksack and brought back some papers. "Here Mama, these are all the songs we had to sing this morning. And we had to say a prayer or something like that. It's written on the last page. But I don't know what it says."

Hilda looked at the papers one by one. "Now tell me, will this happen every morning?"

"Not sure." Vera shrugged. "It seemed like the other students knew it was happening and they definitely knew what to do. So I guess it's something that they do every day."

"How long does the singing and praying take?"

"I didn't look at the clock. We turned around to face the flags and the picture. But I liked the singing. Did you like the singing?" Vera asked Rosemarie.

"Sure." Rosemarie nodded.

Hilda handed the papers to Oskar. He read a few sentences and blew a low whistle expressing his surprise at the amount of verses. "That's quite a bit."

"No, Pappa. We only sang the first verse."

"Obviously, I never heard these songs. After you have a chance to sing them a few more times, I hope you'll sing them for us. Unless, of course, you want to sing them now. We'd all be interested in hearing them."

"No, no, Pappa, I have to memorize how to pronounce the words first, and I want a chance to learn the meanings. And then I will be happy to sing them for you. I just need some time to practice."

VERA CHRISTA DÖDERLEIN HASTIE

10

The household settled into an easy kind of harmony. Each member fell into their own routines and navigated the small apartment. When they decided to cross the Atlantic to start their lives anew, Oskar and Hilda had planned to only stay with their son and daughter-in-law for a week or so until they could find their own place. Although they hadn't discussed it with Günter and Ruth or even their daughters, the parents were quite happy living with their family under one roof.

Rosemarie looked in the mirror and smiled at herself. Her fourteenth birthday was just around the corner. Canada turned out to be fabulous. English was difficult but not impossible —just a matter of learning, memorizing. Mrs. Brent smiled at her once in a while and took time to help her. Mr. Kirkpatrick was the best teacher she ever had. The pretty girl, Julie, whose desk was immediately in front of her smiled at her a lot. When they tried to converse a couple of times, both broke into laughter.

Oskar was surprised and pleased at how much his daughters enjoyed trying to learn English, and even a little French. Perhaps both would also have a knack and ease for learning languages. He had visions of conversing with them in French and English at the dinner table. Maybe one of them would even follow in his footsteps and become a translator. He'd never met a female translator before. But there was nothing his daughters couldn't do.

Ruth was spending more and more time with her young sisters-in-law. She hadn't known them very well when she and Günter had emigrated from Germany. But now that she saw Vera and Rosemarie every day, she rather enjoyed helping them with their homework and styling their hair in the latest fashions. And when the girls were alone walking home from school, not surrounded by grownups and their family, they talked about how much they liked being with Ruth. They were truly interested in the stories she shared about cleaning houses—the tricks and hacks she used to get grout clean and how many different things coffee grounds could be used for. More often than not the girls saw Ruth with a cleaning rag peeking out from the pocket of her colorful house dresses. She was ready to shine a shoe or clean up a mess at a moment's notice.

Hilda had also been thinking about getting a job. Once she had mentioned to Mrs. Blatt how much she enjoyed making her girls' clothes. And the baker had given her the name and address of a dress manufacturer on Sherbrooke Street. Although Mrs. Blatt didn't say, Hilda suspected he might be related to the baker. An easy twenty-minute bus ride took Hilda right to the front door of the building.

The owner, Sam, had been in need of a lady who could bead-embroider fabrics. After Hilda worked on a test sample right in the small factory, Sam inspected the finished work and promptly hired her. To her surprise, this piece-work paid very handsomely and the work could be done at home. As much as Hilda loved her children and would always consider her first and best job being a mother, she surprised herself with how much pride she felt from being employed and contributing to the household in a financial way.

The girls were mesmerized by the beauty of the beads, and the different shapes, colors, and sizes as small as a head of a pin to as large as a real pearl. Oskar procured a suitable table, a good lamp, a much-needed magnifying glass, a round embroidery hoop, and a comfortable chair in their bedroom right by the window for the best lighting possible. Hilda spent considerable time in her bedroom creating beautiful patterns on exquisite fabrics. Often Rosemarie and Vera would rush in after school to see what their mother was working on. They had no idea Hilda was so talented. "Girls," Hilda admonished, "don't even think of coming close to this table. It will take me a year to clean up all the beads if it topples over."

"But Mama," Vera said. "We just want to see what you're doing. Everything is so pretty."

"Thank you. But run along. I need to finish up this dress."

Sam was impressed with Hilda's reliable promptness and her speedy professional work on necklines and cuffs of blouses or dresses. He gave her as much work as she could handle. Inside, Hilda burst with pride. She had no idea how good working would make her feel. She took such pride in her work and loved delivering dresses, blouses and scarves ahead of schedule.

Oskar was thrilled for his wife, but her success only magnified how much trouble he was having finding a job where he could utilize his language skills. So far not one of the ads he placed in the *Montreal Gazette* had been answered. No one seemed to care if he spoke, read, or wrote a hundred languages. He took inventory of himself in the long hallway mirror and saw he was in good shape. His dishwater blond hair was somewhat thinned out, but showed no baldness, and he had healthy teeth.

He had even started answering want ads for any kind of work. He was too proud to let Hilda be the breadwinner in the family. Yet, when he filled out an application for a maintenance worker or a delivery driver, he was met with a polite smile and a promise to be in touch.

Coming home from another fruitless job interview, Oskar lamented to the young elevator operator about his lack of prospects. "You know," the boy said, "our employment office is located in the basement. You might have some luck there."

"Interesting. Thank you. Thank you very much." Oskar stepped out. He touched the brim of his dark gray hat to show respect.

The employment office was straight ahead. It was a small, meager space with a huge calendar on the wall. One of the two desks was empty. From the other desk, a man in his mid-forties, got up and walked to him. "Hello there. Who are you here to see?" The man approached Oskar.

"The elevator operator suggested I come here and perhaps get a job."

The man reached over to the end of the counter and gave Oskar an application.

"Fill it up, then ve'll see." He handed Oskar a pen, but he'd already pulled one from his breast pocket.

A short while later, Oskar handed him the application. The man looked at the information. "Vell, I have only one job. I'm sure an educated man like you vould not be interested. No. I don't sink so." He slowly shook his head and looked at a paper on the counter that Oskar also saw.

"Would you mind telling me what the job is?"

"Janitor. See? Why vould you be interested?"

"Because I have a family and I need to work. Can you give me a try?"

"Oh shua, if you really vant de job. You come tomorrow at seven in the evening, or six, if you vant, and then you get to go home an hour early. I vill leave a note for Raoul to show you de rops." He glanced at the application and saw that Oskar hadn't filled in his phone number. "You have no phone? Check wiis Ma Bell. Dey vill fix you up. Sign here and here, and you're on de payroll as of tomorrow's time clock. One more sign, a time card wid your name vill be by de clock. Don't forget to punch. De rule is: no punch, no money."

They shook hands, and Oskar assured him that he would be there tomorrow.

Sitting on the bus he considered himself lucky to have been hired immediately. As soon as he and Hilda were solid with their income, he planned to order a phone. As long as they were staying with Günter and Ruth, it would be helpful to all of them. Everyone always asked for a phone number, and it would facilitate getting a better grip on employment opportunities. He wasn't planning to be a janitor forever. It was just a stepping stone to a permanent job.

Günter, of course, applauded Oskar's decision and recalled the time when he and Ruth were fairly new in Montreal. He had looked in the telephone book to see if there were any other Döderleins. He found one who owned a photography studio downtown. Ruth and Günter visited the studio and introduced themselves, but it didn't seem as though they were related. But they chatted for a length of time and Günter expressed his dismay at not being able to get a meaningful job with a sophisticated company.

The photographer put him in touch with a friend who owned a small firm that sewed leather items with special machines. He was immediately hired to keep the machines in good running order. Günter did a good job, and his boss was terribly upset when, a year later, he left to work as an engineer for Sperry Gyroscope, a corporation contracted to build airplane, rocket and missile parts.

With Rosemarie's birthday coming up, Vera went to her mother and asked if she could have any leftover beads. She took what Hilda gave her and made a bracelet with one large white pearl surrounded by smaller deep purple beads. She worked on it in the bathroom so Rosemarie wouldn't see. She was quite pleased with herself. It was nothing fancy, but she made it herself and was excited to give it to her sister.

On Rosemarie's birthday, Hilda embraced her daughter and softly stroked her hair. "Ah! My girl. Your birthday is our first real celebration in Canada."

"I know, Mama!" Rosemarie twirled in front of her mother. "Do I look older?"

Hilda touched her cheek. "You look beautiful."

Besides the bracelet Vera had made, Rosemarie received a pair of slacks made with fine English wool fabric. Oskar and Hilda had taken the bus to St. Catherine Street and bought the pants at Eaton's of Canada. A beautiful Scottish tartan of a navy blue and pine green squares with thin black and red lines. The saleslady assured them that these were perfect for a stylish young girl to wear in the winter under her school dresses or alone.

Rosemarie opened the gift wrapped box and held up the slacks. "Oh. They're so fancy. And heavy."

"Günter and Ruth can tell you that it gets extremely cold here in the winter. Extremely. Right?" Hilda looked at both of them.

"Right," Ruth replied. "The ground is already frozen every day when I leave for work in the morning, and in another week or so the temperature will change drastically. Maybe down to ten degrees at night. Isn't that right, Günter?"

"Yes. Your slacks will come in very handy. Especially when it's windy."

"What shall I wear?" Vera asked.

Hilda was ready for that question. "You have Günter's old ski pants. As you know, they are plenty warm."

"You actually brought those?" Vera looked disappointed. "How can I ever look like a real Canadian? I think I'd rather freeze than wear those old pants. Why can't I have new ones like Rosemarie?"

"Because your birthday is a coming soon, just a handful of weeks away. And listen, young lady, I don't deserve your long face," Hilda admonished.

Vera puckered up. "I really like the colors. They'll go so nice with your tunic. True, true, I'm so envious, that's true, but glad that at least one of us can start looking like the real thing. You know, Canadian. Can I borrow them sometime?"

"Sure. But not while they're new-new!" Rosemarie held up the pants again. She was so pleased with them. Finally, she put them back in the box and picked up Vera's gift folded in paper, and she opened it.

"Oh, it's beautiful. I really like it." Rosemarie held out her wrist while Vera clasped it.

"Really? I liked making it. I went to the bathroom and locked myself in so you wouldn't catch me."

"The bathroom, huh?" Rosemarie giggled. "Hope you washed your hands! Ah, well, I guess there could be worse places! What made you think of putting only one pearl?"

Vera thought Rosemarie didn't have to know that she had only one pearl to begin with and gave what she thought, a clever answer.

"Well, let me tell you what . . . tonight, when you look out of the window again, count how many moons are up there? You'll notice there's one . . . only one."

"Wow! That's special . . . so special." Rosemarie turned the bracelet again to admire it some more. She looked at Vera, "I will always wear it . . . always."

"You mean you'll never take it off?" Vera asked with big eyes.

Thinking carefully, Rosemarie said, "No. Never. Except, uh . . . except maybe when washing dishes."

Rosemarie was delighted to see Hilda come into the living room carrying a platter with a Kugelhupf cake and place it on the table. Right behind, Ruth entered carrying a bowl of whipped cream, napkins, and behind Ruth came Oskar carrying a tray with small plates, utensils, cups, saucers, and a teapot. Günter followed his father carrying a book of matches and some candles.

Later that evening as they stood at their usual spot in front of the window admiring Rosemarie's moon, as they called it, Rosemarie gave Vera her book of the New Testament that she got from their church in Birkenfeld. Vera had no interest in reading it, so she pretended to have enthusiasm by dashing to put it under her pillow.

"I don't want to get it dirty. I'm going to put it under my pillow where it'll be safe."

"Let's give this bracelet a name," said Rosemarie.

"All right. We give names to geese, rabbits, so why not a bracelet?" replied Vera.

"How about calling it Rosemarie's moon? I can pretend this one big pearl is my personal moon."

"Rosemarie's moon?" She looked in the direction of the moon. "Hmm. Sure." Vera shrugged. "Why not? Tell me, do you think people live up there?"

"I read that it's too cold. But who knows what else could be out there? Maybe people. Maybe souls are on another moon and we just can't see them. But, you know just because we can't see something, doesn't mean nothing's there."

"That sounds creepy. Something might be there, but you can't see it. Creepy!"

"I bet there's a whole world out there, or maybe even right down the street, that we know nothing about."

In Rosemarie's classroom the next day, two girls said something to Rosemarie about her slacks. Compliments, of that she was sure. It was a good day at school. She felt like a winner in her new pants. Julie, Margo and she giggled and laughed as they were trying to communicate something to each other during breaktime.

Vera had also made a friend, Claudia. Earlier in the week she handed Vera a note. Her mother had written to Vera's father asking if she could spend time with Claudia to watch Howdy Doody Time. Neither Vera nor Rosemarie could imagine what television was, let alone what Howdy Doody Time could be about.

Oskar needed a reminder. "When does school get out early?"

"Tuesdays, Pappa, Tuesdays."

"Hm, hm," he smiled, "I can't remember everything."

Oskar answered Claudia's mother to let her know that it was all right to have Vera come over. She would go from school with Claudia, and he would pick her up at three.

Vera loved Howdy Doody. What fun he was! The last time she'd seen puppets was in the circus that came once a year to their village. All the kids sat on the ground in front of the puppet theater and screamed, cheered, whistled and clapped hands.

Mrs. McCormick cooked macaroni for a snack and Claudia showed Vera how she drizzled ketchup all over hers. Vera had never even heard of ketchup. While they ate, she heard something in the other room ring. She looked over and saw Claudia's mother holding something against her ear. A curled cord tethered it to a pyramid looking box on the table. Claudia noticed Vera's interest, and after her mother hung up, she let Vera hold it. The only other time Vera had seen one was in the principal's office. Suddenly there were voices coming from it and as if it were hot, she flung it away from her. "Is that magic?" Vera asked her new friend.

"Party line," Claudia said and repeated, "it's a party line."

When Oskar came to the apartment he introduced himself to Claudia's mother and chatted for a minute. On the walk home, Vera couldn't contain her excitement and she said, "Pappa, you can't even imagine this. They have a box and when you jiggle a few wires called rabbit ears, a moving picture appears in grey and black colors. People in the box talk and play music. It's called a television set. Isn't that wild?"

"Maybe we'll own a television soon."

"Oh Pappa, we have to. I want Rosemarie to watch Howdy Doody with me. She won't believe it unless she sees it for herself. It's like witchcraft, only fun!"

At about four o'clock, Oskar leisurely put on his work clothes. Ready to leave, he stopped to hug Vera and went into the bedroom. Hilda was busy bead-embroidering. "I don't think I ever told you how appreciative I am," Oskar said.

"Why? What for?" Hilda asked.

"Because, obviously this unremarkable job I have is not exactly what we had all hoped for, but . . . "

"Ah, don't be silly. No buts . . . you're mine. That means your unremarkable job is also mine." Hilda teased him. She took each lapel in her hands and gave Oskar a full smile. "I'm so glad you're you."

11

Hilda glanced at the clock on the nightstand. "Oh, for heaven's sake look at the time. I know Rosemarie enjoys talking with Mrs. Blatt, but shouldn't she be home by now?"

"What are you talking about?" Oskar asked.

"I sent Rosemarie to the bakery for bread and rolls. She obviously lost track of time. I can just see her convincing Mrs. Blatt to let her sample this pastry and that donut. The poor shopkeeper has probably been trying to close up for an hour now. They get up hours before dawn." Hilda glanced at her husband, who was getting ready for work. He didn't seem concerned and that brought her some comfort. "So, darling, before you head out, could you . . . would you just stop off and let her know it's time to come home?"

He smiled at Hilda's habit of using the word "darling", when she thought her request was something more than a mere favor.

"Anything you say, after all," Oskar whispered in Hilda's ear, "I don't get called darling every day. I'll stop off and remind her to come home. I'll see you in the morning." He headed for the doorway, then instinctively turned back to his wife. "Not to worry, love. She's fine. But I will send her your way."

"Thank you so much. I'll see you in the morning." She waited until she heard the door close, and then she made herself pick up a needle and thread.

When Oskar got to the front door of the apartment building, gusty winds swirled the leaves that had fallen from the now almost bare maple trees. He placed his dark gray hat on his head and buttoned his brown jacket. He felt badly that Rosemarie would have to walk home in such nasty conditions. He put his head down, opened the door and made his way up the street toward the bakery.

When the bell on the bakery door jingled, Mrs. Blatt came to the front and smiled. "Ah, Mr. Döderlein, what can I . . ."

"No, no . . . " Oskar held up his hands. "Please, call me Oskar."

Mrs. Blatt leaned forward. "All right. Oskar it is. What can I get for you this afternoon?"

"Actually, nothing. I'm here for Rosemarie." He glanced around the small space but didn't see his second youngest daughter. "Is she in the back?"

"Rosemarie? She's the older one, right?"

"Yes. My wife, Hilda, sent her here an hour ago to pick up some of your delicious, fresh bread." Oskar glanced around the room again. Judging from the look on Mrs. Blatt's face, he doubted that she'd been there at all that day. "Is it possible she went a different way home and that's why I didn't see her on my way here?" He rubbed his forehead and continued talking, more to himself than Mrs. Blatt. "She must have gotten the bread already and is on her way home by now. I don't know how I missed seeing her. But, obviously, I did. She must have walked on the other side. I didn't see her because of all the parked cars."

"Mr. Döderlein . . . I mean, Oskar. I hate to tell you

this, but your girl hasn't been here at all today. Not to buy bread or rolls or even to chat. I don't think I've seen her since . . ."

"She wasn't here? Not at all? I mean, not in the last fifteen minutes or so?"

"No," Mrs. Blatt shook her head, "I haven't seen her all day."

"Okay. Thanks." Oskar swiftly touched the brim of his hat and rushed home, telling himself there must have been some silly misunderstanding and he would walk in his apartment to find Rosemarie, Vera and Hilda in the kitchen making dinner and laughing.

Hilda heard Oskar unlock the front door. She walked out of the bedroom down the hallway. Loudly she said, "You must have had a real nice chat with Mrs. Blatt, but I need the bread to . . ." She realized Rosemarie wasn't next to Oskar nor had she slipped into the kitchen. "Where is she? She's not with you?" Panic rose from her belly into her throat.

Oskar went to his wife and stood in front of her. "Tell me, did she have any other errands to take care of?"

"No. Nothing. Why? You didn't see her?"

"Let's go to the kitchen. You should sit." Oskar pulled a chair out for Hilda. "Sit down. Please," Oskar said in a quiet, urgent voice, "sit down."

Hilda obliged. "Where is she?" She tilted her head and pulled at her fingers.

Oskar bent down and placed his hands on her shoulders. "Hilda, listen. Listen." He tightened his grip. "Rosemarie was not at the bakery."

"What do you mean she wasn't at the bakery? Who did you ask? Did you speak to Mrs. Blatt? What did she say exactly? Tell me what she said." Her voice rose with each word.

"Mrs. Blatt said she has *not* seen her today. Do you

think there's another bakery around here? Maybe she got confused and went to a different place?"

"No. Not that I know of. Rosemarie never mentioned another one. Go ask Vera, she might know something."

Oskar gave his wife a quick squeeze on her shoulder and went to look for Vera. He found her on the couch holding Snowbell. "Vera."

She startled with the sound of his voice and then turned toward him. "Yes Pappa? Wait, why are you home? Shouldn't you be at work?" She giggled. "What a mixed up day. You're supposed to be at work, but you're home. And Rosemarie is supposed to be at home and isn't."

Oskar sat beside his daughter. "Vera, look. Is there another bakery around here that you know of?"

"No, Pappa, I've never seen another bakery. And I don't know of any others. Why? Did something happen to Mrs. Blatt? Is her place closed?"

"No sweetheart. Mrs. Blatt is fine. I was just wondering. Go back to what you were doing."

Oskar got up and walked back into the kitchen. Hilda was furiously chopping parsley. She always cooked or cleaned when she was upset. He put his hand on hers to stop her from what she was doing. "Hilda." She put down the knife and met his eyes. "Vera says there are no other bakeries in the area."

"Well, she must have gone to a friend's." Although Hilda hadn't heard Rosemarie talk too much about having made friends at school yet. "Oskar, look, you have almost two hours before you actually have to be at work. Why don't you check the buildings that look so similar to this one. I bet she confused the buildings. You know sometimes she can be a little absent-minded. She's probably in the next building over wondering why her key doesn't work."

"Yes, of course. That must be it," Oskar agreed.

"It's going to be dark in another hour, and a cold wind started to kick up." Oskar's heart pounded. "You're right, that's probably what happened. I'll go look for her right now."

Hilda followed Oskar to the door. She watched as he disappeared down the corridor. Then she closed the door and saw Vera on the couch still playing with Snowbell, blissfully unaware of the fright that had taken over the apartment. "Good God, girl," Hilda muttered to herself, "don't scare me like this."

Oskar walked north on Randall Avenue to the first cross street. He entered the first apartment building he saw and tried to get past the vestibule, but the doors were locked. He pressed a number of door buzzers until someone answered. He asked in French and English if anyone had seen a young girl named Rosemarie. But he just got a gruff *no*, so he kept going. He went up and down the alleys between the buildings and called for his daughter. "Rosemarie, bist du dah?" *Rosemarie, are you there?* After walking two more city blocks of flats and knocking on every door he could, he returned to his building. His instincts told him she wasn't there. He thought of other possible reasons for why she hadn't come home yet, but he quickly dismissed them. The bakery, after all, was immediately to the left of their building, only two doors over . . . only two doors. A five year old could find her way home.

Gusts of wind whipped across his face. He only took his hands out of his pockets to hold his hat on his head. Suddenly something made Oskar pick up his pace. At that very moment he clung to an old belief. As a POW, not knowing what fate had in mind for him, he used to think that one hope is better than none. He forced himself to hear her laugh. He told himself he'd return home to find his two youngest daughters giggling on the couch and telling each other about their day at school. There must have been an explanation. He wouldn't even be angry with Rosemarie, no matter what she had to say. He would kiss his daughter, just happy that she came home. And then he would go to work.

He walked past the bakery and stopped. He sniffed the night air and turned around. It was worth going in to talk to Mrs. Blatt one more time. He pushed open the door and the bells jingled. Mrs. Blatt was standing at the counter with a customer. Oskar waited for a few moments, shifting his weight from one foot to the other. Finally, he said, "So sorry to interrupt, but Rosemarie . . . did she get the bread? Did she come in after I left?" His voice was strained with worry.

She replied thoughtfully. "No. Sorry, Oskar, I haven't . . . I haven't seen her."

Oskar's face fell and he felt nothing but desperation. "Thank you, Mrs. Blatt. I appreciate your time."

Oskar entered the apartment. From the front door he called, "Is she here?"

Hilda was in the process of placing plates on the kitchen table. She stopped and turned to her husband. She had vague memories of making dinner. But she couldn't say for certain what she'd prepared. "She hasn't come home yet." She didn't want to meet Oskar's eyes. But she made herself look at him. "Did you check the nearby buildings? Did you see anything? What happened? What can you tell me?"

"I stopped at the bakery again. Mrs. Blatt said Rosemarie hasn't been in at all today. I checked two streets north of here, plus both sides of Randall Avenue. No sign. Nothing." Suddenly his body felt weak and words failed him. He sat facing the table, his head in his hands. He rubbed his eyes and his forehead.

Hilda sat next to Oskar. She started to reach for his hand, but then stopped. Her voice trembled and her pitch escalated with each word. "My God. What do you think? Tell me . . . what are you thinking? Talk to me. Tell me, Oskar, tell me what you're thinking." Her eyes pleaded for answers.

"There has got to be a logical explanation for why Rosemarie hasn't come home yet. She must be at a friend's house. Or staying after school to work on a project. She wouldn't just wander off."

"Of course she wouldn't!" Hilda had never been so sure of anything in her life. "But yes. She's a good girl. Maybe she's erasing chalkboards for extra credit. Should we go to the school?"

"Yes, that is a possibility. But listen to this. I know it sounds crazy, but maybe, just maybe she came back. Maybe you were in our room embroidering and didn't hear her. And who knows. Maybe she's hiding in our closet or in Günter's room, thinking she's funny. She's just a child, after all. Perhaps we should search the apartment before we leave." Oskar surveyed the room. "Is Vera home? Should we tell her to stay put just in case Rosemarie comes home while we're out?"

"She is home. But let's not worry her." Hilda got up. "I'll check our closet. Why don't you go look in Günter and Ruth's room?"

Oskar could tell by the look on Hilda's face that she didn't really believe Rosemarie was in the apartment. Neither did he, but they each got up and searched the rooms. A minute later they both returned to the living room.

"I knew it was a crazy idea. But I just had to look anyway," Oskar told his wife.

Hilda shook her head. "I know." She waved her hand nervously. "I already knew the answer before we went to look. It's going to be completely dark in another ten or so minutes. We can't let it get dark. You know she's scared of the dark." Her voice didn't sound like her own, and something was happening to her head. Her hearing seemed slightly altered. She felt her pulse in her neck. She thought maybe she was having an anxiety attack.

Then they heard Vera trying to copy the announcer's words on the radio and a wash of optimism fell over Oskar and Hilda. A second of normalcy. They smiled.

Oskar took a breath and blew it out slowly, trying to make himself relax. "Hilda, do you think . . . maybe . . . on the way to the bakery . . . she could have bumped into someone from school and gone to someone's home?" Quickly he answered his own question. "No . . . she wouldn't ever have done something like that without letting us know." His voice lost its confidence. "Or would she?"

"No." Hilda shook her head emphatically. "She wouldn't. She doesn't know anyone. Not that she's told me about, anyway. Let's hope I'm wrong."

"Well, if we don't know of any friends, maybe we should go to her school. Could she have forgotten something, a book or her homework, and had gone back for it?" While Oskar talked, he snatched his jacket off the back of the chair and reached for his hat as he headed to the front door.

"Yes, of course. Just like we said before. That must be it. She must be at school!" Hilda's face brightened. She got up too. "But even if she went back to school, why isn't she home yet?" Her hope was starting to fade.

Oskar reached the door and turned back to his wife. "I'm going to find out. I'll be back in a while."

Hilda closed the door behind him and then called

for her other daughter. "Vera, can you come in here for a minute, please."

Vera came to her mother. "What is it?"

"Do you know if Rosemarie has made any friends at school?"

"Where is she anyway?" Vera asked. She'd wondered all afternoon where her sister was.

"Can you answer my question, please?"

"She told me she's been talking to a girl in her class. I think her name is Julie. Rosemarie said she's nice. She also said a girl on the playground complimented her bracelet. The one I made her."

"Do you know Julie's last name?" Hilda's hope sparked again, knowing Rosemarie may have made a friend.

"You know what she named it?" Vera glanced at her own, bare wrist.

"Named what?"

"The bracelet Mama, the bracelet!" Vera was annoyed. "You're not really listening."

"Sorry princess. So, you gave the bracelet a name? The one you made for Rosemarie?"

"Yes, but no. She named the bracelet I made for her."

Hilda tried to keep her voice level. "What did she name it?"

"Uh . . ." She looked to the ceiling for a second. "Rosemarie's Moon."

"Oh goodness. What a pretty name for a bracelet. I need you to concentrate for me. Do you know if there's any place Rosemarie could be or if she might be with anyone?"

Vera thought for a minute. "Where is she anyway? I'm dying to tell her about Claudia's house. She'll never believe that tiny people dance and sing in a gray box. She's going to be so jealous. Ooh, maybe Rosemarie can come with me next time." Vera looked around the room, as if

Rosemarie might magically appear. "When is she coming home?"

"Soon, princess. Soon." Hilda heard the front door open and rushed to it. But it was only Ruth. She needed to talk to her daughter-in-law. She'd been spending some time with the girls lately. Maybe she'd know where Rosemarie might have gone. "Why don't you listen to the radio for a little while." She patted Vera on her back.

Ruth rubbed her hands to keep them warm as she walked into the kitchen. She leaned against the counter and caught Hilda's eye, but neither of them spoke. Suddenly, the hum of the refrigerator was unbearably loud. Hilda entered the kitchen once she was sure Vera was engrossed in some radio program and wouldn't be listening to the adults talk. "Ruth." Hilda fixed her gaze on the bread box on the counter. Tiny violets were painted on the side. Oh how Rosemarie had admired the little purple flowers. "Look Mama," she said the first time she had seen it. "Dark and light purple. My favorite color!" Now Hilda fought tears as she stood before Ruth.

Ruth stepped to Hilda. "Are you okay?" When Hilda didn't answer, she continued talking. "Cold out there. It feels like a strong Canadian winter is around the corner. Let me tell you, Hilda, last year when I had to wait at the bus stop the wind was so bitterly cold and strong it was beyond my belief. I stood at the bus stop feeling naked. But believe me, I was dressed warm. I mean warm. Someone told me it becomes a lot colder if the wind blows over the St. Lawrence River or the Hudson." Ruth realized she was babbling, but suddenly she was nervous and just trying to make conversation. "I don't know how the rivers affect the air temperature. But someone told me they do."

Finally Hilda seemed to snap out of whatever had her attention. "Listen, Ruth. Rosemarie is gone."

"Gone? What do you mean gone?"

"I mean I sent her to the bakery next door and according to the nice lady who owns it, Rosemarie never came in. Do you know where she might have gone? Does she have any friends that you know of? Any place she may have gone?"

"Oh, my goodness. She must be around somewhere. Let me think." Ruth tapped her nails on the counter. "You know, I'm late getting home today because there was an accident on Dorchester Street. The bus had to inch its way up Dorchester slower than a snail, and it came to a lot of stops. If it weren't so cold I would have walked."

"An accident? What kind of an accident? Maybe Rosemarie was involved and she was hurt." Hilda picked up a dishtowel and wrung it in her hands. "I should check with the local hospitals. Where can I find a phone? Or can I take a bus? How many nearby hospitals are there?"

Ruth touched Hilda's hand. "Oh no, Hilda. I don't think Rosemarie could have been involved. It's dark, but as near as I could see, there were only two cars in the accident. There were lots of cars around. But I think only the people in the cars got hurt. Why would Rosemarie even be in a car? She doesn't know anyone who drives."

Hilda stared at the ceiling for a moment. "Are you sure none of the people on the street were hurt? Maybe a car sideswiped her and she's in the hospital?"

Ruth could see the desperation in Hilda's eyes. "There were ambulances on the street. Maybe Rosemarie was there. Maybe she went off with a friend. What do you think we should do now?"

A slight smile crossed Hilda's face. She felt a moment of hope for her daughter. "How many blocks is it from here to where the accident took place?"

"Let's see . . . " Ruth looked up to the round ceiling light. "One, two, three, ah yes! It's four blocks from here."

But before Hilda could ask any more questions, she

heard someone at the door and rushed to it. "Rosemarie?" she called. She knew it had to be her daughter. All this worrying was for naught. "Where have you been, my sweet girl?"

But Oskar stood before her, hands at his sides, his face blank.

Hilda swallowed hard. She could barely form the words. "She wasn't there . . . was she?"

"No." Oskar caught his breath. "The school was already locked. I tried all the doors, but no luck. There wasn't even a janitor on site. No cars in the parking lot. I walked around the whole building and called her name. Over and over. I banged on the windows and doors. I yelled her name constantly. I'm sure she would have heard me if she were there. I made so much noise, I'm surprised the police didn't show up. Not that I would have minded. I wished they had."

"Me too." Hilda acknowledged. "What if she fell, hit her head, and couldn't hear you? Oh, God, I don't know what to think. I just don't know." Hilda reached for the nearest chair. Ruth walked over and Hilda explained to Oskar that she had told their daughter-in-law what was going on. "Oh, and Ruth told me there was an accident a few blocks from here. She can't be certain that no pedestrians were involved. Should we call the local hospitals and ask if anyone fitting Rosemarie's description has been brought in in the last few hours?"

Oskar pondered this for a moment. "On my way to the school I prayed. I asked for God's help. Maybe this is the help we need. Maybe we should start calling hospitals. But I don't know why she'd be that far away. She'd have no reason to wander so far away."

"Who knows?" Hilda said. "You never know what kids might or might not do. What if she accompanied someone from school and maybe on her way back home someone hit her?"

"Ruth, do you know where the nearest hospital is?" Oskar turned to Ruth.

"Yes. Sure. It's Royal Victoria on Decarie Boulevard."

He looked at Ruth. "Do you know which way I take the bus? Left or right from the bottom of Randall Avenue? By the way, tell me, why hasn't Günter ordered a telephone? You can see how useful a phone would be right now. You know what, never mind. Just tell me how to get to the hospital."

"Take the bus on the left side."

"See you later." He grabbed his jacket off the back of the chair again and was out the door. He rushed down the avenue and just caught the bus. Soon the large hospital building was within view.

At the front desk Oskar told the middle aged lady of his predicament and of his hope that perhaps Rosemarie was admitted to this hospital. She took his information and offered him water. She could see the anguish on his face. "Monsieur, sit down over there. *S'il vous plaît*. I will call the other hospitals and clinics. It will take me a few minutes. The local police department will also know the details about the accident on Dorchester Street. I will call them."

She turned her back and picked up a phone. Oskar listened and watched the nurse's every expression and movement. Oskar knew each answer was negative. A few minutes later, she dragged a chair in front of him and sat down. "Mr. Döderlein, the good news is, I'm so glad to say, your daughter was not involved in that accident."

Oskar did know if he felt relief or anguish. "Oh . . . okay. I guess that's good. But might there have been other accidents somewhere else? Could she be at another hospital?"

"I thought that too." The nurse looked so kind,

Oskar thought he might cry. "So I asked the officer if there have been any other accidents in the last few hours."

Oskar's eyes brightened. Never had he thought he'd be glad to learn one of his children had been in an accident. "I'm sorry sir, the police said there were no other accidents. *Mon Dieu.* I wish you much good luck. *Bonne chance.*"

As though something was stuck in his throat, he swallowed hard as he touched the brim of his dark gray hat. "Merci, beaucoup. Merci de votre aide."

Slowly he turned and made his way to the brightly lit corridor. Oskar stopped after a few steps, put his hands into his pockets and sighed deeply, exhausted, anxious, yet relieved . . . The warmth of his pockets gave a sliver of comfort. The hallway seemed to have stretched, giving the illusion of a longer walk to the exit than what it was only thirty minutes earlier.

As he exited the hospital, he sat on a bench under a bright, florescent light. He removed his hat and placed it next to him. He bent down low enough to rest his elbows on his knees and slowly stroked his hair. "Ahh . . . Jesus," he said out loud. He didn't relish going home to Hilda with good and bad news. The cold wind felt good. He almost wished the wind was even colder, more Siberian cold, the kind that feels as though it might freeze your brain. He'd give anything to not have to think right now.

Oskar held the pole of the bus stop sign with both hands and stared at the ground in front of him. He couldn't help but wish he were once again a young boy. He remembered the time he got lost on his way home from a candy store. He'd sat on the edge of the sidewalk and just cried and cried. Someone had stopped and asked what was wrong. Then the kindly woman helped him find his way back to his home. Oh how he wished for someone to take his hand now and help him find his daughter. Now he had flashbacks from World War II when episodes of sheer helplessness forced more than one man to his knees. He shook his head just as the bus arrived. This helplessness was different. This was a killer.

He stepped off the bus and walked again to the apartment building. His legs felt like boulders, each step slower and more effort than the one before. This gave him a chance to practice one of the drills he was taught in the military. Oskar gave himself a pep talk to help get rid of unwanted scenarios that had conjured up in his troubled mind. He had to stay positive, for his daughter, his family.

He reached into his pockets and found a dime. Feeling somewhat renewed, he stopped at the corner telephone booth and dialed his boss and filled him in on what was happening. His boss told him not to worry and to concentrate only on finding his daughter, and wished him good luck. He hung up the phone and looked up to the sky and thanked God for the decent people He created in this world.

"I'm home!" Oskar called, forcing an uplifting tone as he entered the kitchen. He smelled the familiar aroma of meat. If this had been any other evening, his stomach would have rumbled with hunger. But tonight he felt nothing.

Hilda and Ruth sat at the table with a cup of tea, and Ruth quickly got up to pour a cup for Oskar. "What happened?" asked Hilda. She placed her cup on the delicate saucer with beautiful dark burgundy roses painted on it.

"Let me have a couple of sips first. I need it."

She waited while he drank. When he placed the cup on its saucer she could wait no longer. "Now tell me what happened at the, what's the name of the hospital? Royal . . . oh, whatever." Hilda's hands were fidgeting, almost as if they were doing so by themselves.

Ruth retreated to the rear of the kitchen. As usual,

she leaned against the countertop with a cloth in her hand. For some reason, she sensed her in-laws needed some privacy.

Oskar had a couple more sips, breathed deeply, and recounted his experience at the hospital. "I also called my boss from a phone booth to let him know that in all probability, I won't be there tonight." Oskar called into the kitchen, "Ruth, shouldn't Günter be home already?"

"I'm sure he'll be home soon. His hours vary."

"When he comes home, we could drive around the neighborhood," Oskar suggested.

"No." Hilda clasped her face and quickly shook her head. "That's not good enough. We need to go to the police. We need help. I'm getting my coat now."

"You're right." Oskar got up and grabbed his and Hilda's coats. "Ruth." He turned to her. "Would you please fix a plate for Vera and not let her know what's going on?"

"Don't worry," Ruth said. "I'll stay with her. Maybe we'll play some card games. I'll keep her busy until bedtime." She turned around to wipe the counter behind her. "But if she asks about Rosemarie's whereabouts, what should I tell her?"

Oskar returned with his and Hilda's coats and hats. "Oh my. That is a good question. I suppose just tell her that Rosemarie is staying with a friend. Change the subject if she asks more questions." Then he turned to Hilda. "Perhaps we should wait a few minutes for Günter. If he doesn't come home in the next ten minutes, we'll take a taxi to the nearest police station."

"Yes." Hilda nodded. "That is a good plan." She put on her coat and then started to sit. But she was too anxious to stay still.

"What if . . . " Oskar started to say.

"No, Oskar there are no what ifs. No. No. We need to find her. Tonight." Hilda's voice was strong and confident. She shut her eyes tightly and made a fist. She hit her hands a couple of times on the kitchen table. "Tonight." Hitting the table brought memories of arguing with the SS who, without pity, put her promptly in the town's jail for failing to produce the proper Aryan paperwork. That had been a long hour, sitting in the cold jail. But the last several hours felt like a lifetime spent in hell.

Oskar touched the top of her shoulder, jarring her back into the present moment. "Take it easy, Hilda, take it easy. Right now we need to think. I'm sure Ruth can tell Vera something convincing tonight. But what about tomorrow? Vera will demand to know what's going on. Those girls have never been separated. And what about Hilde? We'll have to call her. She'll want to know what's going on. That her sister is missing."

Hilda touched her husband's cheek. "Oskar . . . my sweet, sweet man . . . God in heaven knows it's not that I don't care about my youngest, but Vera's reaction is the least of my worries. And Hilde is a grown woman on a different continent. I'm not worrying about them right now. All that matters is finding my darling Rosemarie. But yes. I agree, we shouldn't say anything to Vera. Nothing. Besides, there's really nothing to tell. As soon as we know for sure what's going on, we'll get in touch with Hilde." Hilda's eyes glazed, and her stomach hurt as though a weight had dropped into her belly, and that weight kept rolling around.

As if on cue, Vera came into the kitchen carrying her dinner plate. As soon as Ruth saw her, she excused herself to her bedroom. She wanted no part of lying to the child, if she could help it. As long as her in-laws were home, she'd let them deal with the child. And once they left to search for Rosemarie, she would play gin rummy with Vera to keep her occupied.

"Where is Rosemarie?" Vera put her plate and fork into the sink. "Why isn't she here yet?" When no one answered, she continued talking. "I'm dying to tell her the new words I learned." Her voice and face became serious. "By the way, Pappa, I'm better at learning English than she is."

"What makes you say that?" he asked.

"Because I discovered that a lot of English words are almost the same as my German words. I don't think she's noticed that yet."

"Like what?" Oskar asked. He was trying so hard to act normal, but inside he was screaming for his daughter.

"For example, *sandman*. Sand and man are the same in German. Now I've got a whole sentence. *Mister Sandman, give me a dream*." When that elicited no response from her parents, Vera turned to her mother. "Mama, where is she?"

Hilda swallowed hard and looked wide-eyed at Oskar, then blurted, "She's with a lady keeping her child entertained while she works."

Oskar interrupted Hilda's explanation. "When she comes home, you can tell her all about Mister Sandman. But in the meantime, why don't you go look up some more words. Maybe you could tell her a whole story." Oskar patted Vera on her back and turned her in the direction of the living room. When he knew she was out of ear shot he faced Hilda. "Let's go."

Oskar knocked on Ruth's door. She stopped knitting. "Is Rosemarie home now?"

"No. We can't wait any longer. We're going to the police station right now. Thank you for keeping an eye on Vera. And don't worry about talking to her. She already asked about Rosemarie and we told her she's babysitting." He started to leave, but he stopped in the doorway. "And please fill in Günter when he gets home."

"Of course." She met Oskar's eyes. "Good luck

with the police. I hope they can help you." Ruth carried her knitting and instruction booklet into the living room and sat in the armchair closest to Vera, who had turned on the radio. Ruth picked up her needles and yarn. "How nice, you listening to songs and me knitting. Nice evening, just the kind I like. Cozy, huh."

Vera ignored Ruth's banter. There was something in the air. She knew something was wrong, but she didn't know what. Could it be Rosemarie? "When's my sister coming home? Do you know?"

Ruth froze for a moment and then tried to sound nonchalant. "I don't know. I suppose she'll stay with the lady as long as she needs help watching her little one." Ruth was grateful for the lie Oskar had already told his youngest. "But you know what? This stitch is really hard and I need to count each one as I go. Otherwise the armholes won't be big enough on this sweater. Do you mind if I concentrate on this for a while? It's quite tricky."

"Oh . . . okay." Vera felt a bit hurt, as if Ruth were dismissing her. "It's just that I was told she was with a schoolmate and then, with a lady that she's helping with a kid? I don't know. I can't help but feel like there's something my parents aren't telling me. And now they're not even here." She waited for Ruth to say something, but she never did. Finally, she gave up. "Sorry, I know you need to count."

12

Germany, April 1942

While Rosemarie took a nap, Hilda cut sweet-scented white lilacs and arranged them with the silver pussy willows that grew next to the Enz and were in full bloom. She used her favorite cobalt blue glass vase and placed it in the middle of the kitchen table. She stood back and felt the satisfaction of an artist who had created a beautiful painting. Shortly she'd take the train and bring a bouquet to Mrs. Rosenblum. She also loved those flowers and she hadn't even met Rosemarie yet. Besides, they always had lots to talk about. Rose was a widow in her early sixties with no children, yet Hilda found her to be very smart about kids and more than once she sought advice from her.

Hilda was about to go upstairs and get dressed so she could visit her friend. Just as she stepped onto the stairs, the doorbell rang. She wasn't expecting company and contemplated not answering the door. Finally, she tied her robe tighter and opened the door.

And there he stood, rucksack on his back, his jacket dangling open and his arms outstretched. Hilda felt her knees buckling and her body trembled as she fell into his chest and he wrapped his arms around her. "Oskar!" she shrieked through sobs. "Is it really you? Are you really home? Oh thank god. Thank god." Oskar stroked her back while she cried into his shoulder. After a few minutes they broke apart and he closed the door behind him.

"It's me, my love. I'm really home, Hilda. I'm really home."

They made their way into the kitchen where a nice fire burned in the stove drowning out the morning chill. Hilda helped him take off his jacket and kept repeating that she couldn't believe he was actually home. He stroked her back until she composed herself and could talk again.

"Oskar, you're here! You are really, really here! Why didn't you write to let me know?" She wiped away the tears that ran down her cheeks.

"Darling." Hilda saw the love in his eyes as he gently reached for her hands and raised them to his lips. "I haven't seen anything as beautiful as you for a long, long time. I didn't know about my leave until just two days ago. Mail delivery is slow. If I had written you, the letter wouldn't have reached you in time. During wartime, there's not much chance to think or plan ahead. You just do as you're told and hope to live another day. Did I tell you how beautiful you are? Every night lying there, I dreamt for a chance to live for a moment like this." He bent down to kiss her. "And here I am. Tell me, love of my life, are my children upstairs?"

"Günter and Hilde left for school already and Rosemarie is still asleep. Just wait until you see her, so special, our little Rosemarie. And Günter and Hilde have grown so much!"

"I couldn't visualize anything else and I can't wait. Can I go upstairs now and see her?" Oskar and Hilda stepped lightly up the familiar shiny oak staircase. Rosemarie slept soundly in her small bed with both arms right next to her head. "Oh my sweet lord. She is beautiful." He turned to Hilda. "Just like her mother." He reached down and stroked his baby's cheek. "She is perfection. Just like you." He kissed her fingers and then placed them on Rosemarie's forehead. He gazed at her a moment longer and then they went quietly down the stairs.

Oskar went outside to the back of the house and carried the oval zinc tub into the kitchen. He was delirious at the thought of a bath. A real bath. In his tub. In his kitchen. A proper bath in Italy was difficult. The water was barely lukewarm and the hose often sprayed all over the old, tiled washroom. He placed the tub close to the stove.

"The train ride from Italy, was it comfortable?" Hilda asked while she lifted off the lid on the stove side and filled them with two large pots of cold water.

"You know what? Instead of talking about my train ride I'd rather watch you." Jiggling his hand in the water, he got undressed to step into the tub, his frame thinner than it'd been when he left. "Ah, how nice," he said with his blue eyes that Hilda loved as he lowered himself into the tub. "Just imagine." Oskar closed his eyes.

"Darling, just imagine what?"

"Here I am once again in my own kitchen taking a bath in my own tub. A beautiful woman. A healthy boy and two beautiful girls. What seemed such big obstacles just yesterday seem incredibly small today. I hate to leave again in just a few days."

"What?" Hilda's breath caught in her throat. "You mean you're not home for good?" She felt tears burning her eyes.

"I'm afraid not. This is just a short leave. I should have told you that right away. But I was so enjoying being home as if everything were back to normal." He inhaled and dipped his head under water for a moment and then reappeared. "I feel so . . . I'm not sure what. Privileged? So many men and women will never experience moments like this. Ever. They're dead or maimed. Enemies and allies. In the end it doesn't matter. Countless men will never make it back to their families. This war is beyond miserable. That son of a bitch must scheme at night how to create more misery." He shook his head. "I could easily be one of those. Or you. Or our kids."

"Oh Oskar." Hilda bent down and stroked her husband's hair. "Nothing is going to happen to any of us. We are just so blessed to have three healthy children and you home. Even if for just a few days."

The sound of Rosemarie padding upstairs made Oskar and Hilda smile. "Someone wants to meet her daddy." Before leaving the kitchen Hilda poured the next pot of hot water into the tub and refilled the stove water compartment again with cold water. She wanted him to have a long leisurely bath. She stoked the fire and added more wood and coal.

"Let's hope she likes me!"

"Of course she will. How could she not? She has the best daddy in the whole world." She stood and then turned back toward Oskar. "I'll go get her. Any chance you'd like to bathe with her? She loves the water."

"I'm going to be selfish and hog this bath all to myself, unless of course, there's some chance that *you* could join me, that's my only exception!!" Hilda loved the way he emphasized *you*.

"I'm afraid I'll have to wait!" Hilda laughed and dashed out of the kitchen.

Oskar inhaled his luxury as he relaxed into the water. After a good soaping he stepped out of the tub to pour the last two hot pots of water into the tub. For a few moments Oskar became one with the warm water.

Hilda told Rosemarie that her pappa was home. The toddler loved to talk and Hilda hoped she would tell her father how happy she was to see him. But Rosemarie was more interested in grabbing and playing with one of the small pearl buttons on the front of Hilda's dress. "We waited so long for this, didn't we?" Hilda's eyes teared up while holding her little body to her chest and rubbing her back.

"Let's see little one, which is your best dress and stockings?" Hilda carried Rosemarie into her room and stood in front of her closet. "After all, the first impression is the lasting impression!" Knitted white wool stockings from an old sweater that Hilda wore for many years completed Rosemarie's official debut. "Rosemarie, I just know your pappa will agree that you are so smart looking." Someday, when she was much older she'd tell her baby about her first encounter with her pappa. Rosemarie patted both of her mother's cheeks as Hilda carried her downstairs. Hilda opened the kitchen door to let her toddle into the kitchen by herself. Hilda coaxed, "Rosemarie, say pappa . . . pappa."

He sat up and closed his eyes for a split second while he swallowed hard to find his voice again. "Rosemarie," he said softly and stretched out his wet hand. Hilda stood back with her arms folded and smiled. "Rosemarie, for months and months I wondered about you." She wouldn't take his hand and turned around to hang onto her mother's dress.

"Oh, honey, I guess it's going to take a little time for her to get used to you."

"Sweetheart, can you get me a big towel and something to put on so I can get acquainted with this sweet lamb. Oh God, this bath felt so, so good."

It took Hilda just minutes to assemble everything Oskar would need for the next few days. All his belongings were in the same spot as before he left. Hilda came back into the kitchen carrying pajamas, a robe and his slippers.

"There you go, Oskar."

Oskar dressed, felt tired, but so comfortable. He began talking to Rosemarie trying to woo her over . . . and finally succeeded.

"Pappa." She pitter-pattered to Oskar and he lifted her on his lap and engulfed her in his arms. He stroked the back of her soft hair as if she were a kitten; Rosemarie snuggling into his touch and affection. She babbled and giggled, patting his rough, unshaven cheeks.

Hilda saw a tear roll down Oskar's face. She'd never seen him cry. Never. She didn't know what to do or say, so she just watched her husband of twelve years relish playing with his youngest child. Finally, she spoke. "Oskar, this is May 1942. We've been through much. But I've never seen you cry. Is something wrong?"

"I'm just tired. Sorry. I just thought of some of the things I've seen and heard and here's my girl . . . so perfect and innocent. I can only hope that none of our children will ever know the hell I've seen."

"Don't be silly. It shows that you're a human being." She gave him a quick kiss on the lips.

"Hm sure, just don't tell anybody! When I was a boy and cried my mother used to say that she'd send me to the circus so everyone could laugh."

Hilda laughed along with Oskar when he said that, but inside it made her heart hurt.

In the afternoon Günter came home from school. He let himself in the front door and set his worn, leather rucksack in the hallway. Hilda rushed to greet him. "Günter, listen to me before you go into the kitchen."

"Why? What's wrong?" He could tell she was not the same. She wore her crisp white Sunday apron with tiny yellow buttercups embroidered along the bottom. A new buttercup for every month of his father's absence. There were two rows with another just being started.

"Nothing at all. As a matter of fact, everything is good. Very good. I have a surprise for you in the kitchen."

"Okay." He took off his jacket and hung it on the hook and followed his mother into the kitchen. "Who's—" But before he could finish his question, he came around the corner. "Pappa!" Günter halted in the doorway.

"Yes, that would be me! Oh, Günter. My big, strong boy. Look how grown up you are." Oskar gave the baby to Hilda and stepped toward his only son. "Come here and hug your pappa."

"You'll never believe it Pappa . . . you've been in my dreams so many times!" Günter held his arms around his father's neck as though he'd never wanted to let go. "Especially last night! It was *so* real! You were walking toward me and waved!"

"It goes to show you son, you never know what dreams will bring . . . or what dreams may come true. We're lucky, your dream and mine did come true!!"

Günter tried to wipe his tears away without anyone seeing. Classmates would make such terrible fun of him. He'd seen it being done to others. He got teased all the time because he had to babysit Rosemarie. Teachers did nothing to help unless, of course, the victim had the famous Hitler Youth haircut, which Hilda refused to consider. No one in the Döderlein family would ever support or emulate that wallpaper hanger.

Günter felt like the Vega star, bright and sparkling. Having his father and mother together was all he'd hoped for the last two years. "Pappa, I can't believe you're here. Maybe now our lives will be normal again. Honestly, I can hardly believe it!"

Oskar took Günter's hands and looked him up and down. "Look how you've grown and become more handsome and, I'll bet, smarter as well. Am I right?"

"I hope so."

"I know so. Your mother wrote to me what a great help you are. How do you like having another little sister?"

"She's very cute, but I want her to talk to me. She'd be more fun if she could talk a little more. Hilde seems to know what makes her happy better than me."

"Give it time." Oskar tousled his hair. "Speaking of, where is your sister? Why didn't she come home with you?"

"Oh she wasn't quite ready when I left school to walk home. She'll be here soon enough. You must tell me everything about your time away. I've missed you so much."

"I'd be happy to talk with you and Hilde when she gets home. But we should talk about good things, happy times."

Hilda came into the room after putting Rosemarie in her playpen. "We will all talk tonight, Günter. But for now you should get on with your homework. We only have your father for another few days."

"Only a few days?" Günter was shocked, just as his mother had been. "Where are you going?"

"Back to Italy, I hope. Maybe back to France. After that, I have no idea."

"I guess this means the war isn't over yet?" Günter was curious.

"No, son. I don't know when this madness will end. But, I'm lucky. I work in an office, far away from combat."

Günter was disappointed that his father was only home for a short while. So he wanted to get his homework done quickly. He got his bag from the hallway and settled in the corner at the kitchen table. Hilde came home shortly thereafter, fussed over her father for several minutes and then joined her brother doing homework. Rosemarie played with a toy and Hilda removed the water from the tub with a gallon sized ladle to dump it into the kitchen sink. When she was done, she got out food for dinner.

"Are those potatoes for tonight?" Oskar asked, coming up behind his wife and wrapping his arms around her.

"Yes they are. And I'm cooking your favorite. Red cabbage with spaetzle, potatoes and leftover meat." She felt his tender touch on her breasts and he softly kissed her ear and the side of her neck.

"May I help you peel potatoes, my love?" Oskar asked his wife.

A few hours later, they ate dinner as a family as if they'd never been separated. No anxiety about tomorrow, next month or the next year. The usual excited and happy Rosemarie sat on her mother's lap and chomped away on potatoes and creamed cabbage.

13

At the end of the first magical day of Oskar's surprise appearance he sat on the piano bench and patted the space next to him. Hilda knew the gesture. She sat next to him, stroking his thigh. A loving habit they started years ago and she missed it. She watched his sexy hands move back and forth on the ivory keys and the slow sway of his body to the rhythm of the music. Thank god the children were in bed. Listening to 'Eine Kleine Nachtmusik' by Mozart and dreaming of bedtime felt very good. She thought of him having to leave again in a few days and tears streamed down her cheeks. Soon she wouldn't hear this music again for some time. Truly, she thought. Who would know for how long?

The music stopped. Oskar lifted her off the piano bench and carried her to their bed and undid the pearl buttons of her blouse. Darkness turned into an explosion of magic stars. Hilda shed tears of joy, and more magic stars filled the night.

The early morning sun came too quickly. Oskar saw Hilda had not lost her beautiful habit of stretching her arms over her head. With a tiny hint of a smile she rubbed her back slowly and seductively side to side on the white linen.

The look in her eyes showed the pleasures and love she felt for no one but Oskar—an aura he had always found exciting.

"One of these days darling there will be many, many more nights just like last night!"

Hilda sighed. "I couldn't make it through for even a day if I didn't think you'd be back."

Günter knocked at the bedroom door. "Mama, Pappa," he called through the wood. "I made breakfast. I hope you want pancakes and applesauce. Hilde helped Mama cook the sauce last fall."

Oskar and Hilda looked at each other and smiled, each so filled with love for their children. "We'll be right down," Hilda called. They got out of bed, pulled on their robes and headed downstairs.

Oskar and Hilda leisurely entered the kitchen.

"Pappa. See? I learned how to make delicious pancakes!" Günter presented plates of breakfast to his parents. He beamed with pride.

"I must say, I am impressed." Oskar ruffled his son's hair.

The fire in the stove crackled like a symphony. Günter was already dressed for school and had made several pancakes. Hilde was ready and was pleased with herself for being such a good helper in the kitchen. Everyone helped themselves to the pancakes. "These are the best pancakes." Oskar looked at Günter. "And the applesauce tastes as though the apples were just picked from the tree. Thank you both so much for making me such a tasty breakfast. I'm the luckiest dad in the whole world."

"Run along now," Hilda urged her children. "You need to get to school."

As Günter and Hilde walked to the front door, Oskar followed them and hugged them. "I'm proud of you both."

After the kids were out of sight, Hilda said, "Oskar darling, Rosemarie is still sleeping so now would be a good time to tell me everything that's happened in the last two years?" Like young lovers they meandered back into the bedroom. She sat on the bed with her legs crossed. "Now tell me everything . . . don't leave anything out." She wasn't sure she wanted to know what her husband had endured while he'd been gone.

"Well, let's see. Coming back from Italy to Baden-Baden and finally to Birkenfeld was okay considering the circumstances. At least there was beautiful scenery in most areas."

Hilda gave Oskar a knowing look. "I'm so glad you made it home with little trouble. But that's not what I'm asking about. And you know it."

Oskar sighed. "I know, my darling. But you really don't want to hear about the atrocities I lived through."

Hilda shivered. "Somehow, I can't let you leave again without knowing exactly what is waiting for you."

"Okay. Okay." Oskar shook his head. "Get comfortable and I will tell you what you want to know."

Hilda lay back on the bed and Oskar spent the next two hours telling her everything he had endured over the last twenty-five months. When he was done telling his almost unbelievable tale, Hilda took a moment to consider everything she'd just heard. Then she said, "I'm so glad you're back. But I must say that most people run in the opposite direction when they hear a vehicle entering the town. We've gotten so used to soldiers showing up and snooping around, looking for . . . certain people."

"So true. Most of us privates were friendly enough with each other, but not a hint of a smile on those gray uniforms. They were not there to make friends, only to strictly check your credentials, and you better have them on you, and be who you say you are. They gave me the sense that they would have liked it if your papers were not in order. They lived for the moments they caught people unprepared."

"It would prove that they're doing their jobs and they'd receive another pin on their uniforms if they caught someone not properly identifiable, huh?" Hilda touched her stomach. It made her sick to think about certain people being targeted just because of their religion or ethnicity.

"Probably. The whole war is grotesque. I can't believe I've had to be a part of it for so long. It's gotten so bad that when the grays stand up and do the heil Hitler routine, I go along. I'm too scared not to. Jesus, can you imagine? A man my age being too scared to do what I believe in?"

"But anyway, after arriving in Baden-Baden, I learned that I was getting transferred to France. I ate some of the food that I was allowed to pack in my rucksack and before I knew it, I was off." He shook his head with the memory. "It was a troublesome time. I'm so glad I wasn't there too long, otherwise I probably wouldn't be sitting here having tea with you now."

"Why?" Hilda felt alarm at the very thought of not seeing her love again.

"Well, let's see how I can explain it the best way. As a linguist I was just a private. Some of the French appreciated the Germans coming and taking over, but then there were those who were not happy about it and randomly and radically shot at anything that moved, especially at night. I mean, a cat, a dog. Only God could help them! French soldiers and nervous citizens with a gun or rifle shot at anything that moved, including their own people. The German military finally put a curfew in place because too many innocent people were getting shot and the Germans got all the blame. Going for a walk after dark was out of the question and a stupid thing to do.

"Let me say it this way. Getting out of France and being shipped to Italy was like having the gates of heaven open. We lived more like tourists than soldiers. I was stationed with Mario, the other linguist. We got along right away. It was nice to have that camaraderie."

"Why did they have another linguist? You'd think one would be enough." Hilda sipped her chamomile tea.

"They always have at least two and sometimes even three. One to translate and one other to check for errors or misleading information. The one whose place I took, I believe, got shot for treason. Or so I was told. Trust me. There's no mercy."

"I wouldn't want to be one of those making a mistake."

"No. Me neither! You just don't mess around with these people. And I learned very quickly not to be a hero. If they thought you were committing treason, they'd shoot you dead. But really, this is just what I heard from other soldiers. No one really knows what happens. They expect us to fight for our country, or in my case at least represent my country, but no one will tell us anything. It's maddening."

"Someone knows. You can be sure someone knows. So, what did you and Mario do besides translating for the beasts?"

"In our spare time we did quite a bit of sightseeing. For me Italy is the top in art. My buddies, Peter and Mario and I, we'd all eat together and have a glass of wine with the friendliest old Italian widower who lived just around the block. I tell you Hilda, I've never seen an old man, probably in his late seventies or early eighties with an absolutely full head of white hair and a smile showing several gold teeth that were almost blinding in the sunshine. When it rained he sat outside on his staircase with his cane and wanted to be known as, 'the old man.' When the three of us were bored we'd buy a bottle of Chianti and sit with him, swapping stories about women, war, music, always something interesting. On one of those boring days, right after lunch we went to the store across from the old man's little house and as usual we bought two bottles, one to share while we chatted with the old man, and one for him to keep when we left." Oskar removed the tea cozy to refill Hilda's cup. "The old man would sit on the staircase as he usually did and had our glasses ready on the stone walkway. 'Ah, my buddies,' he would say, 'I hoped you'd come to see me today. It gets lonesome. Everybody who walks by hardly gives a salutation anymore to an old man. They're young and have no use for an old man . . . all my friends, and I mean all my friends and family are dead and gone. I'm glad you three stop off and talk with me . . . drink with me. It brings me back to old times. Right now I can hear the sound of the old time pianos playing in the halls. I see the beautiful women and remember the taste of cherry lips.'"

"The old man had a bit of a cough which he quickly controlled with a sip of wine while we chuckled. We had one or two glasses and gave the proper words of understanding to his woes. We asked what else we should see and he told us to go to the Piazzale Cimitero Monumentale in Milan." Oskar sighed and reached to hold Hilda's hand. "When you see these life-like pieces of art, the artist must have shed tears while working. They're masters, those Italians! One work of art that really made an impression on my friend Peter was a crib carved out of quartz. It stood on the gravesite with a small headstone inside the crib exactly where a baby would have lain. A doll with a lace dress cut out of marble lay face down right next to the headstone. My friend Peter told us then that their seven-month old baby, Monica, died last year from influenza. So sad Hilda, can you imagine losing a child? He said his baby was about the same length as this quartz doll. Mario and I expressed our sympathy and we stood in front of the crib for two minutes in silence and then Mario said a beautiful prayer in Italian. On our way home we became more and more anxious and excited to see the old man to let him know how right he was and how much we appreciated his suggestion."

"Oskar, it gives me the chills. What a sad day, yet filled with beauty. I'm sure the love of these masters' works and the love of those being portrayed will go on and on forever. And if you see Peter again, please say something nice on my behalf. Did any of the gravestones say what the cause was for their early demise?"

"No. On our way back we stopped and bought some more Chianti. We felt we needed it at this point and to thank the old man. He wasn't outside and no answer came to our knock. We saw our usual scene . . . glasses and a Chianti bottle on the usual tray semi hidden between red and pink geraniums. There were only three glasses. A lady neighbor who lives next to the store walked across the street and told us the old man passed away in the afternoon drinking his Chianti on the stairs. We asked if she knew how old he was. She wasn't sure, but she thought he was pushing eighty-five. Right then and there Mario had the honor again of saying a beautiful prayer. We each had two glasses of Chianti in the old man's memory and with our hands and heart we dug a hole by the geraniums and buried our three glasses and the bottle of Chianti. Fine, fine man he was. None of us walked by his house again."

"How sad. How absolutely sad. Yet, so hauntingly beautiful. I would love to visit Italy with you."

He walked over in a cavalier style and kissed her hand. "I would be delighted to be your personal guide, madam! Art, food and music is absolutely exquisite in

Italy."

"Sounds like your military number was very, very lucky for you." She laughed.

"Let's hope my luck continues that way. Too bad there were no operas playing while I was there . . . and I can only imagine what Mario Lanza would have sounded like in there. Mario and I did see a few ballets…Korsar, and also Giselle, a beautiful ballet. What a treat! An incredible love story. The only thing I missed was my love next to me."

"I second that!" Hilda said.

"Giselle takes place in Thüringen by the Rhineland. A magnificent ballet. Like I said, parts of being abroad were not so bad. But I only wish I had my one true love and my beautiful children with me. Oh, how I wish I didn't have to leave again so soon."

"What I wouldn't give if it meant you never having to leave again."

Günter and Hilde came home from school and Hilda told them their father was home for a few days. They wondered why he couldn't stay forever. Günter wanted to go with him, back to the war, wherever he might be going. He didn't want to fight or even hold a rifle. But if it meant being with his father, Günter would do it. He found his father in Rosemarie's room installing a nightlight.

"Oh Günter." Oskar was delighted to see his son. "You're just the person I wanted to see. Would you mind helping your old dad for a few minutes?"

"Sure Pappa. What can I do for you?" Günter was so happy to feel useful and needed.

Oskar pointed to his toolbox. "Would you please hand me the needle nose pliers? They are the thin ones with the red handles."

Günter did as he was asked and waited for further instruction. "Excellent," Oskar told him. "Now come over here and hold this wrench for me. I need to change positions and finagle these two wires together." Günter held onto the wrench for a few minutes until his arms started to ache. He wished for his father to be done soon. But he didn't say anything. He liked that Oskar saw him as a good helper. Finally, Oskar said, "Excellent work, Günter. You can be my apprentice any time. Thank you so much for your help."

"Pappa, I can help you with the war too. Can't you take me? I can learn to shoot a gun. Everybody at school says it's easy. Anyone can learn it." His eyes were pleading.

"Thank your lucky stars, son."

"For what? That you're going to take me with you?"

"That you're too young to understand war. You're too young to be called." Oskar squeezed his shoulder. "You are so valuable right here. Your mother and sisters really need you."

"But you need me too. I want to go with you and help you so you can come home again."

"You're right where you need to be. Your mom has been telling me how grown up and helpful you are. I promise I'll be home again. And soon. Believe me, once I get home, I'm never going to leave my family again."

Günter could tell by his father's tone of voice that their conversation was over. "Okay. Fine. I'll go do my homework. I don't want to get the strap like Hans did today."

"I thought they stopped using the strap. I mean, considering how much kids have to help in the household, allowances should be made," Oskar said.

Hilda had come upstairs to see what her best boys were doing. "I agree." She stood in the doorway. "Günter is such a big help around here that if his teacher tried to give him the strap, he'd have me to answer to."

"Good, honey. I'm proud of you for being so

strong. Speaking of strong, have you ever heard of the
SS or the Gestapo?" Oskar asked.

"Yes, I've heard of them. My butcher friend usually
lets me in on her latest news. I don't know where she gets it
from. Why do you ask?" Hilda was concerned.

"Because the SS became an all-time powerful, don't
mess around with us dictatorship that sprang out from
Hitler's regime. They're a tough, intelligent security system
all of their own within Germany and other countries which
they've been able to conquer so far. Their power is really to
be feared by unknowing citizens."

He took a deep breath. "So, I guess what I'm trying
to say is this, be very, I mean, very careful what you say to
whom. If you're ever questioned, no matter by who, even a
teacher having a social chat with you can be dangerous.
Remember you have our children to think of and if it may
mean you having to dance with the devil, remember
sometimes we have to do what we have to do. You may
hate it, but sometimes there's no other choice. And don't
let guilt make decisions for you. It would serve no purpose
and only stand in the way of any change, any real change at
all."

Hilda glanced at Günter. He should not be listening
to such an adult conversation. "Günter." She put her hand
on his shoulder. "Would you please go downstairs and see
if Hilde needs help with her homework?"

"But Mama. I want to stay. I want to hear what
Pappa has to say." Hilda shot her husband a pleading look.

"Go son. Your mother is right. It's important for
you to help your sister and get your own work done. We'll
be down in a few minutes."

Hilda waited until she heard her son's footsteps on
the stairs. Then she turned back to her husband. "So what
you're saying then, is that I should smile when, in reality, I
want to frown or puke?"

"Yes. Sorry Hilda, but yes. I was told by my comrades that it's the Gestapo, a branch born from an agency who finds anyone who is not loyal or talks negatively about the regime, let alone Hitler. For example, people who don't turn off their radio after five. They round up German citizens as well if they are retarded, crippled or whatever. Believe me, I've heard they take them to a house and do god knows what to them."

Hilda hadn't heard Oskar sound so serious in a long time. She shivered just thinking about innocent people being rounded up and hurt or killed for no reason.

"Heed my words Hilda." Oskar continued. "Be careful what you say to Günter. They get a lot of information from parents through their kids. For now, we need to be cautious and trust these hard times will be over soon."

"That's exactly why I sent him downstairs." Hilda smiled at her husband. But it was a sad sort of face.

"What?" Oskar was concerned.

"The Dietlinger family on the corner with their daughter Doris? Obviously very retarded. She's the same age as Günter and still attends the same classes that Günter did four years ago. According to Günter she occasionally wets her pants and the pee runs to the floor. He said they give her a rag to clean it up and then she has to stand in the corner and face the wall for the rest of the class."

"Yes, I do recall seeing that poor girl. Yes, that is an excellent example. Now if the Gestapo finds her, that will be it for her."

Hilda had a puzzled look. "I've seen the Dietlingers dig a large hole in the back of their house and according to Anna next door, the father supposedly built a box with ventilation inside. I wonder if that's where they hide the girl when the Gestapo comes." Each time Hilda thought about Doris's possible fate for something she could not help her chest felt tight.

"You mean he dug a hole the size of a grave?"

"Yes. And one time word got around that Birkenfeld was being inspected by the . . . well, we always called it the regime, but who knows who they really were? Now that I know what I know, it easily could have been the ones you talked about."

"Yes. They're on the lookout for everything and everyone that might hurt Hitler's reputation or image of perfection. As you know, not even children are safe from this monster."

"That very day when these visitors came to town I happened to walk up our street and it looked to me as though Doris was struggling while her father and mother tried to get her into the box. Of course, I didn't interfere because, after all, I assumed whatever the parents did was for the sake of the child's welfare. Anna told me she observed them removing the planks, opening the box and the father carrying her back inside the house."

"They're lucky that no one told on them. If they had found her they certainly would have brought her to that home. So, is she in school now? Doris, I mean? Because the Gestapo would know of her existence from school records."

"No one in our neighborhood would tell. And the parents are saying that she's visiting her aunt in Austria. Can you imagine having to stick your child into a box in the ground? Makes me feel sick."

Oskar didn't want to focus on everything that was wrong with Germany and the war right then. Not when he had such a limited amount of time left at home. "Not to change the subject but I am looking forward to another blissful night with the love of my life. How lucky can a man get?"

"The real question is . . . how lucky can a woman

get?" She smiled giving her best 'come hither' look. "I will love you 'till the day that I die. It's a song that reminds me of you."

"Mr. Döderlein, you and I will not die for a long, long time," she said in a bossy tone of voice which he found very attractive. She traced his lips with her fingertips.

"You have some dry wood in the cellar, I hope? I'd like to chop up some wood for you. At least enough to last you for a little while. And, when Rosemarie is taking her nap, maybe we can send Günter and Hilde on an errand. And then I'd really like to take advantage of you on that piano bench. How does that sound?"

"Ready, willing and able!"

The whole family took a walk after dinner, strolling along, making idle conversation, appreciating each other as a family. Arriving almost at the first step to the house Günter dashed ahead where he saw a brown envelope stuck at the front door addressed to Private Oskar Döderlein. He handed the envelope to his father.

"Pappa, maybe it's about me. Maybe I can go with you!" Günter was so excited.

"No son, no."

Oskar knew from the look of the envelope that it was something official and Hilda's face showed that it would have to be something unpleasant. He read it.

"Darling, I've had four wonderful days and nights and now it's over."

"Why? What does it say?"

"I have to return. I have to take the train to Baden-Baden again tomorrow morning and wait for specific orders there. I am so sorry." Hilda was shocked and choked back tears.

"Do they know you've been on leave for four days only?"

"Yes, I'm afraid they do. So, before it gets dark I'm going to get busy chopping some more wood. Hopefully I can chop enough to carry you through at least halfway through winter." He was trying to think of something more positive to say to her.

An hour later, Oskar was chopping wood, taking his frustrations out on the logs. Such unwelcome news! How could they take him away from his family after only four days? After chopping wood for more than an hour he felt quite worn out. He admired the nice stack he had split and carefully arranged.

After dinner the children went to bed and eventually Oskar and Hilda went upstairs watching their son and then their daughters in their deep sleep. He left his leather bag again laying on the floor of the hallway the night before leaving. Earlier in the day Hilda took her blouse with the small pearl buttons that Rosemarie always loved to reach for and cut off the bottom button, kissed it and dropped it into Oskar's leather case with a note.

14

The next morning Oskar looked for something in his backpack and saw the button in the early light and placed it in the palm of his hand. He read the note. *You. It'll always be you . . . just you. Our love always . . . Hilda and our children.* Oskar's heart beat rapidly and he put the note with the button in his pants pocket. He walked to the railroad station at four in the morning and boarded the train long before Hilda woke.

After a couple stops with the Gestapo at their usual checkpoints, Oskar arrived in Baden-Baden. He had breakfast at the Adler Inn and then boarded a train to Berlin. A car was waiting to take him to his hotel. He couldn't imagine why he was receiving such special treatment. He'd never done anything heroic, and if it were up to him, he never would have fought in the war.

He had a pleasant dinner that evening and a chance to write a note giving Hilda a few details of his trip. Of course, some topics were off limits such as during the last train stop, two 'gray pants' dragged a man off the train. He wrote to Hilda that he was being treated like a king, but the Grays were strutting around saying 'Zieg Heil', and he still had no idea why he was in Berlin.

Oskar's palms got clammy the next morning when an officer sat at his table. Sipping his coffee, he looked more composed than he felt. Gray uniforms were never good news.

"Private Döderlein?" the Greatcoat asked, removing his cap.

"Yes."

"I'm Lieutenant Schrafner. You are probably wondering why you are here. We know that you are an excellent pianist, and we need an exceptional orchestra for our Führer's birthday party."

"Where is it being held?"

"At the Konzerthaus, two blocks from here. Of course, you'll continue to stay here and enjoy the very best cuisine. We want our musicians to feel at home and be at their best. I will see you here again for a progress report." The gray uniform stood, raised his arm and said sharply, "Heil Hitler." Oskar did not dare not to say it back. He thought his breakfast was coming back up. *Arrogant bastard*, Oskar thought, realizing he had just danced with the devil.

In the first few days in Berlin, Oskar's skill level was tested and he was labeled a number-one pianist. He practiced every day for hours by himself and finally the last three weeks with the whole orchestra. Just about every musical instrument ever invented was involved. It was exhausting and Oskar hadn't known until then he could grow tired of something he loved so much. Finally, it was two days before the event and Oskar was measured for a black tie suit.

"Quite a big deal, eh?" a trumpeter asked in Italian, as they exited the tailor's shop. He stretched out his hand. "I'm Manuel. Sorry I don't know German." They shook hands.

Oskar replied in Italian, "Buongiorno. I'm happy to

speak your language. If I can be of any help to you with German, just let me know. I'm a translator by trade. I'm either at the Adler Inn or at the Konzerthaus practicing. It seems that's all I do these days."

The Konzerthaus was an astounding building built in the early 1800s. Adorned with gold gilded artwork and gigantic chandeliers, lit candles hung like a cloud with crystal drops shaped like rain. The acoustics were the best Oskar had ever experienced. He envisioned royalty and wealthy people in their splendid gowns and jewelry spending Saturday evenings listening to fine music or laughing at a comedy.

A polished black grand piano was at the forefront of the orchestra entrance. The beauty of it tugged at Oskar's heart. A tuner checked its sound every day. Various people worked cleaning every part of the hall. Oskar felt such a sense of pride in what he knew would turn out to be a great accomplishment not only on his part, but all the musicians. He wanted Hilda present. He wanted her smile, her touch, her beauty, her soothing voice. He reached inside his pocket and felt for the pearl button. *Ah! There you are!* He rolled the button between his thumb and index finger, took it out of his pocket and pressed it to his lips.

Giant flags hung from the walls. The orchestra did last minute tuning of their instruments. It was exciting! He truly looked forward to this event, contrary to what he first thought. He couldn't escape performing, so he might as well enjoy it.

Oskar recalled his old music professor with a little stick that he used to whack Oskar's hand when he didn't follow instructions. Mistakes at the piano were a luxury he couldn't afford too often. He loved his old professor and thought he looked a little like Beethoven. He encouraged Oskar to consider a career as a concert pianist, but Oskar had other ideas. He was too fascinated with languages. As a younger man he envisioned himself having an important job that would take him to other parts of the world. Little did he know where his love of languages would eventually take him.

The orchestra played its finest. First, Beethoven's "Symphony Number 3 Eroica." After intermission one of Oskar's musical loves was played, Beethoven's "First Piano Concerto." Not that he didn't play all his music with intrinsic fervor, but Beethoven always had a special spot in his heart knowing that he wrote his most fabulous music after he went deaf. The last pieces were the fabulous Wolfgang Mozart's, "The Marriage of Figaro" and as the finale—"Eine Kleine Nacht Musik". At the end, the musicians bowed to the birthday man, his guests and then did a Zieg Heil. The sound of clapping was the orchestra's sign of success and the musicians' faces looked flushed and satisfied. They knew they were fantastic! Hitler gave one more wave. Looking around, Oskar could tell that the men surrounding him were musicians, not politicians, and just like himself they had no interest in what was said.

15

November 1954

"Let's go." Oskar held Hilda at her elbow and crossed the street to a waiting cab.

"Where to this evening?" the cab driver asked when his customers were settled.

"The closest police station, please." Oskar was trying hard to keep his hands steady.

"That's just a few minutes from here." He started the motor and twisted the knob on the meter. "So what brings you out on this bitter night?" The driver checked the rearview mirror, but neither Oskar nor Hilda answered. He decided that whatever made these nice folks venture out to a police station in this wind wasn't good. So he let it go and drove in silence.

A few minutes later the driver pulled into the police parking lot. Oskar muttered a quick thank you and paid him. Then he hooked his arm through Hilda's elbow and led her into the building.

A slim young officer sat at a desk behind a counter. A nameplate read *Officer Mark Plank.*

"What can I do for you?" he asked as Oskar and Hilda approached him.

"I'm Oskar Döderlein and this is my wife, Hilda. Our daughter is missing. We've been looking everywhere with no success. We need your help." His voice broke.

The officer opened a side drawer and put some forms on the desk. He picked up a pen. "Kids go missing all the time." His tone softened. "I'm sure she's just with a friend. Let me get some information and I'm sure we'll find her in a jiff. What's your daughter's full name?"

Oskar assured Hilda that he would translate everything the officer said, and then began answering his questions. "Rosemarie Helga Döderlein."

"How old is she?"

"She just turned fourteen yesterday."

"How long has she been missing?"

"Since this afternoon. After school."

The officer put his pen on the desk, checked his watch and smiled. "Oh, I don't think you have too much to worry about. No doubt she's probably out having fun and forgot to call home. Kids do it all the time. Would you like to use the phone to check if she's home?"

The officer pushed his phone toward his visitors, removed his cap and with a smile of satisfaction, he casually leaned back in his chair. Oskar quickly gave Hilda an account of what had been said. He then turned back to the officer. "We don't have a home phone. So we can't call. Isn't there something you can do? We're so worried."

Officer Plank picked up his pen again and looked at the additional questions on the form. "Okay, start from the beginning."

Oskar told the officer everything that had happened since Hilda had sent Rosemarie to the store earlier that day. When he was done, Officer Plank said, "What about your other daughter? What's her name? Did she go with her to the bakery?"

"Her name is Vera and no, she was at a friend's house."

The officer coughed and put on his cap. "Missing children aren't my specialty. You'd be better off waiting for Detective McCormack and his partner. They're out now, but I expect him back in about a half an hour or so. If you'd like, sir, you and your wife could have a seat over there." He pointed to a row of empty chairs against a green wall. "There are some magazines. By the way, I see your wife looks rather nervous. It might help her to know that we get calls about this sort of thing almost every day, and mostly all turns out okay." He smiled at Hilda as he talked.

"What is he saying?" Hilda asked.

Oskar translated.

Hilda stood and started to move, but then sat. "Oh Jesus, he simply doesn't realize that this isn't normal. He's just saying that to be nice. Isn't there someone else to talk to? Ask him . . . is there no one else?"

Oskar looked at Officer Plank. "Of course, my wife is on edge, but I'm sure you're right about getting everything resolved tonight. No question. My wife asked, or wondered, is there another person we could talk to? Now? She doesn't want to wait until the other detectives return."

"Yes, of course, we have several people in the back working right now. But," he shrugged, "they all have their specialties and they don't work on juvenile cases. I could have Detective Allen talk with you. But, if I were you, I would wait for Detectives McCormack and Talbot. They're tops when it comes to missing children." He looked into Oskar's eyes. "Believe me, sir, they'll know what to do. They're the best."

Hilda turned to Oskar and said, "I need some air. I'll be out front." Oskar started to get up and join her, but she put her hand on his shoulder. "No. No. Stay here. I'd rather be by myself." Hilda left and stood in the corner of the police department's front door. Cars, with their bright lights, came and went down the boulevard. Through her tears, they all became a blur. A cold wind stung as it whisked past her. It didn't faze her. Her mind felt numb, but waves of pain rippled through her body. Quickly she grasped the handrail to steady herself. She consoled herself knowing that at least Rosemarie had on her new Canadian slacks that she loved and her purple jacket with the hood. She'd be warm.

Hilda stood outside for what felt like a long time. The wind was fierce, but she didn't even feel cold. She could only think about one thing—Rosemarie. When she heard Oskar pull open the door, she looked at her watch and saw that only five or six minutes had passed. He motioned for her to come inside. "Darling." After just a few seconds, he was shivering. He marveled at his wife's strength. "Come inside. They're here and ready to help us find Rosemarie."

Both police officers stood as the couple entered the conference room. Detective McCormack offered Hilda his hand and said, "Mrs. Döderlein. It's good to meet you. Don't worry. We're going to find your daughter." He waited for Oskar to translate, then he began the interview, starting with the basics. "You live at 5370 Randall Avenue?" Oskar nodded and then the detective recapped what was in Officer Plank's notes. "I see she just turned fourteen. Might she have a boyfriend?"

"No. No chance."

"Your daughter doesn't speak any English at all?"

"Just a few words. Not enough to let someone know she's lost."

Hilda waited for some magic words. Words that would solve everything and make the unbearable pain go away.

"Would you ask your wife how much money she gave to Rosemarie for the bakery?"

Oskar translated asked his wife, and then reported to the detective. "Fifty cents."

"What is she wearing?" Detective McCormack asked.

"A wool tunic with a white blouse and plaid slacks. Primarily pine green and navy blue with yellow and red stripes. They're new. A thick dark purple jacket with white lining, a hood also lined in white. The jacket has a white furry collar. On her wrist she's probably wearing a bracelet with navy blue and purple beads with one pearl. A fake one."

"What's the name of the bakery that she was supposed to go to?" the cop asked.

"Bread 'n Rolls."

"Where is it?"

"On Randall Avenue, just two doors from where we live."

"At what point did Mrs. Döderlein suspect something was amiss?"

"My wife says that Rosemarie likes to talk to the baker's wife, Mrs. Blatt. So it wouldn't be unusual for her to be gone longer than needed. But, when she didn't come home by four or so, she started to worry."

Detective McCormack smiled at Hilda. "Thank you." Then he turned his attention back to Oskar. "Did you look for your daughter before coming here?"

"I went up and down Randall Avenue, Milton Street and one side of St. Dorothy. I looked inside the buildings any place I could get in. I also went to the school, banged on the doors and windows, called her name over and over."

"Why did you go in the buildings? And the school?"

"Just in case she got confused. We've only been in Canada a few weeks. A lot of these buildings look similar.

And we thought she might have left something at school and had gone back for it."

Detective McCormack held up his finger and turned to Detective Talbot. "You have the name of the school. Call the superintendent. Find out how soon we can get in that building. Where we get the keys and so on. We need to get in as soon as possible. Tonight. Tell him it's a missing child case." Detective Talbot left the room. "Mr. Döderlein, would you ask your wife if there's anything she hasn't told us? Something we don't know yet? That is, anything Rosemarie did or said that would raise a red flag . . . especially right after coming home from school. It's imperative that we know of any little detail, no matter how insignificant it may seem. Anything at all. Has she complained about anything or anyone, for example, at school, at the bakery, at home? Anywhere?"

The only new thing Hilda could think of was that Günter had come home unexpectedly to pick up some papers for a project he was doing with his friend, Albert. The detective asked what time that was. Hilda suddenly recalled that both Rosemarie and Günter had left about the same time.

Detective McCormack looked at Hilda and Oskar. "Your son's name is Günter? He lives with you?"

"Yes. Actually, we live with him. His wife as well," Oskar replied. "Like I said, we only emigrated from Germany a few weeks ago. We haven't had time to find our own place yet."

"How old are they?"

"They're both twenty-three."

"How is your other daughter adjusting?"

"Oh, very good. Both are adjusting extremely well. No trouble at all."

"Does Günter come home every day at two-thirty?"

"I'm not sure. Since we got here, yes. But I couldn't

tell you what he did before we came," Oskar said.

Hilda looked at Oskar. "Are they doing anything to find her?"

"Yes. They're getting the school's keys." He squeezed his wife's shoulder.

Detective McCormack redirected Oskar's attention back to him. "Did she ever say that a kid or anyone else doesn't like her? Was she afraid of anyone at school or anywhere else? A teacher perhaps? Anyone? Anything at all she may have said about the people at school, in your apartment building, at the bakery that I should know about? Any little thing could be important."

They waited for Oskar to translate and Hilda shook her head. Officer Plank came back and handed a note to Detective McCormack. He read the note, stood and said, "Mr. Döderlein, we just received the keys for the school and we'll have a search party of approximately fifteen trained people. Tell your wife that, if Rosemarie is at the school, trust me, we'll find her. Why don't you two go home? She might be back now. At any rate, after we're done here, and if we have no success at the school, we'll stop at your apartment. We'll want to talk to everyone living in your home, that is, of course, if you aren't reunited already with Rosemarie."

16

Oskar and Hilda walked across the street and waited for a cab. They didn't speak at all. Neither had anything to say, except to shout to the sky to ask for their daughter back. When one finally pulled up, Oskar gave the driver directions to Günter's apartment and then gazed out the window. Their legs felt like lead as they climbed the stairs to the apartment. They found Ruth in the living room knitting and Vera reading one of her school books.

Vera dashed to them. "I missed you, Mama. Can I have a snack?"

"All right, darling, wait for me in the kitchen. I'll be right there." To Ruth, Hilda said, "Is Rosemarie here?"

"No. Sorry. She didn't come." Ruth pulled a cloth out of her pocket and started to wipe the already-clean dining room table. Hilda had noticed that Ruth cleaned when she was stressed or nervous.

Hilda walked into the kitchen and said to Vera, "I'm going to heat your favorite. Chocolate milk. Good? Go ask your pappa if he'd like some."

Vera dashed out of the room and quickly returned. "Yes. He said he doesn't care what he gets."

After a few minutes he came to the kitchen and picked up his cup of cocoa. "I'm glad we didn't wait for Günter."

"Why?" asked Vera. "Wait for him for what?"

"Oh, nothing, child. No reason, really," Oskar muttered and got busy sipping his cocoa.

"Is Rosemarie okay? Where is she?" Vera asked.

"Yes. Of course. She's helping a lady and her baby." Oskar couldn't look at his daughter.

"I thought she was with someone from school. Is she coming home tonight?"

"Drink your milk. It's already eight o'clock. Almost time for bed." Hilda tapped her watch.

"She's helping someone with a baby?" Vera tried again.

"Hilda, aren't you going to eat something?" Oskar ignored Vera's question.

"Not now." To Vera she said, "Do you want something else?"

"No. I just want Rosemarie to come home. I'm dying to tell her about my afternoon. And now since her new slacks are not so new-new anymore, maybe she'll let me borrow them tomorrow. Oh, I would feel like a queen wearing those."

Günter came home and hung up his coat and scarf. Ruth followed behind him to their bedroom. A few minutes later he and Ruth entered the kitchen. "Oh Mama," he started to say. But Hilda gave him a sharp look and then glanced at Vera. "Oh . . . " he stuttered. "Um, how was your day?"

Hilda forced herself to smile. "Oh Vera. Look at the time." She put her hands on her daughter's shoulders and turned her toward her bedroom. "Make sure you brush your teeth before you get in bed. I'll be in in a little while to kiss you goodnight." All four adults watched Vera leave the room, seemingly none of them breathing. Finally, Günter exhaled and turned to his parents. "Oh my god! Tell me this isn't happening."

"Günter, we need your help." Hilda grabbed her son's hands. "I sent Rosemarie to the bakery this afternoon. And she hasn't come home."

Günter loosened his hands from his mother's grip. "Let's sit down." The four of them moved to the living room and took seats on the two couches. "What do you mean she hasn't come home? Which bakery?" He ran through all the bakeries nearby. None of them were so far away that his sister would get lost coming home. "There must be some mistake." Günter couldn't believe this was happening. He was so much older than his littlest sisters that he'd always been super protective of them. Almost like he was their father. Especially during the years when Oskar was away at war.

"I don't know what else there is to say," Hilda said. "Rosemarie knows this area. She knows the lady at the bakery. It's only two doors down. When she came home from school today I asked her to go pick up a loaf of bread. I could have done it myself, but I know how much she enjoys talking to Mrs. Blatt. I thought it would be nice for her to spend a few minutes there."

"Have you talked to this Mrs. . . . "

"Blatt," Oskar interjected. "And yes, of course. She said Rosemarie never made it to her shop today. I checked all the nearby streets. I even went to her school. But nothing. No sign of her anywhere."

Günter got up and paced. "Well, she must be somewhere. Let me call some friends and we'll go out and search for her. She must be so cold."

"Hold on, Günter." Oskar got up and led his son to the couch. "Your mother and I just got back from the police station. The detectives got the keys to the school and are checking it as we speak. They told us to stay here in case she shows up. And since we don't have a phone, they said they would stop by when they'd completed their search. I strongly feel like we should stay here until the police come."

"Detectives? You talked to the police already?" Günter asked.

"Yes. We thought the sooner they start looking, the better."

"Well, if you don't want to search for her, what do we do now?" Günter ran his fingers through his hair.

"There's nothing to do right now but wait to hear back from the police. Why don't you try to eat something?" Ruth was already busy heating up leftovers for Günter.

Günter picked up his plate. "I don't think I can eat right now. But I'll try." Just as he sat at the kitchen table, the doorbell rang.

Hilda dashed to the door. Her hopeful mind whispered *Rosemarie*. Her heartbeat pounded in her neck. She touched her chest as though she wanted to stop her heart from jumping out. She opened the front door. No. She wasn't there. Rocks in her belly took a tumble. She stepped past the door jamb, then past the two men. She looked around the landing hoping her girl was simply being silly and hiding. She looked the other way. No. She wasn't hiding. Another, stronger tumble of rocks took place within her belly. Rosemarie wasn't being silly. She wasn't there. Hilda swallowed hard. Oskar touched her shoulder. "Let me Liebling, let me talk to them."

Detective McCormack and Talbot stood without his girl. For a split second he visualized her peeking out from behind Detective McCormack with a mischievous smile.

"May we come in?" asked Detective McCormack. Both held their hats against their chests.

Oskar found his voice. "Come in. Yes . . . of course,

please, come in." He stood aside to let the detectives follow Hilda into the kitchen. Oskar introduced them to Günter and Ruth. Then he sat across from Detective McCormack and Hilda faced Detective Talbot who tapped his side pocket and retrieved his notepad and pen.

"We're so sorry, Mr. Döderlein. And please give your wife our regrets. We did a very extensive search at the school. As the saying goes, no stone was left unturned. We talked to the janitor. He locked up after he was done with his job and didn't notice anything out of the ordinary while he was working. He saw and heard no one. Please," Detective McCormack looked at Oskar, "tell Mrs. Döderlein we are very, very sorry. We wish we had better news." Oskar translated.

Hilda already knew. She knew. She could tell by the look on their faces. She knew as soon as she had opened the door. Of course she knew that they hadn't found her. And now, as she listened to Detective McCormack's voice, it was too soft, too guarded, showing no smile at any time. No English was necessary for Hilda to understand the outcome of the search. She looked at their blue eyes and saw sincerity.

Detective McCormack exhaled. "Mr. Döderlein, look, I've got to tell you, I have an eleven-year-old daughter, and I cannot possibly tell you how much this affects me. Tell your wife that we'll do everything, and we do mean everything, within our means to find your girl."

They heard Hilda suck in her breath. They witnessed tears freely roll down her cheeks. As she stood, they heard her whisper, "My Rosemarie, my girl."

"Excuse us for a moment." Oskar stood. "I'll be right back. She's very distraught." Oskar touched her back as they walked to their bedroom. She lay on the bed and Oskar removed her slippers and smoothed a blanket over her. "I'll be back as soon as I can," he said softly. He left her sobbing into her pillow.

When Oskar got back to the living room, Detective McCormack said to him, "We would like to talk to the rest of your family. We'll ask Vera a few simple questions. Naturally we don't want to scare her or upset her."

"Of course." Oskar glanced toward his daughter's room. "Whatever you need. Would you like to talk to Vera first? But I must tell you. We haven't told her yet that Rosemarie is missing."

The detective closed his notebook. "Sure, okay. Well, we're going to have to tell her. We won't be able to assess if she knows anything if we're not honest with her."

"What do you mean, assess if she knows anything?" Günter asked. "Do you think my little sister is hiding something?"

The detective spoke. "No, of course not. But she might have seen something, seen someone that she didn't think anything of. But it might be important. We'll be gentle, I promise."

"And of course, we'll want you nearby while we talk to Vera." Detective Talbot had his notebook and pen ready.

Oskar called Vera. Pressing a small book against her chest, she cautiously entered the living room and stopped for a second or two to look over the two men.

"Sit down." Oskar pulled out the chair next to him and forced a bright tone. "There's no need to be afraid. These men would like to ask you some questions. This is Mr. McCormack and Mr. Talbot. I'll translate for you." He looked at the two men. "Gentlemen, meet our youngest, Vera."

Vera sat and held the book on her lap.

Detective McCormack asked gently, "Vera, we're here just to ask a few questions. Don't be afraid. We do this all the time. Is there anyone you know who might not like your sister?"

"No." She turned to Oskar. "Pappa, why are they asking about Rosemarie?" When he didn't answer, she said, "She's not really babysitting, is she?"

For a moment, Oskar thought about keeping up the front. "No, sweetheart. She's not. It seems as though she might be lost." Panic flashed across Vera's face. Oskar touched her shoulder. "But don't worry. These men are here to help us find her. They just need to ask you some questions."

Vera glanced at her mother who nodded. "It's okay," Hilda assured her. "Detectives McCormack and Talbot are going to help us. You can talk to them."

"Okay." Vera sounded tentative. "What do you want to know?" She swallowed the lump in her throat, telling herself to be brave for Rosemarie.

"You love your sister a lot, don't you?" Talbot leaned forward and lowered his voice.

"Of course. She's my best friend."

"That's good, that's good. Do you tell each other secrets? Things that no one else knows?"

Vera thought for a moment. "I mean, we tell each other everything. But we don't really have secrets."

The detective snickered. "Okay. Well, what kinds of things does Rosemarie tell you?"

"Just stuff about school. The English words we're learning. That there is one nice girl in her class that she thinks she might be friends with."

"Excellent Vera," McCormack said. "What is this friend's name?"

"Julie, I think. Yes, definitely Julie."

"Do you know where she lives?"

"No. I don't know this area yet. I'm sorry. I'm sorry. I should have asked her." She started to cry.

"No no, it's okay. We can call the school tomorrow. You're being very helpful." He waited a minute for her to stop crying. "We just need to ask you a few more questions. You're doing great."

"Okay." She picked at a hangnail.

"Do you know if Rosemarie had any problems at school? Is there anyone who is mean to her? Anyone who gives her a hard time?"

"No. She never said anything. She likes school."

"How about here in the building? Did she or you talk to anyone in this building?"

"No. Not really."

"What do you mean by 'not really'?"

"One time she pushed me when we walked up the stairs. I fell against someone's door. A man opened it and he was mad. But everyone here speaks English and we don't. Well, not really, anyway. So we really don't talk to anyone in the building."

"What did he say? Do you remember?"

"I don't know. He yelled at us in English. But, I got up and we ran up the rest of the stairs."

"Do you remember which door?"

"Sure, it's on the second floor on the left side. We were just fooling around, and she just pushed me a little too hard. We didn't mean to make noise. And we didn't mean to make that man mad. We were just playing."

"When did that happen?"

Vera glanced at the ceiling. "Three days ago. I'm sorry, we were noisy. Pappa, we didn't mean to be. I guess we shouldn't have laughed. The man said something, but I don't know what. He looked annoyed and slammed his door."

Detective McCormack put her at ease. "We're not here because of the noise you made at that door. So, no need to worry. Anything else at all that you can think of? Anything unusual that someone did or said to your sister?"

"No."

"Does she get along with other kids? Do other kids get along with her, let's say, in the schoolyard? Did she talk to any strangers that you know of? Take your time."

"No. I don't know anyone who doesn't like her. I love my sister."

"Yes, I'm sure you do. If there's anything else you know, tell your Pappa so he'll let us know."

"There's the man who wears a white thing around his head. He sits in one of the yellow cars. He smiles at us when we walk home from school."

"A yellow car? Do you mean a taxi?"

"Yes. That's it. And the white thing on his head. It's like a towel. But it's not."

"It's called a turban." He looked at his partner and said, "That should make him easier to find." Then he returned his attention to Vera. "Has he ever talked to you or Rosemarie?"

"No. He just looks at us and smiles. Oh, wait a minute. There is a boy who smiles at her."

The detective felt hopeful. "Do you know the boy's name?"

"Gee, no. Just that he's in her class." Vera's eyes got big and she shook her head. "I don't know him, I don't know his name. I don't think my sister even knows his name. Her teacher might know. His name is Mr. Kirkpatrick."

"Thank you, Vera, it was nice talking with you. You've been very helpful." Detective McCormack put forth his fatherly smile.

"What's the name of your book?" asked Detective Talbot.

"*Sunshine and Flowers*. Where's my sister? Where's my mama?"

"Mama has gone to bed already. She has a headache. Since we're finished here, why don't you put on your pajamas and be comfortable?" Oskar urged his daughter toward her room.

"Nice title. Your book sounds cheerful," the detective said. He led Oskar away from Vera. "Mr. Döderlein, Vera is charming. Thank you for letting us speak with her." After Vera left the room, he said to Ruth, "Mind if we ask you a few questions?"

"Sure." Her eyes darted around the room. "But I'm sure I don't know anything."

"It's okay. Just like with Vera, you might remember something that seems like nothing. But it might be a clue. Anything you can tell us would be helpful."

Ruth blinked back tears. "Okay, I'll try."

"Great," McCormack told her. "Has Rosemarie been acting differently lately? Secretive? Unhappy?"

"Unhappy? No. Why? Do you think she ran away?"

"What?" Oskar spun around. "No! Never. Rosemarie is a good girl. She would never run away. Worry us like that. It's out of the question."

"Oskar is right. There's no way Rosemarie ran away. She's only been here a little while. But no, she's not unhappy. She's seemed excited to be here. To start over, learn a new language. Make new friends."

McCormack wrote in his notebook. "Can you think of anything? Anything at all that might be useful? Even the smallest, seemingly insignificant detail might help us. Take your time. Think about it for a moment."

Ruth closed her eyes and hummed for a moment. When she opened her eyes, she shook her head. "No, I'm sorry. I can't think of anything." She clutched her stomach. "I don't feel well. I think I need to go to bed. Do you need anything else from me?"

"You're free to go. Thank you for your help."

Ruth stood and Günter walked her to their room. When he returned, he addressed both detectives. "My wife is struggling. She loves my sisters like they're her own. Is there anything I can do to be helpful? Can I answer any questions for you?"

"Sorry about your sister. We'll do everything possible to find her. And yes, we would love to ask you some questions. The more complete picture we get of the last several days, the more prepared we'll be to find her." Detective McCormack cleared his throat.

"No. Of course I don't mind. How can I help you?" Günter pulled out a chair.

"Where do you work?"

"At Sperry Gyroscope. For a little over a year now."

"Were you at work all afternoon?"

"Yes. I had a late lunch today and came home momentarily to pick up some papers that my friend and I are working on."

"What's your friend's name?"

"Albert Drass."

"So he works with you at the same location for the same company?"

"Yes."

"So what time was it when you picked up the papers?"

"I didn't pay much attention to the time. I'd say two thirty. Maybe a little later."

"Did you see or hear Rosemarie in the apartment at that time?"

"Sorry. Can't help you there. I wasn't paying any attention at all. I thought I heard the front door close. But I couldn't even tell you if she left then."

"Do you know if she had any trouble at school in any way?"

"I don't think so. We're very close and she's never said anything like that."

"Is there anything you can think of that might help

us find Rosemarie?"

"No. Not a thing. Except that she's a good kid and she would never leave on her own accord. She loves us. She's happy here." Günter thought for a moment. "But it's more than that. She's not adventurous. She would never stay out late with other girls or go off with a boy. We're a very family-centered group. My sister would never . . . and I mean never . . . worry our parents like this. Something is very wrong. You've got to find her."

Detective McCormack laid his card in front of Günter. "Thank you for your time. If you can help us with any other information, give us a call, would you?"

"Of course." Günter stood and held the back of the chair with both hands. "Thank you so much. Goodnight. And thank you for helping my family."

They thanked Günter and then asked Oskar for a picture of Rosemarie. Oskar dashed out of the room and returned with one a moment later. "How's this? It's the most recent one I could find. Is it good enough?" He handed over the picture and then showed one taken in their garden in Germany. "This one was taken just before we left Birkenfeld."

Detective McCormack looked at them. "I assume the taller one is our girl. Pretty." He cleared his throat. "Our lab will take several pictures of both. By tomorrow morning, every station will have her picture." Detective Talbot slid the photos into the inside pocket of his jacket. "By the way Mr. Döderlein, tell your wife that the pictures will be brought back as soon as we're done. And may I suggest that you get a telephone as soon as possible. It will assist with us being able to get in touch with you."

"Of course. Of course. I will buy one tomorrow."

"Excellent. Let me know your phone number as soon as you get it. If we're not at the station, leave your number with Officer Plank." The detectives exchanged glances. "I think that should do it for tonight. I know it's not easy, but try to get some rest. We'll find your daughter. I'm sure of it."

Oskar shook hands with each detective. "Thank you both so much. We're just so worried."

"Goodnight sir." Detective McCormack touched the rim of his hat. "Keep faith. We'll find her."

Oskar closed the door and crumpled. Günter rushed to him. "It's okay, Pappa. We're going to find her. She couldn't have gone far. What do you want to do now? Should we take my car and drive around the neighborhood? Maybe she's just a few blocks away, cold and lost. Trying to get home."

"Yes, let's go. Maybe she got turned around and accidentally walked off in the wrong direction."

Günter seemed to ponder this. "Yes, and she doesn't speak enough English to ask someone for directions. And no one knows her well yet. Montreal isn't like Birkenfeld where practically the whole village knew her."

"Get your coat. Let's go." Oskar grabbed his heaviest coat and hat, then told Ruth and Hilda that they were continuing the search and would be back later.

Günter drove slowly around a few blocks while Oskar looked in all directions. It was windy and very few people were out walking. No purple jacket and no Canadian slacks.

Dejected, frustrated and scared, several hours later Günter and Oskar went back home.

17

On Saturday a black telephone was installed in the hallway. Hilda placed it and a small lamp in the middle of a table along with a pad and a pencil. Now the family was ready at any moment to gather information about Rosemarie.

Vera admired it and asked if they could ever use it to call Hilde. She hadn't heard her sister's voice in so long. "Oh honey," Hilda said to Vera as she admired the phone. "We'll write Hilde a letter next week with our phone number. She'll be so excited to talk to you."

Oskar's first call was to Detective Talbot. He gave the officer the number and then found Vera reading in her room. "Come on, Vera. We need to take a little field trip."

She put down her book. "Field trip? Where are we going? The zoo? Do they have zoos in Canada? What about Rosemarie? Should we wait for her to come home? She loves animals. She'll be so happy to see bears and giraffes."

It broke Oskar's heart to hear Vera talk about her sister. She was still too little to understand just how serious the situation was. He sat on Vera's bed. "How about this? We'll go on this field trip again when Rosemarie comes home. But for now, it's very important that you learn how to use a pay phone. Now put on your shoes and coat."

Vera did as she was told. "Okay, but why do I need to learn how to use a phone? I'm already home. And so are you and Mama."

"It's just in case you ever need to call us when you're out. Now let's go." Normally Vera's endless questions didn't bother him. But now he felt like he would be crushed under the weight of her innocent inquiries.

A few minutes later they let themselves out the front door and walked a block to the closest phone booth. "Okay, Vera. This is a pay phone in a telephone booth. I have written our home phone number on the inside of your school bag and put two dimes in it. If you ever get lost and need to call home, this is how you do it. Just find a telephone booth, get one of the dimes out of your bag and put it in this slot." He retrieved a dime from his pocket, checked his new number on a crumpled piece of paper and put the dime in the slot. "See, it's so easy. Just put the dime in and dial the number." He dialed his home number and when Hilda picked up, he handed the receiver to Vera. "Go on, say hello."

"Hello?" Vera asked.

"Oh hi honey," Hilda answered.

"Mama?" Vera's eyes grew big with amazement. "Is that you?"

"Yes sweetheart. This is how telephones work. Pretty neat, huh?"

Vera spoke to her mother for another minute and then hung up. "Can I try?" she asked Oskar.

"Sure thing. Do you remember what to do?"

"I think so." She put her school bag on the ground and thought about it for a moment. "First, I get the dime out of my bag. And then I enter the number into the phone."

"That's exactly right. See, there's nothing to it. Do you want to practice some more?"

"No, I think I understand. What about Rosemarie? She needs to learn how to use the phone. Maybe she doesn't know how to use it and that's why she hasn't come home yet. Maybe she's lost, but she doesn't know how to call us. How are you going to teach her to use a phone if she's not home."

Oskar exhaled deeply. "Don't worry about Rosemarie. I will teach her when the time is right. In case you forget what to do, ask me. It's super important that you always know how to call Mama and me."

Three nights went by . . . five . . . seven . . . then suddenly two weeks had passed.

It was Sunday afternoon and Vera was on the couch playing with Rosemarie's wooden soldiers. Frustrated, mad and helpless she talked out loud. She asked the soldiers questions she hadn't dared ask her parents. "Why hasn't she come home? It's been so long. Why isn't she coming to school?" Vera decided that if she didn't get answers from anyone in her house soon that she would find a way to call Hilde in Germany and ask her if she knew what had happened to their sister. Since her father had taken her down to the phone booth, she now knew how to use a phone.

On Monday Vera went to school. She was learning more and more English, even more than her teachers gave her credit for. She understood what they were saying when she heard them whispering in the corner. Everybody knew that Rosemarie had gone to the bakery and had never come home. What she didn't understand was why no one was talking to her about it. She thought maybe she should tell Mr. Kirkpatrick and Mrs. Brent that she knew what they were saying. But then she decided that they would stop talking in front of her. And maybe, sooner or later, she

would hear something that would help find her sister.
At recess that day, Rosemarie's friend, Julie, came up to Vera as she was sitting on the swings by herself. She talked slowly and pronounced each word very carefully. She only had to repeat herself once before Vera realized she was asking about Rosemarie. She did her best to conjure up some English words along with hand motions in an attempt to have some sort of meaningful conversation. She was able to convey that two police officers came to their apartment to ask questions and look around. Vera pictured that evening clearly. Rosemarie's bed came to her mind as she was sitting there. She found it odd thinking that no one, including her, had moved her rucksack laying on the floor next to her bed.

Julie shook her head. "Well, where is she? Where would she go? You both just got here!"

Very shrugged not knowing what else to say and left the girl.

Oskar picked up Vera at school and walked home with her, as he had done every day since Rosemarie had vanished. He tried to talk to her, draw anything about her day out of her. But she was still thinking about her conversation with Julie. She rubbed her chin with her small fist and thought about how different everyone seemed lately. She didn't know people could change so much so quickly. "Pappa?" She looked up at him as she walked. "Why do Mama's eyes always look as though she rubs them too hard? And why does she stay in her room all the time? She hardly ever comes out anymore. Or talks. What's wrong with her?"

"Oh sweet girl. Your mama is very tired. You know how hard she works." Vera had asked her father about her mother's silence several times, and she always got the same answer. She didn't know why she bothered anymore.

"But Pappa. She's always worked hard. Why doesn't

she talk to me anymore? To anyone?"

Oskar put his hand on his daughter's shoulder as they walked. "Keep the faith, Vera. Keep the faith." Vera waited for him to say more, but he never did.

Each day Hilda seemed to become more and more annoyed when Vera asked about Rosemarie. Vera had hardly ever heard her mother raise her voice. Now she sounded put out just about every time Vera opened her mouth. And she never smiled anymore. She used to smile all the time . . . now it was all gone. She bit her bottom lip a lot and stared out the window. Vera would watch her from the next room, wondering if she had forgotten what she was doing. And what she was thinking. But Vera knew. Rosemarie. Everything was about Rosemarie now. It made no sense because they hardly ever even said her name anymore.

One time when Vera was alone in the kitchen, she dragged a chair to the sink. She stood on it trying to see what her mama saw when she gazed out the window every night. There must have been something out there. Something only her mama could see. Vera looked from left to right and saw nothing unusual—only the sky, antennas on rooftops, chimneys and lots of tall ugly poles with wires. There were also bare trees. So many trees. They all looked like skeletons. For sure nothing fascinating. This intrigued Vera even more. What could her mother possibly be looking at, searching for?

Nothing anyone said or didn't say made much difference to Hilda. She answered every question noncommittally. She'd just mumble an answer and agree with what anyone said, never offering an opinion of her own anymore.

Vera's days were confusing shifts of emotions since Rosemarie had gone to the bakery and hadn't come back. She didn't know what to think or believe anymore. Did

Rosemarie really go to Mrs. Blatt's bakery and not make it back? Or had she been babysitting? Vera hadn't heard the same story twice and no one was willing to talk to her about what was going on and if Rosemarie was coming home. All Vera knew for certain was that Rosemarie never would have left her family on her own. She only had fifty cents and the clothes she was wearing to school.

***

Almost a month after Rosemarie disappeared, Vera came home from school excited and happy. As she burst through the front door, she realized it was the first time she'd smiled in a long time. "Mama! Mama! Guess what? Guess what I can do?" she called from the living room. But no one answered. She went into the kitchen, but it was empty as well. Finally, she pushed open her parents' bedroom door and saw a lump under the covers. She tiptoed to the side and touched her mother's shoulder. "Mama? Are you awake? I have some exciting news."

After a few moments Hilda stirred and sat up. "Vera? What is it? I need to get some rest."

Vera felt like she'd swallowed a boulder. "But Mama. I can sing the Canadian national anthem in English. I've been practicing so hard. Every day during recess. Do you want to hear?"

Hilda looked at her daughter and tried to focus on her. "That sounds nice. But not now. I'm sure I'm too tired."

Vera couldn't believe this was true. She remembered all the cold winter nights in Birkenfeld when her father was abroad and Hilda would tirelessly chop wood, make dinner, mend clothes and take care of all her children. What did she have to do now that would make her so tired? "Please Mama. I feel like I don't even see you anymore. Can't you please listen to me sing? Just for a few minutes?"

Hilda rolled over and closed her eyes. "I'm sorry, Vera. Come back later." She waited for Vera to leave, but when she didn't hear footsteps she said, "Please Vera. I'm tired."

As Vera pulled the door closed behind her, she realized that nothing she did or said made any difference to her mama. Vera was as sad as anyone that her sister, her best friend, was gone, and no one missed her more than she did. But she was still there. Only her mother acted as if she couldn't even see her. She thought of her other sister, Hilde, all the way over in Germany. And she was jealous that Hilde had her own life, in her own country and didn't have to watch their mother disappear before her eyes.

Every so often, Hilda would emerge from her room and grab onto Vera with such force it made Vera cry out. Then she would hold her to her chest to the point where the child felt as if the life was being squeezed out of her. The first few times it happened, Vera couldn't help but giggle. But when she caught Hilda wiping tears off her cheeks, she found nothing to laugh about. Everything had changed. And nothing good was happening.

Almost a month had passed since Rosemarie had disappeared. And Christmas was fast approaching. As usual, Hilda was in her room. Vera knocked once and let herself into her parents' bedroom. "Mama?" Her voice was soft in case her mother was sleeping. "Do you think Saint Nikolaus will come this year?"

Hilda blinked against the light coming in from the hallway. "For what day?"

"December sixth! Remember? I wonder what we'll get in our shoes. Do you suppose living in Canada now will make a big difference to Saint Nikolaus? Will Rosemarie be back in time to put her shoes outside?"

Hilda didn't answer for several seconds. "December

sixth? Is it December already?"

It was clear to Vera that her mother had been sleeping and was still in a fog. "Never mind. I'll ask Pappa when he gets home from work. I mean, we don't even know if Saint Nikolaus comes to kids in apartment buildings in Canada. Right?"

"Right. Sure. Whatever you say." Hilda yawned. "Is there anything else?"

"No Mama. Sorry to bother you. I'll let you get some rest." Vera pulled the door closed behind her. "More rest," she said to herself.

That was that on that subject. Everything had changed. Vera wanted her life back. The one she had, the one they all had, before Rosemarie left. Vera couldn't believe that she would not just come back to see her. Where had she gone? What was so bad that she had to go without even saying goodbye? But then Vera remembered that no one knew Rosemarie better than her. There was no way her sister would leave without her. There was no way she would leave. Ever.

December 6th, 1954 was Saint Nikolaus Day and it came and went. Vera didn't care to put a pair of shoes outside the front door. What did nuts, candy or a new pencil matter? Nothing mattered without Rosemarie. Little did Vera know that Saint Nikolaus day would never be celebrated or mentioned again in her family.

The two detectives came back to talk to Oskar and Hilda several times. But each time they stopped by the apartment, Hilda said she felt unwell and excused herself to her bedroom. Eventually, they brought back Rosemarie's picture. Each time they left, Vera would stare intently at her father, trying to gauge what they had talked about by the look on his face. She could tell by the way he never smiled that it wasn't good news. Regardless, Vera was hopeful that their visits meant something good and after they would leave, she'd always ask her father if she could go visit Mrs. Blatt at the bakery. But each time Oskar got agitated and told her she wasn't allowed to go anywhere without an adult. That made Vera even sadder and she often stomped to the farthest corner of the apartment and sulked.

Ruth tiptoed around the apartment cleaning and didn't say much to anyone. Oskar did most of the cooking. But she cleaned and cooked her favorite meal twice a week—Polish sausage, sauerkraut and boiled potatoes. She had so been looking forward to having her in-laws live with her. But since Rosemarie had gone missing, everything was different and she felt like a foreigner in her own home. She wanted to ask Günter when Oskar and Hilda might find their own place. But she knew the timing wasn't right.

Vera didn't like eating Ruth's stinky meals. In the last month or so, she'd made a habit of taking one of Rosemarie's toy soldiers with her everywhere she went. It made her feel close to her sister to have her favorite toy nearby. Vera held up the toy soldier and smiled. If Rosemarie were home, they would look at each other, knowing they were thinking the same thing. Then they'd wait for Hilda to crack the door just enough to get rid of the stink of Ruth's dinners. But now no one did it and the odor of sausage and sauerkraut lingered in the apartment.

Oskar and Günter still left almost every evening after dinner and drove the neighborhoods. Vera knew they were looking for Rosemarie even though they always told her something different. She begged her pappa a couple of times to be allowed to come with them and finally her wish was granted.

Vera sat between Günter and Oskar. Günter drove around the neighborhoods while Oskar gave him directions. It was a freezing, moonless night and few people were out. The whole trip seemed fruitless until suddenly Oskar said, "Okay. Stop."

Günter pulled over and Oskar opened the door and jumped out. Vera watched as he walked quickly toward a pedestrian with a dog. The street lamp was just far enough away so that she could barely see what was happening. It looked as if Oskar had pulled something from his pocket and was showing it to the person. Vera imagined that it might have been a photograph of her sister and the kind stranger with the dog might have been telling her father at that very moment that he had just seen a girl who looked very similar. But, in reality, the man just shook his head and walked away.

While she waited for her father and brother, Vera thought about how different things were in Canada. She now prayed in school and sang to a queen. She grinned at the thought of singing to a queen. She scratched her scalp. Vera's thoughts became scattered. She didn't know what to think anymore. She felt cold and tired and told herself that Rosemarie would be back for Christmas. There was no way she would miss a Christmas with her family. Vera watched as her father and brother came back to the car.

Vera asked, "What were you two doing?"

Oskar rubbed his hands together. "Man, oh man, it's cold out there."

"Come on Pappa, what did you say to them? Tell me."

"We were just talking. Now it's time to get home."

Vera had thought driving around would be fun. She ended up being cold and bored and never asked to go again. On the way home, she wondered if it was possible that when you turned fourteen you simply got removed? By now she should have known more English, so she could ask the other kids if that's what happened when you turned fourteen in this country. She hated herself for not being more confident in her language abilities. She was sick of wishing for her sister to come home and tired of listening to the lies her parents were telling her about where Rosemarie was and why she wasn't with them.

Hadn't Oskar once said that he'd always protect his children? That he'd never let anything happen to his kids? One question after another swirled in Vera's head. Of course he did. A car drove by. The taxis were not parked across the street tonight. The man with the towel on his head was not waiting for her, smiling at her. Actually, the more Vera thought about it, the less she could be sure if she'd seen him at all since Rosemarie had vanished.

Vera pursed her lips and jutted out her chin. No matter what, she was going to get an answer. For sure! Tomorrow. She'd find out the truth. The joy of knowing there was always a tomorrow made her bellyache disappear. When she got home, she flopped on her bed and for the hundredth time went over what had happened since Rosemarie's birthday. No matter how many times she turned it around in her head or thought about it, she couldn't come up with one single reason why Rosemarie had not come home that cold, November afternoon.

18

Germany, Summer 1942

The Summer of '42, Hilda was pregnant with her fourth child. The regime still controlled Germany, and Hilda and the other townspeople of Birkenfeld had noticed that they had adapted little by little to new orders from the regime. That meant no listening to the radio after five o'clock and no outside activity, including walking after eight p.m. Only approved newspapers were available and soon people realized the only news they would be reading was what they were given. Normal shopping for food with money now turned into strict rationing of food stamps. More and more propaganda enticed very young males to prepare to join the Youth Organization. Günter had turned thirteen on July 7th and thankfully still wasn't very interested in the war.

As Hilda walked home with groceries she could see Anna fussing with plants in her window box. She lowered her groceries on the ground as Anna walked to her.

"Hilda, don't you think it's a good time now for our boys to join the Youth Program?" asked Anna with such excitement in her eyes. "They're almost the same age."

"Absolutely not! I'm not willing to sacrifice my

child for that wallpaper hanger's nonsense. They already have our husbands. They don't get our children too!"

"But Hilda!" Anna exaggerated Hilda's name. "Don't you listen to the radio or read the newspaper? Everything's going so well. I think we'll come out of this war just as we were promised back in the thirties. That's what the Pforzheim News says. We'll have everything we want at our fingertips! Just think, a car for everyone! Instead of walking and carrying groceries in this heat, you could be driving! And you had a nice visit with your husband. Don't you see? If things were going badly Oskar wouldn't have been able to come! Think about it!"

"I have another baby coming around the new year. No doubt I will need Günter's help. At the very least, I can't afford to be worrying about him being in combat." She waved at Anna as she turned and continued to go home. She sat on the front step for a couple minutes.

Suddenly she remembered that Oskar had told her to be careful. People were getting arrested for speaking out against the war or letting their children do the same. Anna had always been pro-war and had supported Hitler. And Hilda had just told her there was no way she would ever let her son join the Youth Program. She got a sick feeling in her stomach when realized that she may have put her children and herself in jeopardy.

Three days later it was pouring rain when the doorbell rang. Hilda invited two young men inside and showed them into her kitchen. They moved slowly into her front hall and their cold leather coats caused the kitchen to cool down. She stoked the fire as she asked what they wanted. "What can I help you with today?"

The tall one with bad skin turned to Hilda and said, "Thank you for allowing us in, Mrs. Döderlein. It's awfully cold outside. May I introduce you to Private Genz." He gestured to a nervous-looking man standing next to him. "And I am Private Kerr."

They shook hands and Hilda motioned the two men to sit at the table where she joined them. "What can I do for you?" she asked.

"According to our records your son Günter is old enough to join the Youth Camp.

Depending on his maturity, of course. You know this training for future service is strictly on a volunteer basis at this age, but you must know that we expect all of our citizens to be united in this war effort."

She shook her head. "First of all I don't remember voting for any war. At one point two men showed up at my house and asked me to sign something about who to vote for. But sir," she looked at the tall man, "I was never asked for my opinion about anything. As you can tell we live in a relaxed village. Are you what's called the SS?"

"No madam. We are not that lucky! We are merely volunteers from Stuttgart who take Germany's war efforts very seriously. We already checked your Aryan status. Everything checks out fine. Be glad, Mrs. Döderlein, that we are very concerned about Germany winning the war." The man with the small mustache shifted uncomfortably in his chair.

Just like a teenager! The idiot copied his mustache! Hilda thought.

The taller one continued. "But we'd like to remind you, that you, as a contributor to Germany, will be looked upon with great honor for your son's service."

With the fury of a firecracker she spat, "Under no circumstances will you take my son from me. After he is gone, will you bring wood and split it? Will you help me with my new baby?" She touched her stomach. "I need my boy. Anything else you need to know?"

"Frau Döderlein," they tried to cajole her into

submission, "Günter is a fine looking and healthy young man. You should be proud!"

"I cannot be prouder than I already am!"

"He is the fine specimen that we need for the program. You should be honored that he even qualifies. Not every young man does! You need to consider this very seriously."

She pounded her fist on the kitchen table. She was so furious she could spit fire. "Listen! First they take my husband and God only knows for how long that will be! I cut my thumb halfway off just two weeks ago chopping wood. My husband's leave was only a few measly days. There's no man to help me now! My husband did his best to chop as much wood as time permitted before they ordered him back to Berlin. I have trouble just knowing why my countrymen are so taken in by his yaki-de-yak. For your information I had to use a regular thread and needle and bit on a piece of wood while sewing my thumb back on so the whole town wouldn't hear me scream! The only doctor who could have helped me is also gone now. Have you ever sewn your skin together with no anesthetic? I doubt it!" Hilda showed her bandaged left thumb. "As you can see, gentlemen, I need my son here! I don't need him groomed for anyone else! You people can't even provide him with new shoes. There are none in the store for the upcoming winter! Come on! And now you want to groom him to be one of the sheep that just follows the trend?" She stood and sneered at them.

Apologetically, the taller one said, "Frau Döderlein, we can tell that you've had an unfortunate accident. We are being very nice to you because we are considering your condition. No doubt you will bring another great Aryan into this world and hopefully you will also reconsider your decision by next year when Günter will be fourteen. The boy who lives next door to you, Peter, I believe his name is?

His mother signed up last week. She is a very proud mother, she is!"

"It doesn't matter to me. My son has not expressed any interest in your program."

They scribbled something on a paper and both signed it. The tall one placed it on the table. They left, rather quickly as though they were looking forward to getting away from Hilda.

After they left Hilda read the paper. It showed dates, signatures and a checkmark that said she was to appear at the Rathaus by 9 a.m. the next day. She put down the paper and did not lose a minute to begin preparing for tomorrow. Who knew, after all, what could happen. She cooked a meal and gave Günter instructions on what to do the next day and evening.

The next morning came too early. Hilda woke Günter much earlier than usual, then made breakfast.

"Keep the fire going in the kitchen Günter, and light the pot belly stove upstairs. Please be very careful. September nights are beginning to get cold. Help Rosemarie get dressed in the morning, her clothing will be on the chair. Read your schoolbooks. Ask Hilde to help with anything. I know you'll be all right. You know I trust you. I love you. Since I'm just going to the Rathaus I hope to be back this afternoon. Anna will help you and Hilde in case you run into a problem." She kissed the top of his head and tousled his wavy dark brown hair and checked on Rosemarie to give her a loving glance once more. Günter smiled at his mother with his hazel eyes.

"Don't worry," he said as his mother picked up her small bag and opened the front door. She walked toward the village, past the center of town. From the Main Street she turned into a short side street and walked to a little brick building where she never thought she would ever end up, not even for five minutes. She wondered how many people must have been in there. There was a sign that said to go next door. She rang the bell and an older man came to the door who knew right away who she was and why she was there. While they walked next door the old man said, "Frau Döderlein I've known you and your family for a long time and I'm sorry to have to do this." Without saying much more he brought her next to the brick house and unlocked the door. Once Hilda was inside he locked the door behind him. It was chilly, but considering what this place was used for, it was very clean with a clean toilet. A square hole outside the wall closed up with a couple of bars. Hilda assumed it was more to serve as window and ventilation rather than prevent escapes. A clean cement sink and towels were at hand. She didn't see anything she felt she couldn't handle. As she put her bag on a chair, a nice looking elderly woman brought her some delicious food and an extra thick blanket. Hilda wore her black cable knit sweater and felt as comfortable as the situation allowed.

"Our leader wants you to be as comfortable as possible. Enjoy your food. If you need anything just yell out of that opening. We'll hear you." Before Hilda fell asleep that night she thought how terrific it would be if only women could wear long slacks like men, and that somehow, by some magic, warm air would come through the ceilings or walls. Her legs would be a lot warmer and homes would be easier to warm up and keep warm. She appreciated having to be here only for one night. She knew it could have been a lot worse and from then on, she promised herself she'd watch what she said and to whom. Oskar was right.

Hilda went to sleep thinking that Inge, her friend who owned the butcher shop, was the only one she could trust. The winds and rain came in ferociously that evening. Günter hooked the outside shutters to the window frames and shut the windows tightly. He did what he was supposed

to do. Feeling like a man he was pleased with himself. He
and his sisters would be safe.

19

January 1943

During the best of times Birkenfeld had only one doctor, one dentist, one midwife, one pharmacy, one baker, one butcher, two small grocery stores, one school and one tavern. The war was raging and, of course, the leader's regime had managed to latch onto the one and only doctor left in the little town. Hilda was about to give birth on a very cold day in the same house and the same room again as she had had Rosemarie. The only doctor was summoned to the war effort and the only midwife had to leave because of a family tragedy.

That meant a very nervous Günter was left to act as doctor and midwife. It wasn't all that long ago that he still believed babies were delivered by storks and deposited into a nest on top of chimneys. It was, after all, a common practice to check the top of chimneys for nests built by storks. His heart thumped double and triple time at each of his mother's instructions but he carried them out as carefully as possible trying not to forget a thing. In some quiet moments he wondered if he was going to have another sister or a brother. He hoped for a brother. His mother's stressed voice kept reminding him to keep the fire going in the kitchen stove for warm water. He had plenty of cloths on hand, towels, and scissors his mother had already sterilized in the fire and then cleaned with alcohol. A crocheted blanket was ready after the baby was bathed and cleaned up and dried. Günter was so scared and wished the whole thing would just stop and go away. But in the end he was a great help and Hilda named her fourth baby Vera.

A few days later Hilda was breastfeeding Vera in the kitchen; Günter and his mother had a casual chit-chat about this birthing experience.

"Mama, the stork story sounds a lot better! Some people, like my teacher, say how lucky I was to witness the miracle of birth. But you know what? It was gruesome . . . nasty . . . and I hope I never have to go through anything like that again. I was so afraid of hurting her, what would happen if I had dropped her? And then I found out it is a girl, of all things!" He slapped his forehead.

"You know son, you were much better than the doctor and a midwife combined. You should be so proud! You handled yourself masterfully and I thank God you were here with me. You'll never know how important it was for you to follow instructions. Your good work was very important. Your father would also be very, very proud."

In the fall of 1944, Oskar was still gone, and food was even more scarce. People had to stand in line for hours to receive measly portions that were never enough for whole families. Every household received 1,000 calories per adult and half that for children. Often all the shelves were bare. Inge always kept some meat or sausage on the side for Hilda.

"Here Hilda, here are a couple of sausages! I hope

you have some kraut at home," Inge said when her friend came in her shop.

Hilda reached across the counter and grabbed Inge's hands. "Thank you. Can't thank you enough. Isn't it ironic how so many people thought we would be provided for and here we are—begging farmers or whoever so we can get additional food." Hilda laughed with a curious air that the butcher lady friend hadn't heard before.

"Most people swallow the hook, party line, and sinker, as the saying goes. Even as bad as things are now, there are still some people who think everything will be fine. Do you think anything will get better before the war ends?"

"No, not really. I guess we all have to do the best we can for as long as we can."

The vegetables and fruit from last summer Hilda had stored in the cellar would carry her and her children far into winter. But basics such as flour, butter, salt and sugar were in very short supply or not available at all. Only pregnant women received butter and sugar. Over the last year Hilda learned quickly what she had to do when their pantry fell short of the basics.

There were only two ways to subsidize the pantry. Hilda, Günter, Hilde, Rosemarie and now little Vera prepared for another trip to forage for food from the farmers and find firewood in the forest. This meant weeding, hoeing, planting … whatever the farmers needed done. This would earn them perhaps six eggs and a half pound of butter and a little bit of flour. Vera would sleep in her pram while Hilda, Günter, Hilde and Rosemarie did some serious work.

These day trips meant that Günter and Hilde had to take time off from school to help their mother gather food. Fortunately, the school excused children to help with their families' household needs and considered it as part of their contribution to the war efforts. Hilde didn't love missing school. She liked her classes. But, Günter didn't mind the break. To him it meant getting away from the constant mocking by his classmates. He liked learning and got very good grades but with his mother's worried looks every time she opened that pantry, he knew he had to ask the schoolmaster for a leave of absence.

Hilda had also learned that she could get food another way. Sometimes she took the train to Pforzheim to work in a factory sewing blankets, uniforms, hats and gloves. She loved the sewing jobs because they were making essential items for the poor men whose number came up just like Oskar's. There was no doubt in Hilda's mind they'd rather be at home in their own beds. Women worked by the piece. The faster they worked the more money they made and Hilda was fast with the foot pedal; maybe because she'd been sewing since eight years old on her Oma's Singer machine. The best feature was that workers could bring little children and take care of their needs during work time.

A visit with her old friend, Mrs. Rosenblum, was also a great feature when working in Pforzheim. Before the war started Mrs. Rosenblum was always a joy. Hilda remembered how prim and proper she was. The children loved her. She would sing songs in Yiddish and make grand gestures with her arms, make funny faces. Hilda promised herself the next time she went to Pforzheim she'd visit Mrs. Rosenblum and bring her some dried fruit. She had no husband or kids which meant no one to help her. Hilda felt a pang of urgency to find out how she was faring these days and show off Vera.

The farmer's men were at war. Only the older men and women were available to hoe, till the earth, trim and plant trees, clean barns, weed, pick fruits or milk cows and goats. Hilda also traded seeds saved from the summer harvest. Farmers liked Günter and admired his ability with a hammer and nails. The women enjoyed working alongside Hilda and her children.

Since the temperature was mild, Hilda and Günter thought about getting some basic cooking items for the pantry, other than what the agency allowed.

"We need to take our small wagon and go to the big farm on Schiller Lane and stop off on the way back to gather some firewood. Rosemarie will have to come with us and we'll bundle her up in the pram with a couple of toys when it's time for her nap. But little Vera, I just hate to do it but she'll have to stay home."

Early the next morning Rosemarie happily played on the floor with a toy while Hilda hugged and rubbed Vera's back. "Poor little one, God knows how I hate to leave you alone again." She patted her little backside. "But don't you fret, we'll be gone for only three hours or so." A small toddler, Vera smiled not knowing what her mama was talking about.

As Hilda did once before, she tied Vera's little wrists to the white rail with the soft cloth kept on a nearby shelf. She made sure the rag was long enough so she could reach for her bottle of milk; but short enough so it couldn't get tied around her neck. This morning Hilda put the last few sprinkles of sugar in her milk. She tied Vera's small doll that she loved to nibble on on her wrist so it was within reach. It was lovingly embroidered with a big red smile and big round eyes made by her Oma. It was her faithful companion and kept her busy babbling with the doll almost all day long.

Before leaving, Hilda put Vera's hand around a cord near her crib and pulled it down to remind her it was fun to turn on and off the light. Thank god for Oskar. Many mothers with children too young to be on a farm had to employ various strategies to enable them to subsidize their pantry and fuel supply and at the same time keep their children as safe as possible. As soon as the room became dim Vera pulled on the cord and the room lit up like magic.

Hours later, Hilda and her older children returned to the house. It'd been a productive day, but she'd been worried about her youngest child, to the point of giving herself a stomachache. Hilda rushed up the stairs and called, "Vera! We're home! I'm coming up to see you! Hold on!"

She stood outside the door listening to Vera babbling, "Ma ma ma ma!" The bottle of milk was empty. Hilda felt so grateful that Vera had such a good disposition. She carried her downstairs to an already warmed up kitchen where Rosemarie, Hilde and Günter entertained Vera while Hilda peeled potatoes. Their day was a success!

The next time Hilda saw Inge, she told her the story about having to leave Vera home alone again and how grateful she was for the kindness of farmers.

The butcher lady smoothed her willowy hair out of her face. "This still has to be rough for every mother with small children. We're getting fewer animals to butcher. Every day I have to turn away customers, because I'm sold out."

"Farmers are generous and if women were smart, they would marry a farmer! From what I see there's always something to eat. You'll never go hungry!" Hilda let out a short chuckle.

"Neither does the butcher!" Inge laughed.

"Good point. I'll remember that and tell it to my girls!" Hilda laughed as she left the shop.

"Guess where we're going tomorrow?" Hilda asked Günter when she got home from the butcher shop.

"Where?" Günter was curious. His sisters came over to see what their mother and brother were talking about.

"Mrs. Gustav, the red apple farmer and Mrs. Graff, the cherry farmer, approached me when I was in the village market. They couldn't find anyone to pick their trees this summer and both ladies are not well. If we're interested, we can have all the apples and cherries we want and for every pound we bring to them they'll pay us fifteen pfennig!" Hilda took a deep breath. "And the apple farm is just a thirty minute walk from here. Not only that, but Mrs. Gustav is willing to loan us her cart. It's bigger than what we're used to, but I think we'll have the strength to push it when it's full of apples. And here's one more thing, all of us can go, including Vera. Her daughter will keep Vera occupied and feed her." The kids jumped up and down.

"I want to help. I want to help," Rosemarie piped in as did Hilde, and Vera drooled and happily babbled.

"So, if it's half an hour to the cart, does that mean it's another twenty minutes or so to the fields? It sounds like it will take all day, but I say we go for it. It sounds like fun!" Günter said.

Hilda thought about that distance might be too much for the little ones. "We can work until the trees are all empty. And I think we should get the cart the day before. Can you handle doing that by yourself, Günter?"

Günter was excited. "Great! Great! Of course. I'll get the cart on my way home from school. I can taste lots of apple pancakes already! We could dry cherries and more apples!" Hilda suddenly noticed the change of pitch in his voice. Knowing Günter would soon be a young man saddened Hilda, but made her immensely proud at the same time.

"This summer we picked wild cherries, blueberries, raspberries, boysenberries, gooseberries, mushrooms from the forest, and snails from the muddy ditches after a rain! And now this! I feel like a king!" Günter danced around his mother.

"Yes, and we're going to visit Mrs. Rosenblum and bring her some of our fruit. You remember Mrs. Rosenblum, don't you Günter?"

"Yes, she's nice, I guess." He shrugged and looked like he didn't know what to say.

"I'm hungry!" said Rosemarie.

"Shush Rosemarie." Günter turned to his sister. "Mother, don't forget the farmer who slaughtered a pig and we brought home meat and pig's feet and delicious grease. I love bread with pig's grease and salt! And chives." His stomach growled just thinking about it.

Farm owners gave generously to Hilda. She and her children worked hard and the farmers also remembered that Oskar helped them with business technicalities. It also helped that Hilda genuinely appreciated receiving a bag of flour, butter or a can of fresh milk.

20

One evening around eleven o'clock Hilda stood on her front steps, listening to the sound of bombs exploding, one after another. She saw the edge of the sky light up where Pforzheim was. *Was Birkenfeld next?* Should she grab the kids and run for the forest? A few neighbors came out of their houses, but Hilda didn't feel like talking. All she felt was horror. Maybe it was the Russians. From what Hilda knew about Stalin, it seemed like he fell into the same category as Germany's leader. Hilda could never call Hitler her own leader.

Hilda thought about Mrs. Rosenblum. She would need help. Hilda decided to take the train the next day and ask her if she would like to live with her. Or, at the very least she wanted to give her some fruit and maybe a few potatoes.

Inge the butcher lady greeted Hilda warmly and neither wasted any time talking about what was on their minds. "Tell me," Hilda began, "do you know what's going on? All those bombs last night. The sky was lit up like it was daytime. Tell me, have you heard anything at all? I have a good friend in Pforzheim and I want to go see her this afternoon. I have food and supplies for her. But I need to know it's safe first."

Inge leaned over the counter and whispered as if someone might overhear them in the empty shop. "You're right. Pforzheim was bombed."

Hilda's stomach dropped. Oh, poor Mrs. Rosenblum. "Do you know who would do such a thing? Was it the Russians?"

"My secret news carrier, as I like to call it, told me the English are responsible. Perhaps the Americans. It's so hard to tell for certain who knows the truth."

"I guess it could be anyone. Germany hasn't made any friends with other nations since that wallpaper hanger got us into this mess."

Inge pulled a rag from her apron and wiped the already clean counter. "You want to hear something no one will believe? Even I had a hard time accepting it."

Hilda wasn't at all sure she wanted to know. "Oh good lord. It can't possibly get any worse. You might as well tell me."

"The French are arresting all their Jewish people and turning them over to the Germans, who in turn, bring them to Poland somewhere and they're being killed. I can't believe that civilized people would do something like this. Newspaper hanger provided the ships."

"You are not serious. Why would they do that?"

"I have no idea. But you better make sure you have your certificate to prove that you are Aryan on you at all times."

"They're not coming for German Jews, are they? Has the whole world lost their mind?"

"I'm serious, Hilda. Make sure you and all your kids have proof that you're Aryan."

Hilda patted her pocketbook. "Yes. We received the notice that we're supposed to carry the certificate all the time. I never thought I'd actually need it. Maybe it's just a sick rumor. Why would the Germans want to kill these people? I can hardly breathe. If what you are saying is really true, wouldn't you think that there would be people objecting, doing something to stop it?"

"I don't know any details . . . but, no doubt I'll hear more. In the meantime hush about that."

"I appreciate you and I promise not to mention anything you tell me to anyone. You can count on it."

"Yes. Yes. I know I can count on you."

"Well, I need to catch a train to Pforzheim. Wish me luck until I see you again."

Even though Anna and she were more than a little distant now, Hilda decided to ask if she would keep an eye on her children while she went into Pforzheim. When Anna came to the door, she cracked it slightly and didn't invite Hilda in.

"Anna, I know we're at odds, but I need to go into Pforzheim to check on a very dear friend. An elderly lady. I'd really appreciate it if you would watch my kids. Please help yourself to a jar of jam. I wish I could pay you for babysitting. It's so important, and maybe I can do the same for you one day."

Anna looked down her nose at Hilda. "I'm happy to look after your children, Hilda. They haven't done anything wrong. They can come over here and stay busy playing or whatever until you get back. You are coming back by tonight, aren't you?"

"Yes, of course. Unless a bomb drops on me."

"Why a bomb?" asked Anna.

Hilda wondered how Anna hadn't heard or seen the bombings the night before. "Oh, nothing, just silly talk." Hilda realized that not everyone heard the noise and had seen the brilliant orange sky. "Listen, I'll leave a note for Günter. And please, if he and Hilde can help you in any way, I'm sure they'll be happy to. Just tell them what you need done. Anna, I can't thank you enough. I'm walking to the train station right away after I leave a note for my kids. Honestly, thanks a lot. I'm really worried about my friend and I'm ashamed that I didn't look into her well-being before now. See you later this evening."

Hilda went home, left a note for her children and packed a brown bag with food for Mrs. Rosenblum. She put on her hat and gloves and walked to the train station. The train stopped quite a far distance outside of Pforzheim. As Hilda walked with big eyes and a pounding heart, she tried to adjust to the shock of the landscape around her. Collapsed buildings lay on the sidewalks. A few people tried to dig through the rubble. She walked several blocks to Mrs. Rosenblum's house. There it was. No damage at all to her residence or her neighbor's house. Yet row after row of homes and buildings were demolished in all directions. Nothing much was spared. Windows were broken and the roofline was gone. Hilda was thankful to be able to check in on Mrs. Rosenblum. She was especially happy that she had the foresight to bring her old friend some food. Now she noticed that the front door had a red X painted on it. *Thugs,* she thought. She twisted the doorbell, then again. She looked around. She saw an old woman peek through her curtain next door and finally open her door. She looked Hilda up and down.

Hilda walked to the neighbor's stoop. "Hello, hello. You're Mrs. Meer, right? I remember meeting you last time I visited Mrs. Rosenblum. I'm Hilda. Her friend. Have you seen her? She's not answering her door."

"Please come inside. My memory is not as good as it used to be, but yes, I remember you. How nice to see you again. I would love to offer you some tea or coffee, but I don't have any. Aren't you from Birkenfeld? Mrs. Rosenblum often talked about you. She adored your kids. She loved and appreciated you."

"Why are you talking in the past tense? Has she passed away?" Tears welled in Hilda's eyes.

"Not that I know of. Didn't you see that red X painted on her front door?"

Hilda nodded. "What does it mean?"

"Did you know she was Jewish?"

"Yes. She used to sing Yiddish songs to my kids." Her conversation with Anna came rushing back to her. "Oh no. No no no. They did not take her!" She couldn't stop the tears from coming. "Please tell me they didn't take her."

Mrs. Meers looked at Hilda with sympathy. "Simply said, they marked her door because she was Jewish. Then they took her away. And I don't think she'll ever come back. Her house is just as she left it. They've been rounding up the Jews and others, mainly the weak or feeble minded."

"So she's somewhere, but nobody knows where?"

"If you look around town you'll see many more doors with a red X painted on them. They're all gone. Whisked away somewhere."

"Poland, you said?" Hilda asked. "Why there? She doesn't know anyone there. She must be scared and lonely."

"I am truly sorry about your friend. I didn't really get to know her very well but she was such a soft spoken little lady. Classy."

"Thank you for talking to me. Here are some things that I brought for Mrs. Rosenblum. I'm sure she'd like you to have them." Hilda reached into her grocery net to pull out the bag of fruits and vegetables. "I need to catch my train back so I can get home before dark." She headed down the steps in front of her.

"Thank you so much for this gift. Goodbye. Good luck to you." She waved and turned around to enter her flat. "Ach mein Gott," Mrs. Meer said out loud and sat down reaching for her bible.

Sick to her stomach Hilda walked over the rubble covering the sidewalk and streets to the train station. What had happened to Mrs. Rosenblum?

An explosion assaulted her ears and she couldn't hear anything for a few minutes. Asphalt on the street burned and smoked. Only a few people ran to the designated marked bunkers. She hurried to the bunker on her left. The calamity was extreme. People seemed to come from nowhere and ran in every direction. Some ran to a cement sidewalk leading to another bunker. Two little boys, maybe seven years old, must have gotten separated from their mother. To her horror, Hilda saw that one of the boys had lost a shoe and she saw red skin on the bottom of his foot. They held hands, running and screaming, hobbling and jumping to avoid things sticking out of the rubble.

Hilda called and waved across the street to let the little ones know to come to her sidewalk. A second siren went off; people pushed her into the opposite direction of the boys and they stumbled out of her sight. She followed a small crowd of people into a theater. They squeezed through a narrow opening to get inside. The stench and horror of what she saw was so incredible Hilda would have trouble finding the words to describe it. Countless dead bodies were hooked together in a circle. She thought maybe they'd been gassed. Their faces were frozen in horror.

She sat on the bench of the small train station in Brötzingen next to a chubby lady, head reeling and sick to her stomach. They sized each other up.

"How are you? You look tired." The elderly lady with bright blue eyes smiled.

"Yes, I had such a long, sad and gruesome day. My mind wants to scream, *Get out of Germany. Get out!* God, I hope you're not one of the regime lovers, but I don't care anymore if someone finds out how I really feel."

"No, I'm not a pro-Nazi, and I'll tell you

something, if I were younger there would be nothing that would make me want to stay either. Nothing! I would move to Canada where my distant cousins live, Montreal." The lady looked down and closed her eyes slowly, shaking her head. "But I'm just too old to start fresh in another country."

"Canada? Where is that? Where?" She tried to get some more information as a train pulled to the station.

"This is my train. *Canada.*" As she got up she turned around and said, "Remember it. Auf wiedersehn!"

She hoped that as soon as Oskar came home they'd work on something. Canada? She never heard of it before but surely he would know.

Hilda was relieved to see her butcher friend again to tell her of her last experience in Pforzheim.

"My friend's door had an X on it. And then her neighbor said some gray pants took her away because she was Jewish. Is this what you were talking about the other day? Is this godforsaken wallpaper hanger eliminating people because of who they are and what they believe in?"

"Jesus, I know. I know. We don't have that situation here, thank goodness. But my news has it that millions of Jews so far were carted away by truck or train and simply put somewhere. I don't know where. Not only Jews, but several million non-Jews. Even the jovial gypsies that used to come through our village."

"I heard. What does our newspaper say about it?" Hilda asked.

"Nothing. Absolutely nothing. It's a nasty business. From my source I also found out that England, France and America all refused entry to Jewish people desperately trying to flee to their countries. They had no choice but to return to Germany."

This was more than Hilda could bear to hear. "I

need to go now, but you know what I was always taught? That our life should boil down to caring for ourselves and others. Learn what true love is."

"That sounds lovely. Bye Hilda. Take care."

Hilda couldn't remember ever wishing ill will to anyone, but in this case she excused herself to God and thought, *He needs to die. That leader of Germany really needs to die.* And his demise came to mind as her second wish.

When Hilda and her children got home from digging for snails, they were drenched from a nonstop rainfall. Günter shivered as he spoke. "The ditches were muddy and freezing. Crawling through wet mud was no party and who knows what we touched that got mixed up in that mud! And we only had such cold water to wash ourselves. We would have been better off using the rain!"

Hilda agreed and smiled, but looking at the bright side she said, "Yeah, but you have to admit that the snails we found tasted pretty good, and some people don't even have fresh water."

"I know, Mother. And I'm grateful you cleaned them for us." He glanced at a grandfather clock in the corner. "I'm also grateful that we made it home before curfew. Do you know why we have to be inside by five p.m. now? Is it because of our enemies?"

"Who told you that?"

"My teachers, kids at school. Everybody knows it." He wrinkled his forehead in frustration.

"No Günter, I think it's because he doesn't want us to know what is really going on."

"Who is he?" Günter looked puzzled.

"You know who I'm talking about. And you know that I don't speak his name."

"Oh right." Günter studied the floor for a moment. "But, it's all so confusing. Some of my teachers think he's doing the right thing and they tell us to respect him. I don't know what to think."

"Günter, trust me. I wasn't born yesterday. I understand their causes. I've been through it before when I was little. Generally politicians are fine people. I'm not sure any of them have a strong moral compass. But this group. My god! They are just a bunch of hoodlums in fancy uniforms."

Günter was shocked. His mother didn't sound like her gentle self. "I guess you're right. But then why do so many people think Hi—" He was about to say the Führer's name, but stopped himself. "Why do so many people think he's going to lead us out of this war in better shape than when it started?"

"Listen Günter, you're a smart young man, but after all is said and done, what really does a fifteen year old know? I can tell you, nothing much. And apparently that goes for half of Germany. All I can tell you is that if that wallpaper hanger were doing a good job and doing right by our country, your father would have been home years ago and we wouldn't have been digging around in the mud for snails!"

"You're right." He sounded relieved, as if he didn't have to wonder who had the country's best interest at heart anymore. "Okay . . . all right."

204

21

April 1945

Anna came to Hilda's house holding a large handkerchief against her face and cried so loud she could be heard from Hilda's kitchen. Hilda had her sit down right away, held her hand and gently asked her neighbor and former friend what was troubling her.

It took several minutes for Anna to calm herself long enough to speak. "Peter's had an accident. My Peter. Can you believe it? He's dead. An accident. I sent him to the Youth Program twice and everything was so good. He loved it so much. He was very happy. He had such a good time. My Peter, my boy."

Hilda wasn't surprised. She'd known all along that that program couldn't be trusted. But now was no time to say that. "I'm so sorry Anna, so very, very sorry. What happened?" Hilda asked in a soothing voice, rubbing Anna's shoulder with her free hand.

Anna could barely get out the words between her crying and screaming. "He got shot."

"What? Where?" Anna wiped her eyes and blew her

nose. Hilda continued to rub her shoulders. The disagreement they'd had about their boys joining the youth program seemed so inconsequential now. "If there's anything at all that I can do, let me know. Please let me know. Any time you want to talk, come and see me. I cannot even imagine the pain you must be feeling."

"Hilda, I should have listened to you. I should have. Now it's too late."

"You couldn't have known. None of us could. Why don't you stay and have dinner with us? I could use an adult to talk to."

"Fred will be home soon. I should go." Anna started to get up. "But thank you, Hilda. Really. Thank you for listening and not telling me *I told you so.*"

Hilda put her hand to her mouth. "What? Of course not. I would never." She felt her cheeks redden with just the thought that she'd been right.

Anna left for her own house, shaking her head holding the handkerchief to her nose again.

The next day Hilda went to the butcher shop and told Inge that Peter was dead.

"Listen," the butcher lady said with a low voice over the counter as though someone might hear. "I speak and read French. I know we're like-minded about this war. Just between you and me, I'll tell you something that I don't think many people would know. Don't tell a soul. I would go to jail for sure if they found out that I get knowledge from somewhere other than their own propaganda."

"Yes, you know I won't."

"My distant cousin sends me French newspaper articles. The latest one told of how the regime used what is supposed to be trained youths to fight in the last row of defense in Berlin. Can you imagine? They're using these young kids as a last ditch effort to fight. Actually have them fight like well-trained soldiers and plenty of them have died." She shook her head and closed her eyes while adjusting her clean apron. "The animals held in the back about to be slaughtered will have had a more purposeful life and a kinder death than those kids."

"No. Don't worry. I won't tell Anna or anyone else. Besides, she probably wouldn't believe me. Chances are, they'll probably pull a poppycock story out of their hats and feed it to her. Sooner or later she'll believe that Peter died with dignity and purpose, not because that wallpaper hanger is a power hungry lunatic."

A customer entered the shop and tapped her toe as she waited for the friends to finish their conversation. "I'll come back later," Hilda called on her way out.

An hour later Günter rushed home from school to tell his mother about Peter. "Mother! Peter is dead! Can you imagine? He's dead! Somebody shot him by accident in the camp! Hard to believe that I won't ever see him again." He tossed his rucksack in a corner and sat at the kitchen table. "He's a hero, Mama. Everybody is talking about him!"

She sat next to her son. "I heard about it and it's a crying shame. I feel very badly for Anna."

"Me too. I'm so glad you don't feel the same way about the war as so many other parents and teachers." He shrugged. "I guess accidents happen. But that's crazy. How does a kid get shot? Do you think Pappa will get shot?"

That question had kept Hilda from getting a good night's sleep since Oskar had left to fight for their country. "No, no. Of course not. He's a translator. He works in an office. He's perfectly safe." But Hilda could tell by the look on Günter's face that he didn't believe her. She could hardly fault the boy. She didn't believe a word she said either.

Günter stoked the fire in the kitchen stove and sat

at his usual spot in the corner to start his homework alongside Hilde. His little sisters played with their dolls and he watched them for a moment, thankful that they were unaware of just how bad things seemed to be.

There was much speculation about Peter's accidental death within the school. Günter's first teacher, Mr. Mertz, a bald-headed man with round glasses, started off the day with a little talk.

"Accidents, my young friends, unfortunately do happen, no matter how careful one is. But we must not let this terrible loss hold us back. We must continue to be supportive and fight to the bitter end, as the saying goes. The important thing to remember about Peter is that he was lucky to have parents who believed in the power and he died doing what he loved best. He had the gift and pride to look ahead into the future of this land. All of Germany is proud to have had this brave young man within our midst. Let's bow our heads and think only of Peter." They all bowed and sat. After a few moments, the teacher raised his head and said, "Let's turn to our work, gentlemen."

All during class Günter had this odd feeling that a few of his classmates were glaring at him when the teacher wasn't looking. And it just got worse during recess. They didn't talk to him, they just sneered when they caught his eye. He couldn't help but feel that they knew something he didn't. He tried to avoid them the rest of the day and decided to cut through their neighborhood in the Kleine Höe suburb on his way home from school.

Günter walked the narrow, seldom-used dirt pathway that ran through fields and apple farms. He spotted his classmates when he reached the new asphalt street.

"Hey guys, what's up?" he asked in a nonchalant manner. He felt a deep knot hitting his stomach as quick as a lightning bolt.

"Listen, you 'kinder' wuss! If everybody was like you and your mother, our leader wouldn't have gotten as far as he did!" a boy in the blue shirt yelled.

"I . . . I don't know what you're talking about." He walked a little faster, hoping they wouldn't follow him home.

"You're a mama's boy," the tallest one mocked. "We all went through the program! See? We helped our leaders! But you, you stayed home with all your sisters like you're a girl too!"

"Ah, listen guys," Günter stuttered. "My mother is going to sign me up this July."

"Ah. . . . ah . . . that's all you can think of saying!" mocked a short kid who shoved Günter to the ground. Two others kicked him in the ribs and Günter gasped for air. The one in a blue shirt spotted a rock that fit perfectly in his hand. He hit Günter three times in the face, blood oozing from his nose, his vision blurred.

One of the boys who hadn't said or done anything turned pale when he saw Günter's face. "Jesus! Stop it. You're going to kill him. Let's get out of here. Now!" Before Günter could even think about fighting back, they took off into the woods.

With his cart and shovel the old cow manure man shuffled his way toward the start of his usual daily route, when, as he came down a small hill he saw a crumpled body on the dirt path. He pushed his cart and shovel and walked as quickly as he could to Günter. He kneeled, recognizing Hilda's boy. He bent down to pat his cheeks.

"Can you hear me?" the man shouted. "Can you hear me?" He saw his eyelids flicker. *Good sign*, he thought. "Listen, I'm going to move you under the walnut tree over here. Just a couple of feet to get you out of the sun. Then

I'm going to borrow an empty cart from the potato farmer to bring you home. Don't try to walk. Just stay still right here." The cow manure man pulled a bottle of water from his sack and wrapped Günter's hand around it.

"Here, take a sip, if you can." Günter had trouble hearing, but swallowed a sip of water and the old man walked hastily to the potato farmer. No one else came along the path and Günter hurt so badly that he didn't think about moving but managed to open his eyes by the time both men came back. The potato farmer brought a clean cart and a blanket.

After only one twist of the doorbell Hilda was at the door. The potato farmer said, "I have your boy in my cart. We don't know what happened. The cow dung man here found him unconscious on the old dirt pathway."

She hurried down the front steps and looked at her son trying to scramble out of the cart.

"Günter can you get out, do you need help?" She was shocked to see her boy's face as purple and swollen as a plum.

"Yes." His voice was quiet. "Help me out of here."

Hilda and the men raised Günter out of the cart. The farmers helped him into the kitchen so Hilda could tend to him. She hurried ahead of them and pulled the table toward the middle of the kitchen to put him on the corner bench. She ran into the bedroom to get pillows and the two men got Günter settled. Thank God Hilde, Rosemarie and Vera were playing with friends three houses away. She wouldn't want them to see Günter like this.

The two men held their hats in one hand. Hilda shook hands with both and hugged them several times, thanking them. "Gentlemen, please wait a moment. I'll be right back." Hilda left the kitchen and hurried down the stairs to the basement and quickly removed two jars of wild strawberry jam. She handed each a jar. The cow dung man got tears in his eyes as he looked at the jar. "It's good jam, nothing to worry about, dung man," Hilda assured him.

"No. No. I'm not worried. It's just that . . . it's just that I haven't had a homemade jam since my mama died. And . . . and I treasure this." Both men mumbled more thank yous.

She turned her attention to Günter. "I'm going to clean you and see if anything is broken. Don't try to talk. Save all your energy. First, I'll make you some chamomile tea. It'll help."

On her way upstairs to get a bundle of chamomile she thought, *Those little thugs. One day there'll be a pay back by someone you won't know. It's called karma.*

22

December 1954

When Vera woke after a difficult night, she felt so grateful that it was Saturday. Strong winds howled past her window. The pillow against the side of her face felt soft, warm and cozy. She felt good and tried not to think. The clinking of a spoon being dropped in the sink came from the kitchen. She put on her yellow robe and slippers and quietly made her way first to the bathroom and then into the kitchen.

Just the person she wanted to see . . . the person she wanted to talk to . . . the person who would give her answers. Her mama sat in the chair stirring a cup of tea.

"Good morning, Vera." Hilda opened her arm for a hug when she saw her daughter standing in the doorway. "Did you see outside? It's been snowing for hours. I watched it fall all night."

"All night? Didn't you sleep?"

"A cup of tea for you, little one?"

Vera didn't bother to ask her question again. She knew her mother hadn't been sleeping well since Rosemarie disappeared. No one had. She pictured her mother staring out her window every night, lost, desperate to get her daughter back. It was more than Vera could take and she fell to her knees. She grabbed her mama's apron at the hemline, put her head on her lap and sobbed. Hilda stroked Vera's hair. Vera raised her head and saw tears rolling down her mother's cheeks. After a few minutes, when Vera had calmed enough to speak, she said, "Tell me Mama. Mama, tell me. Where is she? Where is Rosemarie? Where's my sister? Pappa said she was helping a woman with her baby, but she should be home by now. She needs to go to school. You know she hates falling behind. She wants to learn English. And her clothes. She can't wear the same clothes every day." Vera sobbed again. Nothing made sense to her. Hilda let her daughter cry while she rubbed her back. Vera hiccupped while she talked again. "And what about me? She would never leave me. Never! She's my best friend. So where is she? Why won't anyone tell me where she's gone?"

"Oh Vera. It's okay. You just cry. Get it all out. It's okay." Hilda didn't know what to say to her youngest child. There was nothing she could say that would make it any better for Vera or anyone.

Vera kept up with the questions. "Does she know we have a telephone? It's hard to believe she wouldn't tell me anything. Why wouldn't she even say goodbye to me? Wouldn't she want her favorite book? Her toys? Her red purse?"

Vera stood and leaned on the kitchen counter. "I've seen you cry, Mama, even while you cook . . . I've seen Pappa looking so . . . so . . . different, somehow. It's like we've all been . . . all . . . never mind. I'm not sure what. Tell me what's happening," Vera begged. "You just said that you didn't sleep at all last night. If you and Pappa knew where Rosemarie was and knew that she was okay, things would be so different around here. We wouldn't all be so sad all the time."

"Sit down . . . here, sit down." Hilda wiped away

Vera's tears with the bottom of her apron. It seemed so long ago now . . . when Hilda had sewn the rows of buttercups signifying the years that Oskar was away at war.

"Listen, my little one." Hilda reached for her small hands and covered them with hers. "You can see I'm having trouble talking about this." Tears filled Hilda's eyes again.

With the back of her hand, Vera kept check of her own tears. She couldn't bear to see her mama cry any longer and choked out, "It's okay, Mama. You don't have to tell me. It's okay. I don't need to know. It's okay. I love you, Mama, it's okay. No. No. Don't cry. It's not that important. I don't need to know. Don't cry, Mama. Don't cry." Her hands wiggled around as though they weren't attached to her wrist.

"I love you too, little one. You know that. Believe me, I would give up my breath and give it to you."

She forgot that only a minute ago she told her mama not to tell her anything. "What Mama, what is it? Tell me why she's not here. What happened? Why isn't she here? Tell me . . . Why isn't she here?"

Hilda wringed her hands. "Oh honey. We haven't said anything because we thought she'd be home by now. We really did. The police seemed so confident that they'd find her."

Hilda began sobbing, shaking sobs that Vera had never witnessed. Vera covered her face with her mother's apron. She couldn't bear to see her mother like this. This was all her fault. She never should have said anything. Never!

Vera didn't know what to do, what to say. Should she wake up her pappa? She'd never seen her mama this upset. "Does Hilde know? Why isn't she here helping us look for Rosemarie? Doesn't she love us anymore?"

Hilda put an arm around her daughter and took a

few deep breaths. "Of course Hilde loves us. She will come when she can. But Canada is very far away from Germany and it's not easy to get here."

Vera put a chair next to her mama. Suddenly the words *thought they'd find her* took on new meaning. It was as if something hit her on the head and caused the words to echo over and over. The words seemed to spin. Maybe she misunderstood. She couldn't be found? What? How could it be? Even Hansel and Gretel found their way back home from a big thick black forest, and she couldn't find her way back from two doors down? Worse yet, the police couldn't find her when she'd only gone a few steps away? She wiped her face with the arm of her robe. "Wait, Mama. I don't understand. What do you mean Rosemarie hasn't been found? Is she lost? Did the lady she was helping lose her?"

"No. We . . . we just said that because . . . because we thought she'd come home. We didn't want to upset you. We didn't want to frighten you. But she hasn't been found. Oh . . . I can't talk anymore . . . I just can't. Not just now. Sorry little one. It feels like my throat is . . . never mind. Really, I need to get up."

Hilda stood and found her legs too weak to support her and fell back into the chair. She lowered her head, covered her face with her hands and cried quietly. Vera didn't know what else to do except to take herself with her aching belly and spinning head out of the kitchen.

"Mama, I'm going to bed. I'm so sorry. I didn't mean to upset you." Vera kissed her mother and left her there crying. She started toward her bed, but changed her mind and crawled in her sister's bed instead. She burrowed under the covers and talked to Rosemarie. "You'll be back. Pappa will find you or I'll find you. Yes . . . I'll find you and I'll look at the moon with you. All the time. Anytime you want. I promise I won't complain anymore. I won't make fun of your moon anymore. I promise. You're my only real friend here. I didn't really want your fancy Canadian slacks. I was just kidding when I asked to borrow them. You'll be here for my birthday. I know you'll be here. Can't you find our building just two doors up from the bakery? Just across from all those yellow cars." Vera let herself smile. "By the way, I learned that they're called taxis."

She sobbed until she could sob no more, until her forehead and nose felt like they might explode. Vera didn't have school until Monday so she could stay in her pajamas and do nothing. She could just lie there and think. But she didn't want to think. She didn't want to do nothing because then Rosemarie would fill her head. She took a deep breath and turned around away from the dark spot on the wall. The police. Her mother kept talking about the police. The two men who talked to her the night Rosemarie went to the bakery must have been police officers. That's why they asked so many questions. They were trying to figure out where to look for her.

Vera turned on her side and stared at the tiny dark spot on the wall and cried when she thought about the first night Rosemarie wasn't in her bed. It was so strange. So unreal. Vera recalled that she had barely slept at all that night. She kept waking with the slightest noise, hoping it might be Rosemarie coming home. But she never appeared.

She found it was still empty the next day. She had so many questions. She was eager to ask Rosemarie what on earth had happened. But at the end of each day, all she got was more rocks growing in her belly. Each day's discomfort worse than the last. It was worse than the storms she experienced on the ship while crossing the Atlantic. What Vera would give to be cuddled up with her sister, tucked into the uncomfortable bed on that dreadful ocean liner.

A few days after Hilda had told Vera that the police were involved in the search for Rosemarie, the two men who had talked to her came back to the apartment to talk to Günter once again.

They rang the doorbell and Vera answered. "Vera!" Hilda called from the kitchen. "What have I told you about opening the door before you ask who it is?"

"I'm sorry, Mama." Vera stood, head down, blocking Detectives McCormack and Talbot. "I forgot."

Hilda recognized the men immediately. She put her hand on Vera's shoulder and urged her toward the bedrooms. McCormack waited until the child was gone, and then he said, "Is Günter here? In our investigation, we've come up with a few more questions we need to ask him."

Hilda didn't like the way the taller policeman said her son's name. "You're lucky." She stood, with her hand on the doorknob, unwilling to move. "Günter happens to be here. But you should have called first." Hilda had liked these men so much the first night she met them, the last day anyone had seen Rosemarie. But now, they were different. Their tones seemed accusatory, menacing. "Wait here."

A minute later Günter appeared from the back of the apartment. "Gentlemen." He motioned them forward. "Please come in." He led them to the kitchen.

They sat and put their hats on the table. McCormack spoke first. "Thank you, sir. We'll get right to it. We need to review the timeline again."

"Which one?" Günter got up and poured three glasses of water. He brought them to the table and sat again. "Or what day, I guess I should say."

Talbot sipped his water and then spoke. "What time did you say you left your regular work at Sperry?"

"About one."

"You came in your truck, right?"

"Right." Günter wiped his nose.

"Do you make it a habit of leaving your job in the

middle of the work day?"

The hairs on the back of Günter's neck stood up. He felt the same suspicion from the detectives as his mother. "Ah, no. Not really. I came home only to get some papers that my friend Albert and I needed for a project. Do you not remember this?" Günter tried to keep his tone level, but he couldn't help but feel these two men sitting in his home, with guns holstered to their hips didn't believe a word he was saying.

"We remember just fine." McCormack exchanged a look with his partner. "But the search for a missing person, especially a child, is quite complex. We need to make sure every single fact is documented and backed up. We apologize. We don't mean to offend. It's just how the investigation goes."

Günter searched each man's face for signs that they thought he had done something to his sister. Finally, he decided that they were just doing their jobs. Just like they said they were. "Okay. Go ahead and ask your questions. We all want the same thing. To find Rosemarie and make sure she gets home safely."

The detectives continued asking Günter the same questions as before. Desperate to get his sister back, he patiently answered them. This went on for close to an hour. It eventually occurred to Günter that the cops were trying to confuse him or make him tell a different story. When they were satisfied with the answers to their questions, they stood, pushed in their chairs, thanked Günter for his time and left.

When they got back in the car, Detective McCormack sat behind the wheel with Talbot in the passenger seat. Detective Talbot cleared his throat. "I'm glad we went back. But his answers never wavered. I don't think he's our guy."

"I agree." McCormack started the car and put it in

gear. "He seems like he loves his family. I think we can take the family off the suspect list. They're broken up over this girl."

"Absolutely. They want nothing more than to find this poor, lost child. When we get the photos of the taxi drivers from the lab—maybe the younger sister can tell us something, or, for that matter, any one of them."

"I wonder what bastard got his hands on that little girl. Jesus, it kills me . . . it never stops. The wondering. The worrying. I don't even want to imagine what whoever took her is doing to Rosemarie. Chances are, she's not even alive anymore." Detective McCormack took a long drag on his cigarette and exhaled deeply as he drove off to visit morgues around the city.

Now and then temperatures dipped below zero. Regardless, Vera and her parents walked through their neighborhood and ended up away from their apartment. They took the bus to Outremont and then walked every street that led to Mount Royal Park. Vera didn't understand why they walked these streets. They were narrow with dark alleys and lack of lighting made them look particularly unfriendly. She assumed they were looking for Rosemarie, but if that were the case, why weren't they calling her name or knocking on doors? It seemed like everything her family did these days or didn't do, like laugh or smile, was because of Rosemarie.

"Pappa," Vera finally said when she was so cold she could no longer feel her fingers or toes. "Why are we out here? It's so dark and windy."

Oskar stopped and crouched down so he was nose to nose with Vera. "We're looking for clues."

"Clues? For what?"

He sighed sadly. "Anything that can help us find your sister." Vera had noticed that every day her parents said Rosemarie's name less and less.

Vera brightened. She was happy to have a job to do. "Oh, okay. What are we looking for? Breadcrumbs?" She remembered the story of Hansel and Gretel. Could it work for them too? Why hadn't the police thought of this before now?"

"Tonight we're going to look for Rosemarie's cap. The one she crocheted last winter."

"Oh, I love that hat! Rosemarie said I could borrow it." She held tightly to her father's elbow while they walked. Every time a city bus pulled over and opened its doors, her parents peered inside. After the fourth time, Vera wanted to know what they were looking for. So she stood on her tiptoes and tried to see what they were looking at. At first she thought that maybe someone would have Rosemarie's hat. But she decided that she'd never give away her hat. Not when she had promised it to Vera.

Vera's feet ached and she was so hungry and tired. "Pappa. Is Rosemarie on one of these buses? Is that why you and Mama are looking in every one when they stop?"

Oskar had no answers for Vera. He knew that if Rosemarie was this close to home and she was able, she would have found her way back by then. "You know what?" He took his daughter's hands and rubbed them between his own. "It's cold and late. Let's go home."

When Vera and her parents got back to the apartment, Günter and Ruth were putting up a silvery tree in the corner of the living room. Günter turned when he heard the door close. "Oh Vera," he said happily, "you're just in time to put some ornaments on the tree." He reached into a cardboard box and handed Vera a delicate glass reindeer.

Vera had never seen anything as beautiful as that silver tree. Everything was so different in Canada. Christmas trees weren't real evergreens. The ornaments weren't homemade and no one used popcorn and cranberries. All the change made her miss her sister even more. If Rosemarie were there, they would laugh themselves silly when they discovered that poor St. Nikolaus had to fall through a dirty and hot chimney to deliver gifts to every family. No one in her old village in Germany would believe this story!

But then, it wasn't going to happen. Everything was a mess these days. And Vera felt as if her family would never be whole again.

23

Vera liked her new reading and writing teacher Miss Bell a lot and guessed she was about Ruth's age. She especially liked the dress she wore and promised herself that when she grew up that's exactly how she would dress . . . just like Miss Bell.

Unlike Ruth, this lady smiled a lot and there were times when Vera was convinced that she gave her a very personal smile . . . different from the quick smiles she gave other students. It were as though she knew something that no one else did. She taught reading and writing and said hi to everyone as they filed into the classroom. That made Vera feel so special, like Miss Bell really cared about her.

Miss Bell wore perfume—a scent Vera recognized right away. Lily of the Valley. Each time she walked by, it brought on homesickness when she remembered her spot in the garden where she grew those flowers. Aside from the Crocus, the Lily of the Valley was one of the first flowers to push their way into the world, even in the midst of snow.

One afternoon as the bell rang and all the kids dashed out of the room, Miss Bell quickly walked to Vera and motioned for her to remain seated. She sat next to Vera and smoothed out the top of her skirt. She wet her lips, tilted her head and smiled as she talked.

"Now, Vera, I know you didn't understand what I explained to the class. But I know you'll want to participate in the gift exchange next Monday. Right?"

"Participate? Gift? Exchange?" Vera looked confused as she reached for her translation book while Miss Bell patiently waited with her hands folded on her lap. Vera took too long, and after a couple minutes Miss Bell saw the confusion in her young student's face. Vera didn't understand how the words "participate" and "gift" mixed, or that gift would have anything at all to do with her. She closed the book and pretended to suddenly understand what this was all about.

Miss Bell walked to her desk. As Vera made her way down the aisle, the teacher handed her a small piece of paper. "Here, dear, this is for your father."

Vera bolted home and was almost out of breath as she handed the note to her father. While Oskar read the note, Vera gave her own version. "Pappa, I need to bring fifty cents and some poison."

Oskar said something to Hilda and smiled in Vera's direction . . . something that hadn't happened for some time. "Did you look up the word *gift* in your book?" asked Oskar.

"Yes, I tried, but it was too confusing. Gift is poison. It will make you sick."

"Gift in German is poison. Gift in English is a present, a geschenk."

"This language is crazy, don't you think so, Pappa?"

"No, it's not crazy. A store called Woolworth is not that far from here. We'll go there tomorrow and see what you can find."

The next day just as he promised, Vera walked with her father into the store that had the big red letters *F. W. Woolworth* attached to the outside wall. The farther they walked, the larger her eyes became. She was mesmerized by the music that seemed to come from the walls or maybe the ceiling—she really couldn't tell.

"Pappa, look! Look! So many things! Have you ever seen such a big store? For sure not in Birkenfeld!" She reached out to touch a package of colorful embroidered handkerchiefs.

"They're beautiful. But look over there." She pulled Oskar by his hand to another aisle. "Look, Pappa, look! Ah, who wouldn't want this? Look, look at this bow that's attached to a comb. If you were a girl, Pappa, wouldn't you like to get one of those? Such a dark purple. You know Rosemarie loves this kind of purple. Can I get her one of those? Please, Pappa, please?"

Oskar stopped abruptly and swallowed hard. "For your sister?"

"Yes . . . Yes. I know she'll really like it!" She handled the bow as though it might break any second.

"Listen. Let's get what you need for school. We'll come back again when . . ." Sadness overwhelmed his body. At the same time he forced a chuckle. "The store won't grow legs and run off, so don't worry."

Vera carefully placed the purple bow back into its spot and picked up a red one. "I think this bow is perfect for school. Promise me we'll come to this fabulous store again. Pappa, I can't believe there are so, so many things here."

Oskar gave the clerk a bill. With a smile and a 'Merry Christmas,' she handed a small bag to the beaming Vera and the change to Oskar.

Vera checked inside the bag. "Thank you, Pappa. I love you."

"Just wait a few minutes, then you'll really love me." Oskar led Vera to a food counter.

"What's all this?" Vera asked as she slid on the

round stool next to Oskar and pointed to the items bundled together in an aluminum bracket.

"Napkins. See?" Oskar talked to her in English as he pulled one out of the napkin holder and offered it to Vera. "This is salt and pepper. This is sugar." Vera lifted the salt, pepper and sugar as she repeated each of Oskar's words.

"So, one can just take them?" Vera returned to German.

"No. You can't take it away from here, but you can use them as you need them while you're here."

"Has Mama ever seen anything like this?"

"No." The waitress walked over and talked to Oskar about what he and his daughter were going to eat. Then she looked at Vera. "Chocolate or vanilla?"

"I like to have chocolate, please." Vera spoke slowly and cautiously in English.

"That was nicely said, Vera. Very good." Oskar complimented her.

"Oh! I understand a lot more English than I can speak. And my new reading and writing teacher at school helps me. Rosemarie would do better with English if she'd come to school. Doesn't she have more to learn? It's all so weird." Vera returned to German.

"In Canada they wrap gifts for Christmas. So, before we leave here we need to buy some festive looking paper." It wasn't lost on Vera that every time she brought up her sister's name her father changed the subject.

The waitress came back with two tall glasses filled with ice cream. "Enjoy." The lady smiled as she placed Vera's glass in front of her.

"I enjoy." Vera spoke English to the waitress. She took a bite and smiled at Oskar. "Have you ever had this before? It's so good. I'm not quite sure what it is. But it tastes so good!"

"Yes. I had gelato in Italy but listen, do you know what you just said to the lady?"

"Yes. I told her that I like the taste."

Oskar pursed his lips. "Kind of. You could have answered . . . yes, I will enjoy it. Or even a simple *thank you* would have done."

"Pappa. Does everything have to turn into a lesson?" Vera wasn't allowed to go anywhere alone anymore, and every time her father walked her to school or home from the grocery store, he constantly tried to teach her something. Usually it was about learning English or any one of the languages he spoke fluently. Sometimes it was just chitchat. But they never spoke of Rosemarie.

While eating, Vera swiveled around on her stool to look at the various displays of merchandise and Christmas decorations.

"Look, Pappa . . . over there." She pointed to the right. "There's a bottom part of a large doll. It looks like she's wearing a ballerina skirt."

Oskar turned around. "Ah yes. The doll is called a mannequin. Stores use them to model clothes. And the skirt is made of a material called crinoline. It's worn under a skirt to make it puff out."

"Now I know why Mrs. Bell's dresses are so poofy. I really like it. Pappa can I get one of those?"

"Not right now. Remember we're here to get a gift for one of your classmates. We should get some wrapping paper. Do you see anything you like?"

Vera found some beautiful green and blue plaid patterned wrapping paper that looked much Rosemarie's new slacks and decided on that.

Excited, Vera dashed up the four flights of stairs and found Hilda at the sink peeling potatoes. "Look Mama, look what I got! You should have seen the store. It's huge. They have so many things to choose from. Birkenfeld doesn't have anything like it. I wish you were with us. You should have seen this purple bow I found. It was so pretty and it was attached to a comb. I really wanted to get it for Rosemarie. You know purple is her favorite color."

When Hilda didn't react to Vera, she looked at her father. "Tell her, Pappa. Tell her how beautiful the bow was and that I wanted to buy it for Rosemarie."

Oskar put his hand on his daughter's shoulder. "Why don't we show Mama what you bought for your classmate?"

"Yes, show it to me." Hilda forced herself to smile. Vera went to the sink with the bow in the palm of her hand as though she was holding a fragile bird. Hilda looked at the bow. "Looks nice. The paper is nice too. Oskar, would you help Vera wrap her gift? And remember we're supposed to mark if it's for a boy or girl." She picked up another potato.

On the day of the exchange, Vera was so pleased with the gift she received: a glass globe with a little house and a pine tree in it. When she shook it, snowflakes danced around until they settled on the bottom. She'd never seen anything like it and absolutely loved the present. She felt a little giddy at the thought of showing it off to everyone, but especially to Rosemarie. During the last hour of school she shook the small globe. It was magical how the flakes reacted to her movements. Each shake was unlike the last. *Surely, she'll be home for Christmas. People don't get lost.* Never had she heard of such a thing before. Never. Vera was sure her sister would be home soon.

From that afternoon on, every day became more desolate and joyless. Günter found a station on his Marconi radio that played German Christmas songs. Whereas they used to bring the family so much joy, Vera hardly heard them anymore. Her full attention was on the door and the doorbell. Waiting for Rosemarie to surprise her. She kept staring at the door willing it to ring, but it didn't. *What was taking her so long?*

Just like back in Germany, on the table was a plate with a few candies, some dates and a large box of colored pencils. *Where was Rosemarie's plate? Where was her plate?* She wished she could shout about it. Oskar gestured that the only plate was hers. She, in turn, was surprised that the Messenger of God remembered only her, but not Rosemarie. If only she could have seen Archangel Gabriel . . . oh, the questions she would have asked.

Why didn't the grownups say something? Anything? Thoughts began the torture again. Where was her sister's plate and colored pencils? Why wasn't she there? Did people really get lost? She held her box of pencils against her chest. With a sick feeling in her stomach she admired the cake in the center of the table.

Hilda left the living room. "I have a surprise. I'll be right back." Vera's breathing stopped and time froze for just a moment. *I was right.* She swallowed hard. *Rosemarie would be the surprise.* Hilda returned holding a large brown envelope. She pulled out three drawings of Rosemarie's face and laid them on the table.

"How much did that cost you?" Günter asked.

"Oh no. She didn't ask to get paid."

"Who drew these?" Oskar asked, reaching for a drawing.

"Mrs. Blatt. The baker's wife. She asked me for a photograph and she drew those for us. We can put them in stores. Aren't they fantastic? Don't they look just like our Rosemarie?"

Vera saw her mama's eyes come alive.

"Where is my picture?" Vera asked.

"Imagine, years ago she went to art school. That's where she met her husband. They're so real, aren't they?

What do you think, Oskar? Ruth?" She took a deep breath. "And see? She even wrote her name and the police station's telephone number. Mrs. Blatt hung one on her door already."

"That was so nice of Mrs. Blatt." Günter took one and studied it. "It looks just like Rosemarie. These will help get her home sooner. I just know it."

Seeing the drawings of Rosemarie made Vera feel sad. She excused herself from the table and went to her room. She started to write a letter to Hilde telling her about the drawing of Rosemarie, but she was too sad. She dragged the chair from the corner to the window and stared out into the cold Christmas Eve night. Just like with the little globe, Vera saw snowflakes swirling around a lamp post. She whispered, "I bring to you my pa-rum-pa-pum-pum-pum." It was her favorite song.

24

Vera continued learning English and missed the fun of challenging Rosemarie's skills. Every night she sat by a window looking at the moon and silently talked and cried to Rosemarie's moon. One day, after a good day at school, Vera talked to her missing sister. "I wish you could have been there. A new lady who wears the most beautiful dresses is now also helping me learn English in my classroom. Her name is Mrs. Bell. Mr. Fisher told me my English book contained a list of Canadian Provinces. He showed me the page and said a spelling test would happen the next day. I didn't know how to pronounce half of them, but with Mrs. Bell's help, I was able to figure it out and even memorize how to spell them. Guess what. Mr. Fisher told me later that I was the only one who got one hundred percent. He had all the kids stand up to look at me and they all clapped. Where are you?" Tears rolled down her cheeks. "How can you be gone? Mrs. Blatt said she misses seeing your pretty face. How can you be gone? Did someone take you?"

In the middle of January it snowed almost non-stop. It snowed ferociously. Snow drifts were up to two stories high. The louder the wind howled, the more Vera's tears fell onto Rosemarie's wooden soldiers.

25

1955

It'd been a few months since Rosemarie had disappeared. Vera had finally made a friend in school named Claudia. They were in the same class and stuck together. Vera had a dance at school coming up and Oskar took her to Eaton's and bought her a beautiful dress. It was pink and white gingham with short puffy sleeves. Finally, Vera had a dress with crinoline! Oh how she missed her sister. One night when she was supposed to be sleeping, she turned on her side and pushed her chest toward the moon. "See Rosemarie? I'm getting breasts. But some stupid boy hit me there today. It really hurt. So, I called him a creep. Can you dance? Are you scared? I hope you're not scared. I love you, please come back. We love you all the time."

Vera continued as she spoke out loud to the sister she hadn't seen in months. "Oh God, I wish you were with me last evening . . . I had such fun. My dress and little white high heels were just beautiful. I danced the peppermint twist, I don't know how many times. And guess what? A boy likes me!"

26

May 1945

The war was officially over. Günter was fifteen, Hilde thirteen, Rosemarie four and Vera two. Even though the worldwide conflict was settled, Hilda didn't think anything had changed. The government was still rationing food and Oskar had not returned home. It killed her to see her two youngest children holding their bellies. Then she thought of those boys in Pforzheim running down the smoldering street screaming, "Mama! Mama!" It would haunt her forever and often she wondered if they ever found their mother. If she had been quicker to think instead of standing there like some frozen fool perhaps she could have helped them. Her children were hungry most of the time, but healthy and safe. That was more than she could say for those boys who were probably orphans now.

Günter came up behind Hilda and put his hand on her shoulder. She jumped with his touch. "Sorry Mama. You look like something is on your mind. Are you okay?"

Hilda stood and covered Günter's hand with her own. "Oh honey. I'm fine. I was just thinking about how much has changed over the years. And at the same time it feels like nothing has changed."

"What do you mean?"

Hilda measured her words. "Well, the war is over. But we're still living on scraps, whole villages are bombed out and your father still isn't home."

Günter thought for a moment. "My teachers say we're lucky."

Hilda scoffed. "Lucky? Take a look around. What about empty cabinets and me being a single mother screams good fortune?"

"But we won the war. Isn't that what's important? My teachers think that's all that matters."

Hilda couldn't stop herself and she snapped at her son. "We most certainly did not win the war. The only good thing that came from it is that that coward killed himself. And besides, my brother …" Hilda realized she was saying too much and put her hand over her mouth.

"Uncle Fritz?" Günter couldn't make sense of what his mother had just said. "Is something wrong with Uncle Fritz?"

"I wasn't going to tell you this because I didn't want to traumatize you, but something happened to him."

"Oh no! Is he okay? Did he lose his job as a bricklayer?"

Hilda decided that her oldest child was ready to hear the truth. "On the contrary. He made very good money, even during the leanest years of the war. But every time he got paid, he went to the tavern and drank away his paycheck. And one night he drank more than usual and spoke his mind about *him*." Hilda still couldn't bring herself to say Hitler's name. "And apparently the tavern owner didn't like that very much."

"Oh no, Mama! What happened?" Günter asked.

"He disappeared the same way as a lot more people

have disappeared. More to the point, people were made to disappear by these thugs in gray uniforms … all in the name of … oh, I don't even know what. All I know is he went to work, then the tavern and never came home. His body was never found. And Fritz is just one of so many lost and never found. Look at Anna. She can't stop crying over Peter's death. And we all know it wasn't an accident. I don't know what happened to that poor boy, but I do know no child should get shot. Ever." Hilda moved into the kitchen and focused on cutting a few turnips into chunks.

Hilda continued. "Of course, you never know if the tavern owner turned him in. I know that your teacher, Mr. Mertz, was very war oriented. That's why I always told you to keep your thoughts to yourself. I've heard of parents disappearing if their kids told their teachers they were anti-war or anti that wallpaper hanger. So no no no my brother didn't happen to disappear. Nor did any of the millions of Jews and feebleminded poor souls. The regime took them. They took them all."

Günter could hardly believe what he was hearing. "Then how come my teachers and so many others made it sound like Hit—I mean, that person, was a great man who was doing what was best for the whole country?" He'd been so confused about who was right about Germany's leader and the war in general.

Hilda stopped chopping for a moment. "I wish I knew, son. I wish I knew. I guess they were all brainwashed or too afraid of being shot to speak their minds or tell the truth."

Günter reached for a turnip that had fallen on the floor. He carefully wiped it off and placed it on the counter with the other pieces. "Wait, did you say feebleminded? Like our neighbor, Doris?"

"Yes, Doris. Lucky for her, her father built a box in the back yard. When he got word that the gray pants were coming, he hid her in there so they wouldn't see her. Can you imagine having to hide your own child from the government? It's despicable. She is Aryan, but even that wouldn't have spared her."

"Oh my goodness, Mama. I had no idea. Now I feel bad for going along with all the other boys at school. Our teachers made that man sound like he knew what was best for us."

Hilda picked up a turnip and threw it in a pot of boiling water. "If he knew what was best for us, we wouldn't still be begging for scraps and living off root vegetables. I hope I never see another turnip again. I can't stand another winter of eating them with no salt, no butter, no nothing. Whole turnip, mashed turnip, quartered turnip! Ugh! I can barely look at them."

Günter looked stricken. "I hadn't really thought of it that way. But now that you mention that things haven't really changed, why aren't we allowed to listen to the radio at night still? I guess I understand why we weren't allowed to listen at night during the war. But why now? Like you said, the war is over. But sometimes it feels like it's not."

"That's *exactly* what I'm talking about, my boy. I would love to be able to listen to the radio whenever I felt like it. It would be great to find out what's happening outside of Birkenfeld! All this time with no real news about anything or anyone. Your father. I haven't received anything from him for some time. Not a word. Even our neighbors are still too afraid to talk! It's killing me not knowing when Oskar is coming home or where he is. I can only assume that he's safe. But what do I really know?"

As she spoke to Günter she had flashbacks of being a child during World War I. It was the same again: hunger, cold and never enough of anything. And now her children were in this same predicament: hungry, cold and never enough of anything. This time they called it World War II.

"Believe me my young man," said Hilda earnestly, "one of these days I guarantee you, we will *never* be hungry again. Your father and I will do something so that our children, grandchildren, their children and their children's children will *never* cry themselves to sleep because of hunger. I don't know when, where, what or how, but we'll do something. I love my neighbors and all the countryside but I despise everything about the state of affairs. I just want out! I want your father to come home and then I just want out. Maybe to a place called Canada. A lady at the train station said Canada is a great country."

Finally the newspaper told some news. Germany was divided into sections controlled by the French, English, Americans and Russians. New orders of what you could and couldn't do or say were spelled out. Hilda didn't care. She assumed Oskar would be standing in the doorway any day now.

"God, I hate the damn French. They're lame, nasty and stupid," exclaimed Günter closing the front door. He threw his rucksack on the floor and stomped into the kitchen.

"Why? What happened?" asked his mother. She wiped her hands on her apron and came out to greet him. When she saw his bag on the floor she pointed to it. He dutifully picked it up and stored it.

"The stupid people, you know, they see you every day. Every day. And every day the same soldier guy asks to see your papers. Can you believe it? Wasn't all this supposed to stop when the war ended?"

"Sure, honey. Of course I believe it. I guess the process is a little hard to understand, but in reality it's quite simple. Germany lost the war, the country has been split into fourths. One fourth is controlled by Russia on the Berlin side. Another area is controlled by England, and the other sections are controlled by America and France."

"So who controls us?"

"France. They sort of own us."

Günter looked flabbergasted. "Why? How? We're people. How can they own us?"

Hilda guffawed. "Just like we stormed France and Poland during the war, they just bulldozed right over us."

"Great. Just great. And on top of everything else, I can't even understand what they're saying. Why would I bother to learn French?"

Hilda was struck by how grownup Günter sounded. "We simply have to make the best of it. And you must remember that we're not allowed outside after six o'clock. We've been told on the radio that they are ordered to shoot to kill anyone outside after that time. That means they have the right to kill you, me, and even little children. Anyone. They are in the driver's seat now, and we are the passengers wearing blindfolds. We just have to do what we're told."

"Oh mother, I know why nobody likes them. They took *all* the food from some people who worked *all* day like we have just because they were outdoors a little after dark." He made a gesture with his hand as though nothing that had been said was of any importance. "I wouldn't want to get shot like Peter, but I have to say that helping with the birth of Vera was scarier. And crazier than the French. I think I would rather take on a French soldier than ever deliver another baby."

"You did a fine job. I agree the French are no pussycats, but regardless, Germany started all the fire, by that I mean, the war my dear."

Hilda made many efforts to find out where Oskar was, disappointed that he wasn't home now that the war was over. The rumor was that all Germans who hadn't returned were being held as prisoners of war. Hilda tried frantically to find out if this was true and if so where Oskar might be. But she never got any information.

Oskar was being held in Russia at the worst POW camp. He had no idea why he was being detained or when he might be released. He was forced to work in subzero temperatures and was surviving on less than a thousand calories per day. Hundreds of soldiers didn't make it through the first winter of 1945, many just lay frozen in the snow like statues until the Russians threw them into a mass grave. Soldiers, including Oskar, took the clothing, gloves, hats, money and any personal effects off the dead. The soldiers talked among themselves about the POW camps in the different countries.

Oskar talked to the guards in Russian but failed to get any information out of them. He explained that he was merely a translator for whoever needed him, that he was not a fighting soldier. They either couldn't help him or didn't care because he continued to go to sleep every night wondering if it would be his last day alive.

Every day was a fight to survive. He often wondered if his father and grandfather had also endured such horrific and grueling conditions of wars past. At night he looked at the sky and wondered if Hilda saw the same stars he did. The pearl button was ever present in the palm of his left hand. It was the only thing that really felt warm and warmed his heart.

Then one day at the end of February one of the guards motioned for Oskar to follow. He ended up in the office of someone obviously important. Oskar thought he might be a lieutenant. He had several papers and envelopes on his desk. He motioned for Oskar to sit. He explained in Russian, "I have seven letters here from a friend in Poland. I do not know Polish. I understand that you do, so I want you to translate them in strict confidence since they are from a lady. In return you will get my help to get you close to the border of Ukraine. You'll still have to walk about five to eight kilometers to get to Belarus, then take the train into Poland, from there you'll be on your own. I will give you train permission into Warsaw. It's the best I can do. You'll be given two loaves of bread and a little dry meat. Some money. That's all I can do for you in exchange for your services." He scratched his mustache and looked at Oskar with piercing eyes.

Oskar removed his glove and touched his pearl button in his pants pocket. "Sir, when do I start? I accept your offer and you can count on my confidentiality." He felt hope for the first time since he'd been home the last time. Finally! Finally, he might be on his way to getting back to his family.

"Very well. You'll start tomorrow." He stood and this time he stretched out his hand and shook his visitor's hand.

The guard took him back to his barrack without saying a word. That night Oskar thought that in case it was not an honest and honorable deal at the very least he'd be out of the freezing weather for a couple of days. And if it was honorable, there would be a big chance of getting on a train home.

"Oskar, what happened?" one of the other prisoners asked when he returned to the base camp.

"Nothing really. They just want me to do some work inside."

"Mmm . . . you better watch it, Oskar. Russians can be sneaky. You know what happened to the whole family of the Czar?"

"I know he and his whole family were executed."

"Exactly. And you know that the other linguist hasn't been seen for several days. He hasn't shown up to get his loaf of bread. Be careful comrade. My father always said that with Russians, it's just like being a chicken . . . you've got to always keep one eye open."

Oskar laughed. "I guess it doesn't take much to amuse us these days, does it! Rest assured that I will definitely keep both eyes open and listen with both ears."

There had been no blizzard that day and the sunset was exceptionally beautiful. The little window showed the sky fading from gold to pink and then morphing into a blue violet. It was the only beauty Oskar could find in that godforsaken place. He wanted to feel hopeful about his new job. But nothing ever really worked out there in the frozen tundra. His main concern was that they'd take him a certain distance and then shoot him, calling him a runaway. He was quite sure no one would care. After all, it'd be one less mouth to feed. Nevertheless, Oskar felt the risk was worth the possible freedom and fell asleep, not giving it another thought. In the middle of the night someone from the far end started to cough, then choke. One by one everyone in the area got up and tried to help the man.

Soon the guard came to break up the crowd. He had his gun ready to shoot.

"This man is going purple, sir. He's gasping for air" Otto pointed to his friend's face. "He needs help right away!"

"Oskar," one of the men yelled. "Go get a guard and tell him we have to help this poor soul. He's choking!"

Oskar moved through the men. He explained what happened, but the guard just shrugged and said that the man probably swallowed a cockroach.

"Please!" Oskar begged the guard. "He needs help."

"It's too late." The guard looked away. "Someone will come around tomorrow and take the body away." Then he tapped his hat and left the body on the ground.

A few hours later Oskar was at his new job sorting

envelopes by date. They were all from the same person in Warsaw, Poland. The last letter had a postmark about seven months before and the earliest postmark was from two years prior. They were from a lady named Lena Karowski. They were very brief. She thanked him for the wonderful time they had in Warsaw and that she wished for the war to end. She wanted the Germans gone so they could resume their friendship in person instead of through pathetic notes.

Oskar was alarmed to read that Jews were being forced into crowded camps. She wrote that no one knew what happened at the camps, but someone had said they'd seen people hanging on a fence, only skin and bones. Oskar didn't dare ask about what he translated. It could jeopardize his deal. He was thankful he didn't have to translate a reply to this woman.

When Oskar finished the seventh letter, a man in a green uniform told him that the next morning he should be ready to leave. The driver would have a packet for him. He touched his cap. "Remember, not a word to anyone."

"You have my word, sir." Oskar turned and walked to his bunk.

While the men stood in line to get their daily loaf of bread, a sled driven by a young looking soldier came by the wired fence. Oskar knew it was for him. Without saying goodbye to anyone he tucked his bread into his jacket.

"Hurry, please," said the young man.

Oskar stepped up into the sled carriage and off they went with four horses dragging them. Oskar looked around for a rifle. All he saw was a small package next to the driver.

"How long before we reach Belarus?" asked Oskar.

"Sorry, no talking please."

At least it didn't snow and the winds were tolerable. Oskar's watch was taken away when he became a prisoner, but at some point he guessed that they must have been sledding for at least three hours. He wondered if the horses needed a break. At last the driver stopped and gave him the small package and told him to continue walking along the railroad, about three kilometers. From there he could take the train into Poland. A permission certificate for the train was in the small bundle.

"Good luck," said the driver and turned his horses around for home.

Another half hour or so the night would be upon him. As he walked he looked for shelter but found only trees half buried in snow. There were no houses, not a forest where he could find shelter, just flat land as far as the eye could see. He had to hope that he would survive the night. Aside from his fur cap, he had a shawl wrapped around his head covering his nose and mouth. As he trudged along, he kept telling himself that he was alive and present. He didn't dare go to sleep, but continued looking for a spot to rest. Since it was night time Oskar thought it had to be at least thirty below zero. He could feel his eyebrows and eyelashes encrusted with ice and even with all the protective gear, it was a far cry from being warm. Different thoughts swirled through his mind, not making any sense. One would think that the planet and the moon would freeze in its spot forever. Russians were a tough bunch.

The wind was kicking up hitting his back. He looked up at thousands of stars shining like diamonds in the distance, and he wondered if Hilda saw the same stars. He thought of his new daughter Vera, what did she look like? No doubt as beautiful as her mother. Did Hilda sing Vera the same song about the distant stars as she had with Günter, Hilde and Rosemarie?

Oskar stop dreaming. His only friends here were stars. The moon threw an eerie ghostly grey-blue color on the snow. The windows of his home were probably glowing that warm welcoming yellow light. He could see himself and Hilda being lovers forever in that house. Trudging a little slower he made it to the tree on the right. In the moonlight all the trees looked like black cobwebs reaching for the sky. There was no sign of life in any direction. The tree had a large crevice on one side and Oskar climbed in. He took out his bread and tore off a chunk. *What a friend!* The bread was almost frozen and he allowed his imagination to go wild pretending a fire was glowing right in front him. He played the piano next, the deepest notes as he looked ahead into the dark grey, then a high tinkling of notes when he looked up at the sky. He was afraid of going to sleep for fear he wouldn't wake up, and he knew that he wouldn't be found until springtime. There was a reprieve from the wind. If he could just rest for an hour after eating his bread, he'd be good for another couple of kilometers. By then, he should be close to the train.

Ah, yes, the train. What a beautiful sight that would be. His heart jumped at the very idea of him actually sitting in a train that would take him to Poland. Oskar didn't know Poland or its surrounding areas . . . but he'd think of that when he got there. Surviving one moment to the next was all he could hope for. He dozed off, but woke when he heard wolves howling in the night.

"If the freezing doesn't get you, the wolves will. That's why they only use one guard. You stay here unless you want to end up as a frozen goose for the wolves," another prisoner said every night when they heard the wolves in the distance.

To Oskar wolves were a danger, but he also thought that civilization must not be that far away. Not that he knew much about wolves, but he thought that they preferred to be close to humans, cats and dogs which he hoped would mean a populated area. He had no idea how many kilometers he had walked. He had no gun and his best defense was a tree branch or perhaps climbing a tree.

As he was crunched in the crevice of the tree trunk, he also thought the night was frozen in time . . . daylight seemed so unreachable.

But daylight did come and with it a swirl of snowflakes and such a wind Oskar felt naked. He couldn't hear the wolves and could only see snow blowing sideways. Mother Nature was odd. The railroad continued where the flakes were falling. Before he left the safety of his tree, he took another chunk of bread and a slice of the dry meat. It was delicious. By the time he finished, it stopped snowing, still windy but sunny. The ground and the branches glistened as though they were made of crystal. So dangerous and yet so beautiful. As he walked a little farther he came across what he knew to be a bunker. Oh! If only he had found that last night, he would have brushed away the snow and made himself a bed . . . and then he thought he still could take a good rest and began to remove the snow from the entrance when he came upon a human foot. He rolled him over and saw that it was the missing linguist. He looked through his jacket pocket to no avail. In one of his pants pockets was a piece of paper. It was folded and on the outside was a name and address. Oskar didn't want to snoop but he thought it could help him find something out about this man. He opened the paper to see if any light could be shed about his demise.

Marie, I couldn't deal with prison any longer. I'm taking a great risk going over the barbed wire fence tomorrow knowing I might get shot and not see you or my son again. I hope I make it. In case I don't, know that you always had my true love. If my song in this life ends, then let my melody live on in our son and that is please teach him that we give from our heart, kindness, consideration, understanding, hope and respect each moment that we are given in our lives. Your true love forever.

Oskar sat for a few minutes to take it all in. He supposed his comrade died from hypothermia. "What a shame," he whispered. "My comrade stopped here to sleep and then never woke up again. What a shame." He stuck the paper into his pants pocket, and if, God willing, he made it home, he would give the man's widow the note. The sound of the wind called him to get going again. Without looking back he left the bunker and headed for freedom. He had some bread and surmised that he walked for at least two hours and once he trudged over a hill loaded with a huge snowdrift he couldn't believe his eyes. There was a town. He beamed and felt like waving as though someone would be waiting for him.

"I'm coming home, Hilda. I'm coming home!"

It was a small town named Vitebsk in Belarus with hardly any people outside. *Can't blame them,* Oskar thought.

"You're German, right?" asked the man behind the window when Oskar finally got to the train station.

"Yes. Yes. I am," answered Oskar.

'Where are you headed?"

"To Warsaw, sir."

"Do you have your certification and your ticket?"

Oskar looked into his bundle, and there it was, written in Russian that he was free to head for Warsaw, Poland at no charge. He munched on some bread. It was amazing that trains in this freezing weather were actually on time. It snowed and the wind blew sideways making it difficult to see. The train's brakes screeched. Oskar didn't have a watch so he walked quickly to the window and saw a clock.

His dream was fulfilled. Just to be sitting in a regular seat and getting out of this barbaric and unrelenting wind. He felt the pearl button. It was where it belonged. He removed the last bite of his bread from under his armpit and kissed it. The train was ice cold. Of course, nothing compared to what he'd been through the last day and a half.

As the train rolled by he could see Poland was still

in total rubble as it had been since early 1939. The train to Warsaw would take several hours and possibly longer depending on the weather. Then off to Germany! Back home! Taking a fine bath in his own warm kitchen. Oskar's heart sang! Soon, soon he'd be away from this prison forever; away from this damn war. He was so enamored in his own thoughts that the train steward tapped him on the shoulder.

Oskar quickly produced the official paper he had from the Russian officer and showed it to the train steward who nodded his head to let Oskar know that it was in order for him to be on this train with no cost to him and returned the paper to him.

"Sir, can you tell me which train would be most suitable to go to Stuttgart after this?" Oskar asked the steward.

"Yes, you would take the train headed south to Frankfurt, and after that I'm really not sure at all. Things are kind of messed up so you'll just have to ask. But good luck to you." The train steward touched his mustache and tipped his cap as he walked away. Oskar felt too tired to acknowledge his good wishes. He was so hungry and his whole body ached, he felt the only thing that kept him going was Hilda smiling at him with those beautiful eyes and lips; his beautiful children caused his heart to sing. In just two or three days he would hold them.

After changing trains in Warsaw, he would take the Berlin rail located almost in the area where he had played piano for Hitler's birthday which seemed years and years ago, and it would take him directly into Frankfurt and then shortly after into Ingelheim. The last train would take him into Stuttgart and then to Birkenfeld. He ate a few bites of the bread and the last two bites from the dry meat. But then, in just a couple of days he wouldn't need to worry about eating. He would taste Hilda's creamed red cabbage and spaetzle. With these thoughts he put his rucksack against the window and the seat. He felt his pearl button, rolled the shirt from his dead linguist pal into a tight ball, put it into his rucksack and dozed off again seeing the most pleasant smile from Hilda. Mario's shirt had been a lifesaver during Oskar's awful icy, windy, frozen Russian trek along the railroad, using it to shield his face from the bitter cold. But the icy cold wind was almost forgotten. As usual he kept his gloves on and unsuccessfully tried to keep his eyes open.

Oskar had fallen into a blessed sleep when he felt someone touch his left shoulder and saw two French soldiers looking down at him. They held him firmly by upper left arm, one soldier behind the other.

"Don't make any trouble, monsieur. If you do, remember we have the right to shoot anyone who tries to escape. We are in Berlin now and you need to come with us. You belong to us now," one of the three soldiers said.

"Why?" Oskar asked in French.

"Well, we've got ourselves a smart one!" The dark-haired one laughed. "Let's go! There's no time to explain."

The war was over, he'd done his stint as a POW, the Russians certified him as being a free citizen with a train ticket. Oskar knew this would not be an invitation to a dinner. He could tell their tone was serious and to think about escaping would be futile with these escorts. They walked across the platform and boarded another train. Oskar couldn't tell where this train was headed but it obviously was not to Germany. He still had his cap and gloves feeling the pearl button. Whatever happens, it would be devastating to lose it. Quickly he grabbed for his rucksack and slid it on his back.

"Where are we going?" Oskar asked.

"Mon Dieu! Just relax . . . we'll be there in just a very short time. Then it will be explained to you." The train came to a halt. They stepped off; first the dark haired soldier, then Oskar and right behind him the light brown-haired, skinny one. They motioned for him to walk just a few feet to the street and they directed him to step into a waiting jeep.

Oskar had no bread left and the dry meat was long gone. He clutched his body . . . he was so painfully hungry.

In the middle of the night in the fall of 1945 they arrived and saw the sign at Camp de St. Césaire. Oskar and his only belonging, his rucksack, were ushered into a building. A door was opened for him to enter into a dingy looking office where an official was at a desk that held a lamp, a few stacks of paper and a holder for ink and pen.

"What is this place, sir? Why am I here? Can you explain s'il vous plaît?" asked Oskar.

"You are here because you are a prisoner of war of France," he replied calmly. The officer really wanted to get the paperwork over and done with. He was tired and anxious to get back to his makeshift temporary closet and doze off again. He told Oskar that he felt so miserable having to work this night shift.

"There must be a mistake, sir. A terrible misunderstanding. I was released from the prisoner of war camp on Russian soil. I have papers to prove it." Oskar started to look in his inside coat pocket to produce his paperwork from Russia.

"Here, you see?" He placed the train permission certificate on his desk in front of him in clear view.

"No unnecessary moves, sir," said the soldier who stood against the wall watching Oskar.

"Oui! Oui! I know all about it. But you see here it tells the real story." The officer sounded annoyed. He put the paper under his lamp and asked Oskar to get up and look at it. He bent over the officer's desk and lamp to where he was pointing at.

"You see, mon ami, you had a bona fide freedom while on the soil owned by Russia. And now, Poland is no longer part of Germany . . . it now, in part, belongs to the Soviet Union . . . and the rest to France. The Russians really left you in the dark, didn't they!" He chuckled. "Ah monsieur! Germany is now divided into England, France, Soviet Union and the United States of America. Now you are ours. The territory where you're from is occupied by us. So, just fill out this form here so we can inventory your assets. Pierre here will then take you to your area with your other comrades. Tomorrow we'll have you fill out a few more forms such as where to send your mail . . . notify your wife, if there is a wife, or girlfriend, if there is one, that you are here."

"Any chance for some food?" Oskar asked.

"Tomorrow at five thirty the cook will come. We'll have a delicious breakfast." He explained in his heavy accent and suddenly got up and smacked his hands together and motioned with his hands to Pierre, the dark-haired soldier "Pierre! Take him to house number three."

"Merci et bon soir," Oskar offered politely. No sense in arguing, especially not with the French. The officer walked very briskly ahead of the private and Oskar. As he walked the gloomy hallway, he saw an officer open the door to a room the size of a closet. Inside was a naked female on a cot with outstretched arms. "Ah, mon amour!" was all he could hear before the door slammed shut.

Oskar grinned as he followed in front of the soldier leaving the dingy building and entered another gray cinder brick walled building. Thoughts of what he went through in Russia and especially in the last two days when he thought he'd freeze and starve to death . . . this dingy place started to feel very snug. No moonlight tonight and only slivers of light from a few outdoor lamps came through small windows. Oskar was shown his bunk. The private whispered, "There are guards outside. I wouldn't try to run. There's nowhere to go, and don't create a rumpus. If you do, we'll shoot you. Bon soir." He tipped his cap and left the dorm. Without a word Oskar quickly removed his rucksack and gloves, never forgetting to give at least a quick glance to the pearl button and, as usual, dropped it into his pants pocket, buttoned up his jacket and fell down on the bunk . . . with Hilda and the kids being nothing but a quick thought before he went to sleep.

27

Of course Birkenfeld didn't have a newspaper of its own and sold only Ingelheim's, *Wings of Times*. Hilda read the obituaries highlighting the where and how the death of a loved one took place. She shook her head . . . sad, so sad, young men in their prime. She hoped this would be the last war on this earth, forever.

Months went by before she was contacted by a war organization notifying her that her love was a POW in Russia. At that time Hilda learned from her butcher lady friend that most of the soldiers getting released were from English and French POW camps and they were gravely injured. But in Russia about 20,000 soldiers died every month from disease, starvation or freezing to death. Of course, *Wings of the Times* would never be allowed to print the truth. Hilda didn't think anything truthful had been printed since before the war started. But she knew Inge was telling the truth because the last time she was in Ingelheim, veterans were sitting on curbs or against the wall of a bombed out building selling pencils. Quickly she'd scramble through her pockets and drop a little money into the soldiers' cups. There was one about Oskar's age with a leg and an arm missing and somehow managed to hold and play a zither secured in his lap.

Hilda loved his gift of sound and found out that before the war, he used to play the zither with an orchestra. His two daughters, wife and father all died when their building was bombed. After expressing her condolences she'd asked him how he was feeling, "Pretty lucky. Sure . . . lucky. At least, they say, I'm one of the lucky ones." He smiled up at her and thanked her for the money while tears rolled down his cheeks. *Bastard Hitler,* she thought, walking off to the train station. *How disgusting this war was and still is. Oh hell! Not just this war, hasn't it been like this since the beginning of time? Before the birth of Jesus Christ? Haven't people learned? Pain from every direction?*

"Our government doesn't even finance the soldiers who were willing to give their lives for that miserable wallpaper hanger; but he had money to build an autobahn of five thousand miles," Hilda added to Anna while having some peppermint tea.

"I know things haven't happened the way the Führer promised to the people. I agree with you now. Imagine losing my Peter over nothing. Nothing at all." Anna spoke sadly. "I was bamboozled and should have listened to you. Really, I should have. I cry every day knowing my boy won't ever come home again. I can never hold him again. Never. I go to his grave and leave flowers once a week and the only thing I feel is my guilt eating away at my insides." Hilda got up to put her arm around Anna's shoulders.

"Don't be too hard on yourself Anna. We all do the best we can during such a very, very difficult time. No one gave us a blueprint to the truth. I just wish someone would tell me where Oskar is. Or at least that he's okay."

"Oh yes, that must be terrible. At least I have the peace of mind of knowing where Fred is."

Hilda felt a surge of hope. "You've heard from your husband?" Maybe she would still get word from Oskar.

"Yes. He's somewhere in England. A POW. I finally got word from him. He wrote he'll probably work in the mines but that he'll be free to come home soon. I mean, seriously Hilda, how long can they keep them as POWs?"

"I haven't heard a thing from Oskar. I wonder if I even have the right to complain knowing the heartache we, the people of Germany, caused. It's hard to see a bright side."

"I know what you mean. I don't even feel like growing any vegetables anymore. I mean, who cares if I do or don't? What's the point? That's how depressed I am."

"Anna, we need your gardening gift. If not for yourself, then for others. There's this soldier in Ingelheim . . . why don't you come with me when I take the train again? We could bring him some things. He plays the zither so beautifully . . . just like Oskar plays the piano," Hilda said slowly hoping it would sink in for Anna. "Our food ration was printed for October fifteenth through the thirty-first and the amount of food looks even more scarce than last month. No flour or sugar, dairy and hardly any fat or meat. If nothing else, I could really use your help, or better said, we could help each other to get something better for our meals."

"How?" asked Anna.

"I'll go with my kids to work for some of our farmer friends. We've done it many times before. Besides, it's fall and most farmers whose sons aren't here need extra help. So, if you'll look after Vera I could take more time. But, I'll be glad to share with you whatever we'll bring home. What do you think?"

"Good. Good. Oh, sure! Vera is such a little doll. Will you bring food for her? I really don't have anything much at all."

"Yes, sure. The only thing is, we leave very early. When we've done this in the past it's best to leave early. Is that okay for you? I mean is it okay if I bring Vera that early?"

"It's not a problem. I hardly sleep anyhow."

Before dawn the next morning, without being told what to do, Günter and Hilde knew to help Rosemarie with the stockings that Hilda knitted for her last year. He put a few handfuls of dried apples and carrots into a paper bag with a canteen of water that they all shared. Four small tin cups completed their daily food for the day. Hilda didn't even have to ring the doorbell. Anna was ready and smiled taking Vera. "Good luck!" she said, taking Vera's little bag and closing the door.

They walked downtown to the house where the potato farmer lived. They'd had good luck with him before, and both Otto and his wife were already up and about.

"You have no idea how happy I am that I didn't have to tie Vera into her crib. Let's hope we'll do good and get off the street before seven o'clock. Anna will be happy to get some flour or something."

Hilda and her three oldest children arrived at the elderly couple's house near the center of town. They welcomed the mother and her kids into their living room. "Come in. Come in." The couple motioned right away to Hilda. "We haven't seen you since before the end of the war! It's so good to see that you are all well. Is your husband home or have you heard from him?"

"Thank you so much. I'm so glad to see that you're well. But, no . . . I haven't received any word at all for several months now. I don't even know where he is. And your son and son-in-law? Have you heard anything?"

"No. Darling no. We think Stefan might be in Russia somewhere, but no one is certain. No doubt Hitler had the best interest at heart for Germany, but now, we just pray for all the lost souls, including his."

"I hope you'll have some work for us to do in

exchange for flour and sugar. Anything you can spare . . . anything at all would be greatly appreciated. The rations are less and less every month. My next door neighbor is watching my youngest and I promised to share with her. Her husband is a prisoner of war somewhere in England."

The old woman turned to the three kids. "Günter, Hilde and Rosemarie, you can clean out the chicken shed and fill the cart with the cow manure and take it to the dump. Don't be shocked Günter because it's pretty bad. We old farts are starting to have more and more trouble keeping up the place and we don't trust too many people these days. I'm sure you know what I mean. Hilda, if you have the energy, look at the floor in this room, it's also in bad need of some staining. I have a whole jar of walnut juice from last year tucked away somewhere. This floor gets the most traffic. Maybe in a couple of months you can put on some wax. Spruce it up a bit for Christmas, huh?"

The elderly lady got up and checked a closet and found the walnut juice and a rag. "Do you mind if I start right away?" Hilda asked. "You know the new rules about not being allowed outdoors after nightfall? We don't want to get shot at or have our food taken away."

The old lady walked to the chair by the window. "It's terrible, just terrible. But then, even though we all knew nothing would be easy for our soldiers not then, or now . . . imagine how the Jewish population dealt with their fate. Nasty, Hilda, absolutely nasty. I can't imagine how anyone could deal with such a disaster."

The women talked for another minute before Hilda went back to work. But she was so distracted by learning Mrs. Rosenblum was most likely dead that she couldn't focus. She didn't even hear Günter come in. He stepped toward her, but she stopped him.

"Günter careful. I just finished staining right by the door where you are." Hilda motioned to the still-wet floor.

He stepped back. "I just want you to know that we're ready to take the manure to the dump so we'll be back in about an hour." He scampered down the stairs.

The old woman came back. "You're so lucky Hilda that you have such good kids. I'm going now to wake up my husband from his nap. Otherwise he'll be a pain tonight because he won't be able to sleep." She left the sitting room and Hilda rubbed the floor like a crazy woman until her kids came back.

As usual the couple gave Hilda flour and a small box filled with eggs as well as a loaf of dark wheat bread. By the time the kids came back, the sky was dark and foreboding. Hilda carried one of the nets and Günter took Rosemarie by one hand and Hilde carried the eggs. "Come on, kids," Hilda said. "We must hurry home before the rain starts. I think . . ." she started to say when all of a sudden very heavy cold rain started to pour. She protected the net with the bread with her jacket. Günter raised his shoulders to prevent the rain from hitting his neck.

"Okay kids, we're not supposed to be out any more. We need to walk in the ditch so we can hide easier with our goods. So, please be very alert. If you even think you see someone, tell me right away. You go ahead and walk in front of me. And please, don't make any noise."

Before very long the ditch had enough water to cover their shoes and ankles. Hilda hoped that the rain would keep the soldiers indoors so they could get home without incident.

"Mother," Günter turned around and whispered, "I just saw a man turn by the corner over there. He has an umbrella and is walking slowly. I can't make it out too well, but, yes, I think he's holding a rifle in front of him. Mother, can you see him?"

They crouched in the mud. Hilda situated Rosemarie so that she could put her hand over her mouth if need be. Günter and Hilde stayed quiet. The soldier turned to his right and climbed up the embankment where dirt roads led to farming fields. Not far from where Günter was beaten not so long ago.

"Kids," Hilda whispered, "let's get up. Quietly. Stay on your knees, and really get going. Remember to stay low. Hurry! Hurry! Crawl faster. I don't want to lie in that cold muddy ditch one more minute. And we don't want to get caught," Hilda whispered as she picked up Rosemarie and carried her with her free arm and held her bag in the same hand. She used her free hand to grab brushes inside the ditch to help pull her along. Her dress kept getting stuck between her knees and clung like glue around her calves hindering every crawl. Obviously the soldier also must have taken refuge from this downpour. They reached Anna's home while the rain still poured down and rang her bell.

Anna ushered them into her hallway. "I was so worried about you. It's after curfew, did you notice? Come in. Come in."

"I know. It wasn't easy. We saw a French soldier coming toward us . . . and we had to dash into the ditch and crouch on our knees until it was safe to go on. I've heard that they are quite free with their rifles. But, Anna, look, here's the good news." Hilda opened the nets to show off the flour, eggs and sugar. "Help yourself to half as I promised. We'll wait here."

"Oh, look at that." Anna looked down into the nets and smiled. "I haven't had flour for some time. And bread. Let me go into the kitchen and get a platter."

"Go ahead and help yourself, then we have to get home. Vera did well, I hope? You'll never in your wildest dreams believe what I learned from the woman we worked for today."

"She was such a good child. No problems at all. We did a little bit of gardening until the rain started. I'm sure

she enjoyed it. I'll be over tomorrow to hear your news."
Anna closed the front door and stood by her kitchen table
to admire the items, feeling like a rich lady.

28

On Monday Hilda took Rosemarie and Vera with her to the butcher lady. She wanted to tell her what the lady told her while she was staining the floor. The butcher lady bent over the counter with deli meat in her hand.

"Rosemarie, give this to your mother." Rosemarie was becoming a young lady. Hilda watched her daughter walk across the floor.

"Thank you." She was polite and gave an easy smile. Rosemarie handed the meat to her mother. She divided it between her daughters.

"Can we get some? This is so good. Please?" begged Rosemarie. The butcher lady's dachshund came running out from behind the counter. She laughed. "Good thing we ate our meat already!" Both girls occupied themselves with the dachshund named Lisa. The last customer left the butcher shop. Inge wiped her hands on her white apron as she came across the floor.

"I haven't seen you in some time. Didn't you need any meat?"

"Oh yes. I received some from the cherry field farmer where I did some work for them on the field. Took the last of the cherries down…."

"What else has been happening? Have you heard from your husband yet?"

"No, not yet," Hilda said in a small voice.

"I suppose he must be a prisoner of war. If he is one, do they notify you where they are?"

"You would think so, wouldn't you? But no, I'm always hoping for the best each day. I hope he doesn't suffer or gets maimed. That would be horrible. But listen, I've got a story for you." And then Hilda told Inge everything the old woman had told her.

"I should be getting my next newspaper in about three to four weeks. That should tell us some more details."

"I'm not so sure if I want to know. Of all the audacity of a man, a nation, whoever, to kill those people. It makes me ashamed. I just want to go somewhere else."

"Where do you mean?" asked the butcher lady.

"I've heard of Canada. I don't know anything about it except it's across the Atlantic."

"If we weren't so set in our ways . . . we'd probably consider doing something like that also. We're getting kind of tired." She shook her head. "Anyway, enough of that talk. What can I get for you?"

"I'm allowed to get a hundred and seventy-five grams of meat that's supposed to last for two weeks. How about some pork and a little beef that I'll grind up." As usual, the butcher lady always added a few more grams than allowed.

"Your children are really growing up so fast. Where are they in school now?"

"Let's see. Günter is sixteen and just two more years and he can be done with school and start work in a factory. Hilde is fourteen. Rosemarie is six going into first grade and Vera is almost four and going to kindergarten."

The butcher lady asked Rosemarie, "Do you remember your pappa?"

"No. No Pappa." Rosemarie shook her head and looked shy.

"How about you, Vera? You want your pappa home?" Vera didn't answer and continued to stroke the dachshund's back and rubbed his head.

"Vera has never seen her father. All these horrible . . . " She had trouble finding the right words. "Horrible tragedies make one's head spin, don't they?" Hilda asked the butcher lady.

"I got news for you. I see a lot of people, you would be surprised at the number of our townspeople who are all for it. I just try to stay neutral, neither agree nor disagree. They give me the creeps. Like I said, I'll be getting another paper in two to four weeks."

"Thanks a lot for the extra meat." Hilda opened the meat shop's door. "Come on Rosemarie, Vera get up. The puppy has to go now and take a nap and we need to get home. Rosemarie you need to write your numbers and Vera can string up some pretty beads."

It was the time of day when the butchers were busy. A wide driveway that led to the back of the slaughterhouse area was curtained off by two big, black Rottweilers chained to each side of the buildings. Farther back, not within view, Hilda could hear pigs squeal and a few cows moo frantically as though they knew what was in store for them. She took Rosemarie by the hand and scooped up Vera and quickly walked home.

29

Christmas 1946 was just around the corner. Hilda listened to the radio and learned that that winter was the coldest and most brutal on record for Germany. New coal was delivered in November and though Hilda was frugal, so much of it has already been used. They all wore the warmest clothing and a coat and a cap in the house. Günter put four bricks on top of the stove to heat through, then he took a towel and wrapped each one and put it on the foot of each bed.

Hilda still hadn't received any word where Oskar might be held or if he had died somewhere. Not one organization or the Red Cross in Ingelheim could help her. They only told her that even if Oskar had died, it might take up to a year for her to hear about it.

Hilda's sister, Emma, who lived in Stuttgart with her husband Otto, usually stayed in constant touch. But it was difficult during the war. So Hilda was delighted when she came home and Günter had placed an envelope from her sister on the table.

Dear Hilda,

Have you heard where Oskar might be? I hope and pray that you did. As you probably know, finally the United States president allowed certain organizations to check the lack of food situation in Germany. Especially where kids are concerned. Are the soup kitchens established yet in Birkenfeld? The soup kitchens in Stuttgart became established, but a little too late for my Otto. He became as skinny as a rail. Actually, me too I mean, we know everybody is hungry because of that lunatic. Otto boiled water to make a soup, he said, just three days ago and ate it. I didn't really pay any real attention. What can go wrong? We've had the same soup for the last two winters . . . turnips in water! What else? What could possibly go wrong. I think he just flipped and wanted to die. Strange, he never indicated anything to me. He complained in the last month especially, for some fat or oil, and he showed me a dirty looking can a week before. It was the kind one usually uses to oil wheels. As you know, here in the city we can stand in line from early morning to late afternoon for a little meat or bread, and so often, by the time it's our turn there's nothing left on the shelves for us to have. After Otto got so sick and ended up not being able to breathe any longer, one of my neighbors checked and he found Otto added some black, thick grease into the water with a cut up turnip. He was moaning and holding his chest and belly all night long and by the morning he died. I didn't bother you about it because I know that you too, must be extremely strung out.

I'm by myself now and every day I try to wake up with optimistic thoughts. If you're going to survive this world, you have to be optimistic, don't you think? Can't wait for spring and summer. This winter is as miserable as last year, don't you think? I know you'll pray for Otto and know I'm fortunate that I had the chance to comb his hair and wash him for the last time in this world. Like so many soldiers he could easily have been killed and lay there in the mud until god knows when.

Please write to me, or better yet, if there is even the slightest chance that you and the children could come here, nothing could make me happier. Let me know about you and the children and Oskar.

I love you, your sister, Emma

"What did Aunt Emma have to say? Is everything

all right?" Günter asked Hilda.

"She's doing all right. Do you remember your uncle Otto?"

"Not really."

"He passed away from eating some kind of poisonous oil or grease."

"So are we going there by train?"

"No, no. I can't afford that. We'll think kindly of him and hope Emma will be happy in the future. That's all we can do for now."

"I understand. I will say a prayer for Aunt Emma and Uncle Otto when I go to bed tonight. I'm sorry, Mama."

Hilda hugged her son. "So am I, my sweet boy. So am I."

That night Hilda took out her blue fountain pen and wrote back to her sister.

Dear Emma,

I am so shocked to read that Otto passed away. You can be sure St. Gabriel has carried him into God's arms and he will be forever at peace. I am so sorry for your loss. Obviously the soup kitchens came a little too late for Otto. Yes, we have the soup kitchen here. Günter, Hilde and Rosemarie go every day in the morning, and the lines are so long, it takes hours. But all in all, we are the lucky ones compared to others.

No, I haven't received any word yet about Oskar, but neither did my neighbor, Anna, about her husband. I imagine they both should have been home by now. All we can do is wait. And I personally hope that Germany will never get another lunatic to run the country. I'm glad he's dead. I hope you feel the same way. Did Otto?

Two blocks over from here live the Harten family. Their twenty year old son was on leave and during that time he committed suicide. Shot himself in the head. Rumor had it that he was sent to a concentration camp with multitudes of people, and he was one of many who were ordered to dig mass graves and bury their dead. His mother said that he saw dead babies, young kids, teenagers. All ages. He couldn't eat or sleep or deal with the inhumanity of it all.

So the truth is, my dear Emma, we must not forget that we are truly the lucky ones. I know you'll probably think that I've gone crazy, but I have to tell you that I have a very, very strong desire to do nothing but get out of this land. I loathe the ground I walk on and by the way a lady at the railroad station told me that Canada is a great place. She has family there. I can hardly wait to see Oskar and talk to him about it.

Take good care of yourself, and remember, after all is said and done, just like the soldier without an arm and leg, we are one of the lucky ones. I'm so sorry about Otto and please take good care of yourself. Hilda

A carpenter in town made splendid crafts out of wood for children. His wife painted ducks on wheels, cars and blocks. Hilda purchased a brown wooden flute for Günter, a doll for Hilde, a gaggle of three wooden geese for Rosemarie and a small doll for Vera. She paid with money, dried plums, cherries and sun dried carrots which the wife had agreed to take earlier in the fall. Hilda was so pleased with the items. She knew these toys were worth a lot more than what she paid and she promised the carpenter and his wife that her children would take very good care of all that beautiful work. She hid the Christmas presents in the closet of her bedroom.

When it was time to pick up Vera and Rosemarie from school thick flakes of snow came down. It was so cold that Hilda felt guilty for sending her kids outside with patched up holes in their shoes. It had been so long since she could afford new shoes for her kids, if they were even available. She would instead just cut a strip of leather from an old pair of shoes and soak it in water until it was pliable enough to form it over any holes and sew it on.

Coming home from school, Rosemarie asked, "Do you think it's cold where Pappa is?"

"What a nice girl you are thinking about your pappa. How sweet. You still remember him?"

"No, I don't remember him at all, but my teacher Mrs. Gertrude asked me about him."

"Why?"

"She misses him. She liked to speak French. I don't really know."

There wasn't any more talk. With Hilda in the middle, her two youngest daughters contentedly held hands and swung their arms up and down, up and down, over and over.

They took off their knitted caps and coats and Hilda ushered them into the kitchen. Rosemarie picked up a stool and stood in front of the stove and rubbed her hands together. Vera was already at the table busy practicing her ABCs when Günter and Hilde came home from school.

30

"You're lucky to be here." The thirty something year old German POW sat on the floor across from Oskar.

"Anything is better than the Soviet Union," commented Oskar. "Even this watery porridge, believe me, it's the best food I've had for a long time . . . can we get more of this?"

"No. If you ask for more, you won't get anything tomorrow. And, if you complain, they'll send you to Alsace."

"How can any place be worse than this?"

The man snickered. "If you go there, you'll be cleaning up mine fields. Acres and acres everywhere. And we know from accounts of those who have been there, let's just say not too many POWs come off the fields to tell their stories. They either get killed or seriously maimed. I don't have to tell you that the French are not very generous when it comes to us. The Americans and they see things one way."

"Which is?" Oskar asked.

"They would be happy to see us all dead . . . that way they don't have to feed us. The French have one motto—*Two wrongs make one right. Three wrongs make one right.*

Trust me, I know what I'm talking about." He took the last gulp of his runny, watery porridge.

"Jesus Christ," Oskar explained, "I just spent almost a month in Russia. We were squashed like sardines in pathetic makeshift camps. Prisoners piled on top of each other for warmth."

"I was told by an Italian newcomer that the US president is making sure that Germans and Italians die as quickly as flies."

Oskar was not surprised. "I'm sure there's more who have the same wish for us."

"There's nothing to do here. But let me give you a piece of advice. These frogs are easily wounded. The more you feed their egos, the better off you are. You know what I mean? Lots of 'oui monsieur, no monsieur lessen your chances to end up in the minefields."

"Thanks for the tips." Oskar got up and put his empty tin canteen and spoon in his rucksack and took a long look around the yard. Hundreds, no, it looked more like thousands of men were crammed within the fences. They resembled cages holding so many men. He only saw a couple of barrack-like buildings. Oskar's stomach hurt, but there was no lunch and finally toward the late afternoon he was taken back to the office where he was brought to the night before. He took off his rucksack and noticed a young soldier by the door and another against the wall ready to fire.

"Mr. Döderlein, please empty your bag and all your pockets and place everything on this table," the soldier said, twiddling his mustache.

Oskar did as he was told. "You have my certification for freedom from the Soviets."

"Mon dieu, that doesn't mean anything here. Don't you get it? You're ours." The officer grinned.

"But the Geneva Convention agreements were . . . "

"If everyone did as the Geneva Convention spells out, half of these men wouldn't be here. Please fill out this card so we can inform your family that you are here. You do have a family . . . you do want them to know where you are?"

"I hope I still do. But I'm not really sure. There has been no opportunity to get any information. I want my wife to know that I'm here. Yes, of course."

"After you fill this out, we will send a notification. Now sir, let's take an inventory of your belongings."

"There's nothing much, sir. Sir, I think there's a horrible mistake. I'm sure I'm not supposed to be here. The officer in the Soviet camp said . . . " Oskar tried again.

The officer motioned to the young soldier who took a pad and pencil from the desk and started to list the items. Meanwhile Oskar filled out the address form given to him.

"But, sir, I still don't understand why I'm here. There's no reason. I'm supposed to be on my way home. They gave me a train ticket."

"Well, you know the old saying, everything is fair in love and war. Right? Can you stop arguing, please? It's boring. Every one of you tells us the same story."

"No. This is wrong. I'm not supposed to be here. I'm supposed to be on the train for Frankfurt."

"God, I hate people who argue. Think they're right. A German yet," he muttered. "Leon, get him out of here and make the paperwork ready for him to leave tomorrow morning with the first truck. Can't stand people who argue with me."

The young soldier put everything back into Oskar's rucksack and handed it to him without a word and motioned with his rifle to walk ahead of him. Oskar readily obliged.

Oskar settled himself into a corner of his cell and

put his rucksack on the dirt floor. Dinner was brought to
the men in big tubs pushed in carts outside the wired cells.
All the POWs held out their tin canteens. This time it was a
watery potato soup with a slice of bread. Oskar could have
eaten ten of those. Around the camp it smelled bad and
Oskar noticed that many of the men had bodily function
problems and had nothing to clean themselves with. He sat
against the fence with his face in his hands, but his mind
played, "When the Lilacs Bloom Again." Next to him was a
man who just lay there, and held his belly, moaning louder
by the minute. He was so skinny and white . . . so sick
looking.

"Can I help you somehow?" Oskar asked.

"Yes. Please kill me. I beg you. I don't have a home
anymore. Everyone is dead . . . everyone. I got the news last
week . . . oh my belly . . . my belly."

"Maybe you just need a doctor to give you
something," Oskar offered.

"No doctor here. But even if there were, he
couldn't help me now."

"Why? Tell me why?" asked Oskar, truly wanting to
help this wretched looking man.

"There's a bullet in my side, got some of my ribs
also. It's gangrene. Please help me. I would do it myself, if I
could. Oh . . . God almighty. Who would have known that
there'd be such pain. That bullet should have killed me.
Listen, all you have to do is squeeze on the main artery in
my neck. It won't take much squeezing, just do it."

"How long have you been here?"

"Just yesterday. Even though I gave myself up the
bastards shot me. It's only going to be another day, maybe
two at the most of this horrible pain before I die from this
wound. Oh please, just do it. I'm forty-five, had a fairly
good life except for this fucking war. Hitler sure
bamboozled us. The bastard is lucky that he killed himself .

. . bastard, and stupid me, I believed him. Of course, when that number comes up what are you going to do?"

"I know what you mean. I'm sorry you have such pain, and I'm sorry you lost your whole family."

"Oh God, Jesus make this go away . . . yeah, my whole family . . . gone. I hope you'll get out of here soon. I heard that every day so many soldiers die from one thing or another."

"Did you eat anything today?"

"Oh Jesus . . . no . . . no . . . wish I had a belt or a rope and I would tighten it around my own throat to get out of this hell."

Oskar was at a loss as to what to say or do. Clearly he could tell that this man was not going anywhere except his permanent sleep. *Hopefully, soon*, he thought.

"Is there anything at all that I can do for you, anything?" Oskar asked helplessly.

"If you're not going to kill me, and you can tell, let's say, during the night, that I am near the end, could you? Would you just hold my hand? Not because I'm afraid, only to let me know that I'm ready to meet my God. I'm so ready to meet my real father . . . my father in heaven. Fuck this Vaterland. Tell me buddy, do you believe in God?"

"Oh yes . . . yes, I do. Sometimes I think I've been so lucky so far in this mess, but you know what?" asked Oskar.

"Oh Jesus." Oskar's buddy bit his bottom lip.

"There's no luck involved. My father in heaven has plans for me and so far has taken care of me."

Even outdoors the stench was almost unbearable. The poor man couldn't get up to relieve himself in the one hole that was dug six or seven cages away. Of course, he himself had not had a cleaning or clean clothes for longer than he could remember. So, he figured they, as everyone else there, both stank to high heaven. The man lying next to him moaned, his whole body trembled continuously and sweat dripped down his face. Nothing would have pleased Oskar more than to be able to help this poor, poor man.

"You're the only one who paid any attention to me . . . everyone is so preoccupied. Thanks buddy, I wish you more comfort . . . I wish I had something to give you now. Please, buddy get me a piece of paper and a pen or pencil."

"What for? I think you need to eat something in the morning. I'll bring you some porridge, or whatever they'll give us . . . but I do have paper and a pencil in my rucksack. Hold on." Oskar quickly found it and handed the two items to the dying man. Oskar saw the man struggling to get into a position to write.

"Can't do it buddy, just can't." He dropped both items from his shaking hands.

"Did you want to write to someone? I'm happy to write it for you. Just tell me and I'll write it and give me an address, and I'll mail it as soon as possible. I promise you that."

"No. I have no one left. Thought I would write my will and testament and you can go to my house, what's left of it and take any belongings that may still be there. For example, there is a coin collection and it is buried within the wall of the entryway, right side. It should be worth something."

"Go ahead buddy. I'll write whatever you say. I hope this will bring some peace for you."

"Yes, it will . . . it will. So, here I go. This is my last will and testament. My name is Jürgen Kreuz. I am leaving all my possessions to be had at the following address and a bank account book if found also at that address too . . . " He was very, very short of breath already. "To you." He motioned to Oskar. "As long as you promise to hold my hand when you believe my time will come and hopefully, I can see my Gertrude's face just once more, her beautiful lips and smiling eyes. Oh how lucky I was."

"I know, I know. I hope I will live to see my wife and kids. And soon I hope," Oskar whispered almost to himself.

"My address is seven Köngstrasse in Pforzheim." The POW gasped for air.

"I live in Birkenfeld. It's hard to believe, but I know the street very well. Have no fear, my friend. I will find your residence and your wife, if she's still with us." Once again Oskar pulled the poor man's jacket closed. He was shaking; his teeth chattering. It looked like the POW fell into a sudden nap. Oskar checked his chest, which still seemed to go up and down, but he stopped moaning.

It was starting to be damn cold. Oskar wondered when some food would arrive and hopefully enough of it. The night before was so cold and the ground so muddy. Nothing much more could be expected for that night. Rain or snow and the cold temperature would be his only blanket. With that in mind he dozed off and woke up to see that the line of men were getting their food. Quickly, Oskar got up, touched his buddy by his shoulder. "I'll bring you some, don't worry, and don't move, I'll bring it to you." Oskar walked to the end of the line where he was given a piece of bread and a half a bowl of watery potatoes. He was so hungry.

"I have a friend over there who can't make it here to get his own food. Please, can I get something extra for him in my canteen?" Oskar asked very politely in French.

"He can't make it here?" the serving soldier asked while stroking his mustache very quickly. "That means he doesn't really feel hungry. Wouldn't you agree? Give him yours. Now move on." He waved him away extremely annoyed.

"Seriously, sir. The man is in terrible pain . . . he can't walk."

"My friend Jacques can't walk anymore. He has trouble breathing day and night and his young wife is beside herself." He tilted his head. "Oh, do I have to tell you why he is that way? That one of you bastards shot him? Now get the fucking hell away from me! I'm sick of looking at you. That bastard lying over there means nothing to me. Nothing at all! And now get the fuck away! Get away, you hear me?" The soldier's voice and flailing of arms were quickly going out of control. At this point Oskar went ahead to the fourth line to receive his slice of bread and headed back to his muddy spot. The poor soldier's moaning was hardly audible and his lips were dry with bleeding cracks. The temperature this morning was damn cold, but not as cold as Russia. Beads of sweat formed on his pal's forehead and his hands on his belly were white as though they were bloodless.

Oskar sat and leaned against the same post as before he left to get dinner. He reached into his pocket to retrieve the spoon he had been given in the third line. *Typical Frenchies,* Oskar thought, *creating four lines when everything could be accomplished in just one line.* Obviously the French thought so. He liked the French, but was sometimes amazed at them and almost had to laugh at their ineptness. Bastard! He could have given me just a tad bit more! Just an extra potato for this guy would have helped seeing how small the potatoes were.

"Look, I've brought you some pitiful food. But that's it for today," Oskar said ruefully, moving closer to the man. He realized the majority of the dead had starved to death.

"Can't . . . can't," he mumbled while the man's teeth chattered, his hands shook and his eyes rolled around his eye sockets.

"Just try this delicious bite!" As though he was coaching a two year old, Oskar held up the spoon that held a very small piece of potato and a tiny piece of meat trying to bring on a lighter mood into the moment. The man immediately dribbled all of the spoonful of liquid. Oskar ate several spoons full. He felt so hungry.

"I don't need anything, really, I don't," the man whispered. Oskar didn't waste a second. Potatoes in water with the tiniest fragments of meat would be better than nothing and, instead of using his spoon Oskar drank everything in seconds, not stopping for a breath.

"It's really getting cold, pal. Do you mind if I lie close to you? We'll both be warmer. Not only that, but these clouds look like they'll burst any time. Do they hand out tarps? They did in Russia."

"Sure. Sure. Just remember, squeeze my hand," the man said, his voice shaking and slurring his words slower and worse than earlier in the day. A fine drizzle came down and just at that moment Oskar saw the same soldier that had served the soup. Quickly he weaved his way between the men who were already lying on the wet ground. Oskar caught up with him. "I apologize for my conduct earlier. As I told you, my buddy over there is really not doing very well. He needs at least a blanket."

"Is there something wrong with you?" asked the soldier.

"No. I don't think so, just hungry."

"Well, maybe you can't hear very well. I told you earlier I don't give a damn about you, your buddy, Germans, Italians or anyone else here. If everyone committed suicide I'd be happy. As it is, only a few thousand have died in this camp. I just want to go home." The last words were a mere whisper, rather than anger. Just when he thought he had a second's worth of empathy, suddenly the soldier's face turned into what Oskar perceived to be more on the evil side. With beady brown squinted eyes he said, "I'll be sure to do my best to get your ass out of here very soon!" He turned and stomped off.

"Sorry buddy, I tried to get us a blanket."

"I know. Careful. Don't draw too much attention to yourself, or they'll ship you off to somewhere worse. That's what I've heard."

Rain started with very heavy drops and soon it rained so heavy that the ground became one mass of mud. Oskar pulled the collar up for his buddy and his own. Everyone laid in the mud shielding their head partially with their soldier's cap, if they had one. Oskar started to think about his buddy's request. How was he to know when exactly he would die? How? His chest already barely moved. It would be impossible to see any movement during the night, especially in this rain. He would do his best for this man.

It stopped raining sometime during the night. Oskar fitfully rested and slept a few minutes here and there. The cold wet mud had seeped into every crevice of his clothing, even inside his boots. He shivered violently and realized that he held the hand of a dead man. Oskar checked his pulse. There was none. He bent over the body. He reached for his friend's hands and clasped them in prayer over his chest knowing that Martin Luther's five hundred year old promise of 'freedom' was bestowed upon his friend. Oskar said a silent prayer in his own style, resting his head on the thigh of his friend as a pillow knowing that nothing would hurt him now.

He felt relief and dozed off until five French soldiers came into the camp to collect those who died during the night. Just a few feet away two bodies on a gurney were carried away when one of the soldiers slid on the mud and fell face down. Both bodies fell on the soldier. Two of the gurney carriers laughed so hard dancing around holding their bellies and the other three became so enraged they kicked the bodies around in a circle as though they were made of straw. Kicking around scarecrows that probably didn't weigh more than ninety to a hundred pounds. Oskar was amazed and appalled. He had dealt with so many French people, but none of them had ever displayed such craziness. His father always said war brings out the worst and best in people but that there's a dark side to all of humanity. The French soldiers were now clapping each other's shoulders as if to say this was a great laugh and a fun sport. Oskar watched as they loaded the muddy body of his friend onto the wooden cart. He whispered, "Auf wiedersehn."

Shivering very badly, Oskar heard his name. "Oskar Döderlein to gate two! Oskar Döderlein gate two!" Oskar stood and pulled the muddy clothing away from his skin as much as possible. "Vite . . . vite!" someone shouted in his direction.

"All right! I'm moving! I'm moving! Can't you see?" Oskar glared at the soldier showing his annoyance for just a split second. The French soldier caught the sliver of Oskar's annoyed look. "I'll remember you later on, you little bastard." About twenty to twenty-five Italian and German soldiers were already lined up in front of gate two. A truck with squeaky brakes came to a stop. His empty rucksack was suddenly thrown to him out of nowhere as he was ushered toward the truck bed and had to hop up to join thirty or so soldiers already on board. With a quick glance at the Italians, instant memories of the good times with his old, old buddy and young Italian friends came worming through his mind. With a twinge of sadness he wondered what the hell brought him to this mess. He bit his bottom lip wishing he was home loving his wife and children . . . assuming he still had a wife and children and a home. To dream for a second or two was the best thing this day brought to him.

"What about something to eat? How about some

watery porridge? We're starving! We want food! We want food." Some of the soldiers yelled in German, then in Italian. "Come on, we're men, not frogs!" They all laughed. "We're not French pussies!" And they laughed some more. Oskar was probably the oldest on the truck and felt responsible to remind those younger ones who seemed to be full of piss and vinegar that they should not antagonize their enemy . . . remind them that they have the upper hand what happens to their life. But they were young. Oskar thought some of them were young teenagers. How the hell did they ever get these young kids to fight in a war as big as this?

"You're hungry? Starving? Food in all of France is short, thanks to you pals! So, if you're hungry, and there's no food . . . we say, like Marie Antoinette said so long ago, let them eat cake!" A few French soldiers doubled over laughing. Finally the truck started moving.

"Does anyone know where we're going?" Oskar asked a young fellow sitting next to him. He looked to be about eighteen.

"This is the truck that takes you to the land of you make it or you don't make it."

"This is not a good time to be a smart ass," chided Oskar.

"Smart ass? No, sir, I'm not a smart ass. You'll see when we get to Alsace. Trust me, we've heard about it. Sucking, fucking nasty French bastards. That's what they are. You'll see if you live long enough," he added wiping his nose with one of his muddy hands. Oskar saw two French soldiers at the end of the truck bed with their rifles pointing toward their prisoners, ready to shoot. Oskar gathered his courage, got up and made his way to the one sitting on the left and looked more mature. Oskar approached him speaking clear French.

"Good day, I'm Oskar." He held out his hand.

"What the hell do you want?" He spat on the floor an inch away from Oskar's boots.

"The young fellows in here and myself, of course, are starving. You can imagine, sir, that seven hundred calories per day is barely enough to keep one alive . . . right?"

"Listen you polite bastard, just because you speak my language don't think kissing my ass is going to help you here." He almost hissed the words. "You're probably a Jew lover. Get the hell away. Sit down already before I shoot you!"

Oskar stumbled back to his previous spot. He couldn't make sense out of what this guy was talking about. He brushed his scalp with his fingernails and closed his eyes trying to make sense out of what the soldier said. The boy sitting next him looked to the sky in a daze with his hands folded.

"Are you all right son?" Oskar whispered to the boy.

"Yes, I'm saying my mother's favorite prayer over and over."

"Does that make you feel better?"

"Not really. My Father in heaven didn't help them any, did He. The Jews." His voice was flat. The truck rumbled on with the screeching brakes.

"What happened to the Jews? I know nothing about it. Seriously, comrade, tell me. What the hell has been happening. I'm a translator, and you'd think I should know more than you do…but here you are. What happened? Please tell me."

"Toward the end of the war I was stationed in France. There was no more bombing. But the French still went from house to house to get the Jews into trucks and literally handed them to the Germans. Now, at that time we didn't know what was what . . . typical French, you know, mum's the word. I didn't know the war was over, but the French looked like they were in control. I was told to be one of their guards to make sure no Jew would escape off the truck. Men, women and children. Women and children were screaming and crying."

"What happened then?"

"Nothing. The trucks with all those people drove off. It was only later that I found out through someone that actually thousands of Jewish families had been killed. I'm praying for those people and for myself."

"Praying can be a good thing," Oskar volunteered.

"Well, sure. I guess it depends how one looks at it. They say God is good. But, really? Is he really good? Why did He allow so many men women and children, even babies to be transported to meet misfortune? If He were ever around I would really like to ask him that. Why?" He looked up toward the sky again and Oskar saw his lips barely move.

It was hard for Oskar to believe that considering his position and that he'd heard nothing about the Jews. Another screeching of the brakes. The two French soldiers jumped off the truck bed. Oskar looked around the landscape. Nothing much but fields lay ahead, in front of him and on the side views, there was a building that flew the French flag. Everyone on his side of the truck bed turned their heads to look toward what was behind them. As Oskar did, he saw what looked like wire cages. The cages had signs with numbers. On one side was an open area that had no cages. Oskar looked into the distance squinting hoping to see some barracks.

"Get down. Line up. No talking."

"Shut up French pussy!" someone yelled.

"Who talked? Step forward, now!"

Quickly six or seven French soldiers came out of nowhere. Four stationed themselves in a row in the background pointing their weapons ready to shoot while three came to point their rifles at three of the young German soldiers.

"Was it you?"

"Nein. Nein!" The fourteen or fifteen year old shook his head side to side. "No. No." He never heard the shot as he fell to the ground.

"How about you blondie?" He pointed at another kid. God, what the hell did Hitler have on his mind? Or, better yet, what did God have on his mind? Kids? Was that God's will? Oskar knew this kid was no older than his boy. *Thank 'Whoever' that my boy had the good sense not to enroll in the Hitler's Jugend. How did this kid end up here?*

"Do you know who just talked?"

"No sir. No, I don't. I tell you the truth." His shoulders shook.

"You're lying. How old are you?"

"Fifteen. Almost fifteen, sir." He stuttered and looked at the ground.

"Almost fifteen, huh?"

"Yes. Yes sir."

"Well, you know what my mother always said?"

"No, I don't know sir." He turned the young man around facing the bare fields. "Let me tell you. She used to say that every time a teenager talks, they lie. Tell me something, do you agree with my mother?"

"No sir. I didn't lie. I didn't talk. Therefore she's wrong."

"So, you're calling my mother a liar?"

"No sir. Absolutely not."

"Then, you just lied. Start walking toward the fields." One shot. Oskar couldn't stand the senseless slaughter any longer.

"I talked," Oskar said in French.

"Glad to have at least one decent Kraut here. You'll

be in cage number one. You are going to dig ten holes about one foot deep and five feet wide. You will leave the soil on the side and each time one of you has to crap you go to one of these holes, do your crap, then pile some dirt on top of your pile. Now, stay in line and go to your new home."

Everyone scrambled, glancing at this monster only for tenth of a second wishing they would get enough food to actually make a pile.

Oskar sat in his cage. Literally, a cage. No roof, walls, floor boards, nothing. He sat holding his painful belly when the guard came to let him know it was time to start digging.

"Can I get a shovel?" asked Oskar.

"A shovel? Yes. Your hands. Idiot."

Oskar started to dig and found the soil rather pliable, and as he was told, he put it on the edge of the seven holes he dug. More than once he nearly passed out from hunger and fatigue. And unbelievable pain. He barely managed to get up on his feet to talk to another guard that he hadn't seen before.

"Sir, as you can see my fingernails are so far down they're bleeding. I'm starving, and I just can't continue. May I please continue tomorrow?"

"Of course, mon ami. Of course."

Oskar could hardly believe his ears. This soldier was actually nice.

"Merci. Merci beaucoup." Oskar trotted toward his cage. He had to duck to get in his cage. He sat and put his wounded hands under his armpits until he heard a bell. He saw the prisoners going in single file toward the gate where everyone was given a bowl and some food. It was a rice soup with something else floating around. Oskar hoped it was chicken. One soldier almost choked to death, having stuffed the whole bread into his mouth at once.

"Look, his eyes are bulging out," someone called out while the poor man hung onto the cage and his head and upper body dropped forward. By some miracle a ball of unchewed bread flew out of his mouth as though someone had thrown it. He sat on the ground for a couple of minutes and desperately raked the food with his hands into his bowl. The poor young fellow was small in stature and Oskar thought his little beady brown eyes looked like a wild animal. He held his bowl and bread tightly to his chest. His head and sometimes his whole body flinched and flitted from side to side as if to make sure that no one should dare come close to him.

"So sad," said a dark-haired Italian to Oskar and made the holy cross.

"Yes, true. It's sad. You have any idea how long this will go on?" asked Oskar in Italian.

"I don't know. All I know is I want some real food. I would kill for it. And that last camp where I was, my god." He swallowed hard. "I thought slave labor was abolished."

"I need to go to my cage, but hang in there. At some point it'll all end. Save your energy as much as possible and take your time eating. Your food will last longer." The April sun gave warmth and hope as he walked down five cages to his own. It felt good to sit down, eat the last bite of bread. He closed his eyes, tried to empty his mind and he saw Hilda. She wore his favorite blouse. Soft flowing fabric with the prettiest tiniest flowers that she embroidered around the neckline and wrists. She had such beautiful lips. Such a beautiful smile. Lucky to have such beautiful children. Yes, lucky was his last thought until the bottom of his soles got kicked hard enough to jolt him back to reality.

"Mon dieu, number five, wake up! Let's go! Hurry up! Get in line! Hurry!" Oskar moved swiftly into the single file. A whistle blew and about twenty of them filed into the waiting truck.

"Where the hell to now?" asked one of the younger ones. No one knew just yet.

A blonde bent forward. "I heard . . . oh, never mind, it's probably not even true." He leaned back again, wiping his face with his forearm. It was starting to get very warm and two soldiers jumped on the truck with their rifles ready to be used, if necessary.

The ride was only about fifteen to twenty minutes on a country lane when they were ordered off the truck. Oskar noticed that the little guy with the wild beady eyes was in the group.

"Listen carefully. Your life may depend on you paying attention now. This is what you'll do. Watch and listen." Three of the soldiers who sat in the cab of the truck and the two from the rear of the truck stood side by side and put their arms over each other's shoulders. They walked a couple of steps and stopped, walked two more steps and stopped.

"Keep looking at the ground very carefully. Not just in front of you, but also keep looking right and left to your partner. Your own life and your comrade's life is in your hands. Each one of you has a red flag. The moment you see a mine or something that looks like a landmine, raise your flag and yell, 'here' or, 'ici'. It also means no one in the group should move until the mine is removed and exploded. Do as you're told, and you'll get to eat dinner this evening. Good luck and don't get any ideas to run off. We'll be over there making sure you all do a good job. Again, merci and good luck." They turned around and walked to the edge of the country lane leaning against a shade tree.

After they stuffed their red flag into their pockets the Germans and Italians divided into three teams of seven soldiers each. About half of the field was manned and after a quiet discussion it was decided to walk to a tree in the distance. They would move over at that point and return. Half of the huge field would be walked. With one more repetition of the same strategy, they'd be done.

"Listen. Obviously this is dangerous. We can all lose our lives. No doubt these mines are live. Even if any one of you is not religious, would someone please say a quick prayer for those of us who are, and hopefully get some comfort." They all looked to the ground as a red headed young German recited the Lord's Prayer.

"Hey! Hey! We don't have all day!" one yelled from the shaded tree area and the brave and disciplined soldiers started to walk slowly watching the ground and around their feet. Of course Oskar knew there always has to be a smart ass and that freckled idiot one row behind him lifted up his arm and screamed, "Heil Hitler! Heil Hitler!" Immediately a shot rang out and the kid was on the ground face down.

"Two of you drag him over here, quickly . . . vit vit! The rest of you go! Allez!" They yelled toward the field. Oskar thought he was going crazy. As he scoured over the field he thought what a great place for a picnic. A crazy thought for sure. Not one person spoke again. Everyone's concentration was to stare at the ground using eyes like a well-oiled machine. Oskar was sweating and with a quick glance he saw that each one of the fellows on his sides were sweating so badly it ran into their eyes.

Oskar was in the first row and just opened his mouth to say something to the fellows next to him when he heard a tremendous explosion and screams. He saw one of the Italian POWs on the ground. His legs were gone and another fellow was in pieces. He heard gurgling and moaning. Then silence from the one who lost his legs.

"Good job! Now two of you get over here. You need to pick up this mess . . . vit!" The soldier waved his arm. Two from the middle row ran over and ran back into the field with a stiff square piece of fabric. Keeping in mind that another explosion could happen any second they picked up body parts piece by piece . . . a hand, an arm, legs. The fellow who died without his legs was picked up last. The tarp with the body parts was thrown on the bed of the truck. One POW doubled over while holding his belly only to fall into his own vomit and pockets of blood and bits of flesh from the victims of the explosion.

"Don't stand around like old women, get on with it! We can't return until this whole field is checked. You may miss your dinner. Hurry!"

Having returned, Oskar saw the fear in the POWs' faces and he felt the fear in his body. He held his belly; it was painful and not sure if he would vomit, and not sure if there was anything to vomit. They put their arms around each other and continued to walk, some saying prayers, some sounded like they were whispering to their mamas.

All were terrified. Each wondered whose body was going to explode next. Who would get carried out in pieces on a tarp and thrown on the bed of the truck? Oskar wondered how long this had been going on and how much longer it would go, on this field of death. Everyone was silent again, very focused as they did as they were told. Oskar was too tall for the young fellow on his right and he adjusted so his arm was around his waist and holding on to his coat. Silent tears ran down the cheeks of two of the pro Hitler youngsters who previously laughed and giggled as though war had been nothing but a game.

They managed to walk down to the end of the field to where a white flag had been placed by someone. They turned around and started to walk up the field a few feet over from where they had walked down. It wasn't but a few minutes when a grand explosion threw pieces of two bodies in all directions. Safe on the country roadside the French soldiers immediately had a tarp.

"Get over here!" one yelled and threw the tarp into the POWs' direction. Keeping his eyes to the ground he slowly made his way to the tarp and back to the group who now had the grotesque and grim task of picking up the pieces of two bodies. So much blood. As they walked slowly, the tarp rained down blood as though there was a faucet. Oskar picked up a finger that had a golden wedding ring on the end of the finger, barely hanging on. He thought it belonged to the Italian. Anthony, nice fellow, Oskar thought as he slid off the bloody ring and put it in his pocket.

Every few minutes now, the French guards would yell, "Vit . . . faster . . . we are not done yet!" All of a sudden, the one who looked not a day older than thirteen, dropped the corner of the tarp causing some body parts to fall off. He screamed and yelled as he ran off toward the road. He almost made it, but the bullet got to him first.

"Hey! Hey number one! Come over here and put this idiot in the truck!" Carefully he made it to the boy and carried him to the truck. "Good job," he was told by a soldier. In French Oskar asked him who put in the landmines and found out it was of course the French. He returned to pick up more body parts. A whistle blew to get their attention.

"Back to the truck vit, vit, quick!" Each one stared at the two tarps full of blood and body parts. Oskar put his hand inside the pocket and felt the ring. He looked at who was left in their blood soaked uniform. The last French soldier to jump up and after placing his rifle into the ready to shoot position, he yelled, "Allez!" The truck made a U-turn and rumbled back to camp.

Oskar immediately noticed the additional POWs. There must be at least a hundred more than earlier; before they left. Little do they know what's waiting for them. He made his way to his cage and found two more men were in occupancy. Both Germans.

"We were caught by the Americans. Here we are in Alsace." Johann shrugged.

"Well, look at it this way, Americans only allowed a few lucky Jews off the boat that Hitler provided. Just like England, France, and others, they sent them back to Germany who was trying to get rid of them. Everybody is trying to hand someone over to someone else. I guess it's my turn now. I've been here and there and everywhere and I just want to go back to my home and check on my mother. If my home is still there. If it isn't, I think I'll go to Canada." This soldier, named Heinz, seemed to know the most.

"This is new information I haven't heard before." Oskar was still holding his stomach. It seemed like the ache would never go away.

"Have you lived in a shoe all this time? A translator you were? I would think that you'd know it all."

"I've been very fortunate. It's only thanks to our God's will that I'm still here. Believe me. You'll see. I wish you all good luck."

They joined the lineup for greasy, gravy-like water and a lump of fat meat about the size of a small pear. Next was a piece of bread, thicker than the last time. Oskar still smelled the rancid blood on his uniform and hands. There was no place to wash his hands or face.

"What the hell is with these cages? Where the hell do we sleep? Where are the blankets?" Heinz asked after he put down his bowl.

"Do like I do. You ball up and keep yourself as warm as you can," Oskar said gently.

"What do we do with our dirty bowls?" asked Peter.

Oskar put his bowl into Peter's and gave it to Johann. "Bring it over there where it was handed to you.

You'll see a vat with water. Dip them in. Try to clean them and stack them up next to the vat. You'll see other stacks." Johann took off and came back looking exuberant as though he was just stepping into a circus.

"I wish I was born in Canada. Some time ago I met a Canadian. He talked to me about Canada and a little bit of their history. I loved his stories." Johann said.

"I, for one hope Canada will be in your future, but, look, I've had a long day. If you don't mind, I'm going to lie there in the corner and hope it doesn't rain and hope it will be God's will I'll have another day of hope to see my family. Hope is my daily gift." Oskar closed his eyes and started to doze off.

31

April 1949

Hilde, Vera and Rosemarie sat on the curb of Hauptstrasse adjusting their skirts to cover their legs like young ladies were taught to do. They wore sweaters and skirts that their mama had knitted over the last two winters. Today, they felt special. They were allowed to watch a funeral. They could hear soft trumpets playing. Black horses pulled a carriage carrying a casket. Vera always loved those black horses; their hooves polished to perfection. The horses trotted slowly down the street closer to where the girls sat. The horses had a red and gold trimmed throw draped over their backs and fancy gold tassels adorned the front of their heads. A black shiny carriage with gold art had two windows showing many flowers adorned with a wreath hanging at the rear door. Everyone walked slowly. A few officials in red jackets and hats with gold trim walked with their shoulders back. Vera wished she could touch the shiny gold buttons. Listening to the subdued music of trumpets, clarinets and other musical instruments made dying a festive time.

Rosemarie whispered, "It's so sad that people have to cry when everything looks so pretty." She tapped Vera's arm. "Promise me, that when I die, make sure no one, I mean, no one cries. Just make sure I get to have a shiny carriage and beautiful, black horses." Before they left their house, their mother told them that Herr Eifel was one of the few firefighters in their village. Vera and Rosemarie only remembered him as a chubby elderly gentleman who suddenly lost a lot of weight and died very quickly. Hilde remembered him when he was a bit younger, always spry and friendly. They saw him on his many walks. He was always old fashioned by the way he tipped his hat to greet the girls and of course they always greeted him. They used to stare at his big belly. His belly sort of swished back and forth and usually Vera had to bite her tongue to stop from giggling. To Rosemarie seeing Mr. Eifel and crossing paths with him was always very serious business. It meant a caramel candy for her and her sisters. Their mother always said that when any living thing dies, it means it was God's will and God simply wanted that person in His arms. Rosemarie felt that Mr. Eifel's dying meant the end of their caramel candy. Hilde told them both to be quiet and pay attention to the funeral procession.

The cemetery was a short distance away and sometimes they'd place wildflowers on his grave. Their mother received many compliments about her kids' great behavior. She was so proud. Her face beamed while she wiped her hands on her apron.

After the funeral, the girls rushed to their house to tell their mother all about it. "Mama ….Mr. Eifel, you know he had such a big round belly, is there a hole on the top of the coffin to let his belly come through?" Rosemarie asked innocently.

"Of course not. You said about a month ago how slim he had become." She laughed. "I wonder what you girls will think of next!"

"What about if someone has an exceptionally long nose? What happens then? What if someone had a big nose, I mean a real big nose . . . do they cut a hole then?" asked Vera.

"No! No girls! No one cuts any holes and God, no matter what they look like, loves everyone and everything. Let's not be disrespectful," cautioned Hilda.

"Everyone?" Rosemarie wondered why she had heard such bad stories about some people.

"Mama, do you want flowers?" Rosemarie asked.

"That would be really nice. How about a white lilac stalk and a couple of lilac colors and, oh, go across the street to get some greenery?"

Hilda opened one of the drawers of the hutch in the kitchen and reached for her apron. Life became somewhat better in the village. Food was still scarce, but not as scarce as in those last miserable years. At least now Günter and his sisters could go to the soup kitchen and get some sustenance for the family; otherwise they'd still have to crawl in the ditches.

She had not heard from Oskar for several years, then one day she received a tattered looking envelope with his writing on it. The sparse information told that he was okay as a POW in France but was being moved somewhere else; he loved her and looked forward to seeing the family. He was alive! Her mind sang those words over and over. She sat and thread her needle with yellow yarn and embroidered another yellow buttercup. The fourth one of a new row. The window was open and a fresh April breeze surrounded her body. She missed her neighbor. Anna grieved for her boy day in and day out and her eyes were almost always red.

Then one day in the fall, a little more than two years after the last time they'd seen each other, Anna knocked on

Hilda's door.

"Hilda, now that the train is running again, I'm going away to Calw. Maybe I can find something to buy."

Hilda shook her head. "Anna, I wouldn't go there. Stay here with me."

"Oh, no, no! But thanks Hilda. In case I have to stay overnight, could you just check on my rabbits? They're clumsy and tumble over their water dish. They have plenty of food."

"Of course . . . sure. It's not a problem at all Anna. Not at all. I have to say, you look great! Your hat and that fox around your shoulders looks beautiful."

"Yes, I wore it because it's so warm and soft, but more than that, it reminds me of Fred and much better times."

"Take care and I hope you'll find what you're looking for and don't worry about your rabbits." Anna waved her white gloved hand and turned around to walk to the train station. No one ever heard from her again.

Anna's sister came to clean out her house and Hilda went over to talk to her. "I'm so sorry about Anna," Hilda told her sister. "Do you know what happened?"

"Like so many people I've known, she was probably pulverized. As though she never even existed." Her face showed no emotion. She turned her back on Hilda and continued cleaning out the house.

Hilda's friend, the butcher lady, also died that year. One of the Rottweiler dogs who protected the butcher shop bit her and she died from the infection. Hilda had experienced so much loss and not knowing if she'd ever see her husband again made it that much worse.

32

"Rosemarie, look!" Rosemarie looked where Vera was pointing. They'd have to walk through a thick portion of the forest to get to that particular dirt road. It was a road farmers primarily used, and although forbidden by their mother, Rosemarie and Vera walked it just to help themselves to fruit that may have fallen from trees.

"Quick, get over here," Rosemarie hissed at Vera. She obeyed and Rosemarie pulled her down. "Shh, don't speak." The man kept walking toward them. Rosemarie kept her finger at her lips to caution Vera. The wheat was tall and being on their knees shielded them. His walk was slow and purposeful. He eventually approached the gate to their house and opened the front door. A moment later they heard their mother screaming, "Oskar! Oskar!" Then they heard her calling for them to come home. They ran to the house and saw their mother hugging their father. "Girls," Hilda said to her daughter, "meet your Pappa!"

Rosemarie was just a beautiful toddler when he'd seen her last and of course, this was the first time he'd ever seen Vera. The girls weren't sure what to do or what to say. They stole a glance at each other.

For many years when their mother had Vera on her

lap she talked to Rosemarie as though she were an adult. She frequently talked about their father to both of the younger girls. She called him Pappa. But they'd never been able to picture a life with him. Their friends had fathers, but it had always been just them, Hilde, Günter and their mother.

Hilda cried and dabbed her cheeks with a handkerchief. "Girls, give your pappa a hug. Come now, remember I've talked to you a lot about him. He's come such a long way to be back with us." Oskar reached out for them and they stepped quickly out of his reach.

When Hilde came home and hugged the man as though she knew him, Rosemarie and Vera relaxed and then seeing Günter and this man shake hands and slap each other's shoulder was somewhat encouraging. Günter had been taking care of his little sisters for so long, they couldn't imagine another man stepping into a father role.

In bed that early evening Vera whispered, "How long do you think Pappa will be here?"

Yawning, Rosemarie said, "I don't know. Your guess is as good as mine. But I can't wait to get to know Pappa the way that Günter and Hilde know him."

That Easter with their father was the best one Vera or Rosemarie could remember. They wore newly knitted lilac dresses with white trim. Their hair combs were new. Their boots were dark brown and shiny and the white knitted stockings were a nice contrast. After the church service, the family went for a walk in the forest and Hilda cried out, "Oh, did you see it? Did you? The Easter Bunny was here, you better look around!"

Oskar pointed to a large bush growing next to a tree and said, "Does that look like something over there? Something the bunny left for you?" The basket was full with a red sugar bunny and some eggs and colorful candy.

33

Germany 1952-53

As usual Rosemarie stood at the school gate waiting for Vera to get there. While watching the other students rushing away from the school she wished her sister would get there just a little bit faster. She whisked away a few hair from her forehead and consoled herself with the thoughts that one day Vera will want to be walking home from school on her own without her supervision.

"Rosemarie, guess what?" Vera danced towards her.

"What?"

"Someone brought a big bag of cookies to our classroom and everyone was able to take and eat two. They were dark brown. One girl didn't like them so she gave hers to me and I had four cookies!"

"So, did you save one for me?"

"Hmm....no."

"If that happens again, it would be nice for you to think of me and grab me one too!"

"I will. I promise to think of you. Forever!" Vera

laughed out loud.

They turned left onto the main street and after turning onto several more smaller streets, they were on the last road that would finally lead them to their home. They continued walking the newly asphalted street when, just past the sweet shop they saw their mother waving at them.

"What do you suppose Mama is doing in the middle of the street?" Vera asked.

"Hmmm. Come on, let's walk faster. I'm also dying to know why she's out in the middle of the street waving at us."

Mama had one arm outstretched dangling something from her hand while the other held Rosemarie's shoulders.

"What are you jingling in your hand Mama?" asked Vera.

"I didn't want you girls to walk home only to find no one would be there....we are going somewhere special. And what am I jingling you ask?"

"Yes..." Rosemarie took a step back and squinted her eyes in the bright blinding sunlight.

"They're keys!" Hilda waved them around in the air. "These keys have brought one of my dreams into reality. And thanks to your father I'm finally able to share my excitement with you now. So, just follow me girls."

The girls looked at each other confused but happy and eager to see what was going on. They could hear the excitement in their Mama's voice as she walked and talked with a pep in her step. Hilda turned and walked off the street to this building that was boarded up ever since the start of the war. To their amazement the boards were gone from all the doors and windows. The shop window was alive with wonderful and beautiful items on display. Mama shook the shiny gold key and unlocked the door. She opened it and held it open for the girls to enter.

"Here girls, is your Mama's dream. My beautiful and lovely shop. Our family's beautiful and lovely shop. This store will soon display and sell all my favorite things… crystal, fine china, sterling silver and of course toys, puppets and dolls for Christmas! Yarn and fabrics and who knows what else….whatever else I think I can sell. Are you surprised?"

"Very surprised. I think this is simply the greatest day ever Mama. What and who is in there? I hear voices." Rosemarie asked as she pointed to a small narrow doorway that had a long navy velvet curtain hanging in front acting as a makeshift door.

"Let me show you. Just pull the curtain aside and go through that door." Hilda pointed.

As they went through the door they immediately saw many boxes, a table and a few chairs. Seconds later the back door opened and Günter, Hilde, Oskar, and Aunt Alice with her youngest daughters Junta and Lea all walked through the door laughing and talking.

"Auntie! Cousins!" Rosemarie and Vera ran to them. "Isn't this new shop great? Will you be here every day?"

"What about us?" Oskar chuckled as he held out his arms for a big hug from both of his younger daughters. The girls ran to him next and within moments the whole group gathered together for one big group huddle style hug.

"What's this out there in the back?" Rosemarie peeked through the upper part of the Dutch door which contained a small glass window.

"Well, it's a courtyard where some people have their sheds for their animals and farming goods. Nice people." Hilda assured them right away.

"It's beautiful Mama! May we play outside?" Rosemarie asked innocently.

Hilda smiled and happily nodded.

The young cousins squealed with excitement and quickly opened the door to run outside and play together before the sun went down.

***

Rosemarie and Vera enjoyed coming to the store right after school every day. The butcher shop was just a couple of doors down and Mama would give them some change to get some of their favorite meaty snacks every day.

Günter's favorite moments were spent helping his Mama at the shop while his younger sisters would do their homework. Günter would stop to help them with their reading and mathematics whenever they summoned him to their small desks in the back room.

On several occasions he would stop to laugh when he caught the girls peering through the sides of the curtain door that led to the main shop. They would catch Oskar and Hilda holding hands and kissing one another on the cheeks and start chuckling. After all, this was their mom and dad and any kind of affection always made them giggle and their cheeks blush like little innocent girls.

***

One warm Fall day Günter was in the shop's back room carving a beautiful wood golden angel with a trumpet in its mouth to get ready for the shop's 'Christmas window' as Mama called it. When Vera and Rosemarie got their books and pencils from their rucksacks to do homework, both girls noticed wax sealed envelopes sitting on top of their desks. Rosemarie opened her envelope and read the letter inside to herself. Vera did the same. When they finished reading, they smiled at each other and then placed the letters back inside the envelopes and inside each of their rucksacks. Oskar had written and left all four of his children letters earlier that morning before work. He was the kind of father that every child wished to have, always taking extra time to remind his children in special ways that he and

Hilda's love and devotion to them is forever and unconditional.

They had just finished their homework when the bell that hung on the shop's front door handle jingled to find their Aunt and cousins stopping by the shop. The group of four young cousins immediately embraced one another with excitement and decided to go together into the back courtyard to inspect two big vats that Vera and Rosemarie were scoping out earlier that appeared to be overflowing with grapes. The grapes were still on the vines with leaves and all, and the air smelled sweet.

"Don't you wish you could help yourself to a couple of those big dark purple grapes?" Vera asked Rosemarie and her cousins.

"Yes, for sure. They look so sweet and ripe and juicy." Rosemarie looked around at the buildings as she sniffed the fruity air. She couldn't see anyone. "So, I looked at all the windows and no one was there. Why don't you girls go to one of those big tubs and bring us a bunch or two to share?"

"No. I can't steal." Vera spoke right up.

Junta chimed in. "Yes. You know that's forbidden, Rosemarie."

"Come on...you girls are young and no one will say anything. It's just one bunch of grapes." Lea appealed to Vera and Junta.

"Well hello there girls! It looks like you would like to munch some grapes. Am I right?" A voice came out of the blue and a man's body hobbled out from the shadows between the buildings.

"Yes, we would! May we have one bunch to share please?" Rosemarie said, not wasting a second's breath.

"Tell you what, I'm going to talk to your mothers and find out if you girls are allowed to have some. So please wait right here."

The man came back a few minutes later. "I talked with your mothers and here's what we decided. You girls can have all the grapes you can eat but I'm hoping you girls can also help me with something. My stomper is sick and I need help stomping and squashing them as thoroughly as possible. How about that? Also, in exchange for that, you can take that basket over there and fill it full of grapes and take them home. How about it, girls? By the way, my name is Dieter."

Vera and Junta were busy eating grapes and both nodded their heads for a yes.

"Absolutely. This is the greatest job ever! Do we need to wash our feet first?" asked Rosemarie.

"Yes. Here girls. Have a seat on this bench and please remove your shoes and socks."

Vera, Junta, Lea and Rosemarie sat down and removed their school shoes and socks and placed them under the courtyard bench. The man motioned for them to put their feet in an enamel bowl with soapy water, and then into a clear water bowl, and after that they put on special clean sandals to walk to the big vats. From there the girls climbed up a ladder and then down. On the last step they removed their sandals and tied their skirts together in a knot to keep them from getting too soiled with grape juice. First Vera got inside the vat followed by Junta, Lea and Rosemarie. They all held each other's hands, sang, laughed, and stomped and stomped…and stomped some more! When Hilda and her youngest sister came out to the courtyard together to check on the girls, the smiles and giggles were like music to their ears. What a difference from the years before, they thought.

34

Beautiful days went on and on from one season to another. Hilda was happy planting in the garden. Oskar left every morning for work but always came home in the evening. Rosemarie and Vera went to school and played in the Enz. Vera delighted in lying on a rock face down. "Watch me, watch me Rosemarie! Watch me swim!" Rosemarie would give her a second's worth of a wave. When they weren't in school, Hilde and Günter went with them. It was the season to harvest watercress and dandelion for salads. Rhubarb was another early spring delight. Vera's pet goose Lisele made herself comfortable under one of the giant rhubarb leaves.

"Go! Go!" Vera and Rosemarie would shush her away, so that they could find the best stalks. They'd wash and peel the hairy substance from the stalk, then cut tiny little ridges on each side to sprinkle some sugar. They'd let the sugar marinate in the cool cellar for a day or so and finally nestle against their favorite tree across the street in the meadows and munch away.

In June big white Shasta daisies, blue cornflowers and red anemone profusely bloomed wherever one looked. They'd continue until the end of August. Oh, what a time! The beautiful crowns they made all summer long. Each girl tried to outdo the others in the decor of crowns. Vera deposited her crown on Rosemarie's head and bowed down. "I crown you this summer the queen of bird country!"

Rosemarie picked up the crown she made for Vera. "Hear ye, hear ye I announce to you, my queen, and all who may hear this, that you are, from this moment forth, the queen of Lisele!"

"Look." Vera pointed across the field. "God, did she hear, did she understand or what? Let's see what happens. Don't chase her away! Let's see what happens!"

Lisele honked while waddling across the street into the meadow where Rosemarie and Vera were laughing. "Come, you silly goose!" Vera gave her crown to Lisele and sat her on her lap. Lisele loved the girls and the girls loved her. During the school year, except during winter time, Lisele went everyday half way to school to greet Vera and Rosemarie. Most of the ladies of the village all knew Lisele and her honking was dear to their hearts. Lisele's trek was like clockwork on school days. She'd come two streets up from the house to meet Vera and Rosemarie. Lisele was a highly respected goose by all who knew her! Some people joked that she was very educated.

It wasn't just Easter when the four kids would find surprises waiting for them. In early December on St. Nikolaus Day, they left their boots outside the front door and the next morning they were filled with walnuts, hazelnuts, apples and two or three candies. Then there was Christmas. The kitchen smelled of marzipan, sugar and cream. Hilda closed the kitchen door to keep the aromas in the kitchen. All the past Christmases of despair were a bad memory. The food scarcity was gone; the mended socks and stockings, skirts and blouses made from previous owners' dress materials became just a memory. The kids were truly baffled by their new, good fortune since their

310

father had come home. Certainly Hilda also had a new bounce in her step! For the first time, Hilda was able to make cookies with her kids.

"These cookie cutters are older than Napoleon!" Hilda laughed.

"Who's Napoleon?" Rosemarie asked, wiping her hands on her apron.

"Oh, never mind. What I meant was I received these from your Oma many years ago. They're the best cutters. Promise me you'll never throw them away." The girls promised nothing would happen to them. Hilda opened the door and dropped some more wood into the stove.

"Well, you never know what can happen. These cutters, I feel keep us all together forever…no matter what. Your brother has grown and is already looking at young women and your sister is working at a good job in a watch factory getting ready to be on her own." Poking into everyone's belly button she added, "So, it's you and you and me to keep these special items used and cherished forever."

"I love the star. Can I use the star for the next four cookies?" begged Vera.

"I want the half-moon," Rosemarie announced.

"Right now girls, we can use anything we want. I just meant that we need to take care of what is given to us. Anything given to you should be thought of as being special. I don't know how your Oma did it during World War I when products were so scarce, but she did make the best cookies. She used these cutters. That's all."

By midafternoon all the baking was done and the kitchen cleaned up and everyone got ready to go to church for a Christmas celebration. Beautiful singing, some snacks and then a Santa Claus who called children's names one by one to hand a little gift to each. Rosemarie received a little toy trumpet and Vera a wooden cooking spoon. Oskar talked with some people and Hilda shook hands with others.

On Christmas Eve Rosemarie, Vera and Oskar were sitting at the kitchen table listening to the radio. The Vienna Choir sang beautiful songs about Jesus lying in the crib. All three hummed along until suddenly Hilda opened the kitchen door.

"I believe this is yours." Oskar motioned to Rosemarie and the small table and picked up a book with a beautiful cover. Next to it was a rolled up pair of new stockings and a white hair bow. Then they looked at the large table. There were six plates.

Rosemarie picked the plate next to the one Vera had chosen. Each plate had the same; an apple, a pear, a few of the cookies that they had helped bake earlier in the week and something yellow in the shape of a half-moon. Three or four kinds of nuts and some festively colored shiny wrapped candy. In the middle of the table were platters with open-faced breads covered with delicious cold cuts. Günter and Hilde arrived home and admired the Christmas tree and all the festive productions on the table. Vera came toward Hilde. "Look at Snowbell, isn't she beautiful?"

"Yes, she is. You and Rosemarie were lucky that Saint Gabriel shared God's joy with you. What a nice book!" Hilde gleamed.

Vera put Snowbell in her carriage and rolled it back and forth. Then she went back to her plate to pick up her yellow half-moon and held it up.

"Pappa, what is this?" Vera asked.

"It's called a banana." Pappa smiled. "We don't have banana plants in Germany. But there are many countries where they grow. Would you like to taste it? I'll use mine to show you how to peel it." Oskar tugged a piece of the peel on the top and then another and another.

"There you are, ready to take your first bite of a banana, and if your mama and I have our way, you'll be eating a lot more like these."

Vera needed help peeling her banana, but Rosemarie had it ready to eat in seconds. The first bite was incredible. It was smooth, sweet, soft, delicious and like nothing that they had ever tasted before.

"I promise you Snowbell, I'll have a lot more of these . . . someday I'll eat so many of these things, that my skin might turn yellow, but who cares?" Vera said as she closed her eyes and savored every bite.

Everyone ate and had some hot tea or chocolate. The cookies were delicious. The music and singing coming from the radio was amazing. Since Oskar had been home, the whole family would bundle up and take walks every night at 9 o'clock. While walking Oskar noticed the yellow glows through the neighbor's windows. The stars were crystal clear. It was hard for him to remember that poor Italian soldier choking on a cockroach in Russia because he slept with his mouth open. They continued their walk up a slight hillside which became a little steeper as they went higher. The snow glistened in the moonshine and crunched under their footsteps. They arrived on top of the hill and it was so quiet in the night. Oskar looked at his watch.

"This is our holy evening. Shh. Just listen."

As though he ordered this special moment, three of the other towns and the church of Birkenfeld all rang at the same time. After the tenth tintinnabulation they turned and walked back home in silence.

The summer days rolled in. Rosemarie and Vera ran with Snowbell through the meadows, staring up to the sky and trying to figure out what objects or mythical creatures the different contours of the clouds created just for them. Crowns of daisies and cornflowers adorned their heads while playing queen and princess.

During one summer dinner Oskar talked about how the gypsies found their way back to their village just as though there had been no war to interfere with their lives. After the war people talked about the extermination of so many people, including the gypsies. Of course, Rosemarie and Vera were not included in such controversial topics, but they did hear their parents talk about the gypsies. One lazy summer evening, Rosemarie called out for Vera. She answered from a meadow across the street.

"Listen, do you want to see the gypsies?" Rosemarie asked.

"Why?"

"Just for the heck of it. I always wanted to see them in action, that's all!"

"Sure. When do you want to go? How about asking Günter and Hilde?" Vera was excited.

"No. I think only we should go. We're going to have to crawl in the ditch and be extremely quiet. You're sure you can do that?"

"Not a problem. I mean, we crawl in the ditch when we want to pick snails! In the rain yet! It's okay. I'm all for it! Shouldn't we tell Mama or Pappa?"

"No!" cried Rosemarie. "They'll never let us go to the mill in the evening with those people there. I really want to see what they do. I mean, Vera, have you ever seen a gypsy?"

"No. But someone told me once that they steal kids and I don't want to be stolen."

"Ah, don't be silly. But if you want to go now instead of in the dark, let's go." Rosemarie piloted Vera out the front door and down the street.

As they came close to the mill, they slipped into the ditch by the road and carefully made their way toward the mill with Rosemarie being in the lead until suddenly they were within view of what were surely the gypsy wagons. The grass between the road and the ditch was tall and Rosemarie whispered, "Duck down. Get on your knees." Vera did as she was told. *It was good to have an old sister who knew what to do*, thought Vera. They crawled a few feet ahead. Four wagons were parked on the side of the mill. A roaring fire burned on the grassy area and lanterns hung here and there on the machinery. Music came from somewhere. They saw several young children Vera's age and maybe a little younger.

"Look," whispered Rosemarie, "they have kids…."

"I see. I see," whispered Vera.

Something pulled on Vera's left shoulder.

"What are you doing Rosemarie? Stop it!" Vera shook her shoulder and looked up and saw a man looking down at her.

Rosemarie got up, ran and kept yelling, "Run Vera, run, hurry!" She didn't look back, and continued to run while Vera was frozen in place. The gypsy held her at her shoulder and pulled her out of the ditch, across the street and toward the camp. Vera was so afraid, she couldn't make any sound. Rosemarie was nowhere to be seen. They were now on the cement pad of the mill and the man was still holding onto her while others came around to look at her. They said words to her that she couldn't understand. A fat woman wearing a colorful skirt and blouse sat in front of her. Vera cried. The woman went to get her a rag for her nose and took her hand and made Vera understand to come with her. The woman walked with her halfway home and squeezed her into her abundant bosom before she left. Vera ran home and confronted Rosemarie.

"Why did you leave me?" Vera hissed.

"I was scared. Why do you think? Come on. And knowing that they steal children. What did you expect me to do?" Rosemarie felt bad and guilty. "I'm sorry. I didn't want to leave you. I just didn't know what else to do. Don't tell anyone we went there, or we'll be in major trouble. I mean, major, okay? Listen. I want to know what happened to you."

"Nothing much. Everybody just stared at me and talked, but I couldn't understand anything they said, and when I started crying a fat lady took me by the hand and walked halfway home with me. I was okay. They were nice. They didn't want to steal me." Vera said, exhausted and happy to be home safe.

Hilda, Oskar and their family were the first in the village to get a water heater for the bathtub water. They still had to heat the water with firewood and coals, but the bathtub now had this fancy device attached to it that would make the water hot without having to do anything at all. Many people came by to admire it. Neither Rosemarie or Vera were crazy about it. The bathtub was now in the cellar, and they had to take a bath together. The water only came up to their knees and they were cramped and uncomfortable. They didn't think it was fair that Günter and Hilde got to take baths by themselves.

Günter had a girlfriend named Ruth who lived in the apartment above the kindergarten with her parents. Apparently her father drank a lot, but Ruth was a kind young lady. Hilde married a man named Walter in the city where she worked and didn't have much time to come home on the weekends. Vera and Rosemarie started to feel like it was just the two of them since their older siblings hardly visited the family anymore.

Rosemarie learned how to crochet and Vera became a master with cross stitches. Snowbell's eyelashes were picked off through Vera's curiosity; her lids still closed as usual and she always smiled sitting comfortably in her carriage. Vera never got tired of looking at her or rearranging her little dress over her legs. And the book of fables that Rosemarie received that Christmas was always on her nightstand. Never far away and never too tired or bored to read the stories again and again. Vera bugged her to read them out loud. Life was perfect!

Hilda and Oskar received news from Günter. After receiving a newspaper from overseas, they announced that they would make the move to Montreal, Canada. He felt satisfied that our family would be safer there and wanted to take the first step. He managed to secure an apartment and arrange jobs for himself and Ruth once they arrived. And like a flash of lightening, Günter and Ruth were off to Bremen and on a giant ship across the Atlantic with thousands of other post war dreamers. Hilda and Oskar missed their son very much and Hilda started talking about moving to Canada. She hadn't forgotten the conversation she'd had with that random woman so long ago. Even though the war was long since over, the scars of living in poverty and fear for many years still haunted Hilda. She couldn't get over her fear that the government was going to come for Oskar once again.

One day Oskar surprised his family by bringing home a pine green car. They called it the Adler. They now had the only water heater and the only car in the village. Many people came to admire the car. Oskar shined the car with a cloth. Vera admired her reflection on the side of the newly shined car and smiled with excitement and delight. Her family was so fancy!

VERA CHRISTA DÖDERLEIN HASTIE

35

Canada 1955

Tears streamed down Vera's cheeks as she spoke into the silent space where her sister was supposed to be. "My sister, my sweet, sweet sister. Yesterday Mama thought she saw you sitting on a bus. One that goes down Park Avenue. She said you were sitting in the back. Was it you? The bus drove away. She ran after it and got very dizzy. She could barely catch her breath and had to hold onto a sign and then she fell to the ground. She yelled for the bus to stop, but it didn't. Then some people thought she had too much wine and called the police who in turn called an ambulance. She had had a heart attack.

"After a few days in the hospital she got better, but now she has to take some medicine. When she came home from the hospital Pappa sat with her day and night holding her hand. She cried and cried and cried. She thinks she missed getting to you if only she would have been able to run faster. Oh God, God, if you only knew how much we want you home. Where can you be? Where? Why would you be on a bus? We're still looking for you and Mama pays other people to look for you. They're called investigators and they promise to find you. Every day we look and eventually, some day," she whimpered, "I know we'll find you." Talking to her missing sister like this reminded her that she would have to write Hilde and tell her what had happened to their mother.

36

1956

A little over a year after Rosemarie disappeared, it was Moving Day and Oskar found a new flat on Esplanade Avenue. When they'd first moved to Canada, the plan was to move within a few weeks. But then Rosemarie disappeared and the world fell away. In the weeks and months after, the time was never right. Oskar and Hilda were so intent on finding their daughter that they couldn't focus on anything else.

But more than that, Hilda was afraid if they moved and Rosemarie came home, she wouldn't know where to find her family. It was a ridiculous notion since Günter and Ruth would remain at the address. Even so, Hilda wouldn't hear of moving. In secret, Ruth and Günter talked about it. Their agreement had been that his parents would only stay with them for a few weeks. Ruth felt terrible asking Günter to talk to his parents. But she wanted her apartment back. It was clear by then that Rosemarie wasn't coming home.

It was a new neighborhood, and the first time Vera saw it she thought that they hadn't looked there yet for her sister. She had always agreed with her mother that if they moved it would make it harder for Rosemarie to find them. But when she drove around the new neighborhood with Oskar and nothing looked familiar, she got excited at the thought of having all new territory to explore. Rosemarie was out there somewhere and she was certain that one day she would be reunited with her sister.

On a few occasions Vera tried to get an answer from Hilda and Oskar about what the detectives and the investigators had found. But every time she brought it up, they changed the subject and her mother closed herself in her bedroom. After a while Vera just gave up and told herself that she'd find Rosemarie on her own.

Vera still talked to her sister. "Ah, my sister! Remember how you used to say that? I forgot to tell you that Ruth and Günter have a baby now. She is adorable and they often bring her over to visit. I see so much of you in her. You will love her when you get back. Ah, my queen, I never stop thinking of you . . . only you know where you are. Did you somehow fall through the slot? Did you? Are you laughing at me? If you could only answer me once more, just once and maybe then, maybe my ache might go away. Just once."

37

1957

Vera hadn't seen Rosemarie in almost three years. As she had done since the last time she saw her sister, she sat in her room, stared up at the sky and talked to her. "I hate it here. I hate it when there's no moon. I hate Canada. I hate everything about it. If we hadn't come here, I could still talk with you, see you and nothing would have happened to you. Nothing."

"My friends say you probably got murdered. I refuse to believe it. After all, isn't God supposed to make everything good? I don't think they're right. I don't know about this God person anymore. The investigators are still looking. Every bit of money Mama makes goes to them. What happened to everything that was beautiful. I hate the weather. Your school bag is intact. Same as before you . . . so when you get back you can continue where you left off. Another good news is Mama is getting me some jobs babysitting and I'm saving every penny, and I mean every penny. Sooner or later I'm getting out of this city. I don't know where I'll go and I don't care as long as I get far away from here. You and I can go together!"

"Your soldiers are standing on guard on my nightstand waiting for you. And even better news than that is that Hilde and our nephew Gabriel….who is not so little anymore, are moving to Canada soon. She's not married to Walter anymore. So now she can live near her family. You have to come back so Hilde can see you. So we all can."

38

1959

Vera woke in the middle of a fall night and felt the need to talk to Rosemarie. She climbed out of bed, sat by the window and talked to the sister she was sure she'd see again one day. "Since you've gone, my heart has never once stopped aching. Not even for one day. My belly hurts if I even just see the colors lilac or purple. Remember? Your favorite colors? Last year during summer vacation I worked at Eaton's on St. Catherine Street, in the basement office. I love this store, the people and the merchandise. I've been hired for this summer as a messenger girl and get paid thirty dollars a week. And Hilde has been here for two years. She and Gabriel are settling in quite well and we see them all the time. We often have family dinners with them and Günter and Ruth and their daughter. But, it's not the same without you."

During dinner one night Oskar looked at Vera. "You always were such a sweet, pretty girl, and now you've grown into such a pretty young lady. We're so proud of you.

Hmmm? Hilda?"

Hilda put down her knitting. "Yes. Of course. I always knew Vera and Rosemarie would be very pretty young ladies. And smart too."

"I've been hired by Eaton's for the summer and probably will be employed full time once I graduate next year. I can't wait to collect all the saved money I've asked you to hold for me so I can move to America."

"I can understand why you don't like Canada anymore. Too many heartaches. Where do you want to go?" Oskar felt a deep sadness at the thought of his youngest child moving away.

"I'm not sure. But you know a lot of Canadians go to Florida, especially for vacation. What if, maybe if I do everything right, I get to go to Florida?"

"We would help you any way we can, sweetheart. Any way at all," Oskar said.

"Thanks. I'm going to save more than ever. I'll need the money."

"Good idea, princess. Good idea."

"Oskar, how can you be so casual about her plan? I can't stand the thought of losing another daughter. How far away is Florida, anyway?"

"I'll show you on a map in my Lexicon." Oskar stood and Vera excused herself to go to her bedroom.

"Ach." Vera looked at the moon and talked to her lost sister. "It kills me that you're not here. Are you ever going to come back? We stopped walking around neighborhoods three years ago. Mama says she just doesn't have the strength anymore. She cooks, she cleans and does laundry. But I don't think I've seen the whites of her eyes since you left."

"Some nights the moon is brighter than ever. Maybe it means that, around the Earth, more people in the world had good things happen to them." She let out a short giggle. "Pappa stopped being a janitor and became partners with Pomerleau. You never met him but he is very kind. I'm not sure what they do, but Pappa is glad that his language skills are back in use. He's making very good money, and loves his job. I heard Mama say so to Mrs. Blatt."

39

1962

Oskar bought a cheap piano that he played every day. Every time Vera heard her father play, she remembered how she and Rosemarie used to fight over who got to clean the ivory keys of the one he had in Germany. The piano always made her think of Rosemarie and therefore made her sad. Vera loved it when her whole family was together and Hilde would sing lead vocals on whatever song Oskar played.

Vera ran a finger over the keys and listened to the rain outside. "Such heavy rain tonight. I still don't understand how you could possibly be gone, just like that. I miss you every single day." She wiped away tears. "I wish you warmth and love wherever you are. Please, to whoever is listening, please give her food, love, warmth and shelter. It's not a lamb that's lost, it's my sister. My gold star."

She folded her hands, said her nightly prayers and then begged God for something good on her sister's behalf. Then she thought about her friend Claudia who was always asking her to go to St. Joseph Mount Royal Church. It's a big church up on the mountain overlooking Montreal. Claudia said the nuns and priests sounded like a choir of angel-like singing and chanting. Claudia used to tell Vera that church bored her because she didn't understand the Latin sermons. So Vera started going with her. The priest told Vera that he and his whole congregation were praying for Rosemarie. He also told her that talking about her feelings could make her feel better. So a couple weeks later, Vera met with the priest.

Vera met the priest in a church that reminded her of the gothic church in Birkenfeld. After the initial introduction by Claudia's parents he led her to his office. It had big pictures of Jesus on the cross and the Virgin Mary holding the baby. A vase of flowers and two chairs faced each other. Vera sat in one, he sat in the other. He said a prayer in Latin then held her hands.

"Child, let me ask you first, do other people tell you Hitler was bad?"

"No. Not at all."

"Actually I didn't mean it in that way. But, nevertheless, just let me tell you this. Hitler did a good thing starting a war. Because of him, here in Canada, the United States, England . . . well, almost all over the world jobs were created for the war efforts. People worked and made money again to be able to feed their families. It got rid of the soup lines. Don't ever let anyone tell you that what he did was all bad."

"I'll be sure to tell my parents." She had no idea why this was a topic and thought to herself, *Sure, I'll be sure to let my mother know how grateful she should be that there was a war and that one of her best friends was hauled away, Hmm-mm.*

"Now child, tell me about our lost lamb."

Vera spent the next hour telling the priest about the detectives who still came to her house from time to time and how her whole family used to walk the neighborhoods looking for Rosemarie. All at once, Vera began to cry and couldn't stop. She felt like she was melting. The priest gave her a tissue and then put his arm around her shoulders. Vera couldn't remember a time when she'd cried like that. It was a river of tears and she could hardly breathe. Finally, she leaned back in the chair and stopped crying. She looked at the priest and told him that she'd always believed that if she did everything right that Rosemarie would find her way home. But she never did.

The priest listened patiently. He muttered in a low voice and she didn't know what he was saying, but she found his tone soothing. He sat in his chair again while Vera apologized for the spectacle. With a slight smile on his face he took her hands, and said, "Vera, all of this, what you told me is God's will, and God won't let you suffer more than you can bear. God loves you and he will take care of you."

"What about Rosemarie? What do you mean, it's God's will." She tried to make sense out of what he'd just said.

"Child, sometimes God's will is to make us suffer. Only He knows why. His own son, Jesus suffered. Remember? He died for us sinners. Believe in God and pray. All that happens is God's will and is in His hands."

Vera couldn't bear to listen any more so she told the priest Claudia's parents were waiting to take her home. Sure enough, Claudia and her parents were sitting on a bench in the courtyard waiting for her.

Graduation came and went. Vera had been saving all her money and still had plans to flee Canada when she turned twenty-one. She learned to sew really well and so wished her sister could see her beautiful clothes.

Vera felt badly for her mother who sat by the window every night writing in her journal. Sometimes Vera was curious about what she was writing, but she never asked. She was sure all of it was about Rosemarie. None of them had been the same since Rosemarie left for the bakery so many years before. While Hilda wrote, Oskar played his favorite Beethoven piece, "Moonlight Sonata." Of course, no one could ever forget how awed Rosemarie was by the moon. Vera wondered if she still loved it.

Months after graduation, Vera started working full time at Eaton's in the basement office. Her boss, Mrs. Johnston, was nice and understood Vera's desire to move to the US. She and her husband had been to America and loved it. Mrs. Johnson offered to make a few calls and find out what Vera needed to know to make the move.

Vera began attending a popular secretarial school on St. Catherine Street. She learned Pitman shorthand, how to touch type and bought an Underwood typewriter. She also learned proper office and telephone etiquette. While Vera loved school, it made her sad because she couldn't help but wonder what kind of a job Rosemarie would have had.

40

1963

When the time got closer for Vera to emigrate from Canada to the US, Oskar helped her with the paperwork. Knowing she was leaving soon, she stopped hating Canada. She realized she was stupid to think the country had something to do with her sister's disappearance. She wanted a fresh start somewhere new, somewhere warm where no one looked at her with sad eyes and thought of her as the girl whose sister had vanished. Her parents understood her wanting to get away from a place that had once carried the promise of a better life than they'd had in Germany, but had only delivered heartache.

Shortly before Vera left she heard of another missing little girl. She couldn't help but wonder if Rosemarie and that girl had found each other. The search efforts had gotten much more sophisticated since Rosemarie had gone missing and Vera wondered how many more missing children there were that she never heard about. But it didn't matter. As far as Vera knew, they never found Rosemarie and nobody ever found that girl either.

Vera thought about how much she'd miss her

family when she moved to the US, especially Audrey, Günter's little girl and Hilde's son Gabriel and her two new children. Vera delighted in playing with her nieces and nephews and was going to miss having children around to lift her spirits. And then there were the young man she'd been dating, Raymond. She enjoyed his company, but she wasn't willing to give up her dreams for him. Everything would have been so much easier if Rosemarie had been there for Vera to talk to.

Vera had finally decided on Los Angeles and since she had made up her mind, she couldn't wait to get there. She could already feel the sunshine on her face and feel the ocean on her feet. And she knew it would be a smooth journey because of all the money she'd saved. Her parents had surprised her by matching what she'd saved and so she would be heading to America with $1500 to her name. Oskar surprised her further by taking her car shopping. But again, all she could imagine was flying down the highway in a convertible with her sister. A fantasy that would never actually happen.

Vera was ready and excited for her move. She had gotten her certificate from the secretarial school and could write about a hundred and twenty words a minute in shorthand. She could transcribe sixty words a minute. That was as many as a sportscaster could speak in that same minute. Over the years she had learned many other helpful tips to become a successful secretary.

A little bit before Vera was getting ready to move the doorbell rang in the middle of the night. Vera's first thought was that Rosemarie had found her family and was, at long last, home where she belonged.

But when Oskar opened the door, he saw a young man hanging on to the side of the doorway. He could barely stand up and was slurring his words. Oskar spoke in

French to him.

It was clear to everyone that the young boy was very drunk. Vera just wanted him to go away. She was so disgusted that it wasn't her sweet sister at the door. But Oskar invited him in and asked Hilda to make a pot of coffee.

While they were waiting for it to brew, Oskar said to Vera, "I'm surprised at you."

"Why?" She had to yawn.

"You know this is someone's boy, son, maybe brother. I would never want someone to send my boy back into this cold night. Would you? Honestly?"

"No. Of course not. I'm just so disappointed. I thought it might be Rosemarie ringing the bell. That somehow she had enough sense to look us up in the telephone book. Why couldn't it be her, instead of that guy."

Oskar put his hand on Vera's shoulder. "I know my sweet girl. We all want it to be Rosemarie. But I do feel obligated to find out where this fellow lives and send him back to his parents." He checked the man's pockets and found a library card. It only had a name on it, so Oskar called the local police department and someone came to the house a few minutes later to bring the young man home.

The next day in the late afternoon the doorbell rang again. It was the father and mother of the young man from the previous night. Oskar was at home and answered the door and Hilda helped to usher the couple into the living room.

"Merci, merci beaucoup." Vera heard a man's voice.

"Oui, je comprend," Oskar replied several times after they spoke.

"We have been trying to keep him away from his so-called friends who drink, but we are not too successful," the fellow's mother said.

Vera thought that the man looked decent and smart. She said to Hilda, "He's lucky he rang your doorbell. It easily could have been someone else who would not have opened the door, or maybe someone not at home, and who knows, he could have fallen over an icy curb or a major snow drift and froze to death."

"It goes to show you how important it is to be careful and think about who we consider a friend," Hilda replied.

For an instant, Vera allowed herself to wonder if that was what had happened to Rosemarie. Had she trusted the wrong person and met a terrible fate? No! Vera shook off the thought. She wouldn't even let herself consider that something terrible had happened to her sister.

41

1963

Finally the day came for Vera to leave Canada, promising to call home when she arrived in Los Angeles. Her parents helped pack her car full of her belongings as well as some snacks and drinks to nibble on for the long road trip ahead. Vera could see the sadness in her parents' eyes. She quickly wrapped her arms tightly around her mom for a long warm hug. And then Vera grabbed her dad and hugged him so tight he could hardly breathe. She kissed them both on the cheeks, hurriedly got in her new car, and drove away crying out the window as she drove away out of sight.

"I love you both!" She shouted.

Vera looked in the rearview mirror to see her parents holding each other, tears rolling down their faces. Vera couldn't look back anymore. She had to focus on her new dream of brighter and happier days. But all the way there, she couldn't stop thinking about her sister. How was she ever going to find her when she'd moved almost three thousand miles away. She took Route 66 from Canada to California. Every time she stopped, she scoured phone booths for phone books, flipping through each one until she found all the *Döderleins*. In the margins she'd write, *Rosemarie Helga Döderlein, please call home* along with her parents' phone number. By the time she arrived at her new home, she estimated she'd written that same sentence more than three hundred times. No one ever called.

42

1974

Vera had long since left Canada and had been living in L.A. for more than ten years. She'd met a good man, married him and together they had a happy life including two children. It was a daily battle for her. She didn't miss anything about Montreal, but she'd go back there in a second if it meant finding Rosemarie. The world had given up on her. The detectives, retired now, came to Oskar and Hilda one last time before they moved south to tell them that they were sorry they had failed them. They were sure that if Rosemarie were still alive, they would have located her by then. People just didn't vanish into a cloudy evening. They posited that she had been killed shortly after she'd been taken and buried somewhere in Mont-Saint-Bruno or another one of the nearby national parks that spanned thousands of acres.

Vera remembered hiding in her room when Detectives McCormack and Talbot came to talk to her parents. She couldn't stand the way they looked at her with such pity when she yelled at them that her sister was alive and out there somewhere, just waiting to come home.

Every year on the anniversary of Rosemarie's disappearance, Vera would let herself out onto her back deck late at night. She'd sit in the quiet warmth of Southern California, looking at the moon and talk to her sister, just like she used to in Günter and Ruth's apartment. The moon connected her to her sister. And somehow Vera knew that every year on that date, late at night, Rosemarie was talking to the same moon. It's how she kept what was taken away.

In the winter of 1974, twenty years after Rosemarie walked to that bakery for the last time, there was a fire at Oskar and Hilda's cabin. Like Vera, years before they had fled Montreal for a cabin in the woods in Northern Ontario. The fire itself was small and contained to a trashcan outside. But the effort of trying to extinguish it himself was too much for Oskar and he died of a heart attack as the small fire burned on.

Vera got on the first flight she could and flew to Ontario intending to bring her mother back to California. Hilda was in her early seventies and wasn't meant to be alone. Even during the years that Oskar was fighting for Germany and then held against his will in Russia and France, Hilda was never alone. She had her kids. And Vera was determined to make sure her mother wasn't alone now.

Vera spent a week in Ontario cleaning out her parents' house and getting her mother ready to move. While she was there, she discovered the grave her parents had constructed for Rosemarie. Vera's heart felt immense sadness. After all these years she was struck by the fact that her parents had accepted that their daughter was never coming back. Beside the grave was the same brand of wool slacks Rosemarie had been wearing the day her mother sent her to the bakery for the last time, as well as her beloved wooden toy soldiers and everything else of hers Oskar and Hilda had taken from the Randall Avenue apartment when they moved the first time.

Vera told her mother she was going for a walk to take in the beautiful woods. But, as soon as she got out of sight of the old, charming farmhouse, she sat on the forest floor and wept for her sister. She let herself grieve for thirty minutes then wiped the pine needles from her pants and went back inside. There she found a framed magazine ad for Palmolive atop her father's piano. The model's resemblance to what Rosemarie would have looked like now was striking.

"Mama." Vera brought the frame to Hilda. "Where did you get this?"

Hilda put her hand over her heart. "Oh honey. I know it's silly. But I saw that in a magazine in a doctor's office a few years ago. I always wondered if it was Rosemarie. Can you imagine if she grew up to be this beautiful woman with a beautiful life? I didn't mean to keep the ad. But I couldn't make myself throw it out."

Vera put down the photo and wrapped her arms around her mother. "Of course you didn't throw it away. Why would you? Even if that woman isn't Rosemarie, it's a lovely reminder of just how beautiful she would've been." She was aware that she spoke of her sister in the past tense. But she didn't correct herself. "Should I pack it in your carryon? We should take it with us."

Hilda broke away from her daughter's embrace. "Thank you. That would be nice." Vera started toward the guestroom with the picture, but Hilda stopped her. "Is there room for more? Because there's something I haven't shown you."

Vera knew where her mother was taking her. Of course she did. She knew all about the boxes and boxes of photos from newspapers and magazines articles. Her parents had been collecting anything they thought might help them find their daughter. She acted surprised when her mother showed them to her. Then she said she would have the boxes shipped to her house. Hilda just smiled and thanked Vera for understanding.

Vera loved living in Los Angeles. She had endured a childhood in Germany during the second great war when she never had warm clothes or shoes without holes in them. And then even though her family was financially secure in Canada, the winters there were even more brutal than in Birkenfeld. Wind cut through her heaviest coat and it seemed to never stop snowing for half the year. By the time her mother came to live with her she'd spent more than a decade living in a place with almost no humidity, never any snow and where the average temperature year round was in the seventies.

Southern California changed Hilda. She spent more time outside. She got around easier as the warmth eased her arthritis. She smiled more. Even though they both missed Oskar terribly, moving to America with Vera was the best thing for Hilda. Vera was happy knowing her mother was happier living with her than she had been for years.

Although Vera usually rose before her mother, one day she came downstairs later than usual and found her mother reading the paper at a small round table on the back deck. The sun filtered through the clouds and Hilda appeared dappled in sunlight. When Hilda saw her daughter approach, she pushed a mug of coffee across the table and motioned for her to sit.

Vera sat and then took a sip of the coffee. "Thanks Mama. Anything interesting in the paper today?"

Hilda's cheeks colored. "Oh, it's nothing. Just looking."

But Vera was curious so she stood and went behind her mother. "Mama! The obituaries? Did one of your friends . . . pass?"

Hilda folded the paper and placed it on the table.

"No no. Nothing like that. I just . . . I just always check the papers in case . . . " She didn't finish her sentence but she didn't have to.

"Oh Mama. It's okay. You don't have to say anything." Hilda sat across from her mother and they stayed like that, sipping their coffee in silence, for a few minutes. "How long have you been looking for news of Rosemarie's death?"

"Since the day after she disappeared. Don't get me wrong, I really don't believe she's gone. I know she's out there somewhere. But if she is gone, I just want to know. It's been so long. Too long."

Vera reached her hand across the table and held her mother's fingers. "I think it's nice. Would you mind if we looked together?"

Hilda finished her coffee. "That would be nice. Thank you."

Vera and her mother spent the next year reading the obituaries in every newspaper they could find. Vera also took to placing personal ads in those same papers and several German club newsletters once a week asking for Rosemarie Helga Döderlein to please contact her family.

No one ever answered the ads, but it made Vera and Hilda feel better to continue to place them and read the papers. They'd always been close, but doing this together every morning made Vera feel like she was doing something to help her mother.

About a year after Oskar died and Hilda moved in with Vera, Hilda had a catastrophic stroke. The doctors made it clear that there was nothing to be done for her other than to keep her comfortable. So for three days Vera sat by her mother's hand and just talked. Most of the time Vera didn't even know what she was talking about or even if her mother could hear her. She just wanted to fill the space in the too-still room.

Vera was in the middle of a story about her day at work when Hilda squeezed her hand and struggled to sit up. "My dear Vera." Hilda's voice was little more than a whisper. "What in the world do you think ever happened to Rosemarie?"

The question surprised Vera. In the twenty-plus years since Rosemarie had disappeared, the family had never sat down and actually discussed what they thought happened to her. She didn't want to say the wrong thing, knowing it might be the last thing her mother ever heard, so she stayed quiet for a moment. Then Vera leaned in close to her mother and whispered, "I think a nice family found her. I think she got lost on the street and a really nice family took her in and raised her as their own. She's all grown up by now. So she's probably married to a really nice man. And maybe she even has kids of her own. Wherever she is, Mama, she's happy. I just know it."

Hilda smiled in a way that Vera hadn't seen in years and closed her eyes for the last time. For years after her mother left her, Vera wondered if she should have given her a better answer, a more honest answer. But she didn't know what that might have been. What did Vera think happened to her sister? Could she possibly have been found by a nice family? It was more likely someone terrible had taken her. Was she still alive? Would Vera have felt it if Rosemarie had died all those years ago? She didn't know. She just didn't know.

It was only after both Oskar and Hilda had passed that Vera dared to speak to Günter and Hilde about what they thought may have happened to their sister. By then the three remaining siblings all had families and children and the mystery of Rosemarie's disappearance was passed from one generation to the next like a precious heirloom.

The three siblings, their spouses and their children

discussed their theories. Because Vera was nearest in age to Rosemarie, she felt closest to her. She knew that Rosemarie wasn't unhappy in Canada. On the contrary, she was happier away from war-torn Germany. And she hadn't been there long enough to meet any boys, or even know enough about boys and love, never mind fall in love with one and run away with him. It didn't take much for Hilde, Günter and their families to agree with Vera about the "boy theories" considering they were all born and raised in the same unsophisticated village. None of them really believed that Rosemarie would have willingly left her family. But they didn't like to talk about some of the more sinister possibilities.

Although Ruth had never been much of a talker, she was most familiar with Canada and had brought up the possibility that Rosemarie had been snatched and sold on the black market to a family who desperately wanted a child. None of them knew much about illegal adoptions, but it seemed probable that something like that could have happened. Except that fourteen was older than most kids who were adopted. Still, it provided Rosemarie's siblings with some comfort knowing that perhaps she had been living a happy life.

One of Hilde's sons heard that a Montreal pilot took Rosemarie and flew her away somewhere. This son was named after one of the private investigators who his parents had hired to look for Rosemarie. The entire Döderlein family had spent thousands of dollars on private investigators looking for Rosemarie. They'd collected hundreds of bits of information and leads. But nothing ever panned out.

Hilde's daughters had their own theories. One, a Montreal cop herself, heard that a man in Montreal who lived in a one-room apartment took her and made her write a note to her parents saying that she was taken by a man.

Apparently that note was torn up and left in a trashcan. The other daughter had heard from more than one person that the aunt she'd never meet was taken by human traffickers, put on a ship to the Middle East and sold. Several of Hilde's children had heard from their parents, when they thought they were alone and nobody listening, that a man who drove a taxi had taken Rosemarie and may have taken other young girls as well.

The only option none of them wanted to discuss was that she was in the wrong place at the wrong time, and was kidnapped by a predator. Given that she was never found and that her body was not recovered, Vera and her siblings dismissed this theory. Surely if Rosemarie had met a bad fate they would have eventually found her body.

After her mom's death, Vera promised herself that she would continue to read the obituaries and place classified ads. This went on for years, well after she got married and had children of her own. Vera made sure that Rosemarie was as much a part of her family as she would have been if she were still alive. Her children knew as much about Rosemarie and her disappearance as Vera did. When her kids got old enough they helped Vera scour the internet and they even did their own research on and off again.

43

California 1993

It had been almost fifty years since Rosemarie disappeared when Vera's husband, Al, died after a five year battle with colon cancer. Their children, Christa and Tamara, helped care for Al for many years after his many surgeries and procedures, and through his ups and downs. They spent time with their parents that may never had happened otherwise.

Christa eventually married, had four children, and for over a decade had a full-time career as a software engineer. She was resourceful, a master of all things computers, and most of all a "go getter." Vera knew that her daughter always found a way to accomplish anything she set out to do, despite any setbacks or obstacles. And a few decades after Al's passing, Vera eventually moved in with Christa and her family. The two women became more like best friends than mother and daughter.

Christa and Vera continued the search for Rosemarie over the years. It was never a burden, not an obligation. Just something they wanted to do. A labor of love they felt called to complete. The internet had just been introduced to households across the globe. And it opened a world of opportunities to Vera and her daughter.

They continued searching for any obituary for women named Rosemarie Helga. Through many awkward phone calls and letters, they got in touch with the families of every Rosemarie Helga they could, but either the birth years didn't fit or the demographics were too different. There were so many Rosemarie Helgas both dead and still alive, and none of them were ever their missing family member.

Vera often told Christa that she didn't have to help with the search. She could only imagine how mentally taxing it must have been on her daughter to look for some phantom whom she'd never even met, especially since Vera knew this always became a fruitless endeavor for her and her parents over the decades past. It must have felt like chasing ghosts to her. But Christa never complained. She loved spending that time with her mother and she'd become obsessed with finding her aunt, even if it was only in death.

Over the years their searches never waned. Despite all the dead ends, hours spent, and sadness that came from learning about the millions of other missing people around the world, Vera and Christa kept at it. For more than thirty years they diligently searched for Rosemarie Helga Döderlein.

In 1994 one of Hilde's sons called his Aunt Vera and his cousins, summoning them to Canada. Hilde was dying of cancer and she wanted to see them before she passed. The mother and daughters hurried off on the first flight and to her bedside. And it was not lost on Vera that her sister asked the same question as did her mother when she lay dying. What in the world ever happened to Rosemarie?

Although Vera no longer believed the fairly happy

tale she'd told her dying mother, she couldn't bring herself to send her sister into the afterworld hearing the bleak possibility of what probably had happened to Rosemarie. So Vera held Hilde's hand and whispered that their sister Rosemarie was happy. That she'd been raised by a loving family, met a wonderful man and had four beautiful children of her own. Perhaps two of them had even been named *Hilde* and *Vera*.

Vera had lost her husband the year before and she was still grieving his loss. Telling Hilde that Rosemarie was alive and well was as much for Vera's own benefit as it was for her sister's. She held onto Hilde's hand as she grew weaker, all the while whispering to her that Rosemarie was safe and happy.

It was then, in that moment that Vera promised herself that one day she would find out what happened to Rosemarie. Beautiful Hilde passed away peacefully in her sleep that evening.

44

April 2022

It'd been nearly seventy years since Rosemarie had disappeared and Vera never gave up hope of finding her. Even if she were no longer alive, Vera wanted to fulfill her promise to her parents, sister and brother of bringing her home or at least letting them know in spirit that she finally solved the mystery of what happened to her.

Vera had lived her whole life caught between two worlds—one where she grieved her sister every day and would stop at nothing to find answers and one where she had her own family and tried to make life as normal as possible for her two daughters.

Normalcy included having an annual family photograph taken by a local professional. Vera and her children and grandchildren wore matching outfits and took a beautiful group photo under a weeping willow tree in Christa's backyard. Shortly after, Vera was chatting with the photographer when he mentioned that he collected bibles and prayer books. Vera's eyes lit up and she went inside. Knowing what her mother was about to do, Christa followed her into the house.

"Mama," Christa said, "please don't do this."

But Vera had already gone into a back closet and retrieved one of her sister's prayer books that she'd held on to for sixty-eight years. "Let's face it, Christa." Vera's smile disappeared. "We both know your Aunt Rosemarie isn't coming back. So let's let this nice man have something of hers. Rosemarie would want to do something kind for someone else."

Christa couldn't argue with her mother. She made a very good point. "Okay. You're right. You're always thinking of everyone else. But….can we please keep it…just a little longer?" Christa met her mom's eyes for approval and then gently took the prayer book from her hands and placed it back in the curio cabinet.

Later that night, Vera and Christa were talking about what a nice afternoon they'd had with their family and the photographer. Christa mentioned that even after so many years Rosemarie was still a part of so many of their daily conversations.

"You know, Mama, today got me thinking." Christa's eyes lit up.

Vera put down her cup of tea and met her daughter's eye. "Oh yeah, sweetheart. What about?"

Christa swallowed hard. "Aunt Rosemarie. I know you've never stopped looking for her. But things are so different now. The internet is so advanced and there are so many websites and people and resources. What if we tried one more time. I mean really tried one more time to find her."

Vera seemed to consider this for a moment. "I think you might be the loveliest girl in the world. Thank you."

Christa couldn't decide if she felt hope or apprehension. "Great." She knew her mother would jump at the chance to try to find her sister. But Christa didn't even know where to start.

"What's first?" Vera asked. "It's been almost 70 years. There isn't security camera footage, almost everybody who knew something is probably dead or dying, and most records have probably been destroyed or ruined by fires or floods."

Christa stood and offered her hand to her mother. "Let me think. Let's start with a good night's sleep."

The next morning Christa woke before daybreak and sat at her computer with a cup of tea and her dogs curled at her feet. She started reading every Canadian newspaper she could find from 1951 to the end of 1955. Perhaps Rosemarie had been hit by a car and gotten a terrible concussion and ended up in the hospital? As Christa did her research she realized that not everything from the fifties was memorialized on the internet the way life was in the present day. She read hundreds if not thousands of articles from that timeframe in Canada. Not all of them were useful, but she kept a file of the ones that were. She discovered quickly that the possibilities for leads were endless. She saved all the articles written about the black market for babies and children in 1950s Montreal. Christa was shocked to learn that so many children, thousands of them, had disappeared just steps away from where her mom had lived on Randall Avenue. When Christa read some of the articles aloud to her mom, Vera reminded herself that she never regretted fleeing Canada and moving to the US, and now more than ever, having two children and four grandchildren of her own, she was grateful to be as far away from Montreal as possible.

Many articles caught Christa's attention. So many of them had details that were similar to the circumstances surrounding Rosemarie's disappearance. Young teenagers had been sent to do a quick errand and had never returned. Kids had been just steps from their homes and seem to have vanished without leaving a ripple of alarm. Girls who lived in safe neighborhoods and who played in their yards without care or concern never again came home for dinner. Even other girls that also went to their neighborhood bakeries in Montreal, went missing as if they never existed in the first place.

Christa emailed several of the journalists who'd written those articles in hopes that they may have had some insight. One called her right away and they spoke several times. His name was Christopher Morton, and although he ultimately couldn't offer anything helpful, his willingness to speak to Christa renewed her faith that she would eventually find her long-since-missing aunt.

While reading article after article, Christa came across a book by Danielle Lacasse called *La Prostitution Féminine à Montréal* as well as several newspaper and magazine articles that indicated young girls were taken off the streets of Montreal and sold into prostitution houses, often facilitated by corrupt police officers in the city. A bit more research revealed that Lacasse had written her PhD thesis on the countless girls in Montreal who had disappeared around the same time as Rosemarie. Most of them had been sold to families or forced into prostitution. Although Christa didn't want to imagine either of those situations befalling Rosemarie, she felt they were both strong enough possibilities that she added it to her list of possibilities.

Christa spent hours googling Rosemarie's name and also recreating a timeline of happenings from 1954 to the end of 1955. After a few days, Christa was flabbergasted by all the crime that took place in the city her mom lived in as a young girl and teenager.

After she'd been at it for a week, she was

researching a lead from an article dated December 1955. The byline was a woman whose name Christa had seen on several other articles. All of them referenced crimes, and Christa thought the obvious next step would be to request old police records.

"Mama! Come!" she yelled into the kitchen. There were so many new possibilities that could lead them to Rosemarie. Christa was excited to share what she learned with her mom and put a real plan into action.

45

"The list of leads to investigate just keeps growing and growing." Christa told her mother as she pointed to a giant posterboard she created full of circle diagrams outlining higher-level categories of possibilities for Rosemarie's disappearance. Christa felt it was important to understand the bigger picture of what was happening in the community - at school, with the local police, and in and around the Randall Avenue apartment. Each of those major circles had branches to smaller actionable research items. Anything that both could and couldn't be investigated was added to the appropriate category on the poster.

"Well don't keep me in suspense." Vera rubbed her hands together. "Tell me, tell me."

"So many archives from so many places are online now, it's like a treasure trove of records from Canada and around the world. Who knows what we may find. All we need is something, anything. Just one record or photo. Finding Rosemarie is like a needle in a haystack. But we know the Rosemarie needle is there somewhere, she didn't hop on a rocket and leave the planet. We will identify the haystacks and look into each one." Christa said confidently. She always had a way of making words sound fun. "So here's a plan of action, with many leads to investigate one-by-one." She said as she proudly held up the poster in front of her.

Vera leaned over Christa's shoulder so she could get a better look at the poster. "You're right. Anything is possible."

"Who knows what got published or investigated around the time Rosemarie went missing." Christa felt her stomach twist, but in a good way. "I feel like we're a hair away from Rosemarie, a hair. I can't wait to investigate every lead on this poster."

Vera sighed. "It's been almost seventy years. It's hard to get excited about anything anymore. I've looked for so long. *We've* looked for so long."

Even though Christa understood the chances of finding Rosemarie were very small, she hated hearing her mother so despondent. Usually it was Vera who was the one who always held out hope and made it seem like a foregone conclusion that the Döderleins would eventually bring Rosemarie home to them.

Christa squeezed her mother's hand. "I know, Mama. But we have so many more resources now than we had even last year. We've come so far. Don't give up yet."

Vera stood and patted her daughter's shoulder. "I'm going to get more coffee. Do you need anything?"

"No Mama. I'm just going to sit here for a little while longer and see if I can dig anything up from the archives before we need to go pick the kids up from school. I'll be done in a moment."

In that moment, Christa quickly searched for Montreal specific Facebook groups to try and solicit some help from anyone who may have known the scene back in 1954. She joined a handful of groups and posted of summary of what happened to Rosemarie and asked if anyone knew anything or had had similar experiences. As she anxiously waited for the administrators to approve her posts, she left with her mother to go on a short walk before picking up the children from school. When Christa came back to check on her posts a few hours later, to her amazement hundreds of people commented.

Christa got her mother and together they sat at the table while Christa read all the comments out loud. They learned that the neighborhood the two sisters had lived in on Randall Avenue was called Notre Dame De Grace, or NDG for short. Most of the comments were from people about Vera's age who reminisced about growing up there and how safe it was. A woman who lived just a couple blocks from Vera and her family talked about how safe she'd always felt there. But then that same woman also said that her father was a cop. So Christa thought that that probably had made that woman and her siblings immune to harm.

Christa was starting to think that everyone from NDG thought it was loveliest place in the world. But then she saw in the upper righthand corner of her screen that she had private messages. She clicked on that and read the words of a woman who recalled exploring an abandoned building not far from her mother's apartment. This woman and her friends had been playing hide and seek when they stumbled upon a bathtub filled with blood. Scared that they would get in trouble for playing where they weren't supposed to, they never told anyone about what they'd found. The message sender couldn't remember exactly when she'd made the discovery, but she thought it was toward the end of 1954. It was definitely winter and not long before Christmas because she remembered seeing white lights streamed on trees as she ran home.

Christa wondered for a moment if her aunt could have met a terrible ending in that bathtub. She knew it was possible, but she also understood that this was probably just one of many leads that would come her way. She clicked out of the message and went back to reading the rest of the comments to her mother.

Every time a comment seemed like it could offer a clue, Christa sent the poster a private message asking permission to call. The first week alone she must have talked to thirty people. Every single person listened with interest and sympathy. Some had suggestions for other avenues she could investigate. But most just commented about how sorry they were.

After several days of nothing new or anything that Christa felt was helpful, a few people on the Montreal Facebook groups suggested she join other smaller, more narrowly focused Montreal Facebook groups. One person listed the names of a few groups that were more specific to what Christa and her family were looking for.

That night after dinner while her kids were doing homework, Christa made her mother, her husband and herself hot cups of mint tea with honey and milk and they sat in the living room talking about their days.

"How goes the search?" Ali, Christa's husband, asked.

"Funny you should ask," Christa said, making eye contact with her mother. "Let us fill you in."

Vera jumped in immediately and excitedly started telling Ali some of the various replies to their posts in the Facebook groups.

Christa then proposed joining the new Facebook groups suggested to them, even though the thought of doing this made her nervous as it somehow felt bigger, going deeper into the rabbit hole. "There are a bunch more Facebook groups we can join. The people I've talked to so far have all said we should post Rosemarie's story in these places and wait for people to comment. Is that okay with you?" Christa met her mother's eyes for approval. "Okay.

Then that's what we'll do."

Vera gave her consent and Christa got to work joining all the new relevant Facebook groups. She couldn't believe how many dealt with lost and exploited children. Within hours there were thousands of comments to sift through, hundreds of private messages, and by the next day Christa couldn't keep up. She asked Ali to help her, but even with his assistance, it was too much.

"What if you just make your own Facebook group?" Ali suggested as he sipped tea and tried to organize the leads into three categories of *promising, maybe* and *trash*. "We can invite the people from other groups to join so we can still communicate with them. But this way we won't have to constantly switch between groups to try to follow all the comments. At the very least, it will make it easier to organize the leads."

"A-Team." Christa leaned across the table and kissed her husband. "I'll do that now if you want to flag people you think we should invite."

A Montreal historian was one of the first people to post on the newly created *What in the World Happened to Rosemarie?* Facebook group page. He knew a lot about many missing children cases in Montreal over the years and offered to video chat with Christa and Vera.

"Do you mind if I give you some unsolicited advice?" Very few people looked good on Zoom. The angles and lighting usually gave people wide foreheads and exaggerated noses. But this man, with a scarf wrapped carelessly around his neck, looked like he could be on the cover of a magazine. "Forget about requesting police archives. Call all the police stations in Montreal and speak to an actual human. If they put you through to someone's voicemail, leave a message and call back. Be persistent. Do what you have to do. But don't give up until you have an actual conversation with a real person. It's the only way you'll get any answers."

Christa and Vera thanked this man for his time. Vera Googled phone numbers for Montreal police stations while Christa began calling them. By the next day, Rosemarie Döderlein was no longer a cold case and forgotten. The Montreal police sent a follow-up email indicating that no records were found in their archives and that they would instead open a brand new case file for her and that an assigned detective would be in touch.

The Montreal historian wasn't the only helpful person. Another man from Canada named Rod sent an email to Christa and Vera offering his help including contacts and resources in Montreal that could help locate Rosemarie. He had embarked on a similar search for his 83 year old wife a few decades prior. She was one of many thousands of survivors of a scandal in Montreal and throughout Quebec in the fifties where nuns and other religious folks would scour the streets of Montreal to snatch women, children and babies and bring them to the Catholic orphanages that were reclassified as psychiatric institutions overnight.

Rod explained that this madness started the year the federal government announced that they would dramatically increase the per orphan stipend for any children who were "mentally ill." At the time, Quebec's longest-serving premier in Quebec history Maurice Duplessis enlisted the help of the Catholic community to help round up tens of thousands of children to maximize this federal funding opportunity. Rod said babies, children and girls were literally plucked off the streets for any reason and declared mentally ill, including the "disability" of having a lack of English or French language skills.

Decades later thousands of the children who were raised in these orphanages would later allege that they were abused, kept in straight-jackets and held against their will being labeled mentally incompetent. One particular institution in the West end of Montreal on the side of the mountain called L'Institut Chaumont and was eerily close to the Randall Avenue apartment. Nuns in the area were reportedly always on the trot in that neighborhood. And if they saw an opportunity beyond creating a new "orphan," thcy would simply bring the child to the Montreal Windsor Train Station, get on the train with the kids and luggage, and whisk it off to New York to sell the child. Nobody at the time would say anything because they were part of religious congregations that represented good people.

Christa couldn't believe the horrific and shocking things she was learning about Montreal in the 1950s. Could Rosemarie have been snatched off the sidewalk by a virtuous nun? Christa could easily Rosemarie as a victim in this particular situation. The act of putting a microscope on Montreal's history continued to reveal the horrific possibilities on how her aunt may have met her fate, and in ways she never imagined. All this aside, Christa was thankful for any and all leads and quickly replied to Rod thanking him for taking the time to share his resources and information. She quickly filled out the paperwork with all of Rosemarie's pertinent information and emailed it to the Centre intégré de santé et de services sociaux de la Montérégie-Est's "Accueil Service Antécédents et Retrouvailles" and the National Reconciliation Program for Duplessis Orphans to see if they had any records on Rosemarie.

Strangers from around the world continued to offer their tips and help. Sketch artists, forensic scientists, private detectives, translators, artists and genealogists lined up to help. Christa and Vera checked their messages and emails several times a day. The assistance complete strangers offered was amazing, but overwhelming at the same time.

A one sentence email came in from the Montreal detective later that week. The expectation to receive any help from the police department after almost 70 years had passed and seemed like a big ask. Christa and Vera could detect the annoyance in the tone of the message, they shrugged it off and vowed to themselves to continue searching the haystack for Rosemarie on their own.

When hundreds of people suggested Vera and her family get DNA tests and search those records, Christa remembered that she'd bought Ancestry.com home DNA kits for her whole family an entire decade earlier for Christmas gifts. The first few times they checked their accounts, there hadn't been any matches or requests to connect so she didn't think much of it. But she'd come this far and she wasn't going to let even the most improbable lead get away from her. To that end, she decided to also buy 23andMe, Family Tree DNA and MyHeritage home DNA kits and registered on their websites to increase the amount of potential leads. Christa was feeling hopeful.

46

May 2022

One morning, Christa found some quiet time and logged into all the DNA sites she registered with and found hundreds of DNA matches to her mom, mostly distant cousins. However one specific match stood out that was close enough to pique her attention. The website had labeled the very Italian sounding relative as being possibly Vera's grandniece, but Christa had never heard this name before. The website also indicated that this DNA match could also have been related to Vera in many other possible ways, even unexpected ways such as being a cousin, the child of a half-sibling or an unknown sibling. Christa recalled reading an article recently that interviewed several people whose DNA revealed shocking family relationships and the conclusion was "Never say never when it comes to DNA!" This prompted Christa to talk to her mother about it but Vera never knew her parents to be anything but a loving, faithful couple. But since Oskar and Hilda were long since dead, they had no way of verifying if there were more siblings in Canada or anywhere else.

Christa made contact with this woman whose DNA

was a close match to her mom. Her name was Valentina Rossi and she didn't have much information to offer. She reported that the whole reason she joined these DNA sites was because she didn't know anything much about her father's side of the family. She'd been hoping to connect with paternal grandparents or cousins. Valentina told Christa that she thought her father was born around 1960 because she remembered her mother saying they were about the same age. She also mentioned that her grandfather was named Lucifer and that her grandmother Mary, whom her mother met once at a dinner, was a quiet lady with dark brown hair and dark brown eyes. Rosemarie had disappeared in 1954 at age fourteen, so she definitely could have had a baby in 1960 by age twenty. Even after all the years of silence and wondering, Vera couldn't fathom that her sister would have had a baby and never told her about it. They were best friends. And Rosemarie was Rosemarie and not Mary afterall. And while hair color could conceivably change anytime, anyone who saw her bright cornflower blue eyes would never forget them. This "Mary" couldn't possibly be Rosemarie.

Another close DNA match on Ancestry.com was also a match to Valentina. It seemed likely that this man's grandparents also had the same surname as Valentina's father. Using a hand drawn chart on a piece of butcher paper taped to the wall, Christa created a skewed version of connect the dots. Without a doubt this new match somehow fit into the Döderlein family tree and very well may have been a direct descendent of Rosemarie. Christa sent the person a message and made herself lunch while she waited. She'd included all the major details about Rosemarie's disappearance. She thought for sure that by the time she put the lunch meat back in the fridge, she'd have an answer. But when she opened her computer there was nothing. This went on all day until Christa finally told herself that she was being silly and not everyone was as connected to their devices as she was.

But a day turned into a week that turned into a month. After four months and almost twenty unanswered messages, Christa gave up and resigned herself to knowing that that person wasn't going to help her find her aunt.

So Christa moved on to other possibilities which were complicated by the fact that she learned that her Aunt Hilde had given up a baby for adoption in the late fifties or early sixties before having seven more children by 1969. This made it exceptionally difficult to figure out how Valentina and the other DNA match were related to Vera's family considering Valentina's estimated 1960 birth year of her father.

Stuck and frustrated, Christa turned to their Facebook group to post and see if anyone in the newly formed group had any suggestions on how to figure out how these two DNA matches were related to her mom. Someone suggested to look into using investigative genetic genealogy or IGG for short and suggested posting on one of the largest Facebook groups full of passionate volunteer armchair DNA detectives.

Christa found the group with a quick Facebook search and joined. Within a few minutes Christa crafted and posted a message in the group soliciting help on how to figure out how the unknown DNA matches were related to her mom. Within minutes, dozens of people from around the world replied to her post and sent private messages offering to help. Several chimed in to explain how the IGG process could be used to place the unknown DNA match on the family tree. Christa was getting excited and didn't want to dismiss the possibilities surrounding these DNA matches. She felt that DNA could be the most viable lead that she would have in this new search for Rosemarie.

Investigative genetic genealogists in the Facebook group indicated that a family tree would need to be constructed first. Then free professional online tools on the DNA Painter website would use this family tree to compare the amount of DNA the unknown matches shares with Vera to amounts from known members on the family tree. Christa was also told that she would need to research historical records to establish accurate dates and relationships between everyone.

Undaunted, Christa made her family a nice dinner and sat across from her mom at the dinner table while she asked questions about the family she'd left behind in Germany. Vera didn't remember much because she was so young when she left. She knew that she'd had grandparents, aunts and a few cousins. But she couldn't remember anything other than their first names or nicknames.

"I'm sorry, Christa." Vera fidgeted with her fork. "It was just so long ago and my memory isn't as good as it used to be."

"Seriously Mama, don't worry about it. Maybe we'll get lucky and find some random relatives in the US. God knows you can find anyone any time here. The privacy laws are so lax here that anyone can have anyone's phone number and address served on a silver platter within minutes for ten bucks. But alas Germany is quite the opposite. Privacy laws in Germany are very strict, but we'll figure it out. I even heard someone say recently that you can drive on the Autobahn at 200 kilometers per hour and almost kill ten people and nothing will happen to you. But if you violate privacy in Germany then you are doomed." Christa stopped to laugh out loud for a moment. "Luck is what is needed to find any people who are alive or who were born in the 20th century over there. Sometimes with more luck there are old phone book entries or old newspaper articles online. Building a family tree that includes current living relatives is going to be a huge mission, but once we get it done, the next task will be to track down everyone who is still alive and ask them to spit in a tube. One day at a time."

Vera crinkled her nose. "Oh honey. Don't say spit. It's such a vile word."

Christa bowed her head in mock apology. "Okay, we'll track down everyone who is still alive and ask them to follow the instructions included with their DNA kits. Is that better?"

Vera laughed. "Perfect." She paused for a moment. "So where do we start?"

"I was wondering that exact same thing. I found a German genealogy Facebook group. It's as good a place to start as any. Give me a minute and I'll ask for any help there too. So many people have been kind and helpful, maybe we will continue our good luck."

A few minutes later Christa got a response from a man in the Facebook group who recommended a passionate genealogist and historical author named Carolin who lived near Vera's hometown in Germany. This woman dedicated many years to translating of all the archives Birkenfeld had managed to keep over the many centuries from when Birkenfeld first became a village on the map. She put Vera's grandmother's surname in her custom built software and database and she got a hit of nine generations of her ancestors dating back to the 1500s. Christa tasked her oldest daughters to the monumental task of adding the names and birth and death dates from hundreds of ancestors to the family tree on Ancestry.com. By the time they were done more than nine hundred people were added to the Döderlein family tree.

Carolin took the initiative to cross compare this data with very distant DNA matches appearing on the

DNA websites and after much analysis, emailed Christa her findings that showed how Vera shared many maternal and paternal matches with her DNA match, ruling out the half sibling theory.

When Christa got done reading everything Carolin had sent her, she yelled out, "Woo hoo! We're one step closer to figuring out who these DNA matches are." Vera came into the room and asked what they should do next. "Funny you should ask," Christa said. "Carolin suggested we write letters to the mayors of Birkenfeld and Pforzheim to see about the possibility of receiving any additional family records that might reveal a clue to finding living relatives."

Christa and her mother quickly got to work and wrote to the mayors at the Rathaus' in both towns explaining the situation and the urgent request for records. She snapped a photo of her mom along with her passport and California driver's license to prove her identity and sent it along with her letters via email.

After a few days, Christa opened her email and to her surprise, both mayors had replied with a few records they were able to find and share. Christa and Vera could decipher quickly that Hilda and Oskar had three other children Vera never knew of or heard about. It appeared that all had passed away at birth or as young infants. The rest of the records were undecipherable to both Christa and Vera, and they quickly clicked on the forward email button that whisked the records across the Atlantic Ocean and over to Carolin. From there she began reading and deciphering the documents. A few hints contained in the records prompted Carolin to access the limited public resources in Germany including a search of various databases and newspaper archives. Luck was had when she found two relatives who were still alive.

"Mama! Look! Your cousins that you always told

me about over the years! The ones you hung out with, stomping grapes and playing together at your Oma's house every Sunday? Carolin found one of them!! Junta! She's alive and living in Germany still! We have an actual address, so let's send her a yummy gift basket and write a letter to tell her how excited we are to find her! And a DNA kit of course!" Christa chuckled. "Do you think she will remember you? It's been 68 years!" Christa was so thrilled she could hardly contain herself.

"Yes of course she will remember me!" Vera's eyes lit up with excitement, "I remember feeling sad not being able to say goodbye to her when we left. Always a kind, gentle and sweet girl." Vera continued, "She was one of my best buddies in Birkenfeld. This is so exciting!"

"And look, another cousin from Birkenfeld is here in the US on the east coast! Have you ever heard of this lady?" Christa summoned her mother to her side so she could show her the record open on the computer screen. "She is the daughter of one of your cousins that you used to play with. And wow! She's almost the same age as you too!"

Vera didn't recognize the lady's name but she figured that at the very least she would have fun connecting with a new cousin and other relatives she never even knew she had. So with a quick search on the internet, Christa found the woman's phone number and they called her together on speakerphone. "Grüss Gott!" Vera said in her native Swabian tongue when the woman answered. Switching between English and Swabian German, Vera and her new cousin instantly knew they were related and were happy talking for a few minutes about the old village they both knew as children. The woman also remembered hearing about Rosemarie's disappearance from letters sent by Hilda to one of her sisters. The woman admitted that she didn't know she had any relatives in the US and was happy to make the connection. The conversation ended because she had an appointment but she and Vera vowed to call one another and talk again another time.

A few moments later, Vera made some fresh chamomile tea and got her Chromebook and sat down to start typing up a letter to her old cousin Junta in Germany right away.

At the same time, Christa researched and found a small deli and gift shop in Pforzheim and contacted the shopkeeper. She arranged for her to print Vera's letter and deliver it along with an enormous gift basket loaded with Vera and her cousin's favorite childhood snacks, fruits, deli meat and cheeses, and of course a DNA kit.

The shopkeeper confirmed delivery of the goods the next day and reported back that a lovely woman answered the door and was very surprised and thankful for the basket. The next day Vera followed up with a phone call to her long lost cousin and they immediately reconnected talking in their Swabian dialect as if were back in the early 1950s all over again. Vera learned about the passing of most every family member she remembered and told Vera of the many letters Hilda had sent to her mother about Rosemarie's disappearance and how she often wondered over the years if she had been found.

Christa and Vera were feeling hopeful that with the DNA submitted from this new cousin it might finally put them on their way to being able to use some of the sophisticated IGG tools and finally determine who these unknown DNA matches were.

A week later a young lady named Kharisma replied to one of Christa and Vera's Facebook posts on a DNA related Facebook group. She was a passionate volunteer American investigative genetic genealogist that wanted to really dive in and help figure out more about Vera's unknown DNA relatives, especially Valentina who could be the possible granddaughter of Rosemarie according to the percentage of DNA she shared with both Vera and the other unknown DNA match.

She suggested that this possibility existed: Valentina's *grandfather*, and not *her grandmother*, could be the one that connected all of them, and that using IGG she could help prove or disprove this potential DNA relationship. Christa couldn't help but remember Valentina's words describing her grandmother: "Mary" with the dark brown hair and dark brown eyes. What Kharisma was suggesting as a next step made perfect sense. All this talk about DNA and IGG made Christa and Vera thankful for all the kind people willing to take time to help them understand everything. But thinking about this DNA possibility meant that Vera had another brother that she didn't know about. And while it wasn't uncommon in those days for women to give their babies to another family member, Vera just couldn't imagine this is something her parents would have done and kept it a secret forever. But then flashes of the records from Birkenfeld showing that her parents had three other children she never heard about made her realize that this was a possibility to consider. After reading hundreds of posts in Facebook groups from others seeking help with their DNA, Vera knew anything was possible. Christa and Vera were thankful for Kharisma's willingness to try and take this DNA possibility off the table.

Kharisma got right to work researching old records, newspapers, and databases and within days she had built an exhaustive family tree for Valentina's grandfather's side of the family. It showed that Vera was not related to Valentina's grandfather. Although Vera and Christa were disappointed to learn of a dead end, it was one lead that they could cross off their list. But Kharisma told them that it wasn't a total loss as she found the DNA match's grandfather's name Lucifer in old digitized city phone directories found online. These directory listings included addresses, phone numbers, and names of all employed household members for the grandfather's family for decades starting from 1952 until the late 70s.

"Incredible!" Christa was in shock at the thought that Rosemarie might actually be found after all these years.

"We're getting somewhere! Maybe we can write some letters to these addresses and their neighbors or even call all of them! Maybe Rosemarie still lives there! Maybe one of them remembers Rosemarie!" She quickly used the reverse address feature on the Canada 411 directory website to create a long list of people to call and write. She thought for a minute on how she would approach a phone conversation and then starting dialing.

One phone call after another, Christa gained momentum with her confidence speaking to random strangers. Several numbers were out of service, many had answering machines, and several answered. Christa would explain the story in a basic way: *I heard my Aunt Rosemarie lived in the house next to you a long time ago. She spoke German, had blonde hair and bright blue eyes. She would have been a young teenager in the mid to late fifties, a young woman in the sixties and seventies.*

For every number dialed Christa jotted down notes in her cherry shaped notepad. After first calling the phone numbers associated with the old addresses that had Valentina's grandfather listed many decades ago, Christa learned all these homes had been demolished and new homes built with new owners. But when real people answered from the list of possible former neighbors of these residences Christa started to see a whole different story starting to form. While none who answered would remember anyone named Rosemarie or Mary, several did remember a young woman with several children. At first most people seemed fearful to speak to Christa, as if there was some secret they all knew about. One such phone call was with an Italian woman whose said her father was 90 years old and that he lived in that same house since 1950. After telling the reason for calling, the father only spoke Italian and his daughter translated. "Please, they are gone and we have peace now." Christa inquired further by asking who left. The man didn't want to say. The daughter thanked us for calling and wished Christa luck.

Another phone number dialed found an elderly woman answering. She explained that a young couple lived next door to her for a few weeks one year back in the late fifties. The woman who matched Rosemarie's physical description never spoke a word and had a black eye so black that she would never forget it. She recalled many babies and young children in the small home playing in the small grassy area out front a few afternoons. She said the man clearly spoke German and after a week the family disappeared. The elderly woman always wondered what had happened to that woman.

Another neighbor sent Christa a text message a few days after hearing her message about Rosemarie on her answering machine and offered to do a Facetime call with Christa and Vera. At an arranged time a young woman close to Christa's age called and appeared live on video on Christa's phone. She explained that there were always stories from her late parents about the people who lived next door since she was either not alive yet or too young to remember anything significant herself.

With fear in her voice Christa and Vera could tell the woman wanted to help them understand that maybe Aunt Rosemarie was mixed in with something bad or some bad people at one point. "Mom said there was a young man who was there that was always in rage. Probably drinking or drugs or something. Lots of not nice looking people coming and going from the house all the time for years. And another man who talked to himself often on the front porch. I have no idea if your sister Rosemarie was there. I do know they had a German coat of arms and the German flag displayed inside the house. You could clearly see it through the front house window. It was there forever. Before the house was demolished, an elderly woman was the last person we all saw living there. She was alone and nobody else had come for a long time. Then one day she was gone, the house was gone. That was that."

Three weeks later the DNA results were posted for Vera's cousin in Germany. *Finally, one step closer: one relative on the family tree with a known amount of DNA*, Christa thought.

But one DNA sample was not enough and more DNA from known relatives was needed to make a one hundred percent determination about the unknown DNA match's relationship to Vera. Christa reached out to more known cousins on both Hilde and Günter's side of the family and asked if she could mail them DNA kits. Vera and Christa anxiously awaited the results of these tests to be posted, which typically involved two to six weeks processing time.

47

A student researcher at McGill University in Montreal caught wind of Christa's monumental task and reached out to ask how she could be of assistance. Every weekend she would travel to various archives in and around Montreal and snap and send photos of records she found that looked like they could have been related to Christa's search for Rosemarie including headstones of other missing girls, ship and flight manifests and various school yearbooks. Christa thanked her and told her how helpful it was to have the records put aside so she could review them.

That research student had friends in television and passed along Rosemarie's story. CBC News did a TV story on Rosemarie as well as a national news radio broadcast. An article about Rosemarie appeared on the front page of the Montreal Gazette and Le Journal de Montréal. Several online websites covered the story as well. For the first time Christa truly felt as if the whole world was looking for Rosemarie.

Several months into the renewed search for Rosemarie, Christa and her mother were at the kitchen sink doing the dishes when Christa said, "You know what's funny, Mama?

Your parents spent years going door to door and wandering up and down the streets of Montreal looking for their daughter. And now, seven decades later, we turned it into a global mission with the help of the internet and DNA testing. Just think, someone in China could get a DNA test and be the key to finding Rosemarie."

Vera put down the dishtowel she'd been using to dry plates and leaned against the counter. "I can't even imagine that. I've never given up hope of finding Rosemarie or at least finding out what happened to her. But it seems so surreal now."

A skilled forensic artist in Miami Florida volunteered to created a realistic age progression of her missing aunt to see what she might look like today. Another artist in Poland recreated a realistic portrait of what Rosemarie looked like when she first disappeared. Christa used these art files to quickly create a flier in Photoshop.

"You know what else seems surreal?" Christa didn't wait for her mother to answer. "The fact that now I'm calling and emailing businesses all around Canada and asking them to hang up Rosemarie's flier. And the idea that Rosemarie might *actually* be alive and actually see it!"

Christa and Vera were getting emails with hundreds of leads after the various TV, radio and newspaper articles came out. The leads all pointed Christa in the direction of a few specific neighborhoods in Toronto, many of the same exact places Valentina's grandparents lived in for decades according to the old phone directories. Christa then compiled a list of local businesses in that area and contacted each of them asking for help. If they would place a flier inside their business or taped to the window, maybe Rosemarie or someone who knew her would see the flier and get in touch.

Surprisingly several messages came in from people

who recognized the present-day rendition of Rosemarie and wanted to offer their assistance.

One message: *Hi Vera. I met a lady in Toronto in the late 90s. She went by the name of Helga and claimed to be from Stuttgart. She lived in my apartment building. Give me a few days and I am going to find my old address and message you back.*

And another message: *Christa and Vera, a German lady who looks like your sister has been walking around our neighborhood in Toronto for years. I'll track her down and find out more about her!*

The messages kept coming in, and Christa and Vera started to get excited. Every lead was like a lottery ticket that gave them hope of winning the prize of Vera seeing Rosemarie after 68 years. Vera broke down in tears. "If I saw her, I would tell her we never stopped looking. That we never stopped loving you." Christa held her mom and they cried together.

Christa and Vera kept up their diligence researching DNA matches and eventually another cousin popped up on Ancestry.com. The close DNA match had her full name listed as Kels Hansen, and her profile showed that she lived in Las Vegas. Like with all the other leads, Christa messaged the person on Ancestry.com and hoped for a reply.

A few weeks had gone by and with no response Christa grew curious and eager to place this person and their DNA data on the family tree.

Christa thought quietly to herself. *We just have to figure out a few more DNA matches and we will finally have enough living people on our family tree with a known amount of DNA to my mom. And then finally, finally we can use the DNA Painter tools and finally we can figure out who Valentina and the other unknown DNA match is.*

With a quick search on the internet Christa found

Kels' phone number right away. She mustered up some courage to cold call this woman and explain her story so as not to sound like a typical scammer. *Ring, ring.* A woman answered right away. Christa explained "Hi! May I speak to Kels Hansen please?" The woman confirmed that she was indeed Kel and asked who was calling. "Well Kel, this is going to sound a bit bizarre but I am a long lost relative of yours. I found you on Ancestry.com" Christa paused to laugh a little. Kels laughed along, and explained that it wasn't bizarre at all and the reason why she'd joined Ancestry was because she found out that she had been adopted by a fifties Hollywood movie star and according to her adoption paperwork, she was the biological grandchild of Vera's paternal uncle from her father's side of the family. Both Kels and Christa were thrilled to talk and swap stories. After the conversation, she ran downstairs to fill her mom in on the conversation with Kels. Christa was feeling proud.

A few weeks later Christa logged into the various DNA websites and noticed results were posted for one of Hilde's daughters and grandsons who agreed to help Christa and Vera by sending their DNA to Ancestry.com. She rushed to get her mom so they could see the results.

Christa excitedly opened the DNA Painter website and navigated to their *What Are The Odds* tool. This is a tool that many professional genealogists and investigative genetic genealogists recommended to Christa and Vera on the DNA Facebook groups. They were told that with enough DNA samples and a complete family tree, one can use this tool determine where in a family tree an unknown DNA match could possibly fit. Christa uploaded the family tree they had created and plugged-in all the amounts of DNA every known living relative on the tree shared with Vera. With a deep breath, she hit the submit button.

Within seconds, the tool provided relationship

probabilities for each potential spot for Valentina on the family tree. The probabilities are calculated based on family tree information entered, along with the amount of shared DNA that the match shares with people in the tree. The probability that the DNA match was Rosemarie's grandchild turned to 100%. The other unknown DNA match would turn to be 100% Rosemarie's great grandson according to this tool. Christa's heart was racing and she could not believe what her eyes were reading. She didn't know what to think. *Rosemarie? Children? Grandchildren? Great grandchildren?*

"What, what does it say? What is it telling us?" Vera asked innocently.

"It says Valentina is Rosemarie's granddaughter. That Valentina's dad is Rosemarie's son. I know Valentina said that her grandmother Mary and her mom met one time…the one with the brown eyes. Well this 'Mary' must be Rosemarie and somehow just doesn't remember her blue eyes."

Vera was in awe at what Christa was saying. "Wow, okay so Valentina is my grandniece… how do we find Rosemarie with this information though? That's who I really want to see, of course."

"Of course! Let me email the Montreal Police Department again and see what they say. Maybe they will help us now by running a driver's license search for Rosemarie or her son, Valentina's father! I feel like we are so close!"

Christa enthusiastically prepared a 50 page document detailing all her findings: a family tree full of almost a thousand deceased and living relatives; along with the 100% determination on Valentina's relationship to Vera via the DNA Painter tool; as well as all the tips and leads from social media and fliers; and interviews with dozens of Rosemarie's possible former neighbors; and profiles of all the relevant DNA matches. She presented all her findings by email to the assigned detective from the Montreal Police Department. Christa received an email from the woman detective shortly after stating she was going on vacation for eight weeks for the rest of summer and that she would read and reply to Christa's email upon her return.

Frustrated, Christa felt like giving up. "What do we do now?" she asked Ali one night over dinner. "If we can't find Rosemarie with nine hundred new relatives and a bazillion leads, is there really any hope?"

Christa thought about it for a moment. "We have gotten a lot of tips out of Toronto."

Ali put down his napkin and stared into his wife's green eyes. "I'm sorry, what?" His eyes got big. "Have you ever cared when someone told you no?"

Christa smiled with her husband's teasing. "Ha ha. But seriously. Where do we go from here?"

"Let's look at it from a practical standpoint. So you haven't gotten anywhere with the Montreal police. Valentina lives in Toronto. Why not start with the Toronto PD. Maybe they can help."

"I suppose it can't hurt."

Christa emailed the Toronto Police Missing Persons department with her findings and within an hour Detective Constable Mike Kelly emailed Christa back and said that he personally would be handling the case from then on, and that they'd opened a missing persons case in Toronto on Rosemarie. He explained that normally Montreal would still be the lead agency but because the detective in Montreal had been all but unresponsive that now he would be her lead contact.

Three days after Christa made contact with Detective Constable Kelly over email, he called her before she'd even brushed her teeth that morning.

"Christa," he said, "sorry to call so early. But this is DC Mike Kelly with the Toronto Police Services and I have an update to share with you and your mom. Do you have some free time now?"

She put down the toothpaste. "Oh hi. Good morning DC Mike Kelly! Yes of course. Let me get my mother real quick and put you on speakerphone. I'm sure she will want to say hello and hear whatever you have to say." Christa called for her mom to come join from the other room.

He paused and waited for a moment. "Yes she will. But it's a lot. Before we start I have to warn you that some of the information I have might be upsetting."

"I appreciate the warning," Vera said joining the conversation. "But nothing could be worse than wondering what happened to my sister for the last sixty-something years. And by the way, it is so nice to meet you Detective Kelly. Well, at least meet you over the phone. Thank you for helping us."

They'd been so focused for so long on trying to

find Rosemarie, that Christa had never stopped to consider the consequences. Did she let the genie out of the bottle? What would they find out about Rosemarie? What if someone had kidnapped and killed her immediately and she'd been gone almost seventy years? Christa had remembered reading a novel about a woman who'd spent half her life looking for her twin sister's killer. In the end, she'd thought the woman would have been happier if she'd never found the killer. It'd never occurred to Christa that finding Rosemarie would bring anything but joy.

Mike held his breath for a moment. "OK, are you ladies ready?"

"I guess I'm ready. What did you find out?" Christa felt like she was holding her breath diving into the depths of the ocean.

Vera echoed her daughter's words. "Yes, please we're as ready as we'll ever be."

"I'm just going to say it."

"You're scaring us." Christa and Vera took the phone into the kitchen and sat at the wooden farm table. "But go ahead."

"We found and spoke to one of Rosemarie's sons. We called and asked him to come into the office, and he did."

Christa and Vera couldn't believe what DC Kelly was saying. She couldn't make sense of it. She heard his words, but they sounded like background noise. A strange buzzing. "What do you mean? This is crazy. She really has a child? Is there more than one?"

"Yes. And had. Unfortunately, she passed away a handful of years ago."

Christa thought about that character from the book she'd read. Now she knew how that girl must have felt when she figured out that her sister hadn't been murdered at all. That she had ended her own life. After sixty-eight years, Christa had done the near impossible. She had spent years, literally years worth of time to find Rosemarie only to discover she was dead.

"Christa? Vera? Are you still there?" Mike's voice was soft.

"We are."

"Do you need a minute? I know this is a lot."

"No. No. I'm okay. I just can't believe this." Her head felt wavy. "Did I hear you say you actually *spoke* to her son? That he came into your office? What did he say?"

Mike cleared his throat. "It was a long conversation. Again, you're going to find a lot of this hard to hear, but I think it would be helpful to just listen for now and I'm going to tell you everything he said."

Mike continued. "At first he was in shock and disbelief when I placed Rosemarie's photo from sixty eight years ago on my desk in front of him. He instantly recognized his mother. He broke down in tears and said his mama didn't deserve to always be black and blue. That he and his brothers didn't deserve to always live in fear, to have horrible things happen to them. He recalled the time his father broke his arm when he tried to buy food for his mom and brothers. Anything other than booze or drugs was considered an unacceptable purchase. And they lived much of his childhood and teenage years with little to no food, with rags for clothing most of the time, and nothing but a mattress on the floor for personal effects. His father had what he referred to as a 'bone chilling' psychopathic laugh. On whim he'd hold a gun to his head and threaten to blow his brains out of his skull. To his mom's head. His brother's heads. And a lifelong infatuation with William Tell kept his father carving wooden arrows in his free time: for sport he would make them all sit in a line so he could use his bow and freshly sharpened arrows to shoot apples off their heads."

Mike stopped to take a breath. "Ladies, are you still with me?"

Christa and Vera couldn't believe what they were hearing. "Yes, we are here. Please, continue."

"Eventually his sadness about his childhood turned to anger and he talked about how he knew his father was a monster, but this was a whole new level of hate and disgust for him to steal his mom from her family. He said he didn't go see his father when he was dying a few years ago, and that his 'devil' dad somehow managed to outlive his 'angel' mom by more than a decade. That his dad never left her alone in peace. It was obvious he didn't like his father much. And I'm going to tell you ladies, while I cannot disclose details of anyone's criminal history, what I can tell you is that Lucifer, the man Rosemarie had children with was a very bad man. And Rosemarie's children, most are not the types I'd assume you'd want to be in touch with. Most of them appear to have followed in their father's footsteps over the years. I can point you to a few publicly available resources that will paint the picture of Rosemarie's life with her family if you like."

Christa and Vera were in disbelief. "Wow, just wow, ok." Christa said. "But wait! Did you ask him if she ever talked about my mom? Or her parents? Her brother and oldest sister? Didn't she ever talk about them? Or where she came from. She must have mentioned her little Birkenfeld village!"

The detective continued as Vera and Christa continued to carefully listen to every word. "Yes. I asked these questions. He said his mom always said she was from Hamburg, and that her parents and whole family were blown up in a potato field towards the end of the war, and that she was the last remaining family member. She said she grew up playing the flute in an area of Germany with a crematorium, and that because of this her whole childhood smelled like death. In 1954 she said an American bomber plane brought her and other young women over to Toronto where she ended up meeting their father at a local German social club. He never heard her mention Montreal ever."

"Toronto? Young women. She was barely 14 in 1954!" Christa exclaimed.

"Ladies, I am sorry to say that I'm sure all this wasn't what you expected to hear. But most missing persons cases never have any answers. You are one of the very few lucky ones to at least have some answers. I hope it provides some understanding. I wish I could tell you more, but it's all I have to share for now."

Vera was trying to understand everything she heard. "I'm grateful for all of this man's time and information but I feel like the more I hear the more I'm starting to believe that Rosemarie would only make up such stories because she wanted to keep me and our family safe from this psychopathic sounding man and her children all these years. Did this son of hers have anything else to say? And can we have his phone number if we ever want to call and talk to him ourselves?" Vera asked.

DC Kelly chuckled lightly. "Well, funny you mention that. I actually have a statement from him and his family. He emailed it to me late last night."

"A statement? Like a press release?" Christa was intrigued by the detective's choice of words.

"Sort of. When I asked him if he would like your contact information, or if he would like me to share his, he was reluctant and said he didn't have anything else to say. And he told me to tell you that he is sorry for all the pain his family was responsible for."

Christa felt a weight on her chest. "What? Why? We've been waiting so long for this moment. Doesn't he have photos or any other stories or information he can share with us?"

"Why don't you just let me read the statement?"

"Sure. Go ahead." She took a breath. "We're ready."

"Okay. This is what her son emailed and asked me to tell you and the rest of your family. 'We knew Rosemarie by a different name. Regardless, she lived a full life and has long since passed. She was married and had children, grandchildren and great grandchildren. But we wish to maintain our privacy. We thank every volunteer and detective who spent their time, energy and money trying to locate our beloved family member.'"

Christa felt heat rush to her cheeks. "Privacy? What the hell? My mother's sister disappeared when she was fourteen years old from a good family and safe neighborhood. And now we find out that she had a whole other life, a whole other identity that had nothing to do with us and we're supposed to just let it go? What is going on here?"

Mike waited for her to finish. "I hear your frustration and I am just as confused as you. But since she is dead and her family doesn't want to speak anymore with me, you, your mom, or the Toronto Police, there's not a lot more I can do for you as far as connecting you with her children."

"But . . . but we have so many more questions."

"I'm sure you do. But you do have *some* answers. You know she didn't meet a terrible fate. She got married. She had kids. She lived a good long life."

"Yes. You're right, ok." Christa took a deep breath. "I feel like we need to absorb this all. Just sit with this for a little while."

"I'm sorry Vera…Christa. I know how upsetting this is, but I thought you'd want to know as soon as possible. I'm digging around to see what else I can find out about Rosemarie and still waiting for a few people to return my phone calls and emails."

"We cannot thank you enough for everything you've done for us," Christa said and then hung up. She knew she shouldn't be mad at Mike. Without him, they never would have found her aunt. But she was just so frustrated. How could they have gotten so close and still have no real answers?

Vera put her hand on her daughter's shoulder. It took Vera a moment to be able to speak. "Honestly, I didn't want to ask too many questions. I think I was too shocked. I mean, we did it. We finally found her. I know it's not the outcome we were all hoping for. The big reunion. But now we know she didn't meet some terrible fate right after she disappeared. Maybe she had some happy times. Perhaps we can call Mike back in the morning?"

"Of course, Mama. Anything you want. But take heart in knowing you did it. You finally found your sister."

49

Christa spent most of the day making a list of questions she wanted to ask DC Kelly. She knew he wouldn't be able to answer all of them. But perhaps she now had enough information to piece together exactly what had happened to her aunt almost three quarters of a century before.

She waited until eight o'clock the next morning to call him. He picked up on the first ring and sounded happy to hear from her. "I'm so glad you called. I have another update for you and your mom. But go ahead," he said. "You go first. I know you must have a list of questions a mile long. I don't know how helpful I'll be, but I'll tell you everything I know."

"Thank you, Mike. I appreciate your willingness to help. If it's okay with you, I'm going to put you on speakerphone again so my mom and I can both hear."

"Perfect. Hello Vera. How are you this morning?"

"I think I'm still in a state of shock. But I'm good. I cannot thank you enough for all your help these past few days and weeks."

"Truly. It's my pleasure."

Christa looked at her mother who nodded. "I guess the most important thing we want to know is what happened to her in 1954? She never would have run away."

"I agree with you. But that is something I cannot tell you because I don't know, and I'm not sure it's something any of us will ever know. But I got the distinct feeling Rosemarie did not have the happiest life with her first husband and children."

Vera's breath caught in her throat. "Oh my poor sweet sister. She didn't deserve that."

"Do you know if she was married to that bastard until she died?" Christa was quick to ask another question.

"The short answer is no. Let's me catch you up. I did some digging and found her marriage certificates. The name she used was Anna Mary Rose Fluss."

"Wait. Marriage certificates as in more than one? And what name did you say? Did I hear you correctly? Did you say *Anna Mary Rose?*" asked Vera.

"Yes and yes. You sound like you've heard that name before. Is that name significant?" asked Mike.

Christa could tell from the way the color had drained from her mother's face that the name meant something to her. "Mama? What is it?"

When Vera spoke her voice was barely more than a whisper. "When we were children in Birkenfeld, one summer a neighbor girl disappeared. Everyone was up in arms. Nobody knew what to think. Some were sure that the gypsies had taken her."

"Mama! Why didn't you ever tell me that?"

"It hardly seemed relevant after all this time. I feel like Rosemarie was sending a message using that name. She was taken."

Christa tried to puzzle out the connection. "This is terrible. That poor girl and her family. But what does it have to do specifically with Aunt Rosemarie?"

Vera's voice got quiet. "The name of that girl was *Anna Mary Rose Fluss*. What are the odds Rosemarie would change her name to that same exact name? It's a name I'll never forget."

"Oh my god." Christa felt faint. "She *was* sending you a message. She was abducted. Don't you agree, Mike?"

Everyone was quiet for a few moments. "Wow." Even his voice sounded different somehow, heavier. "While that doesn't change anything, it certainly continues to make me think she didn't run away on her own."

"So now what? What do we do now?" Vera asked.

Mike flipped a few pages. "Well, is there anything else specific you want to know?"

"So many things," Christa said. "Who took her? Why didn't she try to escape? Why did she change her name? Was it really a message to us telling us that she had been stolen like the girl from Birkenfeld? If she was in Canada the whole time, why didn't she ever go home?" She stopped for a moment and fought back sudden tears. "Did she miss her parents and her siblings?"

Mike whistled long and low. "Those are all good questions. And I wish I had those answers for you. Alas I do not. But I do have an update I mentioned earlier that might help answer some of those questions. I have been searching various records and in doing so I located a record from Ontario's official record of land property showing that Rosemarie and her second husband Albert were co-owners of a piece of land in Ontario with another couple. I called and left a message for them last week and this morning my phone call was returned. The best thing I can do is put you in touch with this woman. Her name is Emma. Her husband recently passed, and they were both lifelong friends of Rosemarie and Albert. She would be more than happy to speak with both of you. I would also like to give your contact information to the one son I spoke to with your permission. That way he can reach out if he ever wants to."

"Wow, Emma! Emma is one of my favorite names.

It was my Oma's name. Yes, yes we would love to talk to Emma. And as far as Rosemarie's son, can't we just call him?" Vera asked. "There are so many things that we'd like to ask him."

"I'm afraid that he doesn't want to be contacted. But Emma, Rosemarie's friend, said it would be fine if you called her. As a matter of fact, she's anxiously awaiting your call."

Vera and Christa exchanged looks. "Well, I guess that's something, thank you for everything as always Detective Kelly. We appreciate you." Vera said.

50

An hour later, Christa and Vera found themselves on the phone with Emma Bauer, an upbeat elderly sounding woman with a light but detectable Canadian accent. After Christa introduced herself and her mother, she asked Emma to tell her everything she knew about Rosemarie.

"My goodness. It's so shocking to hear her referred to as anyone but Anna Mary." Emma chuckled. "When I first returned DC Mike Kelly's phone call this morning, I was shocked when I heard about all this. But oddly in some ways not surprised at all. But yes, I'd be happy to tell you anything you want to know. But first I have to say that I am so relieved to hear that's she wasn't who she told me she was."

This took Christa aback. "Really? Why's that?"

"It's just that . . . she never seemed happy. And when I pressed her to reach out to her family for help with the kids back in the day, she would never look me in the eye. She would never say a word. Nothing."

"What do you mean? Like she was lying?"

"She just always seemed to be holding something back. I mean, if I had had six boys one after the other, I would have been begging my parents and siblings, if I had any, for help."

"What did you just say?" Vera asked. "She had six kids?"

"That's right. She must have been close to 30 years old when she had had her last child in the late fifties. But she never had anyone to help her. Nobody. Not that I expected her husband to change dirty diapers. And mind you that was a time when we all still used cloth diapers. But with six young boys, well that's too much work for one person. Trust me, I worked at a nursery school for decades. A combination of six rowdy toddlers and crying needy babies is not a job for one woman."

Vera couldn't make sense of Rosemarie's age according to Emma and started subtracting years in her mind. "Well, the late fifties would place my sister at age 19. She was only born at the end of 1940. And Emma, did I hear right? Are you saying that I have *six* nieces and nephews I never even knew existed? Six?"

"Well I thought your sister was born in 1933, the same year as my husband, because we would often joke about how she never aged like the rest of us! She drank from the fountain of youth! Wrinkle free forever is what we would say! So ah ha! I knew it! She wasn't as old as she said she was! And yes, you heard correct. Six nephews. Well, five nephews really. It's my understanding that she gave her first son up for adoption or something since she and Lucifer weren't married yet. She didn't speak much of this first child. And I never wanted to press her. I can't imagine giving up a child for adoption and never seeing the child again. But it was illegal in Ontario in the fifties to have a baby out of wedlock. And now that I know she was still a child under 16 years old, I understand why even more. In those years an unmarried girl of that age would be considered a child having a baby with a grown adult man, and that was highly illegal. Lucifer could have gone to jail for that one too. And I am also pretty sure all of Anna

Mary's children had children themselves, although I have personally only met a few of them. So I think you have at least a handful or so of new relatives. There were a few summers we had the grandchildren camping with us on our lakefront property just southeast of here. We tried to get them to take them with us to Germany to visit my husband's family and visit Hamburg to see where she lived as a young woman, but she insisted on never leaving Canada. That was okay with us because we loved camping together. There was so much land and privacy there for us to eat, talk and play. We bought the property together with our husbands in the early eighties and loved planning our annual summer camping trip together all year long. And even when Anna Mary and Albert moved across the country, they would still road trip back here every summer to visit with us without hesitation. Our husbands loved to fish together. Anna Mary and I loved to chit chat about the latest books we read, or crochet by the campfire together. We loved taking a boat around the lake to keep cool in the warm summers. Even with her pigeon toe limp she still always went hiking and biking with the rest of us. We never missed a summer camping trip together for almost 25 years, can you believe that? I have some great memories."

"Oh my goodness, she never limped or was pigeon toed when I knew her." Vera felt a buzzing in her ears. She was trying to imagine what Rosemarie must have endured in order to have had acquired a lifelong pigeon toed limp.

"Emma, thank you for sharing all of this. As you can imagine it hasn't been easy to hear any of this but I am so thankful that you've been so open and willing to talk to us. I never imagined this day ever. Do you know where her other sons are or how we can get in touch with them?" Vera continued.

"I'm just going to say it because you've already been through so much." Emma's voice started to sound more nervous. Vera's stomach sank, but she stayed quiet. "Trust me when I tell you that you don't want to know any of her sons or their families. They're not the types of people you want to know."

Vera could not imagine that her sister would have ever chosen an unkind husband or reared terrible children. "I . . . I don't understand what you're saying. Do you know anything about her first husband? Is he still alive?"

Emma sighed through the phone. "No. He's long since dead and the world is a better place for his absence. He never left her alone. Even years after the divorce he would track her down and find her and torture her with fear. There was one summer evening when he drove down the long driveway at Anna Mary and Albert's house with his old pickup truck that sounded like the engine was in desperate need of repair. You could hear it coming from a mile away. My husband and I happened to be there for dinner that night. He pulled right on up next to the house and he came to the door shouting for Anna Mary, knocking wildly on the door. She jumped up like a flash of lightening and asked for us to remain quiet in the kitchen. Of course we wanted to hear what was going on so remained still while we listened intently. My husband and I looked at one another and thought of an emergency exit plan in our minds. Turns out that he just wanted to stash all his guns with Anna Mary while he was in prison again. You could hear a tone of fear in her voice while she talked him down from an angry rage but she remained calm the entire time. It seemed like it was an often occurrence. I don't know, maybe he was drunk. As for her sons, well, there's a story there too. In the seventies, Lucifer told Anna Mary that their sons were old enough to take care of themselves and that he no longer needed her since the 'child allowance' given by the Canadian government came to an end when the boys all reached a certain age. He divorced her and left her with no money, no job and no place to go. The crazy part is that her youngest son was actually not old enough to take care of himself. But he was so dead set on not living with his crazy father that he opted to go into the foster care system. Honestly all of those boys never stood a chance. Anna Mary did the best she could to raise them with what she had, I know she did."

Christa saw that her mother was having a hard time speaking. "So, what happened to her kids after she left and the one was taken away from her? You said they were . . . not nice children. In what way?"

"Do you really want to know?" Emma asked. "None of it is good or happy news."

Christa looked at her mother who nodded with her consent. "We've come this far. The detective kind of alluded to this on the phone earlier but we really don't know too much of anything at all really. So anything that you're willing to share, we just want to know as much as we can about what Rosemarie's life was like from the time she disappeared until she died."

"Okay. Here it goes." Emma paused for a moment. "Three of Anna Mary . . . You know what, if it's okay with you, I'm just going to call her Rosemarie from now on. I feel like she deserves to be spoken of with a name that's associated with her first, loving family."

"You're very kind." Vera's voice was barely more than a whisper. "Please continue."

"Of course. Three of Rosemarie's boys ended up in prison."

"Prison?" Christa could not believe what she was hearing. Every member of her extended family was so kind. "For what?"

"Murder…weapons and heroin distribution… prostitution. It's my understanding that some of the sons have been diagnosed with serious mental conditions from a young age on."

While Christa herself was very happy to finally have some answers for her mother, she was devastated to learn that her aunt must have led a very unhappy life.

"Oh my gosh. This is all too much. It's like a movie."

"A horror movie really. It's almost like it might have been better for her to have met her fate in the Laurentian Mountains 68 years ago." Vera said. Christa expected her mother to fall apart hearing about her lost sister's terrible circumstances. But her voice sounded strong. "Is there anything else you can tell us?"

"Only that I always knew she was hiding her truth."

"What do you mean?" Christa obviously had never met her aunt. But from everything she'd heard about her she couldn't imagine that she'd been a dishonest person.

"She said her family died in Germany. She told the same story over and over about them getting blown up in a potato field when anyone asked about her childhood or family."

"Then how did she explain how she wound up in Canada? Did she ever talk about that?" Christa wished she had been taking notes the whole time Emma had been talking.

"Yes. She said something about an American bomber plane taking her to Toronto from Germany in the fifties sometime. It was an odd tale indeed but she was steadfast in her story that she had no family left, and that she was all alone in this world. As close as we got, and I know I was her best friend, she never wavered from her story."

"Why? If she trusted you, why wouldn't she tell you the truth?"

Emma pondered Vera's question for a moment. "I think that awful man she was first married to must have threatened her. Looking back with retrospect, I suspect he probably told her that if she ever tried to escape or tell anyone about the abuse that he would hurt her family. So she decided from the very beginning that she would never let him find out who she really was and that she had a family."

Christa held back a sob. "That is so sad but that's what we've been thinking too. It's crazy to think that maybe *I* wouldn't be here right now if she had told Lucifer the truth."

Vera squeezed her daughter's hand. "Emma, is there anything else you can share with us?"

"Would you like me to tell you about when I first met your sister?" Emma asked.

Christa quickly replied. "Of course, yes, thank you."

Emma took a deep breath and continued. "Well, it must have been in the late fifties sometime. My husband Manfred and I worked at a Lutheran church off of Bloor in downtown Toronto. He worked as the church custodian and I took care of the babies and young children in the nursery school behind the church. I can still imagine that day when I first met her sad blue eyes, pregnant with a child in each arm. She looked like a child herself. She came limping into church service one Sunday, all of them in tattered ill-fitting clothes."

Christa interrupted Emma for a moment. "Was Rosemarie religious?"

"No, actually no, not religious at all. And to be honest, neither were my husband or me. We had a primarily German congregation, so knowing what I know now perhaps she also found a bit of comfort hearing people speak the language of her familiar motherland. Anyhow, after the potluck luncheon after service that Sunday she noticed me looking at her while she tried to be discreet placing a few dinner rolls and whole fruits in her ripped coat pockets. I approached her and introduced myself, and with a broken smile, she nodded. That was it. She then shrugged and pointed at herself and said 'Lithuania.' Her children always looked sweet but fearful and didn't dare speak a word ever. Every Sunday we would simply nod and smile to one another. Many Sundays would go by when we didn't see her at all. It was then that my husband and I worried most. Every so often I would give her a small bag of secondhand clothing I managed to cobble up from other women in the congregation. And while she never spoke a word, I could tell she was thankful. I know my husband also had difficultly learning English for many years as he was an emigrant from Germany. I was always understanding of new people coming to our country and having to learn a whole new language. And one year Rosemarie managed to get a job working at a little coffee cart stationed on the corner by the church, despite her minimal English speaking skills. Over the years she would walk by the church and nursery school on the way to the coffee cart with sunglasses on. Her eyes were often swollen and black and blue. My husband and I spoke with the Toronto Police privately every so often to see how we could help this woman. She was moving around the area from place to place quite often, and it always seemed that nothing we did helped her. In fact it seemed to make her black and blue marks get bigger, so we stopped. And honestly ladies, it took a long time before she ever spoke a word to me again. I didn't even know her name for years and years. I can remember the day she told me her name as if it were yesterday. We have been friends for a long time and I think of her often."

Vera squeezed her daughter's hand. "Incredible. Thank you for telling us all this. And thank you for being there for her."

"Your sister was a strong woman. She always had a

lot to deal with. And I tried really hard to never interact with her family. As the boys grew up, the newest one was worse than the one before. I don't think you should try to find Rosemarie's sons. She really did do the right thing by shielding her real family from them."

"Thank you," Christa and Vera said at the same time. Then Christa said, "Is there anything else you can tell us?"

"Oh yes. Last thing. I hope you take some comfort in knowing that Rosemarie did have a happy ending. Well, as happy an ending as one could expect her to have. After Lucifer took her sons and divorced her, she bounced around for several years doing odd jobs. She was an exceptional seamstress and provided quite nicely for herself. Then, in the late-seventies she met, Albert, the love of her life. He was a kind man from Germany. He worked as a house painter and together they also ran a small bed and breakfast in their traditional Bavarian style home where strangers from afar would come share their life stories with them."

Once again, Christa and Vera were stunned. "My god," Christa said. "Is her second husband still alive? Can we have his phone number? Or does he have any living relatives who she might have told about her past? So much of what you've told us makes perfect sense and so much doesn't. There must be someone who knows more than we do."

Emma considered this for a moment. "Albert was a young widower when he met Rosemarie and his daughters and their families were still in Germany."

"Albert was good to my sister?" Vera wiped tears from her face.

"Very. He loved her more than anything. He used to say that he was twice blessed because he found such a strong love again after his first wife died. I promise you that he gave your sister a wonderful twenty four years."

"They got married in 1984 and stayed together until he died in 2008, the year before her. Honestly, I always thought that after Albert died, she gave up. The lung cancer took her very quickly and I always thought she just wanted to end this earthly life so she could be with her second husband again."

"Lung cancer? Was she a smoker?" Christa asked.

"No, she never smoked or drank ever. And not Albert either. Lucifer though, he smoked like a chimney. If you would give me a little time, I'd like to ask my grandson to bring down some boxes of old photos and memorabilia from my attic when he visits this weekend. I can't get up on a ladder anymore after my hip replacement surgery last month. I'm hoping I will find some photos of Rosemarie and when I do, I would love to share those with you. Ladies, I'm hoping we can all talk again soon."

Christa and Vera talked with Emma for another few minutes and ended the phone call by exchanging addresses and promising to stay in touch.

51

Christa sat with her mother each morning for the next week reviewing on repeat everything they'd learned from Emma and the detective's communication with Rosemarie's son over hot cups of their favorite Dragon Jasmine Pearl tea. There was immense sadness, anxiety and fear that filled their minds and weakened their bodies with all the information they learned. It felt like letting this genie out of the bottle would take months to process. And that a whole new form of grieving the loss of Rosemarie had begun.

Finally she suggested lunch. "You must be hungry. You need to eat. What can I make you?"

Vera touched her stomach. "Honestly, I am so much at a loss for words these days that I'm not sure I'll ever be really hungry again."

As Christa entered the kitchen to make grilled vegetable paninis, she thought it was probably nearing dinner time. But to her shock, the microwave clock said it was just after eleven in the morning. She grabbed two yogurts and put a frozen casserole in the oven instead, and joined her mother once again on the couch. She offered the mixed berry one to her mom, but she held up her hand to refuse it.

Christa opened hers and licked the lid. She glanced

at her phone and noticed a text message from an unknown phone number. "Wow just wow. Mama. You'll never believe this. Rosemarie's first husband's younger brother is still alive and is willing to talk to us. Apparently he got one of our letters in the mail! You know, the letters I sent to all the addresses we found in the old Toronto phone directories? How cool is that? So what do we do now? Do we just dive right in and call him now? His name is Stefan. And his brother, what was his name? Oh yeah… that's right, Satan."

Vera smiled. "Lucifer. Doesn't it seem like a self-fulfilling prophecy when you name one of your sons after the devil?"

"There's no accounting for taste," Christa muttered. "Anyhow, as they say when it rains it pours. It's just so . . ."

"Much?"

"In a word, yes."

"Let's make a quick list of questions for Stefan in case he is willing to talk to us." Christa opened the catch-all drawer in the kitchen and got out a pen and notebook to start jotting down a few questions.

After a few minutes, they sat with Christa's cell phone on the table between them. "Are you ready, Mama? This man could have all the answers we've been looking for."

"As I'll ever be." Vera pulled on a handkerchief she always kept in her pants pocket. "Let's do it."

Christa willed her hands to not shake as she pressed a few buttons to call the number. When he answered she quickly introduced herself, alerted him to the fact that he was on speakerphone with her mother and began explaining a tale that had spanned sixty-eight years. Christa talked so quickly and for so long that when she was done, she wasn't even sure if Stefan was still on the line. "Hello? Stefan? Are you still there?"

"I am." He had a trace of a German accent. "I'm just trying to process this all. You say . . . what did you call her?"

"Rosemarie." Christa's voice was shaky.

"You say Rosemarie disappeared from her home as a child?"

Now Vera spoke. "Yes. It was November of 1954. She was supposed to go to the bakery next door to buy bread and she never returned home. As a matter of fact, the bakery lady said she never made it there."

"Well," Stefan seemed at a loss for words. "That is not the story my brother told us. Lucifer said he saved Anna Mary."

"Saved? Impossible!" Vera shouted. "She didn't need saving. She had a wonderful home and a big family who loved her very much."

"Vera and Christa, you need to understand one thing, my brother was bat shit crazy." Christa could hear Stefan's voice rise as he spoke. "He said she was a runaway prostitute and he saved her from that depraved lifestyle."

Vera had never heard such blasphemy in her life. "Rosemarie was a child! Nearly a baby. She'd never even kissed a boy. Your brother must have stole her right off the sidewalk and did terrible things to her. That's why she never came home again. He must have threatened her."

"Look," he finally said. "I'm not sure I have answers to all your questions. But I'll tell you everything I can remember about Lucifer and Anna Mary or Rosemarie or whatever she was called. Just so you know Lucifer and I didn't have a happy childhood. Our father was very abusive toward us and our mother. So perhaps some of what you think may be true. I wish I could tell you everything you want to know. Lucifer divorced An—Rosemarie in the seventies and I have no idea what happened to her after that. And to be honest I was a youngster and Lucifer was a grown man living his own life out of the house already when he first met your sister."

Christa felt herself soften toward this man. Perhaps he was as much a victim of circumstance as Rosemarie was. "Thank you. That's very kind. Please continue."

"Is there anything in particular you want to know? Anything specific I should begin with?"

Christa and Vera exchanged looks. "Just start at the beginning, I guess," said Christa. "Your brother's real name was actually Lucifer? And when was your brother born?"

"Yup, Lucifer the devil himself. Let's see. Lucifer was 9 years older than me, so he was born in 1931 and told us Rosemarie was about his same age. Although she always looked awfully young to me. More like my age."

"That's because my sister was born in 1940, not 1931. She'd turned just fourteen years old just days before she was taken from us. Fourteen!"

"Oh . . . I am so sorry. I had no idea. Do you want me to continue?"

"Yes, please." Christa squeezed her mother's hand. "Sorry, we will try not to interrupt you again."

Stefan cleared his throat. "My family was from Danzig, but we had to leave everything we had at the very beginning of World War Two. We ended up at a resettlement camp in the Baden-Württemberg region of Germany." Vera's eyes got wide. *Her stolen sister's husband's family was from an area very close to Birkenfeld?* "It was a bad situation. We resented living in this part of Germany and we were never accepted by the German Swabian people. I think it really changed all of us. We didn't want to be there and they didn't want us there. Nasty people."

"Finally, we were able to escape that dreaded place and my family and I emigrated to Toronto in 1952. I always hoped it would get better. You know, a new country. New people. New everything. But all that didn't matter when both Lucifer and my father were never well. It was never easy living with those two. I'm thankful I had my mom around."

"In what way?" Christa asked.

"Lucifer wasn't right in the head. He heard voices and those voices telling him what to do weren't kind to the rest of us. Same with my dad. He heard voices too and thought the Nazis were listening in on us . . . all the time. He thought they were listening on our phones, through the walls, everywhere. Anytime he went off on one of his rants, we were all scared for our lives. It got so bad that my mother carried a brick in her purse and used it defend herself any time she needed to. He even threatened to beat up my nephews when they visited, and my mom was always the one to stop him. Which was all the time. Oddly, they both had good jobs. They both worked as patient attendants at the psychiatric hospital. It was just a few blocks down the street from us. But, come to think of it. I don't think the hospital was a very reputable place. At the time I overheard stories from my parents about patients getting tortured and being subjected to shock therapy on a regular basis. Turns out it was all true. I read an article recently about this place and I don't know how my parents were capable of working there for so many years. It must have been torture to listen to people getting tortured."

Vera had heard enough about this man's early life. She didn't want to feel sorry for him or his brother. "That's a lot," she said, not unkindly. "What can you tell me about Rosemarie and Lucifer's time together? Did she act like a captive? Did she ever seem happy? Did you ever meet her children?"

"Make no mistake. Her children are all bat shit crazy too, just like my brother." His voice was matter of fact. "Truth be told, Rosemarie led a miserable life. That poor woman even had to give birth alone at home five times.

Five times. She had no family or anyone here in Canada to help her. And my brother wanted her off the radar. No schools for the kids for a long while. It took a lot of convincing from me and my wife to get those boys in school. And certainly never hospitals for child birthing. One time I happened to be stopping by their apartment to drop off some food my wife prepared for Rosemarie and her starving children when another baby came out from this woman. Anyhow, I can tell you that for certain that experience made me never want to even be in the labor and delivery room with my own wife for the birth of my two kids. Nope. And I don't know if you know this, but Canada gives every family a child allowance for each child they have. Lucifer loved this concept. I remember when he mentioned it one winter night to me and our parents over dinner. Why work when you can just have a baby making machine provide a steady paycheck to keep the booze flowing for years, right? I am guessing Rosemarie was his baby making machine and guaranteed paycheck for years. But Rosemarie was never allowed to use any of that money for food or clothing. Oh no. Clearly. She always looked like a total rag. Same with those nephews of mine. My brother drank away every penny he earned or was given by the government. Lucifer always loved the bottle more than his family. And it was worse after his accident at the canning factory in '62. I think the constant pain from that injury got to him. Every time I did go to one of their apartments, there was no furniture, no beds, just a pile of guns and a mattress or two on the floor. And there was never any food. Nothing. I very rarely visited their home because it was too disheartening. It seemed like they moved every few weeks anyway, my guess is to escape debt collectors, drug dealers or bad people with guns. Lots of guns. Lucifer had a huge collection of guns of all kinds. I was never a gun guy personally myself. But. After a while my wife and I stopped trying to keep track of them."

Christa felt as if Stefan was reluctant to tell her more. She had to find out as much information as she could before he ended the call. "Okay, what about when he met Rosemarie . . . regardless of what she was doing at that time. What was *he* doing? We're just trying to piece together how they ever crossed paths. She never would have associated with someone like you're describing."

"Oh, I honestly have no idea the real story on how they met. I never believed she was a prostitute. She didn't wear makeup, she waddled like a duck. She seemed like a country bumpkin in crocheted garb that didn't speak a lick of English. Actually that woman never really said much at all ever. All I know is that she certainly didn't fit the stereotypical provocative prostitute profile as far as looks or attitude, but I must admit that I've actually never seen or known a real prostitute. Just seem 'em in the movies." Stefan's voice sounded lighter. "But you mentioned that Rosemarie lived in Montreal. Well Lucifer loved Montreal. If it wasn't for the added hassle of needing to learn French just after learning English, I think he would have moved there permanently. He was an on and off again seasonal cab driver in Montreal after we first moved to Toronto in 1952. For the first few years we were here, he would rent a room up there for a few months each year. Apparently heaps of money could be made up there, at least in late November and December. You know, for the winter holiday season. I'm sure he pissed every dime away on guns and booze. If you like I can send you at least one photo of your sister. Lucifer loved to take photos of everyone in front of his cabbie car. He kept a whole album of them. I know exactly where it is. It would be shocking if she didn't have one in his album too. I can take a look later today and send to your email address if you have one."

Vera shivered. "A cab driver? In Montreal? Really?

Are you sure?"

"Am I sure? Yeah of course I'm sure. And he was a super crazy driver too. He was always crashing his car. Nobody smart would get in a car with that man. It's possible most driving laws were inspired by Lucifer."

Vera could barely speak and suddenly wanted to get off the phone. "Stefan," Christa said. "I think we have to go now. If we have more questions, would it be okay if we save your number? Would that be okay?"

Stefan paused for a moment. "I suppose so. I'm sorry if I upset either of you. That was never my intent. The fact of the matter is that Lucifer was not a good person. And I'm sorry that all of this happened to Rosemarie, to you, and your whole family all because of my brother. And yes, of course, feel free to call back any time if I can help you in any way."

Christa pressed the end call button on her phone and led her mother to the couch. "Stay here, Mama. Let me get you some water." Vera nodded but didn't speak. Christa returned a moment later with a full glass of ice cold water and handed it to her mother. She took a few sips and then put in on the glass coffee table in front of them. "Mama. Are you okay?"

"I want to see a picture of this Lucifer. There was always a long line of taxis lined up outside our building. Some of the drivers wore turbans, some never looked up from their newspapers and some smiled and waved. But there were a few of them who used to watch us, I mean really watch us, every day as we walked home from school. I told my parents and the police about them after Rosemarie disappeared, but I guess nothing ever came of it."

"Do you think you'd actually remember this man's face if you saw him in a photo? A man you might have seen almost 70 years ago? Are you sure, Mama? There must have been so many taxi drivers back then. And it was so long ago." Christa wasn't exactly sure why, but she felt like she needed to assure her mother that she hadn't seen Rosemarie's abductor ever in her life.

"I appreciate you trying to convince me otherwise, but I have no doubt Lucifer was the same man who used to watch us cross the street every day on our way home from school." She took off her glasses and wiped away tears. "I should have insisted that the police question all the taxi drivers. I should have made them understand. We could have found her. We could have rescued her and brought her home." Vera started sobbing and Christa jumped up to comfort her mother. "All these years. Everything we've done has been for nothing. None of it matters. I had the chance to find my sister seventy years ago and I failed!"

Christa waited to speak until her mother's breathing evened and slowed. "Mama, listen to me. You were a child. Not even a teenager. You did everything you could to help the police. Maybe it wasn't even Lucifer who took her. But if it was God only knows what that monster told Rosemarie or did to her to keep her quiet. Who's to say what he would have done to you if he'd suspected you of knowing he had kidnapped her. She was gone the moment he took her. But look. You never stopped looking for her. You brought her and us and our entire family closure. You found out what happened to her. You did that. She would be so grateful to you. And you should be so proud of yourself." Christa rubbed her mother's back as she began to cry again.

52

Days went by and Christa and Vera didn't talk much about their phone call with Stefan. There was so much more Christa wanted to know. So many details either Stefan had left out or didn't know. But she knew not to push her mother. She would talk about it when she was ready. Christa just really wanted to know if this was the end of it. Was their search for Rosemarie finally over? Did her mom get all the answers she was looking for? Would life feel different now? Would her mother appear lighter? Freer? Christa could only wait until she was ready to talk.

Finally, more than a week later, Vera came to Christa while she was reading on the couch after collecting the day's mail. "My Reader's Digest magazine is here and I'm going to read it right now with my cold glass of lemonade. It says on the cover that laughter is the best medicine and I could not agree more. Mooooove over. There's some mail for you too." She giggled as she sat beside her daughter and handed an envelope to her. "Here you go."

"Who's selling me what today?" Christa chuckled along with her mom. "Wait. Put that lemonade down. It's from ServiceOntario in Toronto. It's…."

Vera smacked her lips and made a sour face as she

took a quick sip of lemonade before putting it on a purple and green coaster she crocheted just the day before. "Tell me."

"Know what, Mama? Can you go and get one of Rosemarie's prayer books? Like now…"

"Sure, of course. It's in her red purse. And I know exactly where that is. Let me get it." Vera got up and went to her bedroom. She returned shortly after and opened the red purse to retrieve the book inside.

"Oh great," Christa said when Vera sat back on the couch. "May I see it for a moment?" Vera handed it to her daughter and Christa opened it to the first page where Rosemarie had signed it sometime in April of 1954, sixty eight years ago at her confirmation in Birkenfeld.

Christa then opened the envelope and pulled out a few pieces of folded papers, carefully examining them. She looked from the book to the paper and back again. Her breath caught in her throat and she wavered for a moment. "Look at this." She tapped the prayer book. "Look at Rosemarie's name in the book. And look here, first marriage certificate. Second marriage certificate. They're different names, but the same handwriting. Right? It is the same, isn't it?"

They took their time looking at each marriage certificate. They studied the curve of each letter, the lilt of the R*s* and the roundness of each *e*.

"And incredible. Do you see what I see? Your parents' names are both here. Your mom's true full maiden name, Hilda Ruhl, and your dad's name, Oskar. Oskar Fluss, to match her newly invented surname. She knew who she was. She changed her name to protect you. She knew Döderlein was too easy to look up in Montreal. She wanted to be found, without anyone finding and hurting you and your family."

"It was her." Vera's voice was quiet. "She signed

416

the prayer book and the marriage certificates. We found her. We really found her."

"No." Christa covered her mother's hand with hers. "You found her. You did it. You brought her back to our family."

Epilogue

It'd rained all night and into the early morning. Christa woke up worrying that Emma's plane would be delayed because of the weather. She told herself not to worry about things she couldn't control and got up to make a pot of coffee. It was summer after all and the days always eventually warmed and dried up any overnight rainfall. But she heard the machine percolating before she got out of her bedroom and knew that her mother was already awake.

"This weather," Christa said, reaching into the cupboard for a mug. "I can't believe it's going to rain on us today."

Vera smiled slyly. "It won't. We'll be fine."

Christa loved her mother's confidence. She'd always been a force. "How can you know that?"

"What time is it?"

Christa checked her watch. "Almost nine."

"And when did it start raining?"

Christa remembered waking up just before dawn to get a glass of water. It was raining so hard that she thought Ali or one of her kids was in the shower. "My guess would be sometime around five this morning."

"My mother always said, 'rain before seven, gone by eleven.' Emma doesn't land for almost three more hours. We'll be fine."

"If you say so. Are you sure we have enough food? I can run down to the market and grab some of those little frozen quiches and more desserts or something if you think we need it."

"We have enough food to feed three armies. It's

one woman and our family. We'll be fine."

Christa poured herself a cup of coffee and topped off her mother's. "Okay Mama. I have a surprise for you. Close your eyes."

"I love surprises. Okay hurry hurry." Vera squinted her eyes while making squealing noises for fun.

Christa ran to the living room and returned back to the kitchen with her hands behind her back. "Surprise! Open your eyes!" She took out a small roll of fabric and handed it to Vera. She unrolled the fabric to reveal a pair of Black Watch Tartan patterned pants.

Vera took the pants and held them up in front of her. "These are just beautiful, I just love them. Let me try them on right now." Vera rushed into her bedroom to change.

When Vera came back Christa smiled at her mom. "Those look simply marvelous on you!"

Vera pranced around like a model getting photographed for an upscale clothing catalog. "Thank you so much. Come on, let's finish getting the food ready. Emma will be here soon and I want everything to look perfect."

A handful of hours later the table was set with a large buffet displaying bowls and plates of fruits, legumes, veggies, dips, nuts, cheeses, and various salads and sandwiches. A beautiful black forest cake sat atop a beautiful crystal cake stand featuring several layers of chocolate sponge cake sandwiched with whipped cream and cherries and decorated with even more whipped cream, maraschino cherries, and chocolate shavings. A tea pot was covered by an exquisitely embroidered tea cozy hand made by Hilda almost a century before and filled the air with the scent of steaming chamomile tea. It sat on an old wood cutting board covered with a doily Hilde made as a child, along with several crystal tea cups and a small wooden sugar bowl carved and painted by Günter in the Birkenfeld shop so many years ago. A beautiful bouquet made from a hodgepodge of garden flowers and clippings that Vera prepared the day before sat right in the center of the table. The scene reminded Christa of a photo of her Oma in the 1930s when she would entertain her family and friends at their home in Birkenfeld. She kept thinking how proud her grandmother would be of her. This was a day Christa planned as a way to honor her mother, her late aunts, uncle, and grandparents. A day to symbolize visions and dreams materialized. Everything they endured, everything they worked so hard for: they truly succeeded.

"I told you it'd be clear by eleven." The sound of Vera's voice startled Christa.

"I should have known better than to doubt you. You're never wrong." Christa giggled.

Just then the doorbell rang. "Well, what do you know, we have another visitor. I'll go to the door."

"I'm so glad you made it….so glad." Vera held out her hand to help Emma with a bag under her arm. She was a tall skinny and spunky elderly woman with the brightest white tennis sneakers, large thick black rimmed glasses, and a blindingly bright neon pink track suit.

"Nothing is easy when you're as old as me. But I'm here! What a beautiful home you have!" Emma smiled and came further into the hallway.

"Christa, guess who's here!" Vera called out.

Christa turned down the music box and wiped her hands as she rushed towards the hallway.

"Oh my gosh, so good to see you. How was your flight from Toronto? Come in. Come in."

Emma freed her hands. All three hugged.

"I'm so delighted to be here ladies! I brought so much to show you and more stories to share with you all."

Christa put her towel away. "Emma, you timed your arrival just perfectly. The sun woke up a little while ago and warmed everything up for us. Let me introduce you to my husband and children outside." Looking at her mom, she added "Mama can you bring the teapot to the table outside and turn the music up a little again so we can actually hear it outside?"

"Okay. Sounds like a plan! I'm hungry. Hopefully Emma is also hungry. We have so much food!"

"Come Emma." Christa helped Emma happily deposit her small suitcase and bag next to the staircase and led her outside.

The older children supervised the younger ones in the little children's splash pool on the lawn while Christa and Ali gave Emma a tour of the fruit trees in the backyard garden. Vera announced that the lunch buffet table was now open and ready for anyone who was hungry. She sat down on a chair at the table, soaking up the warmth of the sun. She then cracked open a few of her favorite walnuts and rubbed the soft outer shells between her fingers before fetching the nutmeat inside. She closed her eyes for a moment and listened to her grandchildren giggling and laughing. The beautiful piano music playing in the background reminded her of her father's brilliant piano playing. The sound of walnuts cracking reminded her of the warm summer days in Birkenfeld when she and Rosemarie joyously sent halved walnut shell "boats" downstream on the bubbling Enz. And as she took a sip of chamomile tea, she felt her mother's trusty flower starting to heal her from within. All of this started to make Vera smile.

After a few minutes, Emma, Ali and Christa returned back to the lunch table where Vera sat. The grandchildren dried off and joined a few minutes later.

"I have a few photos I was able to find and I'd like for you to have them. Oh and a book. She loved reading, and this is the last one she read." Emma said as she pulled out a faded and run-down copy of The Hobbit along with a large envelope that had some old smelling photos starting to fall out. A photo of Rosemarie camping at her lakefront property, one of her and her kids at church service one afternoon, a photo on a Christmas card, and some other candid photos of Rosemarie were placed on the table. Christa and Vera could instantly see Rosemarie's baby face and her famous "apple cheeks" in adult form on all the photos. For the first time, without a doubt, they knew Anna Mary Rose Fluss was in fact Rosemarie Helga Döderlein.

Just then Emma pulled a big box out from behind her chair and placed it on the table in front of here. "Here Vera I also brought this for you." She placed her hand on the box. "In Rosemarie's last days with hospice I was with her every moment. She had this next to her bed the whole time. She insisted that I take it with me when she passed."

"Emma, I have been wondering one thing. Did she ever mention that she had brothers or sisters?" Vera asked curiously.

"Vera, Vera. No, sorry, she never spoke of any of her family beyond telling us that she has none. There was one other time she did mention your parents…in her final hours. She was on morphine for pain and I know that this often makes people say random things. They are hallucinating with such heavy doses. She kept saying that she could hear her mama and papa calling for her outside, and how cold she was, and how she wasn't able to answer back to them. It was certainly unusual, I didn't think much of it. The same types of odd words came out of my husband's mouth when he passed away of colon cancer almost 20 years ago now. He talked about how the holy cow was in the room with us right before he took his last breath. It was a surreal experience for me."

As Emma placed her hand on the box, she took a

sip from her delicate tea cup. "You should know that Rosemarie loved chamomile tea just like you! She always served it to me and my husband when we came to visit and any and all guests in her bed and breakfast. I feel like I am sitting with my old friend Rosemarie right now." Emma said as she smiled and took another sip of tea. And this potato salad that you ladies made is simply delicious. And it is prepared exactly the same way Rosemarie prepared hers. Every camping trip we had a tradition of roasting our hot dog frankfurters and enjoying them along with Rosemarie's famous German potato salad. You know, most people use mayonnaise and not vinegar. Oh, but not you Fraus! I know I may be skinny but I can eat more than men twice my size!" Emma's lips smacked as she reached across the table to help herself to more potato salad.

Emma then handed the box she brought to Vera. Carefully Vera unstuck the tape keeping the flap of the box closed and opened it to have a closer look. It was a beautiful framed art piece with a cross stitch embroidered piece of a bride and groom standing arm in arm in its center. She assumed it was Rosemarie's work and it pleased Vera to see that the fine embroidery skills their mother taught her back in Birkenfeld had carried over into her adult years. The craftsmanship was impeccable. It also had words from an old wedding tradition embroidered on it as well. "Something Old, Something New, Something Borrowed, Something Blue," with an assortment of relics displayed next to each, seemingly a symbol of each one.

"Rosemarie was very talented in so many ways. Ladies to be honest I completely forgot I even had this. When my grandson brought it down from the attic I knew I had to find a way to get it on the plane and bring it safely to you. She loved to crochet and knit and embroider everything all the time. She even won a big contest for her embroidery work one year. She was so proud. And the placemats still sitting on my dining table were a 50th birthday gift from her to me. Talented."

The first thing Vera noticed is that "And a Sixpence in her Shoe" was the only tradition left off the framed art piece. Rather than a Sixpence, her eyes were drawn immediately to two silver 1954 Canadian quarters that were prominently featured atop the "Something Old" words.

Could it really be the quarters Mama gave her to buy bread at the bakery in 1954?

And next to it a bracelet with a single pearl was on display.

Bubble… Promise… Rosemarie's moon. Could this really be the bracelet I made for Rosemarie's 14th birthday?

A tear ran down Vera's face. Memories of locking herself in the Randall Avenue apartment bathroom to make the single pearl bracelet for Rosemarie's 14th birthday flashed through her mind. Vera recalled that before she disappeared, she told Rosemarie to remember that with the moon, there always seems to be a promise for tomorrow.

Well Rosemarie, tomorrow is today, and you're finally back here with me again. The promise of the moon held true. I promised myself I would find you one day and I did.

Vera noticed the blue neck bowtie and handkerchief next to "Something Blue" was the same one Albert was wearing in the wedding photo Emma brought. And that "Something New" had a beautiful red clutch purse with a white handkerchief partially tucked inside and designed with a dozen or so delicately embroidered chamomile flowers.

"Rosemarie absolutely loved red purses. Even when the red didn't match her outfit she always had one anyway." Emma said pointing at the red purse pinned on the artwork. "She had a huge collection of them in every shape and style. And you might have noticed the gloves hanging on there." Emma said pointing to the delicate embroidered gloves placed next to the "Something Borrowed" words on the artwork. In her last hours she apologized to me for not returning the gloves she 'borrowed' from me for her wedding to Albert. As sad as the circumstances were, we both shared one last little laugh."

Everyone continued sipping their tea and nibbled on the delicious food while passing around and admiring the photos Emma brought of Rosemarie. Christa got up from her chair and announced that she had a surprise. Just then a young man came through the patio doors and into the backyard carrying a giant cage full of birds that looked like beautiful white doves. He placed the cage on the ground in front of everyone, and then opened the door. Dozens of birds flew out one by one and peacefully circled around above them all in the air, dipping up and down gracefully with the orchestra of the wind.

Vera looked up to the beautiful clear blue sky and closed her eyes.

Welcome home, Rosemarie.

PHOTOS

Oskar Döderlein

October 9, 1905 - April 27, 1974

Soldbuch
zugleich
Personalausweis
Döderlein
Oskar
3.9.05
Oskar

Oskar
OPERNHAUS
CHARKOW
KORSAR
STADT-THEATER
CHARKOW
RIGOLETTO
MARGARETHE

Oskar

LE COLONEL BAILLOUX
CHEF DE L'ANNEXE DE LA D. G. P. G.
ALLEMAGNE ET AUTRICHE
P. O. Le Sous-Lieutenant KRETZ

ANNEXE V

1re RÉGION MILITAIRE
SERVICE DES P. G. A.
DE LA RÉGION DE PARIS

DÉPOT DE P. G. A. No 222
Fort de NOISY-LE-SEC

ATTESTATION

No 596
B

Numéro d'ordre : V

Le Commandant du dépôt des P. G. No 222

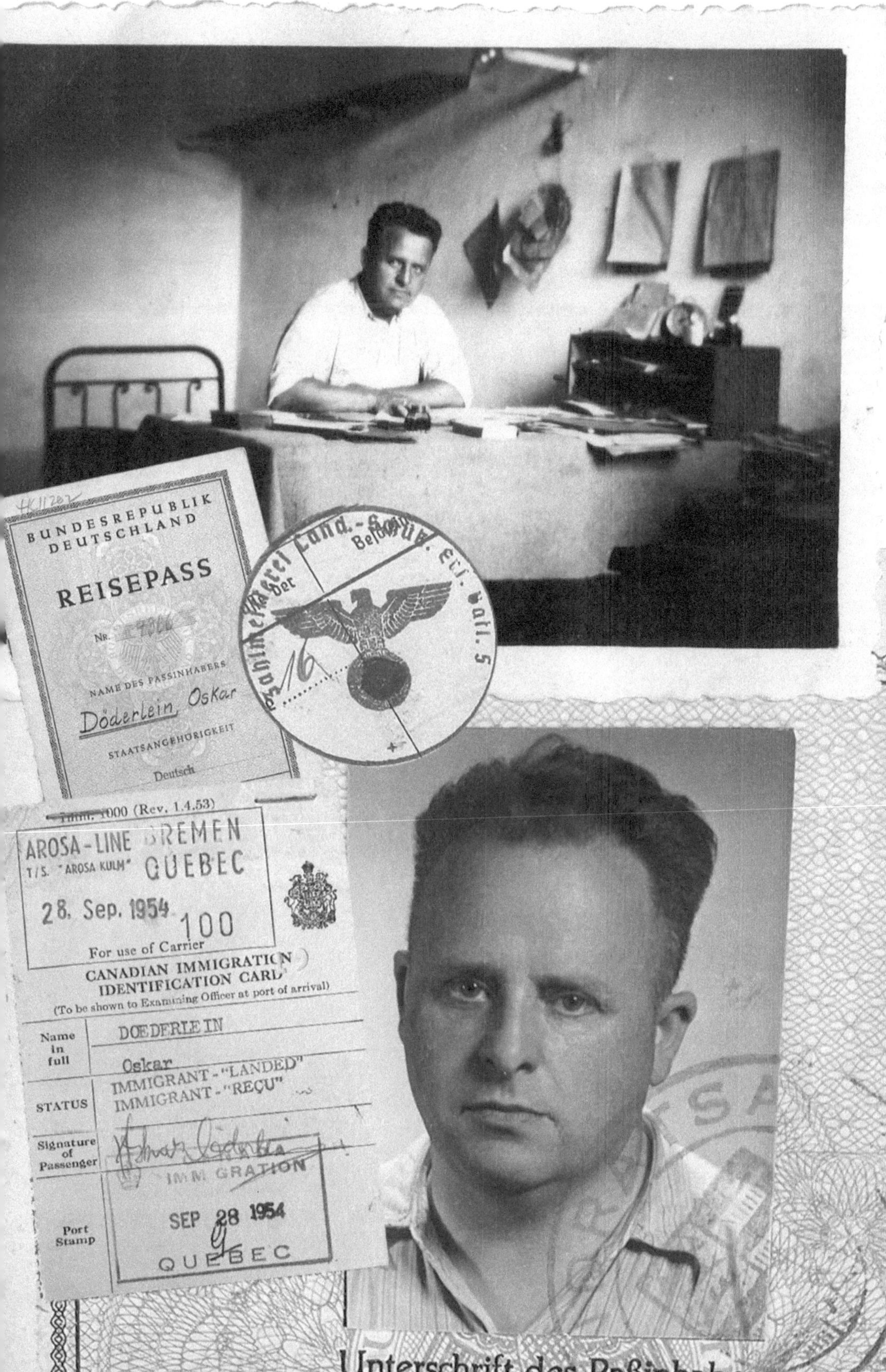
BUNDESREPUBLIK
DEUTSCHLAND
REISEPASS
Nr.
NAME DES PASSINHABERS
Döderlein, Oskar
STAATSANGEHÖRIGKEIT
Deutsch
Thm. 1000 (Rev. 1.4.53)
AROSA-LINE BREMEN QUEBEC
T/S. "AROSA KULM"
28. Sep. 1954
100
For use of Carrier
CANADIAN IMMIGRATION
IDENTIFICATION CARD
(To be shown to Examining Officer at port of arrival)
Name in full   DOEDERLEIN
Oskar
STATUS   IMMIGRANT - "LANDED"
IMMIGRANT - "REÇU"
Signature of Passenger
IMMIGRATION
Port Stamp   SEP 28 1954
QUEBEC
Unterschrift des Paßinhabers

Hilda Elsa Döderlein, nee Ruhl

October 5, 1904 - October 5, 1976

YK11202
BUNDESREPUBLIK
DEUTSCHLAND
REISEPASS
Nr. 5706130
REG.-Nr. 2044
NAME DES PASSINHABERS
Döderlein Hilda Elsa
geb. Ruhl
BEGLEITET VON SEINER EHEFRAU
UND VON 2 KINDERN
STAATSANGEHÖRIGKEIT
Ehefrau
Lichtbild
Unterschrift des Passinhabers
Hilde Döderlein
und seiner Ehefrau

4

Schatzl !

...bei ein paar Kleinigkeiten. Ich weiß nicht recht, was ich   13.1.1944
...cken soll. Das Einkaufen ist oft saudumm. Schadet aber
...Deine Wünsche werden doch erfüllt, soweit es geht.
...und das Portemonnaie haben wir von der dankbaren Stadt
...ihre Befreier bekommen mit einigen Keksen, einem
...und sonstigem Zeug. Die Geldtasche mit Ausweis-
...in Gebrauch genommen. Die Mandeln kann man doch
...auch noch verwenden. Sie waren gerade besonders
...ne Mark 100 Gramm - das geht. Da habe ich sie im
...gekauft. Die Haarspängchen und die Kämmchen wer-
...ht sein, und der Faden auch. Für Hilde ist die
...doch wohl am geschicktesten - nicht ? -

    Dein

Lebensmittelrationen für den 81. Ernährungszeitraum vom 15. 10. bis 31. 10. 1945

Lebensmittel Abschnitte	Brot Nr.	Gramm	Fleisch Nr.	g	Fett Nr.	g	Käse Nr.	g	Zucker Nr.	g	Kaffee-Ersatz Nr.	g	Nährmittel Nr.	g	Milch je Woche
E. über 18 Jahre				175		160		100	—			75		300	E-Milch
1. 15.—22. 10.	1	3400	8	100		50 auf Kl. Abschn.	29	50	—		50	75	36	300	¼ l je Tag a. Abschn.
		1400	9	75	15	110	30	50							¼ l je Tag a. Abschn.
2. 22.—31. 10.	2	1500						100	—			75			
	Kl.-Abschn. 500			250		160	29	50	—		50	75	36		
Jgd. 10—18 Jahre		5000	8	125	15	80	30	50							E-Milch
1. 15.—21. 10.	1	2000	9	125	16	80						75		300	¼ l je Tag a. Abschn.
2. 22.—31. 10.	2	3000									50	75	36	300	¼ l je Tag a. Abschn.

Tag   Tomatensuppe   ...erbraten (100 g)

Brot
Butter 20 g
Wurst 80 g
Käse 50 g

Correspondance des Prisonniers de Guerre
Kriegsgefangenenpost
Frau
Hilda Döderlein
Birkenfeld/Württ.
Kleine Höhe
Württemberg
Allemagne
Lieu de destination
Empfangsort
Rue
Strasse
Département
Land
Landkreis (Provinz usw.)
N'écrire que sur les lignes et lisiblement.
Deutlich auf die Zeilen schreiben
Den 22. Sept. 1945
Hilda-Liebste!! Liebe Kinder!
Ob Euch diese Nachricht noch erreichen
kann, weiss nur das allgewaltige Schick-
sal, das über uns Allen steht. Gerade
kam ich hier aus 12 Tagen Weinlese zu-
rück, da bekamen wir diese erste Schreibge-
legenheit geboten. Vielleicht haben Euch
auch schon frühere Nachrichten aus Le
Mans erreicht, die ich dort zwei Kame-
raden mitgab. Jedenfalls - ich lebe noch

Günter Manfred Döderlein

July 7, 1931 - December 15, 1998

Ruth Ottilie Döderlein, nee Kurowski

July 12, 1929 - March 30, 2009

6

7

Frohes Fest

Hilde Margarete Döderlein

August 4, 1933 - July 11, 1994

Hilde Döderlein

Hilda
Hilde Margarete Döderlein

Rosemarie Helga Döderlein

November 17, 1940 - August 20, 2009

Rosemarie

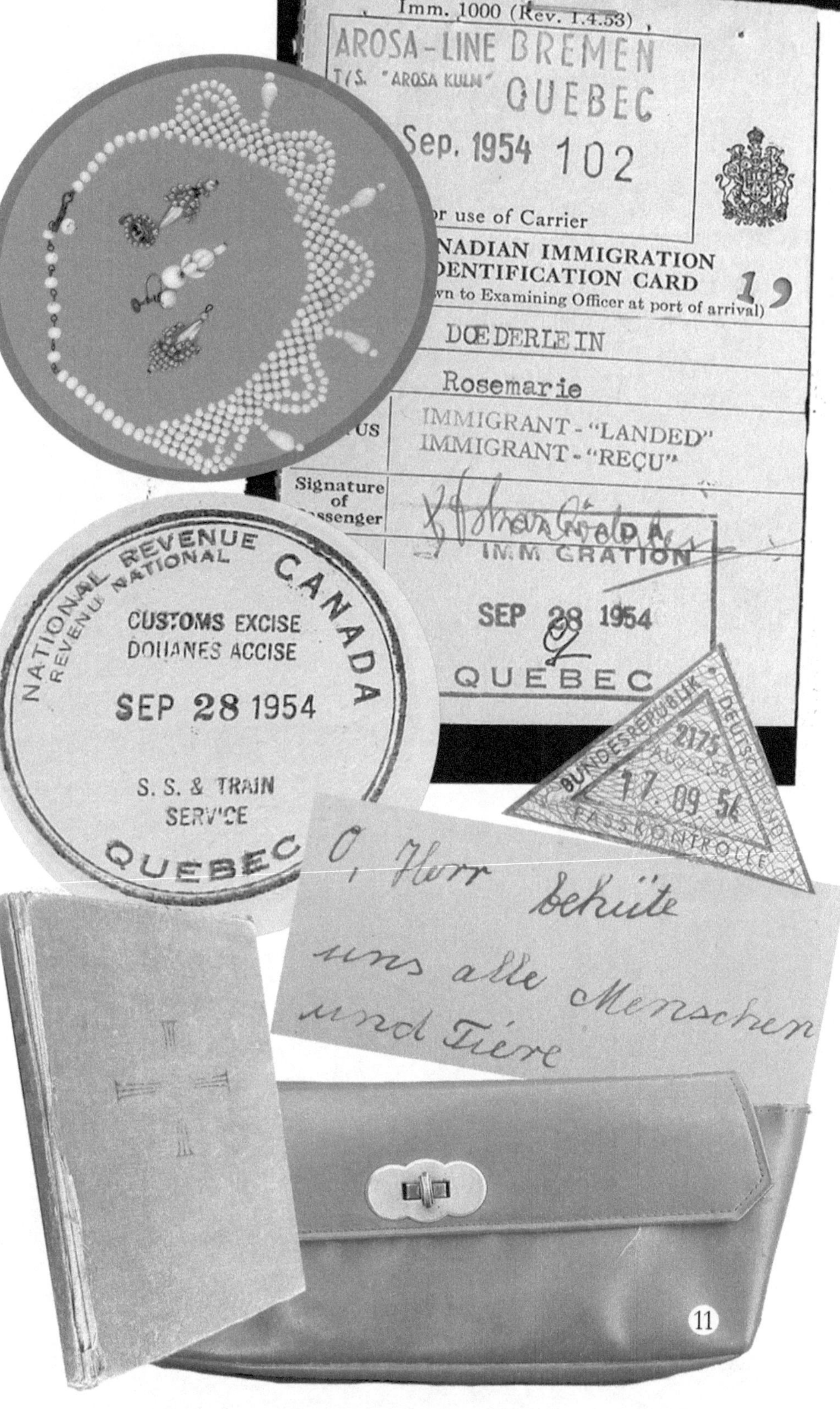
Imm. 1000 (Rev. 1.4.53)
AROSA-LINE BREMEN
T/S "AROSA KULM" QUEBEC
Sep. 1954 102
or use of Carrier
CANADIAN IMMIGRATION
IDENTIFICATION CARD
(Shown to Examining Officer at port of arrival)
DOEDERLEIN
Rosemarie
STATUS IMMIGRANT - "LANDED"
IMMIGRANT - "REÇU"
Signature of Passenger
CANADA
IMMIGRATION
SEP 28 1954
QUEBEC
NATIONAL REVENUE CANADA
REVENU NATIONAL
CUSTOMS EXCISE
DOUANES ACCISE
SEP 28 1954
S. S. & TRAIN SERVICE
QUEBEC
BUNDESREPUBLIK DEUTSCHLAND
2175
17.09.54
PASSKONTROLLE
O, Herr behüte
uns alle Menschen
und Tiere

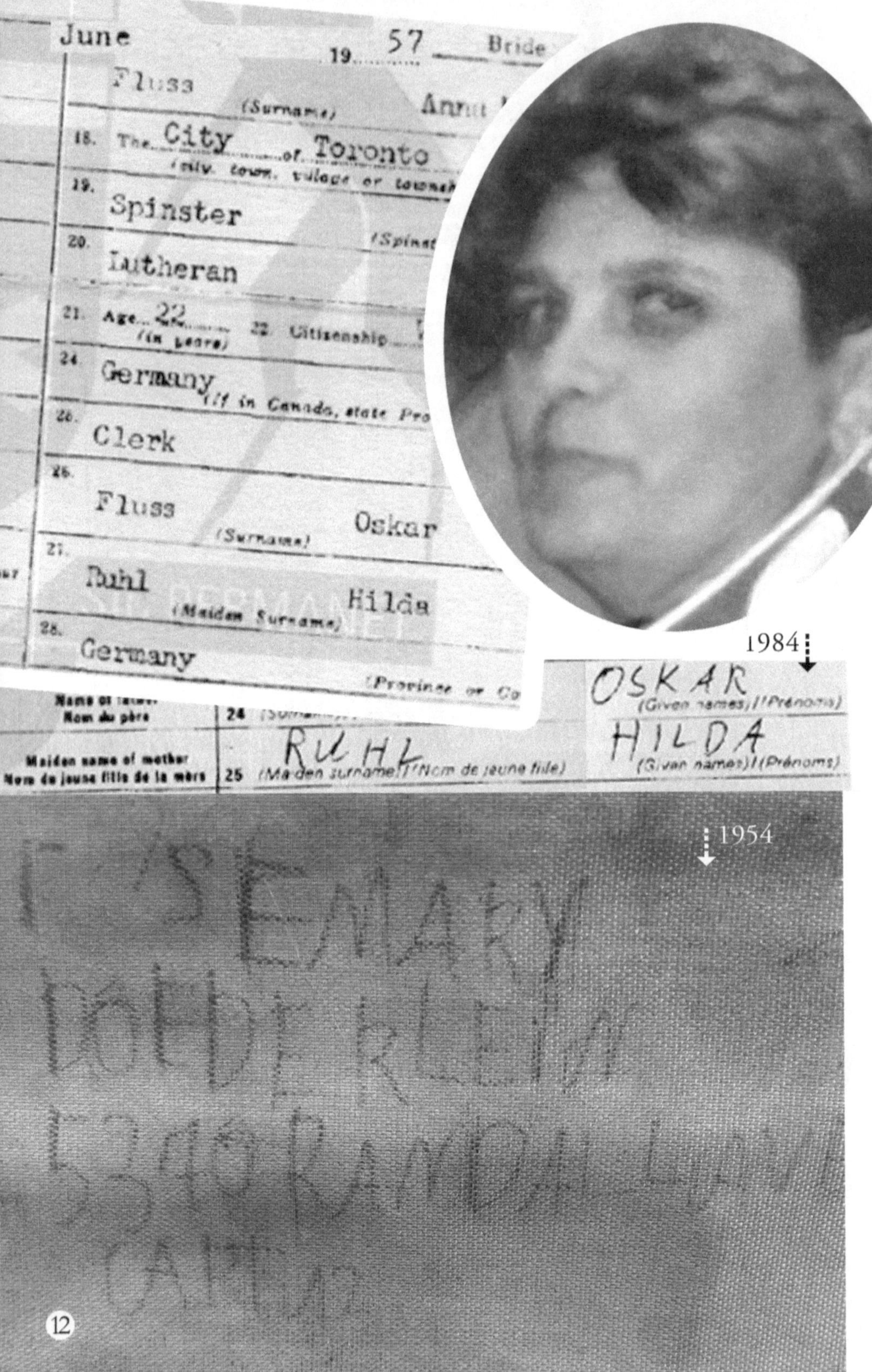

June 19 57 Bride
Fluss
(Surname) Anni
18. The City of Toronto
(city, town, village or township
19. Spinster
(Spinst
20. Lutheran
21. Age 22 22 Citizenship
(in years)
24. Germany
(If in Canada, state Pro
25. Clerk
26. Fluss Oskar
(Surname)
27. Ruhl Hilda
(Maiden Surname)
28. Germany
(Province or Co
Name of father
Nom du père 24
Maiden name of mother RUHL
Nom de jeune fille de la mère 25 (Maiden surname)/(Nom de jeune fille)
OSKAR
(Given names)/(Prénoms)
HILDA
(Given names)/(Prénoms)
1984
1954
ROSEMARY
DOEDERLEIN

13

WHATEVER HAPPENED TO ROSEMARIE?

Woman searches for her sister, who disappeared in 1954 on the way to a Montreal bakery

SUSAN SCHWARTZ

It has been nearly 68 years since Vera Hastie (née Doederlein) last saw her sister Rosemarie or heard her voice — and she says not a day goes by that she doesn't think of her.

Rosemarie Doederlein was 14 when her mother sent her to a bakery a few blocks from their Notre-Dame-de-Grâce apartment one afternoon in late 1954, mere weeks after the girls and their parents had arrived in Montreal from Germany.

She never returned.

MONTREAL GAZETTE

MONDAY, JUNE 27, 2022

COLD CASE

Anyone with information about Rosemarie Doederlein can contact Montreal police officer Linda Bonin, co-ordinator of cold cases, at 514-

WHERE IS ROSEMARIE?

Long search for a lost sister A5

News / Local News

The Gazette

The fate of Rosemarie Doederlein, who vanished in 1954, is at last known

She was 14 when she vanished from N.D.G. What has emerged is a bare-bones portrait of a woman who hid her identity and gave false information about her past.

Susan Schwartz · Montreal Gazette

Published Dec 19, 2022

14

Hypotheses Ranking

Below are the computed probabilities, listed in descending order of likelihood. A greater score indicates a higher probability of a hypothesis being accurate.

Hypothesis 3

Valentina is the child of Unknown child and grandchild of Rosemarie Döderlein

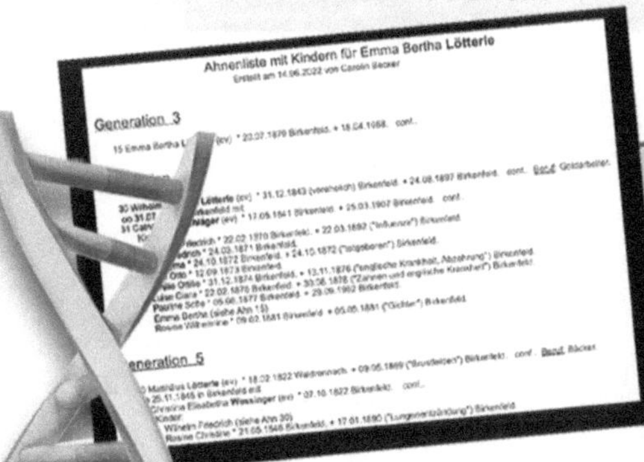

Ahnenliste mit Kindern für Emma Bertha Lötterle
Erstellt am 14.06.2022 von Carolin Becker

Generation 3

15 Emma Bertha L........ (ev) * 23.07.1879 Birkenfeld. • 18.04.1968. cont.

.... Lötterle (ev) * 31.12.1843 (verehelicht) Birkenfeld. • 24.08.1897 Birkenfeld. cont. Beruf: Gelegenheit.
Birkenfeld mit
........wager (ev) * 17.05.1841 Birkenfeld. • 25.03.1907 Birkenfeld. cont.
........redrich * 22.02.1870 Birkenfeld. • 22.03.1892 ("Influenza") Birkenfeld.
........drich * 24.03.1871 Birkenfeld.
........ma * 24.10.1872 Birkenfeld. • 24.10.1872 ("totgeboren") Birkenfeld.
.... Otto * 12.09.1873 Birkenfeld.
........ie Ottilie * 31.12.1874 Birkenfeld. • 13.11.1876 ("englische Krankheit, Abzehrung") Birkenfeld.
........uise Clara * 22.02.1876 Birkenfeld. • 30.06.1878 ("Zahnen und englische Krankheit") Birkenfeld.
Pauline Sofie * 05.06.1877 Birkenfeld. • 29.09.1962 Birkenfeld.
Emma Bertha (siehe Ahn 15)
Rosine Wilhelmine * 09.02.1881 Birkenfeld. • 05.05.1881 ("Gichter") Birkenfeld.

Generation 5

.... Matthäus Lötterle (ev) * 18.02.1822 Weihnachten. • 09.05.1869 ("Brustleiden") Birkenfeld. cont. Beruf: Bäcker.
.... 25.11.1845 in Birkenfeld mit
Christina Elisabetha Wössinger (ev) * 07.10.1822 Birkenfeld. cont.
Kinder:
Wilhelm Friedrich (siehe Ahn 30)
Rosine Christine * 21.05.1846 Birkenfeld. • 17.01.1890 ("Lungenentzündung") Birkenfeld.

25 Juli, 2022

Liebe Junta,

Ich kann es kaum glauben das 68 jahre vorbei gegangen sind seit wir uns gesehen haben im Oma's haus in Birkenfeld. Kannst du dich an mich erinnern? Ich weiss noch das du junger war als wie ich und wir haben ein paar mal Erdbeeren gegessen von Oma's garten hinter dem haus.

Ich bin verwitwet und habe zwei töchter. Die alste is Tamara and meine jüngste is Christa. Hast

EVENT ID: 09-220512-017

MISSING PERSON: ROSEMARIE DÖDERLEIN (DOEDERLEIN)

MONTREAL, QUEBEC, CANADA | MISSING BETWEEN NOV 17–DEC 24, 1954

CASE BACKGROUND

In 1954, two months after emigrating from Germany, 14 year old Rosemarie was asked by her mom to go to a bakery near their apartment at 5370 Randall Avenue in Montreal. She was never seen nor heard from again. She went missing sometime after her birthday November 17, 1954 and Christmas 1954.

Rosemarie's sister Vera Hastie, and Vera's daughter Christa Hastie, are looking for Rosemarie one last time with the help of the Montreal Police Department and thousands of volunteers from around the world.

Please see the full story and updates at: www.MissingGermanGirl.com

INVESTIGATIVE GENETIC GENEALOGY FINDINGS

My mom Vera has submitted Ancestry.com and 23andMe DNA kits, and has also uploaded her DNA to My Family Tree, My Heritage, and GEDMatch.com DNA websites. In this process, we have connected with a DNA match that we believe is Rosemarie's granddaughter. This DNA match has given us permission and access to her data on all of the above aforementioned DNA websites, to be able to compare her DNA data with my mom and other known DNA matches.

Our investigative genetic genealogy findings are as follows:

Vera Christa Döderlein

January 2, 1943 -

Am ersten Schultag
fotografiert.

Liebes Kind!
P.S. Ihr habt eine wundervolle
Mutter. Ich beneide Euch
alle so oft um sie, weil
ich so keine gehabt habe. —
Pa.

ENTERED HERE 21·10·54 MERTON ELEMENTARY | MONTREAL
FAMILY NAME
DOEDERLEIN
GIVEN NAME
VERA
VACCINATED YES
YES NO
PREVIOUS SCHOOL Germany
GRADE THERE VI
PARENT'S NAME OSCAR
PUPIL'S ADDRESS 5370 Randall #12
18
CANADA IMMIGRATION
SEP 28 1954
QUEBEC
BUNDESREPUBLIK DEUTSCHLAND
Nr. B 2719255
DÖDERLEIN
Vera Christa
REISEPASS
PASSPORT
PASSEPORT

No. 9310829
UNITED STATES OF AMERICA
NATURALIZATION
Alien Registration No. A13 719999
Date of birth January 2, 1943   sex Fem
color of hair Brown   height 5 feet 3
color of eyes Hazel
former nationality German
19

Jakob Johann Döderlein

August 24, 1873 - August 18, 1933

Zu dieser Revolution (Elsaß Jordan 1917.)

Durch Veröffentlichung Ihres kleinen Buches „Ist in Deutschland eine Revolution möglich?" haben Sie für die Franzosen ein gutes Werk getan. Es trägt dazu bei, Selbsttäuschungen von Optimisten zu zerstören, die sich, ich weiß nicht welche Hoffnungen auf eine Volksbewegung in Deutschland in den Kopf gesetzt haben. Brotkrawalle sind möglich. Eine Revolution aber kommt gar nicht in Frage. Das deutsche Volk hat weder die Fähigkeit noch den Wunsch, sich ein unabhängiges Urteil über seine Lage zu bilden und eine rasche Entscheidung zu treffen. Nach mehr als drei Kriegsjahren kaut es noch die verrückte Redensart wieder: „Wir sind zum Krieg gezwungen worden" (!).

Nein, von dieser Seite ist nichts zu erwarten. Durch Unterricht, Verwaltung, Literatur, Propaganda, durch einen schlau organisierten Betrug der Intellektuellen, durch den Terrorismus in Amt Schule, Amt und Gesellschaft ist die deutsche Seele methodisch demoralisiert, entmenschlicht und verderbt.

Das deutsche Volk hat Freude an seiner Sklaverei. Es ist stolz darauf. Seine Herren und Gebieter haben es verstanden, diesem Zustand schmeichlerische Namen zu geben. Die Livree nennt man Uniform, die Knechtschaft Organisation, den Sklavengehorsam Disziplin, den Verzicht auf Recht ... und am Charakter heldenhafte Selbstverleugnung ...

We have been forced to fight (!) "

It helps to destroy the illusions of optimists who, I don't know, have hopes of a popular movement in Germany.

The German people just want to enjoy their pianos.

20

21

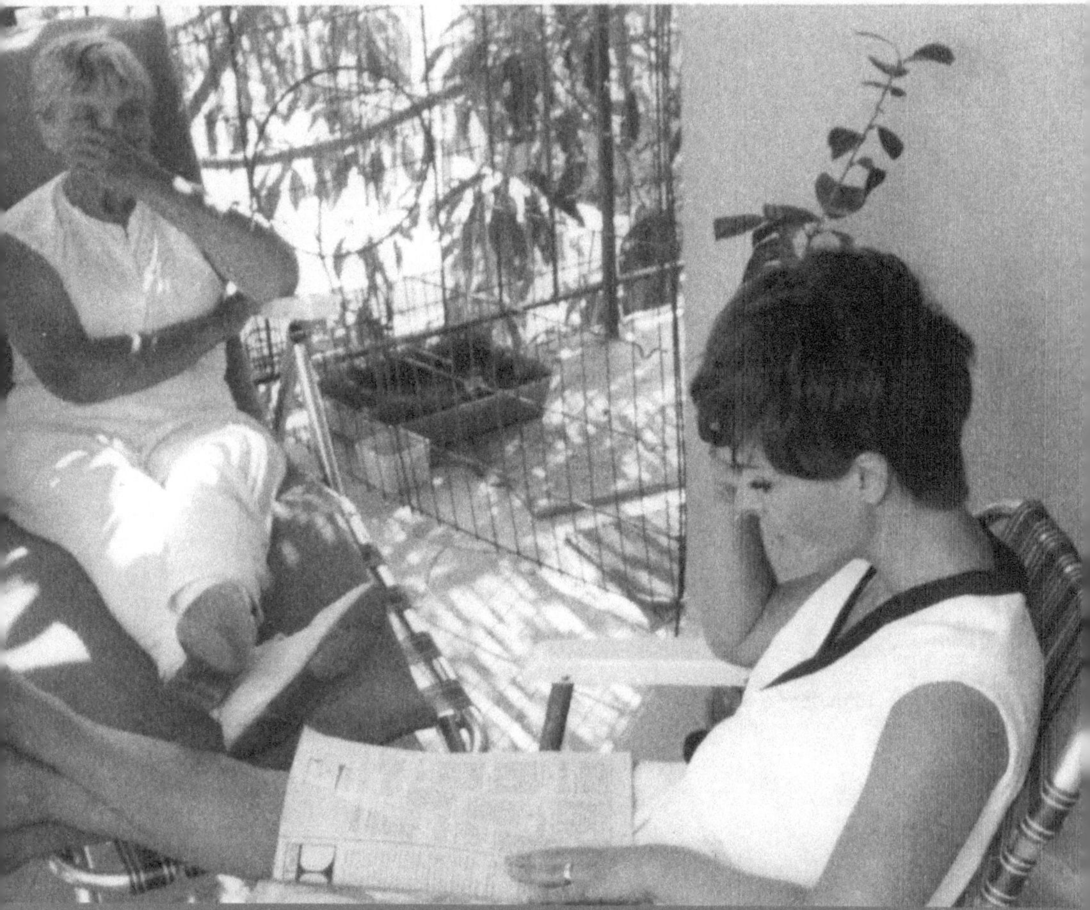

We never stopped looking for you. ♥

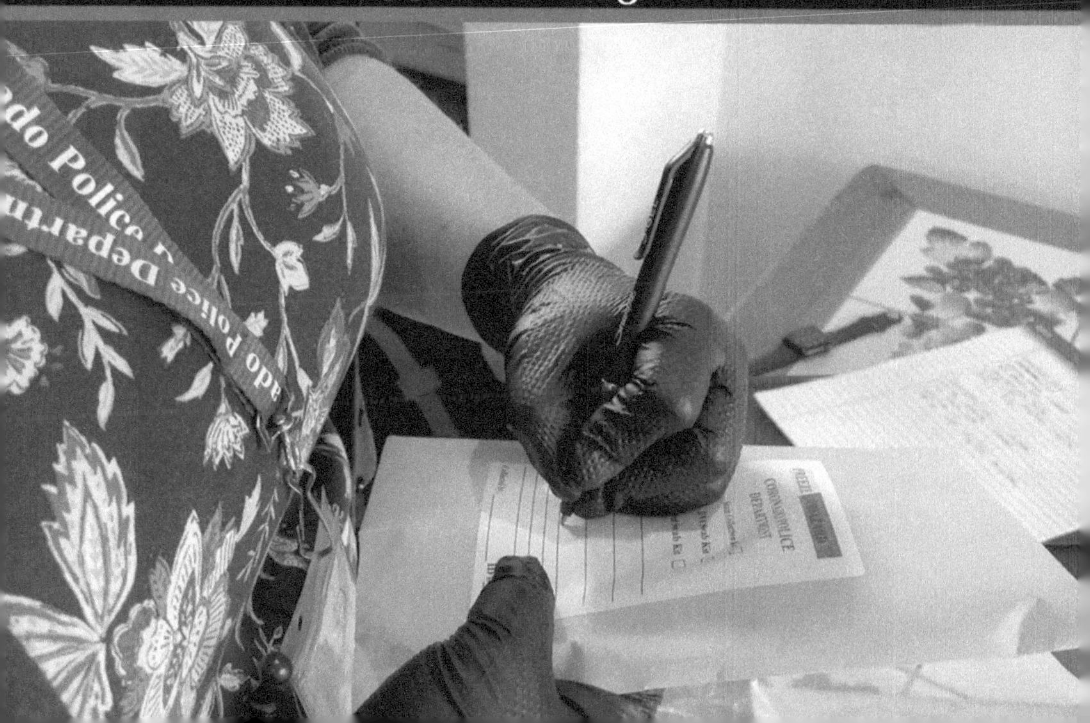

You never forgot about us. ♥

Photo Descriptions

1. Birkenfeld Germany townspeople, 1930

2. Oskar in his military uniform in Italy, 1944; Programs kept by Oskar from operas and ballets organized by The German Propaganda Company during WWII, 1942

3. Oskar and other POWs, France 1947

4. Hilda, winner of the "Spring Maiden" contest, Birkenfeld, 1930

5. Food rations for Birkenfeld townspeople, 1944

6. The Döderlein kids tending to their pet rabbits at their home in Birkenfeld (Left to right: Rosemarie, Günter, Vera)

7. Hilda and baby Günter, 1931

8. Hilda's Christmas themed shop window in Birkenfeld, designed by Günter, 1950 (left); A few of Günter and Ruth's creations: hand carved puppets, wall murals, and handcrafted one-of-a-kind model ships (right)

9. Left to right: Hilde, Rosemarie, Günter and Vera, 1943

10. Rosemarie at her Lutheran confirmation in Birkenfeld, April 1954

11. Rosemarie's prayer book (Written inside: "O, Lord,

Please protect all us humans and animals"), red play purse, and fifties play jewelry kept by Vera for nearly 70 years

12. Rosemarie's first 1957 (top) and second 1984 (middle) marriage certificates using the first real names of her parents, Oskar and Hilda, and her mother's real maiden name, Ruhl; Rosemarie's writing from inside her red play purse, 1954 (bottom)

13. Rosemarie's fishing hook and thimble, two items she loved as an adult

14. Various newspaper articles, 2022: Material republished with the express permission of: Montreal Gazette, a division of Postmedia Network Inc. (top); Flier designed, distributed, and displayed around hundreds of businesses and senior homes across New York and Canada searching for Rosemarie, 2022 (bottom)

15. Collection of documents related to investigative genetic genealogy findings, 2022: Sample result from genealogy tools that can help predict relationships based on shared DNA from known relatives (top); First page of results from German genealogist Carolin Becker's private genealogy software (middle left); Letter from Vera to her cousin in Germany (middle right); Cover page of Christa's 50 page document presenting the findings of her research and investigation to DC Mike Kelly in the Missing Persons Unit at Toronto Police Services

16. Vera and her favorite fox fur scarf, 1945 (top); Vera smelling the white lilac tree in the front yard of the Döderlein house as seen through the front door, Birkenfeld 1946 (right); Vera on the way to school, Birkenfeld 1953 (left)

17. Vera and Rosemarie relaxing at a picnic table while

Hilda works in the field nearby, Birkenfeld 1947;
    Part of a letter from Oskar to Vera, 1974

18. Vera's enrollment form for Merton Elementary
    School in Montreal, October 21, 1954 (top);
    Rosemarie, Oskar, Hilda, and Vera stopping in
    Köln (Cologne) on the way to the Bremen port,
    September 16, 1954 (bottom)

19. Vera's United States Citizenship photo, 1967

20. Jakob Döderlein, Oskar's father, and a letter from
    one of his comrades, 1917

21. Oskar reading magazine and newspapers until the
    day he passed away, to try and find any clue that
    would lead him to his missing child, 1974 (left);
    Hilda and Vera reviewing their latest ads looking for
    Rosemarie, 1976 (top right); Detective Danielle
    Adams from the Coronado California Police
    Department, swabbing Vera's mouth for DNA to
    send to the Montreal Police Department to see if a
    close match exists in their unidentified bodies DNA
    databases, 2022 (bottom right)

22. Shadow box framed art with a hand-embroidered
    ladies handkerchief and gloves, a little red purse, a
    man's navy blue bowtie with a matching baby blue
    handkerchief, two silver 1954 quarters, and the little
    single pearl bracelet that Vera made for Rosemarie's
    14th birthday, 1954

Afterword

By Christa Hastie

"Whooo-hoo!! Go Oma, go!!" Almost a decade ago, it was a warm and sunny afternoon when my kids, husband, mom and I all piled into the family van to drive my mom to a sleek, modern building near the UCLA campus in West Los Angeles. She carried her canvas tote bag containing student essentials: her new Chromebook, her coffee with heavy cream and sugar in a tall silver to-go mug, a bottle of water, a pen, and her inhaler. We led her to the classroom, and lingered outside the door, giggling as we stole glances through the little window on the classroom door to check in on her. My elderly mom, a recipient of the UCLA Extension Writers Program Scholarship, was absolutely adorable sitting in a classroom with dozens of other students that were mostly young, educated and well-prepared. When she finished her first class that day she couldn't wait to share the new word she learned: genre. Apparently when the instructor had each student answer a series of introductory questions, including the genre of their book, she was one of the first to be called. Not sure what to say, my mom replied that her genre was that she was retired! The teacher kindly explained the meaning of the word to my mom. With a giggle from all, the class continued.

This novel is not just my mother's story, but also our family lore. I have felt personally connected to Rosemarie for as long as I can remember. My mother's loss led her to instill a sense of fierce vigilance and caution in my sister and me, which I now instill in my own children. Though I never met my grandparents, I have always felt their presence in our family. I share their unspoken will to persevere. I have always felt their love, pain, triumphs, talents, creativity, and vision for the future of their family through my mom sharing their photos and retelling their stories.

It took many years for my mama to summon the emotional strength to write this novel. The project began as a therapeutic effort to work through the lifelong pain of her loss. The complete void of information on Rosemarie's personal story ultimately caused the project to stall once the story had reached a certain point: my mother could speculate and wonder aloud, but to put fabrications into writing was a bridge too far. I am in awe of the courage and strength she mustered to embark on one final search for Rosemarie, and then again to complete this novel that honors her parents and gives Rosemarie a voice after 70 years. We thank you for taking the time to acquire and read it. We hope you have enjoyed it and will share it with others.

Searching for a missing person is a daunting task. "Needle in a haystack," does not begin to describe the difficulty or the long odds. Nevertheless, I have always felt that everything is impossible until you do it, and also that belief is a prerequisite to achievement. With that mindset and a lot of luck, we were successful.

I will share some opinions I have developed from this experience.

Immigrant education from day one
Immigrant men, women and children need information in their own languages from the moment they arrive in their destination country so they know what to do if they need

help. Concepts like child abduction are foreign to some cultures. Many immigrants come from countries where police are corrupt and not trusted by ordinary people, and do not know where to seek help.

Reporters matter

As my mom and I read old newspapers and magazines from the 50s, we thought a lot about newspaper reporters. In the modern world, news content has an increasingly disposable quality: rapidly produced, rapidly consumed, rapidly forgotten, in the hope of keeping pace with a shortened news cycle. Take a moment to pause and consider that some of these passing articles will be read and referenced a century or more later, by historians and also by ordinary people like my mom and myself. People depend on reporters to listen to the details, and get them right.

Neat writing is everyone's responsibility

All of us have a responsibility to produce neat, legible writing. You never know which seemingly irrelevant scrawl - the writing on the back of a photo or letter, or even a school enrollment form — will be essential to helping future people search and find records to connect the dots of some other mystery in life. Print clearly and accurately all the time!

Help with your DNA

At the end of the day, the key piece of evidence that led us to answers about Rosemarie was my mom's unknown DNA match. Please go online and get some home DNA kits for yourself, your family, your friends - they make great gifts for any occasion: Ancestry, 23andMe, myHeritage, and Family Tree DNA are all great options. After your test results get posted, we would love to encourage everyone to take the extra steps to download your raw DNA file from Ancestry.com or 23andMe and upload the file to GEDMatch.com - everyone has a chance to be a DNA superhero and help detectives solve cold cases and give people like my mom and our family closure. Remember to periodically check your messages on any DNA sites you register for. Other DNA matches may have come online since you last logged in. Go back and see if you have any messages from random people like us. Our DNA match never expected to help solve a 68 year-old cold case!

You can help in other ways too
Scant public resources are committed to investigating missing persons cases. The financial resources of the family drive the search. Many are not financially able and technically savvy enough to create and organize an effective search for their missing loved one(s). Countless people just like Rosemarie have vanished. Take the time to learn about some of these cases. Oftentimes their families will have created Facebook groups soliciting help from anyone and everyone. If you're a talented portrait artist, graphic designer, hiker, or even willing to share information on your social media pages about a missing person, you can help. Every bit helps, even if it's just adding a number to a Facebook group to show support.

Another simple thing is to carefully look at the photos when you learn of a new case. Don't just glance over their faces - inspect the faces and really look. As Jaycee Dugard's case proved, missing people are among us everywhere, hiding in plain sight. If something doesn't seem right, speak up. As the saying goes, "if you see something, say something!"

Say thanks to Facebook Group administrators
When we posted on various Facebook groups in many cities where we clearly do not live, we started to realize that Facebook group administrators (aka "admins") are the silent, tireless volunteers that keep the spammers and

garbage posts and people out, and help support people like us in finding my mom's sister. Some of these groups have tens of thousands of people, and the volunteer job of being an admin isn't small - they approve every new member…every new post…every edited post…all day every day, for years! Many Facebook admins have become our friends over the last few years, and much of our success when searching for Rosemarie came from the community we found in these groups. We would personally like to thank each and every one of them and hope you take the time to do so too.

Talk to old people

Don't forget about old people. Talk to them, hear their stories, and ask them questions. They are the living memory of our world, and have perspectives to share that add depth and context to the written record. Many of our elders who have endured wars and historical events that are unlike anything we've seen are passing away, and we must seize the opportunities to hear their stories. Whether you're 6, 16, 46 or 60, get talking to more old people.

Reconnect with family and friends

The internet has made it possible to find and connect with people, and there's no better time to use those resources to find old family and friends. Newspaper archives and old phone directories that have been digitized, search engines, Facebook mega groups like Search Squad and DNA Detectives, social media, and online background search companies can help connect you. My mom and I have made many new friends from around the world and now talk with a few cousins in the US, Canada and Germany, laughing, sharing stories, and family history. My mom's favorite day of the week is when she gets to enjoy a call from one of her old pals from Birkenfeld.

Read history

In the search for Rosemarie, I read a lot of newspapers and
magazines that shone a giant spotlight on the fifties era: it
was like an explosion of freedom into a whole new era of
excitement and modernization. Modern appliances were
transforming households, new educational opportunities
were emerging, gender expectations were transforming, and
Elvis with his powerful voice and hip-swinging dance
moves began tapping into teenagers and overturning social
norms. Taxi cabs were just becoming more regulated in
Toronto and Montreal after these cities were experiencing
rapid rates of congestion, pollution, and violent crimes. The
school system in Montreal was absolutely overwhelmed in
Fall 1954 when my mom and her family arrived. The
onslaught of record numbers of immigrants moving into
the city sprang a need for makeshift schools in random
buildings around the city causing chaos and confusion for
all. Understanding the backdrop and environment of that
time and place has been illuminating.

We should not let history repeat itself

Hitler's regime was defeated, but the darkness embodied by
the surveillance state as enforced by the SS has not been
extinguished from human hearts. We must always fight
against that darkness. Much has been written about the
surveillance tools of government and large private
companies whose systems we interact with, but there are
other threats to our freedom that are underrecognized and
may be larger. We must be mindful in the way that we use
and consume publicly available information in the digital
age. A controversial opinion, expressed briefly in a social
media post or captured as a snippet on a smartphone video,
can be presented out of context, distorted, and amplified,
resulting in vicious social media takedowns and blacklisting,
ruining careers and lives. Resist the urge to participate in
these types of takedowns, even when you are convinced

that you have a righteous cause. We do not live in a free society when we allow this form of thought control. Our freedoms are not a monument carved from stone, but rather a garden that we must carefully tend.

Voltaire said, "History never repeats itself. Man always does." The mentality of everyday German citizens during World War II is the same as innocent citizens in other countries spearheading wars today: these everyday people just want to live, eat, raise children and work in peace. Many of them keep their true opinions to themselves for fear of being arrested, jailed, humiliated, beaten or worse. I was struck by the personal letter sent to Oskar's father, my great grandfather Jakob Döderlein in 1917 near the end of World War I. The letter echoes this same truth: that the German people didn't want or need a "movement" or "revolution," and that they were forced to fight despite preferring to simply "play their pianos." I cannot offer any solutions to these issues, but felt it was necessary to mention them. As Winston Churchill once said, "Those that fail to learn from history, are doomed to repeat it."

Be kind. You don't know anyone's story
Nobody knows who suffers in silence. We are now extra kind to everyone we meet, and we hope you do the same. You never know who is hiding their entire former life and identity for whatever reason. How many times did Rosemarie put on a smile when she wanted to cry and tell everyone her secrets? Try to be kind to everyone.

Worthwhile Organizations

Please consider donating to these worthwhile organizations that bring awareness and resources to missing persons cases and victims of domestic violence. Even a small contribution to any of these organizations can make a huge difference. Thank you in advance for your generosity!

The Aware Foundation

www.theawarefoundationofvirginia.com

www.facebook.com/theawarefoundation

For years this organization has been dedicated to providing an up-to-date Facebook resource with news and updates on missing persons across the country, serving as an invaluable resource for the missing and their families.

The JAYC Foundation, Inc.

www.thejaycfoundation.org

This organization offers support and assistance to help people recover from abduction or other traumatic events.

Season of Justice

www.seasonofjustice.org

This nonprofit organization is dedicated to providing funding for investigative agencies and families to help solve cold cases.

When Georgia Smiled
The Robin McGraw and Dr. Phil Foundation
www.whengeorgiasmiled.org
This organization supports many other organizations and
programs that help children and families live without fear
of domestic violence and sexual assault.

Unidentified Human Remains Canada
Facebook Group
Founder Jan Guppy has tirelessly volunteered for over a
decade running her Facebook group that helps connect
missing persons with unidentified bodies across the
country, as well as connect families of missing people to
forensic artists, DNA labs, crowdfunding, search
teams and more.

Doe Network
www.doenetwork.org
This organization works to help give the nameless
(unidentified bodies) back their names and return the
missing to their families.

Thank You

We would like to thank the many people, archives, news media and publications, businesses, and organizations around the world who we've connected with on our journey over the last few years. Every person helped, some in big ways, some in small ways. It shows us that humanity is alive and thriving.

~

My Daughters, Grandchildren and Sons-In-Law

~

50+ Nieces and Nephews, Great Nieces and Nephews, Great-Great Nieces and Nephews, and Cousins in the US, Canada and Germany

~

Detective Constable Michael Kelly, My (Once) Mysterious DNA Matches, Toronto Police Service

~

Facebook, Ancestry.com, 23andMe.com, FamilyTreeDNA.com, MyHeritage.com, GEDmatch.com, DNA Painter, Yandex Translation Tools, Google, DNA Detectives Facebook Group by Genetic Genealogist CeCe Moore, Doe Organization, The Aware Foundation

~

Montreal Gazette, Etobicoke Guardian, Le Journal de Montréal, CBC (Canadian Broadcasting Company), Reader's Digest Magazine

~

~

Bonnie Munday (Editor-in-Chief, Reader's Digest
International Editions), Susan Schwartz, Tamara Shephard,
Sarah Treleaven, Martha Beach, Debra Arbec, Kristy Rich,
Matt D'Amours, Brennan Neill, Erica Morris and the entire
CBC News team

~

Marcel Boyer, Andrew & Cynthia Kerr, Joe Demelo,
Gino Pirollo, Elizabeth Robertshaw Watkins,
Brian Peddar, David Mothus

~

Emily Handfield, Joanna Wrench and Stacey Clarke
(English Montreal School Board Archivists), Arolsen
Archives, Ontario Genealogical Society, British Columbia
Genealogical Society, University of Northern British
Columbia, Société de généalogie de Québec, Laurier
Archives, Pforzheim City Archives, Birkenfeld Archives
and Rathaus, Bibliothèque et Archives nationales du
Québec, Toronto Public Library, Library and Archives
Canada, Montreal Accueil Service Antécédents et
Retrouvailles, CHUM (Le Centre hospitalier de l'Université
de Montréal), Centre intégré de santé et de servces sociaux
de la Montérégie-Est Quebec, ServiceOntario, OnLand
Ontario, and hundreds of other newspapers
and archives worldwide

~

Carolin Becker and Family, Kharisma Rodriguez,
Birkenfeld Bürgermeister Martin Steiner, Pforzheim
Oberbürgermeister Peter Boch, Jan Guppy (Unidentified
Human Remains Canada), Rod Vienneau, Annie Richard,
Angela Morck, RN PhD (& Rich!), Anne A. Duff
Zolkiewicz, Alexandre Gagnier Hemmings, Carole
Thibeault, Cathy Collins, Donna Borden, K.F.,

Gerd Hemminger, Dimpflmeier Bakery (Etobicoke, Toronto, Canada), Harald Wolf, Winnie Laning, Judy Koch-Szamosi, Kristian Gravenor, Adam Elliot Segal, Kristine Döderlein, Luanne Frey, Lynn Their, Marie-Chantal Gauthier, Melissa Maude, Melinda Dalton, Nancy Bray, Annette Nußbaum, Nancy Grigg, Shaney Komulainen, Shari LeDrew, Sofia L. Delgado, Sophie Charest, Stéphane Luce (Meurtres et Disparitions Irrésolus du Québec), Steve Mccann, Rob Terry, Sydney H. Pfeiffer, Theresa Segodnia, Fergus V. Keyes, Georgette Smith, Christine Huglo Robertson, Abbe Vance, Kathleen Tansey, Marie Bolen, Sara Goessaert, Tommy Harding, Cornelia Burgeas, Detective Danielle Adams (Coronado, California Police Department), Jana Doiron, Nadine L., The Montreal Police Department, Andre Furlong, Robert Blume, Martina Wessinger, Paul F., Ingrid & Dan, Ingrid A. & W.A., and hundreds of senior home directors across NY and Canada

~

UCLA Extension Writer's Program, Francesca Lia Block, Smitty and Julija, Whitney Hartmann Photography, Samantha Steinberg, Mohesh Km, Laurie Farmer, Deb Nordlie, Evelyn, Caroline, Grace, Virginia Killingsworth (rest in peace) and all my wonderful writing class pals

~

Links

Brothers Get Life For Rape Offences
April 28, 1951 | The Montreal Gazette
https://www.newspapers.com/clip/103031780/the-gazette

German Domestics And Nurses Coming to Canada
October 17, 1952 | Calgary Herald
https://www.newspapers.com/clip/101221331/calgary-herald/

NDG Youth Arrested For Assault
November 28, 1953 | The Montreal Gazette
https://www.newspapers.com/clip/103031780/the-gazette/

Text of Protestant School Board Brief
February 5, 1954 | The Montreal Star
https://www.newspapers.com/clip/119620460/protestant-
schoolboard-formation/

Urgent Needs Related By Protestant Board
February 6, 1954 | The Montreal Gazette
https://www.newspapers.com/clip/119620687/protestant-
school-board-needs/

Rosemere School Not Ready Yet
August 31, 1954 | The Montreal Star
https://www.newspapers.com/clip/119621581/schools-not-
ready-in-1954/

Lost Girl's Dad Blames 'Silly' Story
September 24, 1954 | The Montreal Gazette
https://www.newspapers.com/clip/103011802/the-gazette/

Tip-off ' Finds Missing Girl In Sherbrooke
September 27, 1954 | The Montreal Gazette
https://www.newspapers.com/clip/103155152/the-gazette/

Missing (German) Girl
October 5, 1954 | The Montreal Gazette
https://www.newspapers.com/clip/103011712/the-gazette/

Boy, 15, Missing Since Oct. 7, Is Being Sought
November 5, 1954 | The Montreal Gazette
https://www.newspapers.com/clip/101649639/the-gazette/

Holiday Deaths, Seven In Area
December 27, 1954 | The Montreal Star
https://www.newspapers.com/clip/101433937/the-montreal-star/

2,126 Lost, Police Bring Back 2,050
December 31, 1954 | The Montreal Star
https://www.newspapers.com/clip/101435265/the-montreal-star/

Police Query Woman Who 'Borrowed' Child
February 25, 1955 | The Montreal Gazette
https://www.newspapers.com/clip/101436650/the-gazette/

Police Report Pair of Girls As 'Missing'
March 18, 1955 | The Montreal Gazette
https://www.newspapers.com/clip/101649504/the-gazette/

Aid Sought In Locating Missing Pair
March 31, 1955 | The Montreal Star
https://www.newspapers.com/clip/101649719/the-montreal-star/

Girl Here Believed Victim of Amnesia
April 18, 1955 | The Montreal Star
https://www.newspapers.com/clip/101649735/the-montreal-star/

City Police Seek Data on Girl, 16
April 21, 1955 | The Montreal Gazette
https://www.newspapers.com/clip/101649560/the-gazette/

Police Alerted To Keep Watch For N.D.G Youth
April 28, 1955 | The Montreal Gazette
https://www.newspapers.com/clip/101649744/the-gazette/

Baron Byng Student One of 3 Missing Girls
June 17, 1955 | The Montreal Gazette
https://www.newspapers.com/clip/101649779/the-gazette/

Englisch-Klassen für Neucanadier
September 22, 1955 | das Courier Toronto
Laurier Archives has a copy

Baby Ring Charged As City Woman Held
November 17, 1955 | The Montreal Gazette
https://www.newspapers.com/clip/101206499/the-gazette/

New Guide For Couple Eager To Adopt Child
July 29, 1957 | The Ottawa Citizen | by Mary Haworth
https://www.newspapers.com/clip/101354544/the-ottawa-
citizen/

Orphans Went From Normalcy to Idiocy in 1 Day : Canada:
Thousands of children were reclassified as mentally retarded so
institutions could get more money from Quebec. Schooling
stopped and torture began, they contend in lawsuits.
June 6, 1993 | LA Times | by Jeffrey Ulbrich
https://www.latimes.com/archives/la-xpm-1993-06-06-mn-171-
story.html

From Thornton Blackburn to Uber: a brief and varied history of
Toronto taxis
April 9, 2016 | CBC News | by Joshua Errett
https://www.cbc.ca/amp/1.3526912

Black Market Babies
July 18, 2017 | Maisonneuve | by Adam Elliot Segal
https://maisonneuve.org/article/2017/07/18/black-market-
babies/

Old Bones Tell Tales: Scientists Use Ancient DNA To Identify
Unmarked Graves
March 10, 2020 | Forbes | by Farah Qaiser
https://www.forbes.com/sites/farahqaiser/2020/03/10/old-
bones-tell-tales-scientists-use-ancient-dna-to-identify-unmarked-
graves/

Opinion: Duplessis Orphans have yet to receive justice
October 17, 2022 | Montreal Gazette | by Arthur McCaffrey
https://montrealgazette.com/opinion/opinion-duplessis-
orphans-have-yet-to-receive-justice/

Book | Child protection in Canada, 1954
By Canadian Welfare Council Family and Child Welfare Division
https://search.worldcat.org/title/18088362

Book | La Prostitution Féminine à Montréal
By Danielle Lacasse

Book | Collusion : The dark history of the Duplessis Orphans
By Rod Vienneau

Website | The Great Ghost: Lost Schools of English Montreal
By Christopher Milligan and Wes Cross
https://lostschools.mcgill.ca/

Website | Duplessis Orphans
By Canada's Human Rights History
https://historyofrights.ca/encyclopaedia/main-events/duplessis-
orphans/

Website | News articles about Rosemarie Döderlein
By Vera and Christa Hastie
http://www.MissingGermanGirl.com

Website | DNA - Help With Home DNA Testing Kits
By Vera and Christa Hastie
http://www.DNAsuperHero.org

Have you seen me?

Here I am at age 13 & what I might look like at 77 today

My family arrived in Canada by ship from
Germany June 18 1956

I have brown eyes, once had brown hair, spoke English
with a slight European accent, have a small brown mole on
my top right cheek, & may have gone by the name
Katherine

Both my parents went to work that morning, and my sister
Ingrid went ice skating with friends nearby early afternoon.
Sometime after this, I disappeared from inside or around
my High Park neighborhood home, and was last seen
walking westbound along Harvard Ave toward
Roncesvalles Avenue.

I could have been trafficked or taken into New York
or elsewhere in Canada and the USA

There have been sightings of me in New York
and around Ontario, Canada

My little 74 year old sister Ingrid is
forever still trying to find me

Please help us find Helga!
www.HelpUsFindHelga.com

HELGA
KATHERINE
KASERER

HAVE YOU SEEN ME???

On Dec 29, 1960
at age 13, I went
missing in
Toronto, Canada

ABOUT THE AUTHOR
Vera Christa Doederlein Hastie

Vera is 81 years of age and is "proud as a peacock" to have published this one novel in her lifetime that she considers an honor to her entire family. She is grateful to have been a recipient of a UCLA Extension Writer's Program Scholarship in 2015, which helped jumpstart the writing of this novel.

In Vera's younger years, she worked as an executive secretary in Southern California. She was married to her late husband for almost 20 years, is the mother to two children, and "Oma" (grandmother) to four grandchildren. She enjoys movies, cooking, gardening, sewing, knitting, and crossword puzzles in her free time.